T0128020

Letter to Potential Publisher

Unlike the other umpteen million rubbish books ye likely receive on a daily basis, I'm not an illiterate and inarticulate booger picker. So I implore ye to give me at least through the first chapter. This manuscript is an artfully unusual satirical medieval fantasy with undertones of dark tragedy that grips the reader's attention with offensive quip and brutal violence. If it doesn't cause ye a laugh or capture yer interest, then feel free to cut and paste the rejection letter below, which I have crafted to spare ye yer valuable time.

To Chris Curtin,

In regard to your manuscript, I do believe that I have irreparably damaged brain cells that I can never get back. The fact that someone could produce such a mind-shattering offensive piece of rubbish such as this has severely damaged what little faith I had remaining for humanity.

Thank you sincerely,
Not going to be your publisher

Book Reviews

"That movie was awesome."
          —A random homeless man I gave a six-pack of cheap beer to

"When I think about you, I want to touch myself."
          —An inmate thankfully incarcerated at the time of review

"This book is so deplorably sinful I had to ask Alex, my altar boy, to leave my bed while I read so that he wouldn't be tainted by its evil."
          —A priest

"I wish I could speak Irish so that I could understand him."
          —Not actually said in reference to the book, but the best jokes
                aren't scripted. A delightful young blonde gal said this
                in reference to the manner in which I speak.

CALLAHAN
THE
FALCON

TALES OF CALARR

Chris Curtin

Order this book online at www.trafford.com
or email orders@trafford.com

Most Trafford titles are also available at major online book retailers.

Printed in the United States of America.

ISBN: 978-1-4669-8602-2 (sc)
ISBN: 978-1-4669-8601-5 (hc)
ISBN: 978-1-4669-8600-8 (e)

Library of Congress Control Number: 2013904912

Trafford rev. 03/27/2013

 www.trafford.com

North America & international
toll-free: 1 888 232 4444 (USA & Canada)
phone: 250 383 6864 ♦ fax: 812 355 4082

CONTENTS

FOUR PRISONERS SUFFERING FROM an inexplicable case of amnesia found themselves waking in dingy cells with ragged clothes their only possessions—a witty and charismatic rogue, a barbarian warrior, a priestess of light, and a female ranger. So here our adventure begins, and where it goes depends on your choices from this point on.

For the rogue's perspective, choose 1; the barbarian's, 2; the priestess's, 3; and the ranger's, 4.

1. Now, my dear player/reader, it is time to select the appearance of your new character—

"Whoa, whoa! Hold on a minute. First off, I don't have amnesia, and second, I'm not having some pimple-popping, junk food-feasting virgin turn me into a large-breasted blonde woman to circumvent his complete lack of feminine company, and finally, why can I hear everything yer saying?" The rogue looked to the ceiling as if speaking to the heavens. "I'm not speaking to the heavens. I'm talking to you, jack bag, and my name is Callahan, not just the rogue. I'm the leader of the Falcons, a well-known guild in the city of Lados. So the only lack of memory I'm suffering is in regard to how the fuck I ended up in a cell absent my collection of magically enhanced trinkets, clothes, and weaponry."

Hmm. Well, an interesting twist this is turning out to be. So our rogue seems to need a bit of time to calm himself. To continue his tale, please go to section 5.

2. The barbarian, immense in stature—

"HEY! Bloody hell, ye fucking voice from wherever. Get yer arse back to section 1. I've got some questions, and I feel that I've a very valid reason for getting frustrated at the lack of answers I'm receiving from ye . . .

"Just a bloody second, I know what you know, er, um . . . I mean, I know what the dingleberry writing this knows, not particularly what you—whoever the fuck you may be—who are reading this knows.

"So if I'm gathering this correctly, what to me is a very real and pain-in-the-ass existence is to you a mere hobby to occupy yer time in between yer random bouts of masturbation and cigarette smoking. Boy, do I feel like I got the shit end of the stick here. Well, now that we have that established, I'm not going to play into this whole mindless 'I'll do whatever dumbshit idea the reader comes up with just because they're too unoriginal to craft their own story.' Instead, how 'bout this—if we're going to work this like a Choose Your Own Adventure book, have them select scenarios, and I, in turn, will react as is my nature, and as far as these other three characters, ye can do whatever the hell ye want with 'em. So if the readers want to envision themselves in those roles to forget their own pitiful existences, well, piss on 'em 'cause I only exist insofar as this story remains about me. Secondary characters are fine, but don't go trying to time-warp my ass out the picture."

Not in the mood to negotiate with mere mortals, the gods—

"Come on! What the . . ."

That's quite enough cussing. If I have to negotiate with a fictional character I am crafting, then at least have some respect for your creator because as far as you're concerned, I am God.

"Really now, if that isn't arrogance. Besides, how the fuck are ye gonna call me disrespectful when ye started off my existence broke and imprisoned with no memory? Ye want to talk about not only disrespectful but mind-numbingly cliché. Next, ye'll have me forge an escape through countless dog-sized rats down an irrationally designed maze of corridors.

Every so many kills, a random *ding* sound will pop up, and I'll be blessed with more strength, speed, and knowledge. Seriously, if I were an adventurer that gained so much from killing a fucking rat, don't ye think it would be high time to reevaluate my line of work? Oh, and not to mention the fact that as they died, these rats would magically shit gold and equipment well over twice their size.

"Then we move on to phase 2 of yer brilliant tale in which I have to open barred and locked doors. The bars—of course, due to some act of engineering genius—will be activated from this side down another ridiculous set of corridors guarded by an altogether way-too-weak guard captain. Who will, by another act of sheer brilliant planning, be holding the key or a note telling me that the key is somewhere else in this vermin- and guard-infested shithole."

You piss and whine about cliché, but isn't it just as cliché to have a smart-ass rogue somewhat comically arguing with the narrator about video game clichés?

"Ouch. OK, ye got me on that one. Touché."

So if my premise for action/adventure RPG isn't to your liking, how, then, should I continue to keep our readers interested? Unfortunately for you, no one likes to read. It started on a warm, sunny day. It went rather well, and it ended splendidly. So no matter how we cut this out, looks to me like you're gonna get screwed.

"Perfect! I love it. Ye want to appeal to a whole bunch of video game geeks and medieval fantasy junkies? Well, what better way than to have a snarky rogue in a whorehouse with an unlimited supply of coin and booze. We can even institute yer Choose Yer Own Bullshit by allowing the reader to select which prostitutes I get laid by."

The sad thing is I am sure that is actually a marketable idea, but I really don't want my name being associated with such mindless drivel.

"That's why ye use a pseudonym, like Harry Steele or Barry Bulge. Not like ye actually have to pin yer name to it, and really, come on. Don't ye remember I know what you know, and let's look at the reality of it. Ye have no public image, yer uncouth, and even if it were mindless cartoon smut, ye'd celebrate anything that got yer name out."

My turn to say touché, but we really are digressing.

"Ah piss. Well, all right then, I'm in a prison cell adjacent to three others. At this point, I retract the comments about our readers being pimple-popping masturbation addicts in hopes that they would envision the ranger and priestess as being well-endowed rather floozy women with plump round—"

OK, we get the picture, mate, and really, you were right about the prison cliché, so instead—

"No, damn it, don't ye even bloody well start to envision me as some farmer's son, city orphan, or otherwise useless nobody, who has to scrap together an existence from nothing in the effort to save some random woman, probably of nobility, from some random nefarious character. I'll tell ye right now, no matter how rich and beautiful, no woman is worth half the shit I know ye'd put me through. Sometimes quantity is better than quality. I'll take ten fat women who know when to leave over one damsel in distress any day."

You like your guild, right?

"What're ye on about?"

You like your semi-immortal state of being?

"Oh crap, yer about to pull out that card, aren't ye?"

Damn right, I am pulling out that card. I wrote you, and I can unwrite you.

"Not sure *unwrite* is a word, mate."

Listen here, you collective of sentences I put to paper. You exist in whatever capacity I so choose for you to exist, and for today, that will be . . .

"Writer's block, eh? Absolute bitch, that is. For both of us, mind ye. So for today's tale, why don't we stick to what we both know and tell my story? Ye've dreamed of writing it but could never get the motivation to do so, and well, frankly, I'd really like to exist in more than just yer head. We can dual narrate it so ye'll have a somewhat original writing style, and so I can ensure ye don't go misconstruing the events of my existence."

Good, I think we have come to an accord in what will now be the preface to *Callahan the Falcon*.

"Ah, bloody hell, that in no way is going to be our title. Are ye really that drab and unoriginal?"

OK then, construct of my imagination, since your creative streak is oh so vast in comparison to mine. What do you want to call it?

"Ah piss, we'll come back to that. For now, chapter 1, "Entearra Gharu, Game of the Gods."

Chapter 1

ENTEARRA GHARU, GAME OF THE GODS

[NARRATOR] HIS MOTHER, DAUGHTER to a butcher, was given to his father, a captain of the Lados guard, as payment to avoid extortion by the guard. In those days, before the rise of the guilds, the guards ran the criminal aspects of the city unchallenged. Hating her forced union with Callahan's father, his mother often sought the company of sailors and passing adventurers that frequented the inn she tended. It was suspected that one of these unions was the cause of Callahan's conception; thus, his father looked on him with contempt and disgust. A love for the drink, gambling, and women kept Callahan's father from the home for the most part. When he did happen to be home, the sight of Callahan would send him into rage. He would verbally rip apart his wife until the words were no longer enough to satiate his anger, at which time he would beat her mercilessly.

[Callahan] Yep, Mom was a slut. I say *slut* and not *whore* because at least whores get paid for it. Dad was a drunken moron who had no concept of holding on to money. Suddenly, the lack of memory and a prison cell isn't sounding like such a bad gig after all.

[Narrator] Drug down into a depressive state of hopelessness, the best she could muster for her son was setting his room in the loft of the home, where due to the confined space and rope ladder access, entry was not easily managed by a raged-out drunk. As he got old enough to gain some

1

self-awareness and understanding, the beatings turned in his direction, so Callahan quickly learned not only how to make himself scarce but also how to scrape out an existence on the streets.

By the age of twelve, he had engineered a false floor in his loft, which provided him sanctuary when outright escape seemed unlikely, as well as a hidden rope with a knotted stick he would latch under his secured nightstand so he could drop down next to the front door and, with a quick snap, unlatch the stick from the dresser legs. A good deal of practice while his parents were away got him in the habit of being able to catch the stick as it fell, so he could enact the process quickly and almost silently.

During those years of his young life, he took an orphan boy named Selfin under his wing and started teaching him the ins and outs of acquiring what one needs to survive. During the course of his younger days, Callahan found his quick wit and knack for impressing himself upon people to be his greatest allies. Information and knowledge were key to him. He found that the shifting and acquiring of those luxuries was a far more worthwhile endeavor than petty theft and carried a less immediate threat if handled with care.

[Callahan] Selfin was a good kid. None too bright, mind ye, but a good kid nonetheless. My first real friend, he was. I remember the time I went out in the morning to find him, only to see the dipshit being pummeled by a street merchant. He had got himself nicked for snagging a loaf of stale bread. Course, he had to pick the surliest merchant on the block to steal from. I'd taught him better than that but wasn't about to let him go down on his own.

[Narrator] "Whoa, ye burly ogre, lay off that boy there!" Callahan deftly hopped from his perch on the rooftops to an overhanging sunshade, then down to the ground with a light roll.

Turning his attention to the new kid, the merchant growled, "Mind your own, boy. Caught this 'ere thief fair and square, so what I do with him is what I do with him, and I don't want to hear a word from you about it. 'Less, of course, ye want yerself a healthy dose of it too."

"While an ass whooping would be entertaining and shave more than a little time off this otherwise drab and boring morning, it would not accomplish either of our purposes." Well outside the merchant's reach, Callahan smiled his wry half smile. "I propose an offer. You want profit. I want bread and an end to me mate's ass whooping, deserved as it may be. So what I propose is ye not only give me the loaf of bread he tried to steal but a second one, and within the hour, I will return with four times the payment for both."

"Do I look that stupid to you? Don't answer that, ye little puke. Now bugger off." The merchant raised his hand to strike the boy again.

"Swear to me upon whatever ye hold dear that ye won't hit him again. Give me the loaf he tried to steal. I will go on me own and, as I said, return with four times the profit for two loaves. If I cheat ye, ye'll still have me friend to pummel on, and all ye'd have lost is one loaf of stale bread. If I don't cheat ye, then yer up a healthy profit, and ye don't have to go bruising those soft, lovely hands of yers." Winking to Selfin, Callahan removed his raggedy old cloak as he spoke, then tossed one end out next to his friend. Selfin, catching the hint, snagged the loaf he had tried to steal from the dirt, where it had fallen, and dropped it on the end of the cloak.

Pulling the bread quickly to his grasp, Callahan grinned again. "We have an accord, then. As I said, look for me within the hour." Bolting off with calculations running through his brain, Callahan figured twenty minutes' travel to Horuce's guard station, eight minutes for negotiation, and twenty minutes' return time left him more than ample room to err.

Taking to the rooftops, Callahan smoothly traversed the distance to the guard shack, placed more as a guide between the noble sector and the middle class than as an actual position of danger. His father placed his most unreliable guards at this post, and Callahan delighted in the dependability of Horuce's stupidity. Horuce was his father's least favorite employee and often wound up on duty at this particular station.

"Sleeping yet again, ye lard-ass lout!" Bouncing the stale loaf of bread off Horuce's head to land it in his lap, Callahan grinned wide at Horuce as the large man tried to stir himself to attention. "Last time me dad caught ye wasn't lesson enough for ye, eh?"

"He only came out this way 'cause you ratted me out, you little pissant, and if I heard right, what cost me a month's pay and a lashing cost you a few weeks' worth of beatings. So thanks for the bread and the memory to keep me laughing." The fat man took a healthy bite out of his bread, still snorting contemptuously at the boy before him.

"Ye cheated me on my due when I completed our deal. I brought ye yer flask of wine and some fresh cheese to go with it, and ye refused to pay me. Said, if I remember right, 'Thanks for the drink and food. Now go get a job, you oversized sewer rat.' So I told me father ye would be sleeping later that day, and bugger me if yer big dumb arse hadn't drunk all the wine and dropped yerself into a stupor. Just bad luck that noblewoman happened to overhear him yelling at ye, and me dad's image was tarnished because his guard was asleep on duty." Callahan's grin spread to a wry half smile as he watched the fat guard cram another bite in his mouth. "Ye do make a fine argument, though."

"What's that supposed to mean?" Bread crumbs sprayed at Callahan as Horuce spoke.

"Means I did pay for turning ye in by getting beaten for a few weeks. So debt stays unsquared for when ye tried to stiff me on me pay. Price just got larger for that bread you're munching and my silence about ye sleeping on post again." The smile upon his face remained unchanged.

"Listen here, you overblown shit wad, I am not giving you a copper, so fuck off." Horuce returned Callahan's unwavering smile with an exaggerated one of his own.

"Right, then, I've a deal to keep this morning, and yer delaying me far too long. One of two things is about to happen. One, ye give me yer coin purse with all its contents and we part friends, or two, I turn ye overto me dad, miss meeting my deal this morning, catch a beating from a merchant, a month's beatings from me dad, but not before watching yer bloated arse bounce off the ramparts swinging from a noose." His smile remained solid, but the look in Callahan's eyes became undeniably stoic.

"Give you my coin purse? Bah, damn near a gold's worth of coins in it. I'll be damned if I give that to you." Horuce's voice shook as he feigned confidence.

"Look me in the eyes, dear Horuce. I like ye despite our past squabbles, and so I don't want to see harm come to ye, but a deal is a deal in my world. So ye can fear damnation all ye want, but look again at my eyes. Test me, please. Come, Horuce, deny me what I ask that ye can meet yer gods. I'll take each beating with the image of yer bloated corpse hung aloft to ease my pain, and ye know the depth of truth in my words, so please, test me. Dance with me." Callahan deftly caught the hefty coin purse none too gently thrown in his direction. "Good, I see we can part friends. By the way, Tavinicus carries on him a favor from me father's favorite whore. He's been cavorting with her short of my father's blessing. Do with that tad bit of information what you will, makes no never mind to me."

As Callahan started his rushed jog back to the merchant, he could hear Horuce belly-laughing and calling after him, saying, "You blighter, how in the fuck can you manage to damn near get me hung, rob me blind, and leave with me still loving the shit out of ye?" The fat man crammed another oversized bite of stale bread in his mouth, smiling and releasing his stress in an exaggerated sigh. He knew that small piece of information was his ticket back into good graces and, thus, worth far more than the coins it cost.

[Callahan] That fat sack of useless crap actually used that info to get Tavinicus hung from the ramparts. This, in turn, did put him back on me father's good side.

[Narrator] Withdrawing a silver piece and stashing the remainder of his coins in a thin multipouched roll of cloth he had devised to silence jingling, which was hidden under his belt, he returned to Selfin and the merchant, displaying the silver piece proudly. "Selfin, did he hold to accord?" A quick nod was his answer. "Good then, here ye are, mate. More than ample pay for two loaves of bread."

"A silver. Bah, I charge . . ." The gleam in his eyes and surprised response that he had quickly hidden would've been enough to dispel the truth in his haggling had it not been for Callahan's impatient lack of care.

"Shut up. I'm done bartering with half-wits and knuckle-dragging primates this day. A silver is well more than what is owed. You and I both know it. I've more than met our time frame, and to top it off, I'm going to toss ye a bone due to my generous mood. Two blocks east, three blocks north. That's where yer gonna move yer little stale bread cart so ye can actually make sales. Right 'ere, yer one block from a fresh bakery and two blocks from a well-stocked inn. Where I told ye to go is a frequent meeting spot for guards who want quickies with the cheap streetwalkers and where a commune of those said streetwalkers spend their days." Helping his friend to his feet and then removing a loaf of bread from right next to the merchant, Callahan flashed his wry half grin and, without further verbal exchange, walked casually away.

Out of the merchant's sight and earshot, Callahan slapped the back of Selfin's head. "Ye blighter! What in the fuck is wrong with ye? Damn near got yerself killed there. Couldn't wait a bit longer for me to show up, could ye?"

"Just wanted to get us some breakfast. He wasn't paying any attention. I almost—" Selfin cringed as another shot echoed off the back of his skull.

"*Almost* is an epitaph! Ye don't almost shit! Ye do it, or ye don't. Besides that, since when did we become common street bums stealing bread? I mean, who the fuck wants to eat this stale, bland excuse for food?" Callahan held up the loaf he carried for emphasis.

"I'm really hungry. I could really use some of that. I don't care that it's stale." Licking his lips with longing, Selfin leaned slightly in toward the bread in Callahan's hands.

"Forget it. This is to pay Hemrick. I know ye haven't eaten since last night. So don't worry, I'll get ye a veritable feast if ye just give me a bit of time. This morning's unfortunate circumstances have led to our good fortune. Just trust me, OK." Callahan patted his friend on the shoulder as they hurried on to find the ever-starving bum, Hemrick.

A few moments later found the two boys standing before a ragged older man sitting in the shade of an alley next to a foul-smelling pile of old burlap sacks. "See, yer as odorous as ever, my good friend. So what have ye to earn yer breakfast with this fine morn, mate?" Callahan displayed the loaf to the man.

"Ugh, well, um . . . the nobles be getting together in the next week or two to select our next governor." Looking hopefully, Hemrick feebly reached out for the bread.

"Bah, that bit of well-known trash isn't worth a bite of this bread after me and Selfin have done and recycled it." Callahan pulled the bread well outside the bum's reach.

"What's that supposed to mean?" Forlorn Hemrick's eyes refused to leave the bread.

"If yer not smart enough to decipher when I'm ridiculing ye, then ye should just take it as gracious compliment that I'm endeavoring to expend the vast amount of effort necessary to indulge ye with my presence." Callahan flashed his wry half smile. "Now clear the shit out yer throat and give me something worthwhile, or ye can watch as me and Selfin here enjoy yer breakfast."

"Right, um, well, 'bout an hour past, I heard a mage and one of those Malaki scholars pass on by talking 'bout some magic trinket they had on 'em and some other gibberish. Said they would talk more this afternoon at the inn called King's Grace." A smile lifted his matted beard as he greedily dove into the bread Callahan tossed to the ground before him. "Thank ye, thank ye."

[Callahan] Malaki, god of knowledge and neutrality. His followers believe in learning, study, and complete apathetic indifference to all manner of conflict. They refuse to side with anything or anyone, abhor violence in any manner, and believe the pleasures of the body such as sex, alcohol, and smoke detract from the strength of the mind. Absolute drab, head-in-the-sand morons, if ye ask me, and if ye don't ask me, it still doesn't negate the fact that they are oblivious to a little fact called reality.

[Narrator] Just as Callahan turned to go, Hemrick spit bread crumbs as he made a gross attempt at a whisper. "Hope there is something good in it for me. Yer always generous to dear ole Hemrick, but I got a spot of info I know ye'll love."

"I might have a copper if ye hurry up. Yer stench and mannerisms are making me lose my appetite." Callahan couldn't help but look a bit eager. Hemrick rarely disappointed when it came to discovering rumor and gossip.

"Word in the underground, whispered among those in the know, says that the crown is becoming quite angry with the Lados nobles and their lack of compli . . . complem . . . com—" Stuttering and stumbling over the words, Hemrick continued to make a horrid attempt at whispering.

"Do ye mean *compliance*, ye illiterate lout?" Callahan interjected, stemming his frustration.

"So the king issued an offer of amnity, er, amer . . . uh, ye know, the thing where he doesn't lop off 'is 'ead." Hemrick still bumbled.

"*Amnesty*, ye tit! Now out with it. My patience is running a bit dry." Callahan impatiently tapped his foot in the dirt, producing a slight cloud of dust around the bum.

8

"Whatever, as to what I was saying, the top-shit king offered it to the pirate Namion in return for him doing no more or less here in the city than he does out to sea." Hemrick's eyes shot wide as saucers as he looked at the silver piece dropped before him. "That's a bit more than I'm used to. Not that I am not grateful, but I am mighty curious as to what ye be wanting."

"For services past and future, me dear friend. Selfin and I will look into the mage and scholar. I just want ye to keep yer eyes and ears open and find out all ye can on this corsair. I think ye might be uncovering a gold mine with that one, mate, and I don't forget those who don't forget me." With a wink and a skip in his step, Callahan guided Selfin on to their next stop: the King's Grace.

[Callahan] Many who would read this might ponder how a twelve-year-old boy could adapt a level of articulation that most likely far exceeds their own in a medieval fantasy realm devoid of any formal education. I, my dear friends, am an autodidact, which most likely explains nothing to most. I acquired the ability to learn, and I then refused to let it go.

I saw as a youth that those who had, read and wrote. Those who had not, did not. So I, with great frustration and effort, taught myself to decipher words, and from there, once I knew how to read, I did so. In my exploratory endeavors into the many residences of Lados, I started to borrow manuscripts and books. Many were the candles I burned through in my little loft.

[Reader 1] Our heroes walked into the King's Grace, where the young large-breasted blonde barmaids immediately indulged them in drink and fellatio.

[Callahan] Whoa! I'm twelve in this story, not even sure I knew what a hard-on was as yet, much less the workings of oral pleasure. On top of that, don't ye think these women would have done and been nicked fer blowing off wee ones? Even in our world, that's not OK. Furthermore, I'm in no definition of the term a *hero*, and Selfin is a lackey at best.

9

Finally, alcohol dulls cognitive thought, and at this point, I endeavored to spy upon presumably intelligent individuals, so I required clarity of thought.

[Reader 1] In the preface, you said I had choice over the scenario.

[Callahan] Who the fuck are you? How the fuck . . . what the . . . holy shit!

[Narrator] What better way to interject the voice of the reader than to . . . well, interject the voice of the reader.

[Callahan] If ye all haven't gathered this by now, I'm not one who likes surprises. By the way, how did you enlist this person? Did ye just go round to all yer mates and say, "Hey, would ye like to come and be verbally abused by a figment of my imagination with me?"

[Narrator] Actually, yes. That is exactly how I did it, except that I added to our accord that if this story contained any marketability, he would be excluded from it.

[Callahan] In that case, brilliant! I'm game. That just leaves one further question—who the fuck are ye?

[Reader 1] I am Sir Pwnzalot, level 64 ninja mage.

[Callahan] Sir! Sir! Who the fuck knighted ye? Where the fuck did ye even come from that ye could debase yerself enough to even utter that mind-shattering stupidity? Level 64 mage, the only way ye can prestidigitate is with a bottle of moisturizer and some pornography, and even with that, the fact that yer mommy keeps walking in on ye in yer basement dungeon means yer not nearly stealthy enough to be deemed a fucking ninja, are ye? A level 12 tit is what ye are.

[Narrator] Now, now. No need to get cruel. He is doing us a favor by adding outside perspective.

[Callahan] Yer fucking with me, right? Right? Ye really can't be serious. Level sixty . . . oh shit, just thinking about it causes my mind to nigh implode. OK then, ah, so now that we have thoroughly established that we really don't give two shits who ye are, for all functional purposes, ye will just be Reader 1, and ye'll learn to like it or ye'll up and bugger off now, won't ye?

[Reader 1] But I'm Sir—

[Callahan] Stop! For the mercy of all, just stop. Suffice with being the insignificant brunt of punch lines that ye are, and leave it at that.

[Reader 1] All right, smart-ass, where does one take a shit in this realm of yours?

[Callahan] By the gods, by all that is holy. Under the guise of complete and utter stupidity, ye've managed to craft a functional and engaging question. Seeing as I live in a city as vast as the eye can see, one would be led to wonder how we manage waste disposal. An expansive river system flows beneath the streets we walk upon. Engineers of this city tapped into that water system so that its natural flow ushers our waste to the ocean cliffside waterfalls, thus why those of us in the know don't consume our local fish. Further, waste removal in the form of garbage is also disposed of in the aforementioned manner, burned, or otherwise altered for reuse by magical means.

[Reader 1] Oh, the old magic dodge. Isn't that just original?

[Callahan] Level 64 Sir Whacksalot did not just bitch about the use of magic. That did not happen. Granted, if I were but a quarter of how retarded he must be, I too would vicariously live through fictional characters. Now really, if ye have a problem with conceiving of magic as a possibility, one, ye must be an atheist because magic is but a term to describe inexplicable energy exchange and, thus, is no more or less real than yer world's religions, and two, ye really screwed yerself when ye picked this genre of a story.

Now before we digress too far as to sound like a geeky campfire circle jerk, can we return to the pertinent story at hand, or do ye have any further interjections that I summarily need to abuse ye for?

[Reader 1] That's all for now.

[Callahan] Go ahead and use the stale sock next to yer chair there, and wipe those tears of yers.

[Narrator] Still early in the afternoon, Selfin and Callahan found themselves to be the only two people in the common room of the King's Grace. Spread before them was a meal of pheasant, potatoes, vegetables, rabbit stew, and some warmed cider to wash it down. "This is amazing," Selfin muttered between bites. "How do we intend to get out of here when they find out we haven't any coin?"

"Ha, ye think even as dumb as these people are, they would make a spread like this for two kids without being prepaid. Don't worry yerself. Today has, thus far, been paid for by a friend of mine, and I've still a bit of me own savings if need be. Every coin spent today has been a well-spent investment toward future dealings. One must spend coin to gain the ability to make it." Callahan had positioned himself with his back to the wall and maintained his vigilant lookout for the two interesting prospects.

"I hope you don't take this wrong. I mean, you're the best friend I could ever ask for, but how are you able to walk about tossing coin around like a noble and speaking down to people like they are below you, when really, you are just like me? You're not but a low street urchin." Selfin seemed hesitant as he questioned his friend.

"I do not hide ignorance with flowered words. I express intellect with eloquent and pointed articulation. I do not make threats I am unable or unwilling to back up. I do not make pacts I am unable or unwilling to fulfill. You are a street urchin trying to ascend into society, and I am a god fighting to not descend into the circumstances placed around me. I carry meself in the manner I do because of one simple equation—I am who I say I am, and I only say who I want to be." A wry half smile lit Callahan's face as two robed men entered to be seated across the common room. "Bah, bears to reason. Course they would be seated all the way cross the room. Hmm, sorry, mate, but take this next step in stride, please."

Lifting his cider to his lips, Selfin was brought a slight pause and a puzzled expression at Callahan's last words until a swift and very painful kick to his shin sent the cider mug spilling its contents all over Selfin and the table. A few seconds passed before a barmaid rushed over.

"Terribly sorry. My friend here is a horrible klutz. So that we don't get all sticky and messy, can I perhaps offer ye a copper to move us? Maybe even over to the table in the sun on the other side there? I wouldn't mind a bit of warmth on me back." Flashing a full sweet smile, Callahan met the bedraggled woman's frustrated gaze with his icy blue eyes softened.

The barmaid responded with a light sigh and returned a smile. "Is all right, me deary. Ye two li'l charmers just move on o'er there, and I'll bring yer vittles rightly on by."

As they were shifting tables, Callahan leaned in toward Selfin who, in great frustration, was trying to keep his soaked shirt from sticking to his chest. "OK, when we sit, start telling me the story of when we chased the stray dogs and ye fell in the sewer. Use a great deal of detail, and feel free to pause for eating."

Doing as instructed, Selfin started to launch into speech as Callahan, seeming to intently listen, honed in on the two strangers and their conversation which, due to Callahan's maneuvering, was being held only a table away now. The dark blue-robed man was in the middle of talking. "And so I stopped wearing it. After the discomfort and awkwardness, I reasoned it would take a bit of practice before my old bones would get used to the added agility."

The brown-robed man responded, "So it silences one's footfalls and motions as well as adds to dexterity and speed. Hmm, absolutely fascinating and deserving of more study, I agree. So the manuscript and your ring will be secure here, you think? I don't want to take the manuscript to my brother's in the monastery for fear that I would never again be allowed to study its rare words. The document I have uncovered describing Entearra Gharu could well be the greatest intellectual and theological find of our lifetimes. To have it in my grasp and lose it so quickly would be a tragedy I would not soon forget."

Food arrived for the two men, then as the barmaid departed, the blue-robed man spoke in a quieter voice, causing Callahan to have to read his lips to fill in the blanks for the few parts he could not hear. "Fear not, dear friend. Just as I have taken measures with our door, I will, after our meal, fashion no less an invocation for our chest just to be sure. Then we can take the partial copy you have, as planned, to your brother's to see if they can give us the key we need to unlock the book's secrets."

Interrupting his friend's story with an out-of-place chuckle, Callahan leaned forward with a quick whisper and said, "Five minutes, make a scene. Spill your drink again, cry out, kick your chair over, and run out the door. Meet me in front of place 2." Raising his voice, he bellowed, "I said I have to piss. By the gods, do I have to announce to the whole room for ye to hear me?"

Heading toward the stairwell in the back, Callahan found himself before the barmaid. "Oh, deary, the privy is off to yer right there, down in the hall."

"Oh, thank ye very much. By the way, those two look really important. I even think one might be a mage. They aren't staying here, are they? I mean, you don't actually get to work in the same place a wizard sleeps, do ye?" Feigning boyish excitement, Callahan bounced around a little.

"Well, deary, I'm not to be knowin' their business, but he might be, and yes, they have a room 'ere." She smiled at Callahan's youthful excitement.

"Wow, well, maybe I could get the chef to send a special treat up to their room. Ye know, maybe if I'm nice enough, he'll show us a trick or two later. I'm gonna run on back with yer leave, and ask the chef, but first, which door do I leave it at? Please, oh, please. What a treat it would be to see real magic." Callahan fought back the vomit he wanted to spew.

"Fourth door off to yer right, up the stairs 'ere. For mercy's sake, calm down before ye wet yerself. They seem like busy men. I'm not sure they'll be friendly with ye. Now I'd best be back to see if anyone's needing fer anything. Ye hurry on along to the privy now." The barmaid headed back into the common area as Callahan walked on toward the privy.

Soon as she left his sight, he turned back and bolted up the stairs to the third door on the right. Slowly opening it, he said, "Order's ready. Be ye wanting anything more 'fore I bring it on in?" When he received no response, he moved into the room, closing the door behind him. Noting the room to be vacant, Callahan delighted in that small favor. Moving to the back window, he slid it open, assessing the surroundings. "No drain, no lattice, ah fuck!" Whispering to himself, Callahan surveyed the alley below to ensure that no one witnessed as he pulled his body out the window. Standing precariously on the window ledge, looking to the roof, he knew he would get only one chance. Quick calculations fluttered through his mind. *Broken leg, sprained ankle, possible head injury, and maybe get caught, have to play dumb boy again. Rewards equal magic ring, invaluable manuscript.* With that thought, he leapt, grasping the roof's edge; his left hand dropped, not finding a hold, as the ledge ripped into his right.

"Ah piss." Gritting his teeth, he forced his hold to stay despite the pain then returned his left hand to find a hold. "Why do I always have to believe I'm part monkey? Can't just keep me feet on solid ground, can I? But fuck me if this adrenaline isn't delightful." Muttering to himself, he started sliding along the roof's edge until his legs hung in front of the two men's room. "Oh, come on now. Really, it has to have been five minutes by now." It seemed like an eternity as his right hand throbbed, but Callahan remained in a state of stasis, waiting patiently, until *crash.* "Agh! Not again! WAH!" *Bang.*

As the first crash sounded, Callahan swung his legs back then forward, letting loose his grasp. Clumsily lurching through the window, his body intermixed with the broken glass on the floor. Cursing his luck and his newfound cuts, Callahan sped to the only chest he could find present. Tossing it open, he dug through some robes and a few papers and books until he found a cloth-wrapped old-looking book. Opening it, he saw footnotes folded into it. One of the footnotes contained the words *Entearra Gharu*, which was all he needed to wrap it back up and stuff it in his shirt. Digging a bit more, he found a small velvet pouch containing a ring.

Slipping the ring on his finger, Callahan felt a sudden rush, both physically and mentally. He visibly trembled as he delighted in the energy coursing through him. He could feel an insatiable hunger awaken within him. The power he felt coupled with the knowledge that there must be countless items imbued with magic led to an immediate addiction toward the acquisition of such items. Allowing himself no time for doubt or second-guessing, he bolted toward the window to make his second story-leaping escape.

Unfamiliar with his newly acquired speed, his muscles and mind awkwardly wrestled, causing him an all-too-quick and underprepared tumble out the window. Dusting himself off and stumbling painfully, he did his best to maneuver the alleys en route to the park that he and Selfin had deemed as meeting place 2. A sprained ankle, several cuts and abrasions, a deep cut in his right hand, and a headache of the caliber to drop a full-sized ogre were his incurred cost, but Callahan did not for a second think himself shorted on the deal.

[Reader 1] From what I have gathered, Selfin is a thief who falls into sewers and is a good place to throw your cider. Why do you hang out with him again?

[Callahan] As I have gathered, for the same reason the narrator hangs out with you. I mean, who doesn't want someone to follow them around like a grateful puppy even when ye delight in not more than kicking 'em about.

[Reader 1] Ouch, touché.

[Callahan] This does raise the question of who held you down and shit a brain into yer noggin, though. That's a halfway decent question, and really, it's not like the boy just got abused by me. Fuck, when I found the poor bugger, he was very near death in an alley all alone. I could count his ribs from about a block away. So not sure why. Perhaps I just wanted to know what it would feel like to have a friend. I fed the guy and helped find him an abandoned house to flop in. So it went. I'd help him get food and places to stay as houses would fill and empty on a regular basis, and in return, he took my crap in stride and acted as my lackey.

[Reader 1] All right, so you have a magic ring, a cloth-covered book, and a sticky lackey. Where did you go from here? Wash down the lackey, hock the book, and use the ring to avoid falling into the sewers?

[Callahan] Ah, thought we lost ye for a minute there, but here ye return to prove that intellect must have direct connection to snot which, by looking at the decorative nature of yer walls and the base of yer table, would explain clearly why ye are just that fucking stupid.

[Reader 1] I don't really get what ye mean by that.

[Callahan] Yer not by any chance relation to Hemrick, are ye? Pawn the book! Are ye really fucking serious? I mean, how retarded would I have to be to gain possession of the rarest article of knowledge currently known to exist and pawn it. When each translated sentence would be worth my weight in gold. No, ye flaming jack bag, I undertook great and lengthy efforts to translate that manuscript. Thirty-two fucking languages later, I had still only scratched the surface of its contents and had uncovered priceless jewels of information that would craft the very history of Calarr. So eat shit.

[Reader 1] Interesting thought. Your friend is homeless, and you are by no means well-off, so it raises the question, what shit did you normally eat?

[Callahan] Well, there was obviously a reason we'd been chasing them stray dogs before Selfin fell in the sewer, and you, my friend with clueless luck, just stumbled upon it.

[Reader 1] You mean . . . you ate . . . oh god.

[Callahan] Nope, got that backwards. It's spelled d-o-g, though I'm curious what god might taste like. But yes, it wasn't every day a fat sack of shit placed his neck on the chopping block for me to extort a full purse of coins off him now, was it? Unlike yerself, my mom failed to supply me with a near-unlimited quantity of cheese-coated corn puffs and piss-flavored carbonated water, so I dealt with what I had. I would have ye know that if cooked properly, they can be rather flavorful.

[Reader 1] OK, disgusting as that is, let's get back to the topic. Are you trying to tell me that you stole the holy grail of books, and everyone just shrugged it off and went about their days?

[Callahan] Why do ye continue to insist upon referencing yer singular deity and the items related to such? Ye do recognize that even if I were to be religious, I would be a pagan/polytheist, but due to what I found about Entearra Gharu being a pact fashioned between mortals of vast power that acted as a semi-peace accord so that they could reign as gods, yer continued religious references just further secure my belief in yer vast mental deficiency. Though to answer question at hand before I delve too far into insult, there was an investigation into the theft, and in fact, my dolt of a father was set in its lead. Most disbelieved in the existence of a written book that would outline the pact of the gods. So though it initially stirred a huge ruckus, it was eventually reasoned out that someone must have just been out to rob the mage.

Belief that the theft was centered on the mage did eventually lead to the questioning of Hemrick. Be it of loyalty or just forgetful stupidity, he never did divulge having talked to me and instead wound up leading them after phantom ruffians who had apparently been wandering through the same streets as the mage and scholar after they had passed him.

The scholar insistedthat his partial copy illustrating the game of the gods was in fact a real part of his uncovered holy doctrine that had been stolen. Even his fellow followers of Malaki fell short of believing that the gods had made a pact that placed one adversary against another in a great celestial chess match, where no direct contest or transgression could be enacted. Nor could any pawn be given any directive toward such an end. The gods locked in a constant power struggle had crafted Calarr as their own game board. In which they tried to enlist followers who would, without direct influence, seek to further one god's supremacy over another. In essence, the only way one god could kill another is if a follower chose without direct order and out of his own free will to do it for him.

Now perhaps you can gain a bit more perspective on what I mean when I speak of the book's value to me?

[Reader 1] So I take it that Hemrick was of little use after this point. Being questioned must have given him quite a scare.

[Callahan] Actually, he remained one of my greatest informants in the years to come and was the entire reason I was able to closely follow the rise of the Corsair, Namion, and his gang, the Talons.

Hey out there! Bloody narrator, where did ye bugger off to? Our story here is drowning a quick death, and this reader is tossing me bricks to aid in treading water. I mean, I get it—we are at a lull in the plot that lasts from my age of twelve until I'm sixteen and are stuck in a position of having pertinent information the reader needs to gain prior to us continuing the story line. So we are left with few options, most of which are altogether boring or detract from the pace of the story. Well, our above display has done both of those, I fear, and though the reader has extracted head from arse and given proper prompts, I'm feeling as though, despite it being a massive cliché that stretches all too frequently through all genres of story, it may well be time to queue a cheesy music number and bust into a montage.

We can show scenes of Selfin and me engaging in near-daily swordplay/combat training as was our frequent course in between bouts of further extorting lesser mortals. We can show the many nighttime borrowing sessions I had to undertake to get a hold of books to aid in translating the manuscript about Entearra Gharu. Having been scripted in countless tongues as I alluded to earlier, its translation was, to put it lightly, difficult. I was able to decipher thirty-two of the many languages and obsessively studied it.

How the power structure of Lados itself started to shift as Namion and his gang went about buying up the debts from all the underground gambling would also have to be illustrated. In the years to follow, the Talon thieves' guild, as it was called by the general populace, exploded on to the scene of Lados, quickly threatening the influence and strength of the guard as well as the nobles' pseudorepublic.

Namion was a scarred and rough-looking individual who delighted in power, prestige, and infamy. Those who bore the tattoo of his guild, a large gray talon placed upon the underside of one's left wrist, followed without reservation or question. Rumor and fear of his intellect, strength, and swordsmanship were only overshadowed by word of his cold and calculated cruelty. His men were given a wide berth by the wise and the unwise; well, they didn't remain such for long.

[Reader 1] One more question before we continue. Being so superior, self-sufficient, and smart, why the hell did you stay in your parents' house? That sounds pretty dumb to me.

[Callahan] Ouch, out of nowhere, Reader 1 punches me right in the groin. Our realities will never coincide, so I needn't conceal, reserve, or otherwise hide. Be careful what ye ask; sometimes ye'll get yer answer.

It's not like I woke up one morning and said, "I wonder how I can villainize meself and hurt people." No. When Selfin and I trained, when we played, we saw ourselves as heroes fighting the corruption of the guards, the tyranny of the crown, or the monsters that plagued the outlands. I didn't really want to be what I was. I needed to be it because the truth was I'm human, and I was a boy.

What does any child want? I wanted to be loved. I wanted to love. I didn't want to have to be strong. So many hours were spent with and without Selfin, on rooftops, in shadows, at a distance, just watching people and longing. Not always just watching for further prospect or heist, but more often, I saw child fall in the park, scratching knee. Watched as parent rushed in and, with very real magic, kissed the pain away. I watched parent pull child into embrace as questionable person passed on the street—an embrace that said, "I am here, you are safe, and I love ye." I watched from the outside, praying, wishing, and hoping that someone would invite me in. That someone would breathe life into the fire of my humanity that all around me seemed to delight in pissing on.

I stayed in that house against all logic and rationale because maybe one day, Mom would climb out of herself and tell me I was needed. One day, Dad would accept me and tell me how proud he was to have me as his son, embrace me, and tell me not to fear because he would vanquish all the threatening demons.

That need wasn't fulfilled. With the absence of such fulfillment, a void formed in me, vast and insatiable. A void that was held at bay during those years by my friend Selfin's need for my strength. He wasn't enough to fill or remove the void, but he did breathe just enough life into the fire that was my humanity to keep it from being completely extinguished. In such regard, he was at once my only real strength and weakness in those years.

I remember one time when I was about fifteen. Selfin was no longer settled with having me as his only friend. So he tried to get in good graces with a group of local kids. They told him to get them a thorough lunch, and they would let him hang out with them. He refused my help in the matter and said he wanted to do it on his own. I think it was his way of trying to show me he could make it even without me. Took him all morning to assemble what would've taken me only an hour. He did it, though, as I watched, unseen, from a distance.

All that work and I could see him beaming with pride as he took a full satchel of food to those kids. They took the food, laughed at him, and said, "Bah, in what world would we ever hang out with a weasel like you?" They kicked dirt at him. I saw the tears starting to fill his eyes, so despite overwhelming odds and a previous request to stay out of it, I charged up that alley to stand in front of that group.

"Ye ungrateful shits. Me mate doesn't need yer kind. 'Ere he was just trying to grace ye all with his presence, and yer all far too daft to even see it." I spat at the feet of their leader. I dodged the first punch with a quick duck and came up under him with a solid right just under his ribs that toppled him breathless. Sidestepped the next fella's attempt and palmed his face with enough force to hear his nose snap. A third grappled me, and as we toppled, I managed to force him under me so that I got a few good shots on his face before the fourth and fifth kids rang me head so hard with nearby boards of oak that stars lit my vision. Selfin tried to jump in but was quickly overwhelmed, and the two of us were catching quite the ass whooping until, through my punch-drunk fog, I heard a newcomer rising to our defense.

With our foes distracted by this new person's presence, I was able to gain an advantage over my adversaries, regain me feet, and get to where I could stand over Selfin. Magic agility or not, superior numbers and experience still won out. Feeling worse for the wear as the boys hit the road running, I took my first look at who we owed our skins to.

Cropped jet-black hair, slightly scarred face, hefty muscular build, looked to be in her late teens the gal who stood before me was homely at best. She threw me a disapproving glare. Despite that and her appearance, I found meself engrossed with her. She must've seen the lost puppy look in my eyes as I stepped forward to shake her hand in thanks because I curled forward when her knee connected to me groin. She leaned in and, in a soft whisper, said, "Boy, you have a lot to learn. Watched that whole show you just put on, and though admirable, you really should get it in your head that bravery, compassion, and courage are traits of the remembered."

Head over heels in love, I was, right then and there. Unable to find my voice through the waves of nausea and pain, I couldn't even ask for her name before she disappeared from sight. Selfin, a little better off than me, aided me in finding my feet, and we went on with the grind of life as it had been.

That day taught me a very dear lesson. Having agility, strength, and even knowledge did not make up for the fact that, being a quick-tongued little shit, I had no real combat experience. For the next year, Selfin and I took our little training sessions a bit further and started hunting groups of young punks just like the ones that had stitched us up. In quick order, I was learning to fully utilize the advantage provided by my ring and even studied a bit into the realm of human biology to know how best to manipulate via pain.

[Narrator] As any good creator knows, sometimes it's best to just let the story unfold itself instead of trying to force uncomfortable, unnatural progression. Thank you both for making my job easier.

[Callahan] Bollocks.

[Narrator] At age sixteen, Callahan's dirty blond hair hung in a jumble down to his shoulders. His thin frame and small stature did well to conceal its unusual strength. His piercing icy blue eyes entranced those who looked upon them with the depth they contained. He walked with the strut of a commanding general and spoke, as always, with snarky cynical pessimism. The sincerity in his self-believed divinity could easily be seen in his countenance.

He was, in his eyes, ascending into manhood and had started storing away savings he kept with his prized book in his loft. Having learned to hold his own, his father had again returned to the process of ignoring his existence while seeming to delight in the torment of his mother. He had amassed quite the local reputation as the guy in the know for anything and everything. With that came the reputation that he was not to be trifled with, but such reputations can draw unwanted attention. He found himself more frequently needing to dance around the lingering and all-too-questioning eyes of the local guard. Also, he had noted on more than one occasion individuals bearing the Talon tattoo tailing him in an attempt to monitor his activities.

Their rusted old rapiers clanked together as Selfin and Callahan circled each other. Selfin's right heel dropped flat, indicating to Callahan's observant eyes that a thrust would immediately follow. The ring allowed his muscles to move as quickly as his mind could calculate, so with blinding speed and perfect accuracy, Callahan made a ducking half spin in front of and behind Selfin. His rapier drawing a light scratch as it slid across the front of Selfin's throat, Callahan chortled, "Bah, getting better, boyo, but ye still lead yer moves."

"It's not natural how you're able to move around me like that, as if I were standing still." Frustrated Selfin pushed Callahan's blade away and slid his own in his raggedy sheath.

"Well, just be glad I'm on yer side, mate." Callahan flashed a half smile at his friend.

"Are you? I mean, you, who would sell your own mother for a copper. Callahan, are you really on my side, or am I just another lesser being to be used as a tool for your disposal?" Selfin's voice rose with his anger.

Put back on his heels, Callahan gained a sincere and stunned expression. "Ye ungrateful shit! Of all people, who the fuck are you to question my loyalty? I, who have always stood by yer side. I, who have saved yer arse countless times. I, who have taken ye on as a brother."

"That's right! You YOU YOU! That's all it is, isn't it? Just you. Where is the *we*, my friend? Maybe just once, I want something to be me. Maybe just once, I want to save *yer arse*. I am not OK with just following your shadow. I would walk by your side as equal, not follow like a lost dog. I need a breather. I'll see you tomorrow." Selfin stormed off.

Left alone in the park, Callahan cursed to the open evening air. "Well, fuck him! Not my equal, shit. When have I ever shorted him? Save my arse—yeah, that'll be the day. That incompetent ungrateful fuck!" Full of frustration and anger, he cursed his way home and stormed in to hear his father yelling at his mother once again.

"Ah, boy! Come back 'ere again, have ye? Well, get on out my sight 'fore I mess that ugly face of yers up even more." The drunken man slurred while leaning on the dining table.

"Listen well. Tonight is not a good night to test me. I'll cut yer fuckin' tongue out and sodomize ye with it, even though the act will be interrupted by my need to puke in doing so." Deftly flying up the rope ladder to the loft, Callahan left his father stunned with a bewildered look of disgust on his face.

Giving it a few minutes to ensure there would be no reprisal for his words, Callahan then started his nightly studies. Frustration clouded his mind, so he put his studies away as light faded instead of lighting a candle. Stowing his books away, he lay staring at the ceiling while spinning the ring ever present on the middle finger of his left hand. Anger subsided, and he felt for his friend; no one wants to be second best all the time. His mind started to drift to sleep, fluttering through plans to help Selfin excel, until harsh whispers from outside lit every instinct within him.

Having left the park to cool off, Selfin reflected upon the harshness he had used with his friend. He wanted Callahan's respect as an equal, and his inability to measure up ate at him. He wanted to stay angry, but that quickly gave way to the knowledge that he owed his friend an apology. As dusk set in, he found himself near Callahan's home.

Four men walked with a purpose toward Callahan's home. Selfin watched them converse outside the house and saw one kick the door in and rush in, followed quickly by two of his companions. The fourth figure took a solid look around the streets then confidently strode into the home. Slipping from his rooftop vantage, Selfin moved to a knothole in the home that lended a view of the scene unfolding inside.

Callahan lifted his loose floorboards and slid into his makeshift false floor. It creaked under the strain of his weight. It had been so long since he had used the area for anything but book storage that cramming himself in it was a highly uncomfortable process. The effort was rewarded by the crashing sound of the house's front door being kicked in. Listening carefully, he heard three people rush in; his mother cried out and started shrieking. Her cries drowned out most of the other activities until, through the din, Callahan heard steely unwavering voice say, "Get the boy. We do the whole lot."

Callahan listened to someone's clumsy ascent of his rope ladder, listened as someone crawled right over his hiding place. "Sir, he's not here." The man could be heard climbing his way back down the rope ladder.

"Drag him out here." A few seconds passed. "Where is your son?"

"I'm a captain of the Lados guard. Boy, did ye pick the wrong house to rob." Callahan heard his father's drunken bravado.

"Men, have your fun with the woman while he watches." That voice contained command, depth, and something about it instilled fear even into a heart as calloused as Callahan's.

Compelled and driven by an inner instinct, Callahan rushed to action. Rolling out of his hiding place, he retrieved his rope, set it in place, and slid down. The silence provided him by his ring in combination with the noise below prevented anyone from hearing his descent. Two men were tearing his mother's clothes, one was holding his father's arms behind his back, and the last was only a few feet from where Callahan landed.

As though he were born for this very moment, Callahan maintained his calm and immediately rushed forward. A quick assessment of the closest man found a sheathed dagger on his right upper thigh within grasp; sliding the blade from its sheath, Callahan pushed it toward the man as it withdrew, digging its blade into his hip.

Time seemed to slow, and Callahan felt a rush the likes of which he had only felt the first time he had slid on his ring. Visions of death, torture, rough seas. Memories that were not his own flooded his mind. Then a hunger previously unknown lit within him, and his vision returned.

Strengthened and energized, Callahan surged forward, driving the dagger into his mother's first assailant. Pants around his ankles, the man wasn't even afforded a death cry as the blade ripped through ribs and lung, siphoning his life through to Callahan. The second assailant reached for his sword, but before his fingers touched its hilt, Callahan had rolled over the collapsing man's back and, with an upward thrust, drove the dagger through the base of the second man's jaw and into his skull.

A flood of energy roared through Callahan's mind and body. Unknown to him, a deep and sincere smile spread across his face from ear to ear. Life seemed at peace. The void that plagued his inner being sealed up, and he knew contentment previously unimagined. The third man had thrown his father aside and drawn his short sword. Callahan watched the seemingly clumsy sideswipe as though it were in slow motion. Stepping forward, he slashed the dagger upward, removing the man's hand. Catching the falling blade with his left hand, he spun it and thrust. Letting forth a victorious roar, Callahan released the short sword now stuck through the man's gut and slid the dagger deep through the man's throat as he spun around to face the dagger's owner.

Visibly shuddering with orgasmic pleasure, Callahan stood confident and self-assured. "For once, the drunk was right. Ye really picked the wrong house to fuck with. To what do I owe the great pleasure of getting to make yer acquaintance, Namion, leader of the Talons? What could ye possibly want with little ole me?"

Namion, rapier in hand and readied, laughed uproariously. "Boy, you are impressive. You had me. You should have followed it through while you could, and do not flatter

yourself. The only thing I want of you is your death. I am here
in regard to your father, not you."

"Good job, boy. Now—" Callahan's father started to rise,
but a sharp backward kick to his jaw from Callahan sent him
back to the ground. Near-inaudible groans ushered forth, but
no further motion was made.

"Shut up! Ye fucking wanker. Shit, if all ye want is him,
then be my guest." Callahan cautiously took a step back as
though providing access to his father.

"You are a smart one, but you still have so much to learn.
He is a message. Not just him, but you and her as well. I am
Lados now. Your deaths will scream a message to the very
heights of this city's nobility that none can skirt debt to me.
That none are above my reprisal." Chuckling again, Namion
shook his head. "I really wish I had met you under different
circumstances. You would have gone far in the guild."

"Ye speak in past tense, but here I stand, my friend. Offer
accord, and I'll see if it's to my liking." Callahan did not for an
instant let his muscles relax.

"No, Callahan, don't bargain—" His mother, gathering the
shreds of her clothes, kneeled on the ground before Callahan.
Punching the dagger's hilt against her cheek worked to silence
her words, but not her sobbing.

"Do us a favor, boy, and off that woman that we may
speak awhile before you follow her to the afterlife. Her cries
annoy me. How can I hope to focus my amusement upon
what proves to be the rather entertaining and original plea for
mercy you will deliver?" Like Callahan, Namion's pose never
faltered or relaxed.

Ignoring his mother's sobs, Callahan spoke. "Yer wounded,
and I have yer dagger. We both know the advantage this blade
offers, so bears to reason I've the upper hand here."

"Impudence will only go so far with me, boy. I know that
dagger all too well, and you are right. In a seasoned hand, such
a thing would lend advantage over me. I am also well aware
that unfamiliar as it is to you, the siphoning process will cloud

and contort your thoughts and movements. Adrenaline fading in this lull, you're feeling those experiences, memories, and movements colliding within you. So do not mistake me a fool. You and I both well know that unless I allow otherwise, your death is a foregone conclusion this night. So be quick with it if you care to appeal to my mercy." In spite of his wounded leg, Namion's muscles shifted ever so slightly while he spoke, indicating to Callahan that an attack was imminent.

"I'll not plead. I'll not beg. I don't disagree with yer assessment, though. So I offer pact. Yer an intelligent man, it seems, but I'm willing to bet my life I'm smarter. I don't offer any kind of groveling. What I offer is a challenge. Yer so damned great, then humor me, for I offer ye the pact of Entearra Gharu. I challenge ye to the game of the gods itself. Now if ye can't beat me in that fair competition, go ahead and kill me because I'll meet the afterlife knowing that even the great Namion feared me so much he had to cut me down while underprepared because he knew I would best 'im." Fighting to keep his mind in order, Callahan found great difficulty in his attempts to focus on his opponent.

"You do not cease to amaze, do you, boy? Here I am expecting to hear promises of silence and servitude, but no. You invoke the name of something wizened old men only whisper rumor of. Great lengths were taken on my part to learn of that pact. You realize the scope of your blasphemy in even offering such, correct?" Namion softened his stance ever so slightly, desiring to hear more.

"Can gods commit blasphemy? You and I aren't like others. We're not constrained by mortal law. No. You and I, we ascend to such height that we set law." Kneeling, Callahan pulled his mother, still sobbing, close to himself and said, "Be thankful ye needn't witness what's to come." Driving the dagger into her heart, he felt her life quickly vanish and, at once, felt his hunger subside and burst to new heights in a kaleidoscope of contradictions. "That is a show of good faith. I offer to eliminate all who've witnessed power of yer blade. I offer to serve, in its full capacity, as an inducted member of the Talons. I offer to, in accordance to Entearra Gharu, bide my time until I can properly best ye, assuming yer position and the return of this here dagger into my possession."

"I add to such accord, you will burn this home upon our conclusion. You will burn with it this life you have led, and you will adhere verbatim to what you have said. For you and I both know the pact forces such. To insure truth of your knowledge, draw a slight bit of your blood upon my dagger before you toss it back to my feet. If these terms are agreed to, then you, my boy, have a pact." Looking both puzzled and delighted, Namion forcibly finished, saying, "I, Namion, leader of the Talons, agree to enter with Callahan into the great pact of Entearra Gharu."

"I, Callahan, agree to enter with Namion into the great pact of Entearra Gharu." Callahan then kneeled before his father and lifted him to a sitting position.

Slapping him roughly, Callahan watched as his eyes fluttered to recognition. "Boy . . ." A scream replaced words as he felt the removal of his thumb. Several moments later, the scream faded due to the process of disembowelment. As the scream faded, Callahan heard the gasp from outside, and as only a best friend could, he instantly knew the source.

Cutting his hand lightly, he tossed the dagger to Namion, who caught it easily. "Holding to accord, let me see your rapier."

Having a tight grip on his dagger, Namion's puzzlement gave way to his act of adherence. Callahan caught the well-balanced blade. Not knowing if it was the hunger placed in him by the dagger, an outside force to uphold the Entearra Gharu, or just his own choice, he slid the blade through the knothole and could feel that it met its purpose.

"This just keeps getting better. Your only friend." Namion sheathed his dagger and walked over, retrieving his rapier from where Callahan left it. Looking at Callahan's stunned expression as he kneeled bathed in blood, Namion continued,

"You still live. That is an accomplishment. Now there is more to our pact you need fulfill."

"Let me retrieve some personal effects from upstairs. Drag the other body in, and then I'll burn it." Callahan started to find his feet under him again.

"No, get the body. Burn it all. As I clearly said, your life and everything here burns. Hurry, I am a busy man, and with having to get you tattooed in an unorthodox induction, I just got a lot busier, did I not?" Namion walked toward the front door. "You have more than proven strength of pact, so I will await you outside."

In completing the task, Callahan looked upon his friend's mangled face. He knew that what fire had burned of his humanity was just doused. Leaving only one dying ember in its wake, an ember that found itself being buried deeper and deeper within. He cringed as he lit the house, knowing that his only escape route, being the hidden secrets contained in the book of Entearra Gharu, would burn this night.

Walking up to stand before Namion as the fire roared to life, Callahan nodded at his new employer. Namion's hand grabbed a solid chunk of Callahan's hair and drove his face into an uprising right knee. Chuckling at the stunned and sitting boy, Namion explained, "Lesson one, boy. The human form is awkward and lanky enough as is. Do not further it by adding handhold. Cut that mop of hair, and remember that you serve me. Never again will you bark command at me, question me, or correct me."

Spitting a bit of blood, Callahan growled at the man, saying, "When pact is made and order is given, I'll adhere no less than I did. I'll follow yer orders even if they take me through ye. So cut the ruffling of feathers bullshit. Stop trying to intimidate me. I know ye can best me with blade. I know yer smart. I know yer dangerous. So saying such is just redundant and boring."

Grinning widely, Namion pulled the boy to his feet. "I am going to enjoy this, boy." The two headed calmly down the street just before crowds of onlookers started gathering before the fire.

[Callahan] Anyone else get the impression that our narrator has some seriously deep-seated parent/interpersonal issues? Years, me friend. Long, long years of therapy are needed.

[Narrator] Hey, I'm not the one who took out my parents and best friend in one fell swoop.

[Callahan] Nope, you just imagined it enough to write of me doing it.

[Narrator] Touché, count this as my therapy.

[Reader 1] Uh, yeah, you're not the only one who needs intense therapy after that.

[Reader 1 pretending to be Narrator] What's that supposed to mean?

[Callahan] Hold on a sec. Since when do ye think ye get the luxury of offering yerself leading questions? One good question earlier in our story does not afford ye any lasting respect, so shut up, and know yer place.

[Reader 1] For whatever reason, I ventured away from my happy-go-lucky, carefree world of cheesy poofs and masturbation to follow our narrator, the twisted prick he is, and come here and have to endure this—

[Callahan] Whoa! Hold on there. Is there really any call to disparage the narrator's character in the presence of his character? Budda dum dumb. Thank ye for that little spot of opportunity for a really bad joke.

[Narrator] Really, guys. I craft what I feel is one of the best pieces of writing I have ever produced, and in ye both dance to piss all over it.

[Reader 1] And that's the thing that worries me, man. The gleam that is all too visible in your eyes can only be described as . . .

[Callahan] Careful there, mate. He just scripted me offing my best friend, who wasn't half as obnoxious as ye.

[Reader 1] While I don't usually take my life advice from fictional characters—

[Callahan] Oh, yer atheist too, eh?

[Reader 1] I feel that your words of wisdom are valid in furthering my very real health and well-being.

[Narrator] OK, OK, now that did conclude chapter 1, so what were ye envisioning for our second chapter, Callahan?

[Callahan] I still like the Choose Yer Own Adventure whorehouse. I'm rather partial to loose women and copious amounts of coin.

[Reader 1] I second that vote.

[Narrator] Fuck ye both. Ah hell, now I'm even typing myself in a bad accent.

[Callahan] Fine, on we go—chapter 2, "Rise of the Falcon."

[Narrator] How cheese dick can you get? I mean, talk of cliché, drab, and unoriginal titles. Let's just leave that at . . .

Chapter 2

THE FALCON

[NARRATOR] "IT IS A long walk to the temple of Vertigo, where we will be acquiring your tattoo. So do try not to look like you just killed your best friend, would you?" Namion smiled and chuckled lightly. "Never mind, I guess you did just give him a new eye socket, did you not?"

Ignoring Namion's verbal stabs, Callahan queried, "The god of evil, why would we be getting me a tat from those blighters?"

"Evil?" Namion chuckled again. "You still believe in fairy tales of good and evil, do you? I will let you in on a secret—there is no good and evil. No, the world is not black and white. There are only people. People with shades of gray, granted some of us are darker than others. Vertigo is not the god of evil, my friend. He is merely the god of power. His priests managed to magically imbue the ink that goes into the guild's tattoo so that every bum and transient cannot just manufacture their own." Namion extended his left wrist to Callahan's view. "Look upon mine. What do you feel?"

Doing as asked, Callahan got an inner feeling of the tattoo's legitimacy. "Well, aside from the ever-present contempt and disgust I feel for ye in combination with my bore of yer love of yer own voice, I catch yer drift."

Laughing again, Namion shook his head. "Never had someone who could speak so candidly to me. I kill anyone who tries. It is actually proving to be an entertaining endeavor. Though I suspect you will not survive the six months of induction training."

"Training? That's not part of the deal. I'm to be given leave as a full member, not as a prospect." Callahan glared at his new employer.

"How do you know what it is to be a member without a proper initiation? You will retrospectively go through training as a full member. You will be treated like the other prospects but will be held to the rules of a full member. You did not think I would make this easy on you? We will get your tattoo, which will most likely, due to the process of magical imbuement, be the most excruciating thing you have ever endured. Then we will take you down into the caves under the sewage waterfalls, where I will explain to the current prospects that you have superseded the process of induction they are struggling to survive. I will return to those said caves in a week's time to hear tale of your death. Fun, is it not?" Namion gave one last laugh. "Now I refuse to afford control of my movements to an animal, so we will not ride horses or carriages. We will walk. Take this herb. It provides rest for one's muscles and body while not diminishing their mental capacities. Use it carefully, though. Overuse can lead to a breach from sanity due to an overtaxed mind. Now smoke that, and shut up. I order silence for the remainder of this trip."

Callahan accepted the pipe and herb skeptically, but in view of Namion's words, he feared any negative reactions to the herb far less than the jealous reprisal of the untold number of prospects he was destined to meet. Horrible as Namion seemed, Callahan didn't think him a liar, so he lit the herb. Moments later, he was amazed by the pep in his step. He traveled the remainder of the walk to the temple district, which took well into the morning, feeling as though he had slept all night.

[Callahan] He wasn't lying. That tattoo hurt like crazy. Every pierce of the needle sent surges of energy through me body. He sat there watching me the whole time, waiting for me to cry out, but I refused to give him the satisfaction. While the tattoo was being done, another priest, on direction from Namion, lopped off me hair and, using a straight razor, smoothed it off. I actually rather delighted in the freeing feel of it; since that day, I have kept it short, but I never did go full skin again. Of course, the temple décor was meant to intimidate with its dark, demonic furnishings and color scheme, but really, I was unimpressed. Religious sorts just make me ill with their illogical thoughts and irrational mannerisms.

The herb was not marijuana, so for all ye antidrug dipshits, drop it, and for all ye who would celebrate my use, that's probably a significant contributor to yer inability to move out yer parents' basement. Yer world has nicotine, caffeine, yada yada, and so forth; our world also has mood-altering substances, hallucinogens, and so on. As for the particular herb in question, its effects were limited to the revitalization of one's body, leaving the mind no more or less effective than it was prior to use. In other words, if ye were to use it, ye would still inevitably be less intelligent than myself.

[Narrator] "How original, thieves and brigands having their secret hideout amidst shit-smelling underground dwellings." Callahan snorted his disdain at Namion as they walked the beach up to the sewage waterfalls.

"I thought I ordered silence." Namion reached for his rapier.

"That was pertaining to the leg of the journey that led to the temple now, wasn't it? So stuff it up yer arse, ye blowhard." Callahan flashed his wry half smile. Mocking Namion's deeper and more properly pronounced dialect, Callahan continued, "I order silence for the remainder of *this* trip."

"I will delight in urinating on your corpse." Despite his frustration, Namion couldn't help but smile at Callahan's persisting insolence. "It took a good deal of effort to evict the dwarves who resided in these halls we travel to. You are right, though. It is a ridiculous concept, and that is why we force our prospects to endure six months of training there, while the lot of my inducted members reap the benefits of their tattoos. If you survive the next six months, you too will no longer need to pay for such trivial things as shelter, food, sex, weapons, and armor. Just flash your tattoo, and you will be amazed at the respect and fear it will reward."

The stench was nauseating. Callahan found great difficulty in holding back his gag reflex. A wry half smile lit Callahan's face. "By the way, how's the leg? Ye seem to be lacking a bit of pep to yer step. Must be a real bitch to have to do a daylong trek on it."

Namion's grimace in light of the foul odor softened to a slight grin. "Doing a lot better than your friend's, I would wager."

The natural cave walls gave way to intricate dwarven stonework. As they progressed further into the halls, Callahan could hear the roar of flowing water through the stone above him until the sound was drowned out by the shouts of men and the clanking of metal on metal. They entered a vast underground valley via a platform with a descending stone stairwell leading into the valley. Callahan found himself impressed by this small town stretched out before him that kept itself relatively unknown to the surface city above. Two men were in the process of a dice game on the platform but immediately stood tall when they noticed Namion enter.

With surprising volume, Namion's shout drew the valley to silence. "Hadrick, Bring the prospects before the entry." Quieting his voice, he looked to Callahan. "Let the real fun begin, my friend."

Callahan watched as about two dozen men gathered in rows before the platform, all looking to be in their mid to late twenties. A large man in thick leather armor stepped before the assembly and said, "Here they are, sir. They are honored that you would show your presence before their unworthy selves."

"Damn right, they are. I hate this shit-smelling underground pit. I am here in regard to a new trainee. This boy by my side is an inducted member of the Talons and rightly wears the tattoo as such. Despite not having spent a single day in this pit with the lot of you. He has not had to fear the very real possibility of death throughout the training process, but now that changes. He will be held to the laws and rules that guide our members but is to be treated and trained as though he were a prospect. As a member, no other member may kill him lest they suffer public torture and death excepting, of course, if proper challenge is issued and publicly addressed. Who would be first to prove their worth and challenge him?" Namion smiled at Callahan.

"That's no different than ordering me death. Yer in breach." Callahan's features twisted with anger as he whispered.

The strongest fighter in the lot forced his way through the ranks, stepping next to Hadrick. "I challenge him!" With a nod from Namion, Hadrick pulled his short sword and lopped the man's head off from behind him. A shocked gasp ripped through the ranks.

"Collect yourselves! Do you think this is a fucking summer camp? Do you think you are here to play at being soldiers? Do you aspire to lead or be heroes? Because if you do, kill yourself tonight to spare yourself my hands. Bravery, courage, and compassion are traits of the remembered. Do you want to be remembered, or do you, like I, want to live and be feared?" Namion's expression was emotionless as he addressed the prospects. "Worry not, that lesson is concluded. Know that this boy is a Talon and will be afforded the protocol of such, but is in no way or shape under any special protection. Acts that adhere to our rules in his regard will be treated as they would with any other member. I would wish you all luck, but I do not cater to the lucky. I reward the skillful. Hadrick, the boy is yours to command." Lowering his voice so that only Callahan could hear, he whispered, "Be back in a week to hear of your death, boy."

Callahan gritted his teeth as he watched Namion depart. Walking down the steps, he cursed his foul luck in regard to the ranks of prospects glaring death at him as well as the puzzled look of anger upon the instructor's face. Curiosity lit his mind as he pondered the bravery line; he had heard that before, heard it said by a gal he would do near anything to meet again. Storing that thought, he continued into the valley. Having arrived at the valley in the early evening, Callahan was spared any lessons or work prior to dinner. Wordless shaking heads were his only greeting as he watched the ranks break and head to a nearby building that the cry for mealtime had originated from.

He noticed that the prospects lined up behind the last of the men bearing tattoos, so he proceeded, muttering, "Here goes everything." He cut in line without apology between the last tattooed man and the first prospect.

"Hey! Get yer . . ." The man started to reach for Callahan's shirt. Driving a knee into his groin then head-butting him, Callahan drew the rapier from the man's side.

"Skip this meal! Dare to lay hand on me again, and ye'll starve a slow death. Thanks for the sword." Sliding the blade into his belt and swallowing his fear of all potential results, he turned as though nothing were unusual about having to put a prospect back in line. The tattooed man in front of him snorted his disgust at Callahan.

The line progressed until Callahan retrieved a tray with some kind of stew and a hunk of bread. Turning to find himself a seat, he hopped back a step as the man that had been in front of him tried to push back into his tray. "Unless ye want to issue a proper challenge, I suggest ye stop trying to fuck with me."

"Save yer tongue for prospects, boy! Know yer place." The man walked off to a table filled with other members.

Looking at the sparse number of tables already filling up with prospects, he saw an open seat near a man bearing membership. Upon approach, he watched as the man pushed the stool near him under the table. Knowing that further words would be pushing his luck, he decided to take a more familiar route of action. Walking the hall, he stepped up to the now-seated man whose rapier he had taken. Placing his meal in front of him, Callahan offered his wry half smile. "Ye need this more than me, mate. As I'm sure ye'll be needing this." He placed his rapier on the table next to the tray. "Point me in the direction of the armory. Meal and blade are payment fer such."

In quick order, the man gave him directions then dug ravenously into the meal. With a self-appreciating smile upon his face, Callahan strutted straight into the armory. The blacksmith offered only a glare as he entered the forge area. Presenting his tattoo, Callahan ordered, "A rapier and a dagger." The blacksmith took a second look at the tattoo then pointed to a rack adorned with weaponry then to a table with sheaths.

This isn't so bad, Callahan thought to himself. He exited with a rapier sheathed on his left hip and a dagger sheathed inside his left boot. Some act of dwarven ingenuity allowed a mere dozen torches to reflect off the stonework, lighting the entire underground valley as if it were daylight. Appreciating this fact and assessing the layout of the town around him, he caught on to a group of prospects heading in his direction justas they got within a few body lengths of him.

"I offer challenge. Ye huff and puff, but yer nothing but a boy. Boys don't belong down 'ere, and I'm suspecting that if I take ye out, it may be met with reward." A solid large-framed man stepped out from the front of the assembly.

"Think well before ye answer this next question. Ponder it. Roll it about a bit. Then spew yer ignorance. Do ye really want to offer a challenge to me?" Callahan drew his rapier, setting the blade upon his shoulder.

"Aye, the center arena. Now. I challenge ye to—" The man's bravado was cut short as Callahan's blade ripped down through his left collarbone into his chest.

Pulling the blade free, Callahan calmly wiped it on the man's pant legs. A roar of protest was rising all around him, reaching moblike heights, when Hadrick finally rushed on to the scene. "What the fuck is this?"

"That peon thought himself of a position to be able to challenge an inducted member of the Talons. So I politely corrected him." Callahan's wry half smile only worked to further infuriate the head instructor.

"I don't know who the fuck you think you are, but I am about to gut you, boy." Hadrick drew his short sword and stormed on toward Callahan.

Flashing his tattoo before him, Callahan spouted, "Well, I have deflowered this blade already. Quenching its thirst a little more would make this drab evening a bit more exciting. Do ye care to offer challenge as well?"

Calling his bluff, Hadrick smiled. "Damn right. I am Namion's head prospect instructor. I teach men to survive using blade and fist. I will delight in giving the real future of the Talons a good lesson." He waved his hand over the assembled mass of prospects.

[Callahan] As we marched on toward the . . . arenalike . . . center of the valley, I couldn't help but curse my luck again. I pondered to myself, *What the fuck am I doing? Talk about a really bad ad-lib. Namion was right, though. He has the upper hand on me, and if I don't pull off something drastic, me arse is gonna be floating that shit river outside. So best to go out with a bang, having fun and making a show of it.*

[Narrator] Entering the arena, Hadrick reached for his back, producing a small shield in his left hand; adjusted his grip on his short sword with his right hand; and addressed the gathered audience now containing numerous Talons as well as all the prospects. "This boy thinks that just because he gained a tattoo, by way the gods only know, he can mouth off to anyone he wants and strut like a king. Let's cut him down in size a bit, eh, fellas?" An approving roar answered in response.

His rapier held in preparation via his right hand, Callahan gave his signature smile. "A shield? A fucking shield? Really? I mean, come the fuck on, yer training a lot of street thugs. What the fuck do ye need with a shield? Do ye suddenly think yer a gladiator?" Callahan lurched a few quick thrusts and found himself shocked that his enhanced speed was met easily as his blade was deflected by the very shield he was mocking.

Ducking, he could feel the wind as an inhumanly fast swipe just missed his head. Thankful for his newfound lack of hair, Callahan backpedaled and worked to regain footing, but the skilled man's pressed advance was working to keep him off balance and underprepared.

Parrying a few feinted thrusts, Callahan came to the conclusion that he was outmatched. Somehow, Hadrick was able to match his speed and was superior in experience and strength. His shield easily batted down another thrust then came a wide sword swing at chest level. Raising his rapier to parry, Callahan audibly groaned as the short sword cut easily through it. Throwing himself back, Callahan felt the blade's tip rip into his chest, scraping ribs then sternum as it passed. Lit with pain, on his back, and lacking his rapier, Callahan cursed his luck one more time.

Turning his eyes to the onlookers, Hadrick let out a howling laugh. "See! Arrogance and pomp might play well with the weak, but in circles of strength, you need experience and . . ."

Rolling diagonally by Hadrick's legs, Callahan drew his dagger. Finishing the roll, he cut deep through the back of Hadrick's knee, then spinning to his feet, he swapped hands so that he held a right-handed reverse grip on the dagger. Stabbing through right collarbone, withdraw. Left collarbone, withdraw. Finishing with a slash to the back of Hadrick's neck, Callahan smiled from ear to ear and roared at the onlookers with primal glee. Sticking out his tongue then licking his lips, he roared one more time. Blood oozing down his chest and shirt, pain lighting his senses, Callahan maintained his composure the best he could as he started looting the body before him.

Placing his hand upon the short sword, he felt a familiar surge of energy that delighted his senses. His muscles tightened, and he could feel their density increase, lending explanation to Hadrick's ability to keep up with his speed. Turning again to the onlookers, who all sat stunned without noise, he shouted, "It's not arrogance when yer just this damn good! Perhaps if he'd paid more attention to finishing the job and less attention to celebrating himself, he'd still be here to speak to ye all. Any others care to die this night, or will someone guide me to my new room? Hadrick's ole room, if ye all were too fucking stupid to catch me drift." Having taken what coins he could find and the short sword, Callahan kicked the shield and muttered, "A fucking shield? Really?"

Not gaining a response from any of the onlookers, Callahan grabbed the nearest prospect he could reach by the shirt collar. "Lead me to that corpse's prior dwelling, or join him." Pointing to the prospect sitting near the one he was holding, he ordered, "Fetch me a needle and thread. I need to stitch this new window that bum opened on me chest." Speaking loudly again, he addressed the lot of onlookers one last time. "Age does not equate to wisdom and experience. Test this boy, and meet yer gods."

Following the prospect he had selected, Callahan found himself in a comfortable solitary room. Head light from blood loss, he smoked a bit more of the herb Namion had given him in hopes that it would have healing properties. It did not. Soon, the second prospect arrived with the necessary equipment. Gritting his teeth and sending the man out, Callahan crudely fashioned stitches through the wound in his chest until pain became too fierce, sending him into a deep sleep.

[Callahan] Trying to stitch meself with the materials that numb nuts brought me was much akin to a pack of chimps trying to rape a gorilla.

[Reader 1] In a disturbing way, I think I get the metaphor. Maybe?

[Callahan] One, isn't the word *metaphor* well above yer juvenile vocabulary, and two, when was the last time ye were raped by chimps that ye would have personal understanding of it?

[Reader 1] My uncles were short and had real hairy arms now . . .

[Callahan]Holy fucking . . . whoa! Though this explains a lot, I really didn't want it explained now, did I?

[Narrator] Yeah, that's a line that really just shouldn't be crossed. Well, yeah, that's so far behind us now. I can't even see it anymore. Will you two just shut the fuck up?

[Callahan] . . .

[Narrator] Beauty of typing the story is I have the ability to make them shut up now, don't I?

[Narrator] "Sometimes what we want is not as good as what we have." Callahan awoke to see Namion finishing up a professional-quality stitching of his wound. "Supposed to return in a week to find you dead, not be requested back to a mass of chaos. You threaten members and prospects alike. You, within your rights as a Talon, slaughter an outspoken prospect. Then you not only kill a member in justifiable challenge, but you kill my instructor. Not a has-been, not a never-was, a holy-shit head instructor." A sincere smile unfamiliar to Namion's cold features lit his face as a heartfelt laugh burst forth uncontrollably. "My fucking instructor! I mean, how in the world do I plan for that? How could I ever possibly foresee you securing your rights among the men by offing one of my best on your very first night? That is not a possibility. I really wish I could kill you, but even if it were not for our accord, I absolutely adore you." Further laughter worked to rouse Callahan.

"Ugh, I wish I could share in your revelry. Fuck, this hurts, though. And not in a good way. Ye really have put me through a wringer, mate. I'll not relent. I hope ye know, and if I must go, I will go in such a way as to tear out the heart of yer guild with my passing." Groaning, Callahan shook his head, still cursing his luck.

"Bah, we have a contest, you and I, but that does not mean we cannot delight in the friendship of it. Your actions are not unnoticed. The men whisper of nothing but you this day. They speak of the boy whose sharp wit, lightning reflexes, and vicious streak reflect that of a falcon hunter. So your new handle or moniker, if you prefer, will be just that, the Falcon.

Furthermore, Owl, the head of the order of Avian assassins, has, in an unprecedented move, offered to act as head instructor until I can find an adequate replacement. He has done so to pay price for sponsoring you into the Avian assassins. Your weekend rest and relaxation will be replaced with further training toward that end. You had to know that stunt you pulled off yesterday would carry weight. Hefty risk you took. Congratulations on not dying."

Laughing again, Namion walked to the door. "Fucking instructor, simply astounding. This room is yours for the remainder of your training. You earned as much. In such regard, everything in it is also yours. Enjoy that sword of his. An increase to strength, it will never lose its edge, and it slides through nonmagical weapons and armor as if they were cloth. Hefty reward for that hefty risk, if you ask me. The instructor." Another laugh ripped the air as he opened the door. Then as he prepared to close the door behind him, he added, "By the way, I have a favor to ask of you. Please do not die too quickly. This is proving to be far too entertaining. The poultice applied to your chest will alleviate the risk of it reopening, though it will do little for the pain. Your training starts in the morning, village center. Just as a show of good faith, I will ensure a prospect comes to call on you so that you will be sure to be punctual. Takes a bit to get used to the perpetually lit valley here underground, could throw off your concept of time."

An hour or so passed after Namion's departure when Callahan heard a light knock on his door. Pulling his newly acquired short sword under the blanket with him, he called out, "What is it?"

"Sir, my name is Dedrich. I mistakenly disrespected you in the meal line yesterday evening and have come in attempts to make good on that." Callahan recognized the voice of the prospect from the night before that had given him directions to the armory.

"Aye, come on in." Callahan still held fast to his sword under the blanket and sat up, prepared if necessary. The man entered and bowed his head slightly in a nod. He carried with him a large tray containing a full meal and an odd flask.

Setting the tray on a stand near Callahan's bed, the man then spoke. "I am going to reach to one of the swords at my side now. Not in disrespect but because, from what I saw, you left a short rapier last night. So on top of the meal and elixir that should aid in your healing, I brought you another one." He removed one of the sheaths containing a rapier from his belt and placed it on the floor.

"This isn't a fucking social club now, is it? So out with it. What am I to be doing to earn this generosity?" Callahan, ever skeptical, kept a strong hold on his blade.

"Far as I see it, I'm not dead now, am I? You're not wrong, though. What I want is to kiss your ass." The man let a light chuckle and seemed relaxed as he found a seat across the room. "You could've started by killing me to set your example yesterday. You didn't. You made a fair bargain. Then you went on to carve a name for yourself the likes of which no one has done before and probably will ever do again. So I ask only that you look kindly upon me. See me as ally and, in such, help me survive. Half of us prospects will not last the stretch of this, and really, I don't want to fucking die, especially not in some underground shithole."

"I can understand such a sentiment. In light of my recent arrival and warm welcome, I missed a lot of the ground rules. So I would take it as a good show of what ye offer if ye were to fill me in." Callahan turned so that he was sitting on the edge of the bed, feet on the ground. He laid the short sword across his lap.

"Hey, now is . . ." Dedrich stared questioningly at the sword now produced from under the blanket.

"Ye do remember yesterday, don't ye? Don't really have to ask why, do ye?" Callahan just smiled his half smile.

For the next hour or so, Dedrich went over some of the common training practices, ground rules, and procedures that Callahan would have to know to keep himself alive. Callahan held a bit of hope that he might have actually found an ally in the midst of all the surrounding chaos. He knew it would be a long lonely road, and with the absence of Selfin, he knew he could use a new follower. "Well, mate, this could be the beginning of a very productive and mutually beneficial arrangement. Let us honor this friendship by sharing a meal. Go ahead and eat a bit of that meal ye brought me."

"No, that's a generous offer, but I'm able to go to the meal hall. You eat that and save your energy for the training to come." A kindly smile lit Dedrich's face.

"OK, so gentle nudge didn't get through. Eat some of the fucking meal, ye snake-tongued wretch, and if yer still good, I will apologize for doubting ye." Callahan placed his right hand back on the hilt of his sword.

"That's fucked, mate. You would think I am out to poison you?" After taking a few exaggerated bites of each part of the meal, Dedrich picked the tray up to carry it to Callahan.

"All right, my mistake, but can ye blame me? Everyone has been trying to kill me lately. Been a veritable slaughterhouse round me, so go ahead and take a sip of that elixir, and then our healthy friendship and allegiance can begin." Callahan still gripped the hilt as he grinned slightly.

"I'm not wounded, am I?" Dedrich paused and shook his head.

"Get off it! We're in a den of thieves and murderers. I've killed eight people in less than a week. So unless ye want to be wounded, recognize that I'm not in a mood to pretend that we trust each other. Drink the elixir, or I'll start the process of yer slow and painful death." Callahan stood up, short sword at the ready.

Dedrich sat back in the seat he had been occupying, placing the tray back on the table. He pulled the flask off the tray, popped its top, and placed it to his lips. Callahan watched the slight trickle at his lips and the absence of movement in his throat. "There now, stop being so damned paranoid, would—"

With his blade drawing a bit of blood from where its tip pressed into Dedrich's neck, Callahan laughed. "Crap." Letting out a sigh, he said, "If it's too good to be true, then it isn't true now, is it? I'll live with the pain, but now that ye've a cut of yer own, let's see that elixir at work. Drink the whole fucking thing, and if ye spill another drop, I'll open ye. I'll remove pieces of yer insides that I recently discovered, through study of my father, can be removed while ye yet live. I'll take those pieces, and after a nice light sauté, I'll feed 'em to ye."

"OK. It wasn't gonna kill you, I swear. Just make you sleep real deep. I wanted you to oversleep tomorrow's training so that I could regain my lost reputation and stance with the prospects. There was a reason I was able to stand in front of that food line, and you came and fucked that all up. I wasn't trying to kill you." Callahan could see the deep-seated fear in Dedrich's eyes as he confessed.

"Then you better hope that you don't oversleep, eh? Drink that elixir! It's no longer a request, nor was it ever. It's a fucking demand, and it'll be met by choice or force." Callahan watched the man as he drank every last drop of the elixir. "So how long does this usually take to work?" The question was met by light snoring. "Thanks for the meal. Looks like another long night, eh?" Callahan sat to enjoy the meal while lighting a bit more of the herb given him by Namion.

Chimes rang through the valley, indicating the hour. Callahan knew he was off by a minute as he walked into the arenalike center of the valley that next morning. The prospects were assembled in ranks before a gray-haired man in casual clothes. A long sword was sheathed at his side. Behind him were two other men and a woman. One of the men was a weasely short man. The other had a crooked nose, wild eyes, and a sneer showing gnarled black and yellow teeth. The woman had short black hair, her face slightly scarred, and it dawned on Callahan—it was her.

"So no one among you can explain this to me?" the gray-haired man asked in a steady loud voice while he pointed to the large makeshift cross Dedrich's sleeping form was tied to in the valley center.

"Well, actually, that would explain me tardiness this morning, wouldn't it? Takes a good spot of one's night to crucify a man without help." Callahan took a place at the front of the ranks, displaying his wry half smile.

"Oh, the conquering hero finally decides to grace us with his presence." Owl's hand subtly and lightly rested on his long sword's hilt.

"Aye, my apologies, Owl. I don't wish to disrespect the compliment that is yer presence. Nor that of what I am assuming are others of the Avians. That man tried to poison me yesterday while offering allegiance." Raising his voice so anyone within a block of the arena could hear, Callahan continued after quickly pointing to the crucified man. "Let any man who would accept such allegiance, as that man offered, take him from that cross. I will accept any substitution. Anyone feeds that man, gives him water, ends his suffering through death, or releases him will take his place. To all members, take that as a preestablished challenge. To all prospects, take that as a promise of fatal reprisal. To everyone, how many? How many must I kill? Before ye all learn the very real lesson that I'm not to be fucked with!" Shaking slightly from his frustration, Callahan awaited vicious reprisal for his tardiness.

"Falcon, why do you stand next to lesser men? Join your kin that we may begin the day." Owl pointed to the three behind him.

Callahan walked to join the line as directed. Something alerted his senses, and he yet again felt as though things were too good to be true. Scanning the area with his peripheral vision, Callahan lurched to motion.

From a nearby building's darkened window, an arrow sped toward Callahan's heart with perfect accuracy. Cursing his luck but thankful for his magically enhanced speed, Callahan batted the arrow aside as he drew his rapier with his right hand, drew his magic short sword with his left, and lurched toward

Owl. Easily grabbing both of the boy's wrists, Owl stepped in, face-to-face, with him having to spin slightly as Callahan pressed his advance.

"Ease!" Ducking, Owl spun Callahan back. "Eagle, show yourself and join ranks." A well-dressed man leapt lightly from the darkened window and jogged to his place near the dark-haired woman.

Callahan's blades still held at the ready, he shouted at Owl. "What the fuck? It would be real fucking nice to go ten fucking minutes without someone trying to fucking kill me!"

"You were late. Put your blades away, and join the elite." Owl turned to look at the amazed prospects, but Callahan could feel Owl's eyes still upon him. "He knew enough to not trust offer of friendship. He knew enough to kill the head instructor. He knew enough to put me between further arrow and himself. He knows enough."

"My apologies again, sir." Callahan sheathed his blades and stood beside the weasely short man.

"I only waste my time with the mass of you street thugs and peons because of Morgian's young messenger you see behind me." Owl pointed to Callahan as he referenced Morgian, the human name for the god of death. "Namion offers him no protection. In such, there is no rule or law of our order against his harassment. Know this—as of now, he is one of ours. We protect our own in so long as they protect us." He pointed one at a time to the people behind him. "So if you are that bored with life, please step forward that we can just end the dance before it begins."

[Callahan] Though it wasn't safe and it wasn't gentle or easy, that moment was the one that turned it all from survival to actual training. The weasely little man was Sparrow. Ugly, creepy dude, Vulture. Wondrous, strong dark woman, Raven. Well-dressed bowman, Eagle. Gray-haired wise man, Owl. Then last but not least, snarky, cynical, pessimistic rogue, Falcon. That, my friends, was the crew that made the Talons feared throughout our known world.

It was quite a change I went through from easily trumping Selfin in the park to eating dirt on a daily basis. The assassins were not sympathetic to my wounded state. I was held to the higher standard I had placed upon myself those first few days. Failure meant death. If I wasn't the best, if I didn't come in first in every aspect, then I would've been labeled a failure.

I didn't train with the prospects. They trained in their usual fashion under inducted members guided by the ever-watchful eyes of Owl. Owl would take what evenings and time he could to go over contract planning. He taught me that the most important part of any job as an assassin is the setup and planning. He reconfirmed my belief that friends were by far more dangerous than enemies. He taught me that strength comes from calculation in all facets of life and that relationships were no more or less than any weapon of metal except in the intricacy of their implementation. We also went over the layout of Lados in great depth and even extensively studied the geography of Calarr.

I sometimes imagined seeing hope in Owl's eyes for me during those months of torment. I imagined that he saw me to be the answer to unraveling the tyranny of Namion. I imagined that he saw a new order guided by a skewed but solid pact of honor under the leadership of the Falcon. When physical pain became too much for me, I would lose myself in such imaginings and find myself stronger on the other side.

I was put through rigorous physical exercises intended to build strength, increase stamina, and improve dexterity by Eagle. He instructed me in the ways of silencing one's actions and movements. I laughed at these lessons in view of having my ring but paid attention regardless, for I'm not one to shirk off useful knowledge just because it's not immediately pertinent. We also spent an extensive amount of time in the study of archery and throwing knives. Like all other aspects, I excelled above all the prospects but found little love for the use of bows. Knives were a different story. I crafted a tight leather vest with six integrated sheaths down its front, in which I placed throwing knives. As natural as my gift of gab was my ability to send those knives to purpose.

Sparrow instructed me in poisons, herbs, and other alchemic processes. He taught me how to properly apply such additives to weaponry, food, and even a person's clothes. He taught me the subtle approaches necessary to ensure that the materials remained undetectable. He taught me of antidotes and even put me through the process of building immunity to some poisons by forcing me to endure doses. Under his instruction, I also learned how to maintain myself despite mentally impairing chemicals such as alcohol and many of the commonplace sedatives found throughout Lados.

On top of the negatives learned in studies with Sparrow, I also learned a lot about the healing aspects of herbs and chemical combinations. In some minor respects, he taught me about magic detection and counteraction. I tried to push him more toward the end of learning in that regard but quickly discovered he neglected those lessons because he just didn't know.

Vulture taught me about human biology in the regard of rather disgusting and disturbing methods of torture and lengthened pain delivery. To say that he was a man of no moral compass would be a lie. He was, in fact, a man of reversed moral compass. As has been portrayed, I didn't live a soft, censored, or sheltered life, but all the torments that would haunt a mind, even one as calloused as mine, Vulture delighted in bringing to reality. He was Namion's instrument of fear. He was a skilled, strong fighter who put his dual-handed axes to brutal art but had no business being an assassin. His was not an art of stealth. His was not an art of skill. His was an art of crushing enemies' resolve and spirit.

Through his lessons, I did manage to interpret the proper stitching method and other useful battlefield medical practices. I learned to further detach my emotions and mind from other people, turning them into objects so as to feel no reservation in their regard. Others' regard of Vulture was a lesson in how useful reputation can be when applied to the masses properly.

Despite the physical torment of exercise and poison. Despite the mental exhaustion of constructing constant backup plans for backup plans. Despite the frustration built by having to maintain peace of body and mind through the chaos of distraction provided constantly in that underground pit. I hated my time with Vulture the most. His lessons were not physically testing or mentally straining but were by far my hardest. Knowledge is like herpes. Once ye learn it, ye've got it. Ye can pass it on, but ye can't get rid of it. What I hated most about the things he taught me was the fact that, deep down inside, I wasn't disgusted.

The opposite side of that coin came in the lessons I looked forward to—lessons of manipulation, seduction, and socialization delivered by Raven. Still of muscular build, she was no longer of a form I'd have described as hefty. She seemed annoyed by my presence at the best of times. She taught me how to lose my accent when necessary to fit in properly with higher society. She taught me etiquette and social graces necessary for passing oneself off as a noble. She also taught me some of the cultural habits of other races.

I couldn't understand her obvious disdain for me and constantly prodded her toward discovering that end. She also aroused my curiosity in her lack of the Talon tattoo. When I was well into my training and it was becoming more and more obvious that I was surpassing the skill levels of my instructors, she decided to answer my questions. "Callahan, I once met a young man." Of all the people around me during those years, she was the only one who used my given name and not my moniker. "That young man showed honor that impressed me. He was a hero in the making. One who was willing to sacrifice his own health in the face of overwhelming odds. He did this for no purpose but to save face for his dear companion. He was a man I could have fallen for. Before me today is a man crafted in blood and villainy. Strong without measure, intelligent, wise, and deathly agile but lacking any humanity. Standing before me today is a cookie-cutter copy of a younger version of the father I hate."

Her lack of tattoo was due to the fact that her allegiance was of blood. Being Namion's only surviving heir, he didn't have her branded so that she could move undetected among the citizens of Lados. She, like the rest of us, was not but a useful tool put to purpose, and no less than I, she resented that fact but knew of no way to escape her plight.

If yer curiosity is roused by the amount of things I describe having learned in what should have been six months of training, then I would call ye quite astute. Owl didn't get replaced quickly. Unknown to me, the Avian assassins had been put to the purpose of crafting me. I was to become the all-around assassin. As such, two long years was my sentence. Namion would show his face every few months, and I would see his delight when he found me yet alive. Not only had I saved my life on that fateful night, I crafted pact with him. I also forged an admiration and friendship toward myself from him. The only thing more dangerous than being Namion's enemy was being Namion's forced apprentice/friend.

During these visits, Namion undertook the task of training me in the ways of leadership. Which, being guarded in regard to his knowledge, really just became his outlet for getting to tell stories of his past. Having ordered me to silence in regard to our private conversations, he saw me as his one opportunity for real human contact.

[Reader 1] That must have been a boring endeavor. I thought you gained all of his knowledge through that dagger of his? I don't know about you, but I despise being told the same reheated war story over and over again.

[Callahan] Does yer reality often have cases of alien abduction? I ask because the individual pretending to be to Sir Wackshisminystack has actually been respectably engaging. I only drew a bit of blood with the dagger ye reference and, as such, was only granted brief images and feelings. So no, just as he didn't know all I knew, I didn't know what he knew. Just some feelings and intuitions.

[Reader 1] So did your crucifix stunt do its intended job? Other than Eagle's not-so-subtle reminder of your mortality, it would seem that even the deranged Vulture has taken you under his wing.

[Callahan] Any person's real strength isn't found in their skill but in the culmination of combined skill held in the allegiance around them. Owl's proclamation that I was part of the Avian assassins was more than enough to quell any further attempts against me. To answer the question, yes, Dedrich had a less-than-pleasant two weeks before I cut his lifeless and much lighter corpse off the cross. Some of the other members had crafted an interesting betting game that revolved around small darts and his hanging body. I did find a few objections when I went to remove him, and in fact, they kept the cross up so as to utilize it in future executions. I allowed the game and told them such as long as the losers of said betting pools cleaned excretions because, given enough time, starving men dying of thirst and suffocation cause quite the mess.

[Reader 1] Wow, I don't think I'll ever look at a friendly game of darts the same way again.

[Callahan] I'm starting to get a more personal grasp of why the narrator finds us so obnoxious. I was in the middle of telling a story, ye know. It was flowing, and I had a rhythm, so bears to reason, when in comes Reader 1.

[Narrator] Callahan had spent two long years being crafted into the Falcon. The end of a long day of physically and mentally demanding training was met by the presence of Namion in Callahan's room upon the day's conclusion.

"Evening, friend, I come with good news. Your training has taken you as far as it can and much further than I suspected it would. In you, I have created the greatest instrument of death ever known to Calarr. Which, due to the agreement of Entearra Gharu, I know cannot be turned against me because it has always been against me. Keeping you closer than any other being, I am able to watch those around you, thus alleviating your threat to me. You are amazing and honor our guild well, so time has come to unleash you. For far too long now, the Avian assassins have been preoccupied.

"In their absence from the surface, a man has stepped forward to challenge Talon authority. He is an ex-champion of the crown turned rogue. Bradier spent many years in service to the king, slaughtering monster and brigand threat. One occasion in the past, he cost me one of my ships. After said servitude, he found retirement to be boring and unprofitable. Taking to mercantile bounty hunting, he found greater profit. From that point, he found even greater profit in moving from hero to villain. So he took to raiding merchants en route to and from the wildlands to Lados.

"He has undertaken those endeavors for the last few years but recently became unsatisfied with his profit margin and wildland lodgings. Moving his activities into Lados, he poses a threat to our guild, and assuch, I want him removed in a less-than-pleasant manner. That being stated, he has a remarkable skill with his long sword and has numerous companions who are also not shabby in their use of weaponry. More than that, he has a knack for detecting and avoiding ambushes, assassination attempts, and other acts made against him. It is very likely that he, like yourself, improves upon his vast skill with magically enchanted trinkets." Namion watched Callahan move through his evening rituals as though he were not speaking. Normally, such an action of disrespect would be answered with death, but in the case of Callahan, it had just become commonplace behavior.

Ignoring disrespectful neglect, Namion continued unabated. "Yes, I used plural—trinkets. I did not attain my current status by being unobservant now, did I? The ring you carry is obviously the only explanation as to how you could have snuck up on me that fateful night so long ago. I am angry with myself that it took me this long to piece two and two together."

Callahan's interest now fully piqued, he sat on his bed facing Namion. "Two and two?"

Namion smiled at his young friend. "Yes, two and two. Along with the alleged manuscript describing Entearra Gharu, a magic ring was taken so many years ago. I was unable to track the book because the thief was intelligent enough to not sell it. Had he, I would have known. Great were the lengths I had undertaken when I heard rumor of that book's existence. It just disappeared, though, because you didn't want to profit from it, did you? You wanted to study it, unlock its secrets. That's how you knew, wasn't it? So I hate to use such a cheap and easy route, but where did you hide it? Somewhere safe, I'd assume. Somewhere you could survive through training then return to it to find an escape from our bargain. Somewhere no one would suspect it could be."

Laughing, Callahan delighted in his answer. "Well, that's the kicker, isn't it? Ye made me burn it, remember? Not like I didn't try to save it, is it?"

"No. Really? You had a book of that magnitude in that house?" Namion started shaking his head with a grin spreading across his face.

"Well, it surprised you, didn't it? So yeah, it was actually a real effective hiding spot till ye had me burn it." Callahan chuckled again.

"You never cease to surprise me. You burned your only escape from our pact and managed to never whisper hint of that." Namion looked with fondness upon his young protégé.

"My only escape was, by extension, yer only escape as well, so I couldn't rightly tell ye about it now, could I? I was still holding on hope that a manuscript containing secrets of the gods would have some form of magical safeguarding against fire, but that ye just asked me its whereabouts means it wasn't recovered, was it?" Still chuckling, Callahan's mirth was quickly joined as the two men burst into an outright fit of laughter.

"All right, well, upon Bradier's death, you will no longer be subjected to this pit. Make sure you take with you anything you desire to keep. Congratulations, Falcon, if you manage this, then you will have earned your place as elite among my elite." Still chuckling, Namion made his departure.

Heading out with near immediacy, Callahan found Owl overlooking vigorous sword exercises undertaken by prospects. "Ah, dear friend, I have come with good news. The Avians have been issued contract."

Without turning his head, Owl responded, "This is how you ask for help?"

"Well, I apologize. Didn't realize it would be such an affront to offer ye a break from changing diapers and chasing booger pickers." Callahan flashed a wry half smile.

"I'll assemble the crew. It'll be nice to go back to doing what we should have been doing all along." Owl turned toward a nearby tattooed member. "You! Congratulations on your new promotion. You are now head instructor." Owl turned back to Callahan. "We will gather at the dockside pub. See you there."

[Callahan] Now before ye all go freaking out by my disrespect of Owl and his lack of reprisal, recognize that in the Talons, there is Namion, there are tattooed members, then there are prospects. Beyond that, there is no distinction of rank.

[Narrator] As Callahan stepped onto the beach en route to the meeting place, he took a moment to stop and revel in the smell of fresh night air, breathing it in, relishing in the freedom he had long been denied.

[Callahan] Really! Are you fucking dense? Seriously, I walked out from under a waterfall of piss and shit, danced a jig, and celebrated its refreshing odor!

[Narrator] Correction: Callahan, now a mile or two away from the cavern's entrance and thus the smell, paused and reveled in his freedom.

[Callahan] I wasn't really free, was I?

[Narrator] Sullen, hateful, cynical, and sarcastic as usual, Callahan rushed on to the warm meal and drink provided by the dockside pub.

[Callahan] Far more like it there.

[Narrator] After a few hours of listening to the drunken revelry of sailors, the other Avians filed in. "Hmm, five men, one woman. That thing is probably beat all to shit." The group just smiled as a volunteer stepped forward to aid in clearing out prying ears. With a nod from Owl, Vulture smiled.

Moments later, five dead and the protesting proprietor opened from groin to neck, the group settled back in at their table to begin their conversation. Owl led by saying, "Bradier is a crafty target. He disrupted a previous Talon attempt by winning the inn proprietor's confidence. Gaining his room information from that proprietor, the men were led into the wrong room, which became their grave. More than that the man, those Talons were tailing was a body double. Bradier has yet to even set foot in Lados to our knowledge. His men are very loyal, and most of them are not even afforded the knowledge that the man they follow is not, in fact, Bradier."

"Well, sounds as though it's my turn to prove me worth, then, isn't it? Give me a day to track a few ole contacts and meet again at the King's Grace Inn." Callahan gave his signature smile.

[Reader 1] I get it! You cleared the pub because you will then have Avian assassins posing as workers and sailors. Then when the fake Bradier walks in, it's time for another full-scale slaughter. That's brilliant!

[Callahan] I would like to ridicule and demean ye, but if this pub were anywhere within the vicinity of our target, that wouldn't be a bad plan. It would take weeks of integration to properly pull off. Actually, no, we just wanted to teach that smart-ass a lesson and clear out any prying ears.

[Reader 1] So you killed everyone to say five sentences and drink some free beer?! That's fucked.

[Callahan] I can't disagree, but ye can't argue its effectiveness, can ye?

[Reader 1 says nothing but does move his chair several inches farther away from where the narrator is seated.]

[Narrator] What had been a regular hangout for inducted Talons set to task in the underground valley now came into the ownership of such. With the untimely passing of the proprietor, actions were set into motion that transferred full property ownership to the guild. The guards took little notice as none of the shipping routes were disturbed, and technically, the docks and small surrounding beach suburb were not officially part of Lados proper.

Resting lightly, Callahan did enjoy his stay in one of the pub's rooms. He leaned back, throwing daggers against all entries, and kept himself on high alert for their fall. Such preventative measures had become commonplace for him. Part of his training had consisted of multiple attempts to break into his room and otherwise get the jump on him—attempts he had, in one way or another, managed to trump.

Callahan knew he had to act swiftly, so he rose before the sun to start his journey up the cliff stairs into the city proper to hunt his old friends Hemrick and Horuce. His curiosity was piqued at the delay with which Namion had asked him of the book. Having departed the underground shortly before Callahan, he had not given himself much of a head start in the regard to finding its whereabouts. This fact in mind, Callahan took extra care in watching his surroundings for any telltale signs of unwelcome company. He knew that Namion, like himself, would be unsatisfied with believing the book to have burned and, in such regard, would not rest until it was rediscovered.

As he entered what should have been familiar territory, he came to a quick realization that much of the scenery and populace had shifted and changed in the last two years. He was also well aware that given two years, the old and unhealthy homeless man who had been so pivotal a contact before was very likely to be dead. Pondering such possibilities and unsure as to where to start his search, Callahan decided to first look into the site where he had last left his treasured book, the same site where he had left many an emotion and possession, his old homestead. Callahan paused a moment to appreciate the well-kept nature of the house now in its place.

Callahan watched a captain of the Lados guard and three of his men approach the house and stop to talk in front of it. Callahan couldn't believe his eyes or his luck as one of the men addressed the captain as Horuce. "We've some catching up to do, you and I, dear Horuce." Callahan openly approached the group.

"If you've a grievance, sir, please take it to your district's local station and report it appropriately, or if you persist in this line of action, we will be forced to detain you." As he calmly finished his statement, a well-built and in-shape Horuce turned to face the man intruding on his conversation. "Holy shit! Ah, uh . . ."

"Wow, always suspected that fat sack of shit I knew to have swallowed a man of actual worth. Yer looking good, mate, and it seems as though yer doing well professionally." Callahan looked him up and down as Horuce remained slack-jawed before him.

"Men, you know your orders. This man is not wrong. We do have some catching up to do." Waiting until the men left from earshot, Horuce pointed toward the house that stood where Callahan's had previously. "The dead walk. Let's head into my home for a spot of privacy."

Following him in, Callahan immediately lost any ill will toward Horuce residing on what should have rightly been his property. The family abode was comfortably fashioned in a welcoming way. It could easily be seen that a woman's hands had taken part in its décor, and a crib portrayed the presence of a young one. "Gone family man, have ye?"

"You're dead young, Callahan. We found your body amidst the rubble. Three rogues your father had managed to slay, your mother, your father, and you. Like a phoenix, I see you risen from the ashes a formidable-looking young man." Horuce placed tea on a dining table before Callahan and bade him to sit. "In a time when I felt no worth or purpose, you presented mewith an escape. I owe you, and knowing you, that's why I'm seeing you again. It's OK. My wife, my son, my health, my job—I owe it all to you. So ask and see my purpose set."

Surprised by Horuce's words, Callahan nodded. "I only seek a few bits of information and wish to reestablish old ties with ye under new name. Yer not wrong, friend. The Talons burned Callahan that night. He's dead. I'm Falcon." Showing his tattoo, he saw a shocked and puzzled expression light Horuce's face. "Don't much know what all ye mistake me for having done fer ye aside from taking a purse of yer coin and almost getting ye hung."

Chuckling lightly, Horuce smiled and looked at the table while he talked. "No, you wouldn't, would you? There was a young man of no status or place. There was a young man with no aid toward future or prospect to prosper. Yet that young man carved his way with word and wit. He carried himself as a noble. Yes, you took my coin, and I'm sure you'd have followed through on your threats, but you saw enough worth in me to give me information we both knew would change my world. Aye, you didn't do the rest of it. No, I did that. All you did was show example that no matter who we are seen as, we can be so much more if only we strive to such."

Feeling the ember of his humanity heating, Callahan stored what Horuce told him then proceeded to douse the ember again. "OK, that's wonderful. Terrific 'we can be whatever we want to be if we only try hard enough' story, but please go drown yerself in yer privy if ye intend on continuing it. I don't give two shits as to why ye give me what I want. I just care that ye do. Ye'll tell me all ye know of Bradier. Ye'll tell me anything ye may have heard on me ole friend Hemrick. Ye'll continue to maintain loyalty to me. Ye have no allegiance to the Talons. Ye answer to me and work only with me. This first occurrence, ye will grant me due to that wonderfully sappy hogwash ye just spewed. Further engagements will be paid appropriately in accordance to their worth."

"So different, yet so much the same. I took grievance to your passing, exposed your father's crimes, and started a personal war against the very men whose tattoo you now hail. The information I disclosed on your father's extortions, gambling, and so forth led the district representatives to feel less inclined to respond to the Talons' actions. So they quelled any response. I refused to relent, so I waited until Namion's men preformed bold action in assuming ownership of some housing near the noble's district then pushed again for response. Still reluctant to make any direct actions against the corsair and his men, they did give me clearance to enlist outside aid as long as I kept it out of public knowledge." Smiling at Callahan, Horuce found amusement in the approving look of respect being cast toward him. "I take pride in who I am. In such, I carry myself as a man worthy of pride today. I have more than just assumed your father's job. I have excelled it to new heights."

"I would be lying if I said I wasn't impressed, but ye really haven't told me a fucking thing yet, have ye?" Callahan's half smile lit his face.

"By the gods, I hate that dangerous smile of yours. I hired Bradier to contest Namion and help push him out of Lados. Seeing your tattoo, hearing your questions, I'm led to believe I'm going to fail in that endeavor, aren't I?" Horuce continued, not looking for an answer to his rhetorical question. "Hemrick was known to have dealt with you. Due to that, I enlisted his services the same way you did. He started information-seeking on Bradier's regard and was put up in a stable residence. Bradier is not in the city. His friend and second-in-command poses as him for any and all contacts here. I don't know his actual location. I don't even know where the body double is currently. I'm sure Hemrick would know, though." Scribbling directions, Horuce passed them to Callahan. Standing to leave, Callahan was stopped by Horuce's voice. "I was sworn to secrecy but guess there is no harm in telling the dead, eh? During my investigation, I recovered a book unscathed by the fire. It was old and in an odd language, had lots of footnotes in it. I didn't know what to make of it, so I took it to the only ones I thought who might. The brothers of Malaki in the temple district paid me ten gold and told me to never speak of it again. I would have returned it to you if I thought you had lived. It looked important."

"It was important, and that little bit of information was enough to buy you some. I bought my life with service to Namion. I have excelled. There is a storm coming, and I'm at its forefront. I hold no love for the Talons but do what I must. We may come into conflict, you and I, but know I do not forget those who do not forget me. Thank ye, and know that whatever ye hear of the Falcon, he counts ye an ally." Hurrying on to where Hemrick now resided, Callahan pondered the vast changes that had occurred in his absence.

"Appears as though Horuce isn't the only one to have cleaned up, eh, my previously odorous friend." Callahan slid easily through a side window only a few body lengths from where a decently dressed older man sat for his noon meal.

"By the gods." Gasping aloud, Hemrick had started to rise to meet the intruder but was put right back in his seat by the vision that stood before him. "I haven't drank in a while now and have been off all the other junk too. Please tell me you're real."

Releasing two throwing knives, Callahan drew a light scratch on each of Hemrick's arms while pinning his shirt to the table. "I come in friendship and peace. Let that light pain awaken ye to my reality and serve as warning to what would await any who wouldn't greetmy friendship and peace in like kind."

"Savior arisen before my very eyes. Of course ye've me friendship." Hemrick leaned back, gaining a widespread smile.

"Holy shit! Really! Not you too. I'm no fucking savior, am I? Someone took a shit in the place where Horuce and yerself are supposed to be stowing yer brains. Bradier—I need to know all ye can give me on 'im. Callahan is dead, me friend. I'm Falcon. Know me as such, and use today to purchase allegiance." Callahan took a seat across from Hemrick and pulled his knives, replacing them in his vest.

"Bradier has a body double who poses as him here in the city. He is always on high alert for potential assassination plots, and I afford him such information whenever I can for a healthy price. Be warned, Falcon, I'm not their only contact, and they may know of your approach already. You should go after this guy with care. He wears an earring that seemingly detects lies. I looked at it once, and it was a week before I lost the warm and fuzzies toward the guy. So I'm thinking it shifts a person's perception toward the wearer as well. There are eight followers who go wherever he goes and know what they're doing. I delight in your return, mate." Hemrick smiled at his old friend.

After giving Callahan directions to the inn housing Bradier's double and describing in detail its layout, Hemrick stopped him as he started to leave . . .

[Callahan] HA! Anyone else catch the absolute lack of tact used by the narrator when he couldn't think of an inn name? Not that it has any bearing on the story whatsoever, but I just like to point out when I see things that are lacking.

[Narrator] Really, why don't we just give them an architectural breakdown of it while we are at it? That and I could vividly describe the position of the sun while you make the walk there or how your trousers find themselves riding a bit high, so you frequently pick them out of your ass.

[Callahan] OK, I'll give ye this one. I agree that being overly descriptive kills the pace of the story and loses reader interest. So in that regard, I will just say that the architectural layout crack is hilarious because, in small part, that does play into the next scene.

[Narrator] You really can be an ass, you know.

[Still Narrator but this time returning to the actual fucking story] Hemrick stopped Callahan as he—

[Callahan] Already said that bit.

[Narrator] Fuck all!

"Falcon, hold up a few more minutes, mate. Going after the body double isn't necessary. Heading two days out toward the mage tower, Calleigh, you can find a brigand campground. They have six Ssarrin captured and enslaved. Bradier is amongst their number. If he is killed, his men will lose all heart and disperse." Hemrick spread a sincere smile and added, "You may not recognize what you have been to Horuce and meself, but know that if you ever decide to stop being a servant of Namion's—" Sword to his throat, Hemrick's smile faded.

"I serve no one! I do, as I did when ye knew me last, what I must. Ye yet live because ye've been a great help this day. Seek Horuce, stick close to him. In such, serve me. A war will soon light this city the likes of which has never been seen. Yer a lot smarter than most give ye credit for. That's why I have always delighted in our business together. Stick with me, and I'll see ye through the horror that will come." Callahan sheathed his blade and headed for the front door.

"Please use the window. I don't want ye to stumble into any of Bradier's men, and as I was gonna say, if you would only lead, many would follow." Hemrick's grin returned. "Ye always did take good care of ole Hemrick now, didn't ye?"

[Callahan] Narrator, by the way, we just had a semientertaining interjection, and I didn't hear a word from our illustrious level 64. He must be busy being a ninja, eh?

[Narrator] No, he's just been in the pisser for quite a while.

[Callahan] So he's busy conjuring some prestidigitation, eh? Told ye he wasn't all that stealthy, didn't I?

[Reader 1] Did I miss something, or earlier, did Hemrick mention six slaves? Inquiring minds want to know, are they hot?

[Callahan] The Ssarrin are average seven- to twelve-foot-tall unisex lizard humanoids with toxic saliva that works well as a paralysis agent.

[Reader 1] Uh, how does one go about enslaving such a person?

[Callahan] Level 64 lacks the ninja skills to chain a lizard, eh? I would assume that a skilled sword arm, strong steel, and some distance weaponry would aid. Though in real answer, the Ssarrin are followers of a power much like orcs or goblinoids of any nature. Kill their strongest, and ye are their strongest.

[Reader 1] Point taken.

[Callahan] It has to be taken for ye, doesn't it? Not like anyone would let ye give yer point to 'em, would they? On to regard of the story as it sits now. Two of my old contacts and the closest people to what you could call friends of mine that yet lived are directly and deeply integrated with my first contract. Which led me to wonder, *What the fuck did Namion have in store for me this time?*

I pondered that very question as I left Hemrick's place that day. Having some time before evening fell, I took a preliminary glimpse at the inn that held the body double, ensuring to keep distance and discretion. My mind was reeling, just so many questions and so many options at this point. Hemrick told me that Bradier's double was no longer a necessary target. Well, if he was tainted by Namion, Namion would want him to tell me such to lead me out the city, wouldn't he?

I went on to the King's Grace and was grateful to see that Owl had secured the establishment for the purpose of our meeting. In other words, he rented the building and made everyone leave without dying. I told them the gist of the information I had gathered but that my sources were potentially compromised. After some heated discussion, the Avians agreed to my plan; it was an order given to me, so failure or success would fall on my shoulders.

Placing faith in Horuce and Hemrick, we would follow their leads. Owl and the other Avians would keep the brunt of our manpower focused on our primary target, and I would solo our secondary target. The other five would leave the city and handle the brigand camp and Bradier. I would case my target and wait. On the third sunrise after their departure, I would take out my target, giving ample time and coordination for the acts to be accomplished simultaneously.

Now for our more astute readers, I did just uncharacteristically use the word *faith*. I didn't hold faith in their loyalty. I held faith in the predictability of their stupidity. Even if those two blighters had tried to set me up, odds were good that they would have at least given me the proper destinations. Worst case, they would have disclosed the location for the ambushes. If the desired targets weren't present, I was confident in mine and Vulture's ability in regard to information extraction from anyone unfortunate enough to not die quickly.

I spent the next day in alternating observation of Horuce, Hemrick, and the inn housing my target. Horuce and Hemrick both seemed legit as far as my observations could tell. I managed to take in quite a bit of the regular operations of the men in the inn, and it seemed just as Hemrick had told me until the evening of that next day. A courier arrived, and a sudden rush of activity flowed through the inn. They were preparing for something.

That night, I paid a visit to good ole Hemrick, who had no idea what the excitement was all about. When I told him to go in the morning and find out what he could, he told me that they contacted him. He said that short of having life-or-death news, he was not to contact them. I couldn't take my target without knowing what had stirred them. Remembering that the man had an item that could derive truth, I told Hemrick to tell them that the Avians were on to Bradier's camp and were en route to assassinate him.

Don't say it. Don't think it. I'm an assassin with a track record of killing my best friend and parents in one night; betraying other assassins didn't even give me a second of hesitation. It wasn't really betrayal anyway; no courier would make the trip in time to stop them, and even if he could, worst case would lead back to Hemrick, and if that looked to be a possibility, I'd just take care of it myself.

So I sat there in Hemrick's dining room till he returned just before noon the next day. Stumbling in, the poor bastard looked pale as death.

[Narrator] "Falcon, mate. Please, I didn't have a choice." Hemrick's words caused Callahan to draw both his blades, kick the table over, and slide back the chair he was sitting on so that it obstructively sat before the side window. "Whoa! No worries, they're not here, but he did ask if anyone knew where he was, and I had to tell him the Falcon did. I didn't want to, but they'd have killed me."

Swords still drawn, Callahan cracked his wry half smile. "I hope ye've something really worth me while for that blunder."

Hemrick dropped to his knees with a look of pleading in his eyes. "Bradier himself is showing up at the inn this evening. The double laughed himself crazy hearing 'bout the Avians. He seemed a bit worried when I told him 'bout you, but I did catch eye on something." Callahan was stepping from behind the table toward Hemrick as the old man stuttered on. "That rickety house of cards could easily come tumbling down if someone were to just burn or break two beams. Give me a chance, and I will lay it all out for ye."

"OK, give me the rundown. I have some materials to get, and ye're to head right on back, and I don't give a crap if ye tell 'em everything ye know on me. Just tell them that I plan on killing Bradier tonight." Smiling, Callahan sheathed his swords, cursed his luck, and set his mind to task.

[Callahan] Aye, I have the best worst luck of anyone I know. Send all me manpower on to a recluse's camp, a recluse who never comes to the city. Get meself all prepped and ready to take out a few skilled men, and then out of nowhere, here comes said recluse and the opportunity for untold amounts of fame or a torturous death against ungodly bad odds. So I did what I do best. I headed off with the intention to surprise everyone and leave death in my wake.

[Narrator] A few short hours later, early in the afternoon found Callahan with a satchel of supplies, walking nonchalantly through the front door to his target's inn. He entered about a half an hour after he watched Hemrick finish conducting his business there. Taking in the scene quickly, Callahan took note of several innocent bystanders, a few potential brigands, and his target, sitting at a table with three other men, all of whom dropped their hands to their weapons upon seeing him. Having expected an attempt to be withheld until nighttime, the men were unsettled and underprepared.

"Hold on there, mates. No need to make a scene in front of a bunch of bystanders and risk collateral damage." Dropping his satchel on a nearby table and grabbing a chair, he quickly continued, saying, "I'm not here to kill ye." He looked directly at his target's earring as he made the last declaration. Then he sat in the chair and scooted in uncomfortably close to two of the other brigands at the table. Placing his unarmed hands casually on the table, he grinned at the man with the earring. "So what's good in this dive? Stew, perhaps?"

Having waved his men off from drawing their arms, the body double chuckled. "You've a lot of gall. If you're not here to kill us, what plea do you offer?"

"Oh, ye mistake what I said. I said I wasn't here to kill *you*." Raking his fingernails across the faces of both men sitting next to him, his hands then shot back to his chest.

[Callahan] Having had Ssarrins in mind, I took a bit of that time I had between Hemrick's house and the inn to stop at a Talon-friendly apothecary, among a few other stops, to pick up a few things and paint my fingernails with a paralysis agent. I had read much about the monster races and their traits as a child, having delighted in my own imagined battles against them. Who knew that knowledge would become professional aid

[Narrator] The first throwing dagger entered the third brigand's eye. The second entered the body double's right armpit. The third removed the ear with the earring. The fourth entered the neck of a man rising from a corner table. The fifth and sixth surged on toward the man charging down the stairs, who, surprising Callahan, caught both of them; one he caught with his right hand, the second he caught with his Adam's apple.

On his feet, Callahan drew both his blades and, with the left-handed short sword, cut down one paralyzed man, spinning through to lift the second paralyzed man before him, as two crossbow bolts found their place in the man's chest. Dropping the body, overturning the table, and grabbing the wounded and scrambling body double, Callahan dropped behind the cover of the table before the two men at the top of the stairs could reload their crossbows.

"HA! Having fun now, aren't we?" Callahan, with a full smile spreading across his face, listened to the chaos within the inn. In a low whisper, he asked the body double, "Mind taking a look?" Pushing the top of the man's head up as though he was peeking, Callahan delighted as two bolts split through it.

Diving over the table and using his magically enhanced agility, he leapt atop the bar, sheathed both blades, and then leapt up, grasping the base of the banister. Flipping over the railing, he found himself between the two crossbow wielders as they raised their freshly drawn weapons for a third shot. Drawing weapons as he burst into a roll, he heard the dual twang and thuds of the bolts released, finding targets. The two men had let their shots off, not accounting for inhuman speed, so groans could be heard as each received the other's shot. While finishing the two, Callahan watched back on the ground floor as the two rear door guards rushed in. He also noted the makeshift doorstop he had dropped and slid into place in the front door doing its job to delay the panicked crowd's escape. Dropping from the banister, he landed, driving both blades into the back of the first incoming brigand and, with a dual sweep, opened the second man's face and gut.

"Whoa! Silence!" A quick count brought seven total bystanders to view with noises accounting for four more upstairs. One thrust finished the last surviving brigand he had just slashed open. "Anyone leaves and I'll not only hunt and kill them but also everyone they've ever loved. I suggest ye all come down to the common room, and those already here take seat." Keeping his eyes and ears alert, Callahan gathered up the earring and removed it from its prior place in the body double's now separated ear. Pushing it through his own ear, he gritted his teeth at the slight pinch then delighted in the beloved feel of magic coursing through his body.

A woman, two children, and an old man came down from the upstairs. A bit of questioning later with the aid of the earring's ability to detect lies, Callahan had discovered that his attempt at shock and awe had worked out with all present brigands dead and no bystanders escaped or harmed. "All right now, folks. I want for us all to get on friendlylike. No sense in tearing up over these scum, eh? No one leaves, not till after tonight. So ye all gather on down in the cellar, all right, and on the morrow, ye can go 'bout yer lives." Ushering the lot into the cellar, he slid a wine keg on top of it, collected his knives, looted the bodies, and then went about preparing the establishment for the night to come.

[Callahan] Now before ye go pissing and whining 'bout how I could just ignore the magic charm of the earring. Let's remember, I'm not exactly yer usual sort, am I? I killed me own best friend without hesitation, so it wasn't that I didn't feel the tug. I rather liked the guy even after I cut his ear off and used his head as a catcher's mitt. It's more of a magical suggestion and less of a magical demand anyway. It doesn't control one's mind; it just guides one's intuitions and instincts. Also, I hadn't lied; I wasn't there to kill the guy. That was just the unfortunate turn of events that followed. I would've been perfectly happy with locking his mangled arse in the cellar with the rest of them, and I didn't really kill him, did I? His own buddies did.

Also, for any who may have caught the body count, Hemrick had told me the body double traveled with eight guards, yet I killed nine. The courier had never left and, as such, was one of the three men seated near the body double.

[Narrator] As darkness gripped the city, Callahan watched a procession of twelve heavily armed men walk to the door of the inn. Having informed the cellar dwellers of the multiple Talons in place around the building, Callahan had released the citizens from the cellar, allowing them to roam the inn as they wished. With aid of his new jewelry, he knew from their answers that his bluff would hold them fast. So he had taken his place on a rooftop overlooking the inn's front door. As the first few men entered the inn, Callahan started raining arrows down on them as quickly as he could draw them. This, in turn, caused the men to huddle around Bradier, inadvertently betraying his identity, and quickly rush into the safety of the inn.

Lighting a tar-coated bolt on a torch he had strategically placed behind a makeshift barricade to hide its light, he released it in through one of the inn's windows and watched as his chemical setup danced to life throughout the inn. The tar caught powder, which ran to more tar and so on, until the two main support beams, as Hemrick had described, lit, and the inn crackled and groaned. Picking his bow back up, Callahan rained arrows on the front door and any trying to escape from it.

The first beam snapped, and the building started falling in on itself; Callahan's bluff was no longer enough to contain the bystanders, who now rushed the windows and the back door. Shield held in front of him, Bradier dove through the front door as the second beam snapped, and the building toppled in on itself. Fire uncomfortably at his back and the screams of his dying men urging him on, Bradier held his shield aloft, absorbing several arrows with it as he slowly moved in a crouched position.

Letting his bow drop, Callahan lightly hopped from his perch, rolling as he landed on the street. He drew both his blades with a large smile on his face. Bradier drew his long sword and swept his shield clean of arrow hafts. Preparing for mortal combat, both men found themselves surprised as a frantic woman ran up, grabbing Bradier's leg. "Please! My babies, they're still inside."

That distraction was enough for Callahan to close the short gap between them and thrust his rapier under the shield at an upward angle, piercing leather armor and finding the heart. Ducking the dying man's swing, Callahan turned again to see the pleading woman's eyes upon him. "Please, oh please, I can't bare it."

Looking to the burning structure then to her, Callahan lost his smile. Calculating the odds, he knew any rescue would be a lost cause. He shook his head as he slashed his short sword through her. "No one needs to live with an image such as that." Grabbing Bradier's body, he pulled it off into the night with him.

[Callahan] Where did I get the torch? How about the bow and countless arrows? Well, jack bags, I didn't head out there completely unprepared. Aside from the apothecary, I had hit an armorsmith, a bowyer, and a general store. Why the armorsmith, you ask? Considering nothing I used would have really needed to come from a smithy aside from the weapons I was already equipped with. Well, in answer, I had snagged a few plates of metal, punched holes, and fashioned a chest and back guard just large enough to cover vital organs. The holes had been punched so that I could fit the leather strips used to fasten them tightly to myself. The whole elaborate setup wasn't really needed and is only being described to lend further weight to the following statement of "Shut the fuck up, and stop analyzing the damned story."

[Narrator] A few days later found Callahan sitting across a table from Namion. "The city is in an uproar with news of my new right hand, the Falcon. Who sent the Avians on to slaughter Bradier's camp while he single-handedly massacred Bradier and his second-in-command? The Falcon, who burned an inn down around his foes with no regard forcollateral damage, who slaughtered a woman begging for her children'slives, who killed two Lados guards when they tried to stop him from hanging the corpse of Bradier above the noble district's gate with a talon carved in his chest, who delivers Namion's vengeance with unprejudiced mayhem and has no mercy." Tossing a coin purse to Callahan, Namion nodded his approval. "The tattoo affords most of what you could want, and what it does not buy, use that ten platinum to pay for. Serve me as you have, and you will never want for anything."

"That's just pay for a difficult task." Callahan found himself in awe of the fortune he now held. "One question if I may, though. There were far too many coincidences. You knew of my contacts, and you knew Bradier was coming to town, didn't ye?"

"I knew of your contacts as well as their past heralding of your name. I knew Bradier was on the move in this direction but was unsure as to his intended destination. I knew that the best time to strike was now, and the best way to yield information was through your contacts using you. I expected you to go after the magic trinket you now boldly wear. I did not expect you to honor the guild by sending the brunt of your manpower after Bradier's camp. I figured you would find an excuse to take the Avians to get your trinket for you." Namion nodded his approval. "In regard to your earring, its pull carries no weight with me, and I have no reason to ever lie to you, thanks to our pact. Assuch, congratulations on your new acquisition. You have started the war, Falcon. I will rain death upon any who oppose me, using you as my blade. I am Lados, and all will respect that or rest uneasy with fear of the inevitable reprisal brought by the Falcon."

[Reader 1] OK, you execute above ragtag plan in perhaps the goriest fashion possible and leave the reader feeling like it's the only logical thing to do. I just want to state that if our obviously schizophrenic author ever decided to trade places with Callahan, I'm straight fucked. What's worse than that is that I'm completely confident that he would convince a jury that he did the only logical thing to do at the time.

[Narrator] I'm not a violent man.

[Callahan] Says "the Ripper" to his whore.

Chapter 3

LIFE DURING WARTIME

[CALLAHAN] READER WARNING: WHAT is to follow is a less-than-brief intermission instituted by the narrator to grant the reader a backstoryof Calarr. For those who just want to speed along to further snarky comedy and reckless slaughter, please skip on to my next interjection, where I'll give a quick summation.

[Narrator] Calarr consists of a large singular continent and multiple islands. The gods had divided the Pangaea into three parts using a vast wall. The realm primarily of forest and jungle was gifted to the elves. The realm of varying terrains was gifted to the humans. The realm of desert was populated by the more turbulent members of all the races.

Aside from the elven and human realms being able to exile people to the desert realm, no other mortal entry or exit was allowed between the realms. Currents of the ocean converged into tumultuous maelstroms in line with the great walls, preventing any water-based circumvention of them.

In the youth of Calarr's human realm, southern barbarian tribes banded with various seagoing and jungle tribes, forming a monarchy. The first several kings were just and honorable, seeking only to unify and protect humanity against the countless monster races of Calarr. As tends to be the course of humanity, the crown turned unification and protection into a progression toward subjugation and tyranny. Seeing this progression, some of the seagoing men moved north of the unified lands to form Lados, city of the free. Farmers, fishers, and hunters alike gathered to form a community where individuals were granted an equal voice in matters diplomatic and political.

It didn't take long before the populace grew to such an extent that individual voice became impractical, so districts were fashioned, and representatives were chosen when deciding upon matters became necessary. As time progressed and the city grew immense in its populace and size, constant political meetings became necessary, so lifelong district representatives were chosen.

During this phase, the ever-expanding monarchy of the southern realms grew to such an extent that conflict with Lados seemed imminent. The crown at that time was worn by a fairly honorable man who recognized that rebellion would be the reprisal of conquering Lados. He crafted a pact of allegiance on terms that if Lados were to refrain from creating further settlements or taking action against the crown, then the crown would allow them their republic and take no actions within the walls of Lados without direct consent of its representation.

Lados grew to over ten times the size of Calarr's next largest city and thus became the trade hub for the whole of the human realm. During this growth, the district representatives left nothing but an illusion of choice to the people. Calling themselves nobles, the representatives formed a district specifically for themselves. The city found itself under the control of the collective of them. They selected among them a governor to oversee in a kinglike fashion. In the time of our current tale, the governor in place was Kaville, and Callahan's stunt in regard to posting Bradier's body above the noble district's gate had caused Kaville to summon an emergency gathering to decide upon a response.

In that meeting, a declaration of bounty was made against the Talons at two gold per tattoo turned in. Further bounty was offered in regard to the members of the Avian assassins, and yet further reward was offered in the personal regard of the Falcon and Namion. The gauntlet had finally been thrown down, and the city was cast into war.

With Horuce's aid, the Falcon constructed a list of all nobles who had cast a vote against the Talons. More specifically, any who were particularly outspoken in the matter. Upon delivery of this list, Namion double-checked his sources and fashioned a hit list. The declaration of bounty had caused the Talons to move their operations underground. Many members were lost in the initial sweeps. The Talons' superior training and experience accounted for little when it came to the sheer mass of the Lados guard and outraged citizens.

The citizens, long oppressed, seemed to delight in the fashioning of a tangible enemy. All the rage built with their lack of voice could now be released on a viable target. Knowing the tentative nature of his position, Namion wisely chose a discreet course and ordered his members into hiding. Biding his time, Namion gave the nobles a month to enjoy their imagined suppression of the guild.

[Callahan] Gods create Calarr, men fuck it up, Kaville is governor of Lados, and Namion wants control of Lados. There, now that the doldrums of historical diatribe are complete, we can get back to me, which of course, in my opinion, is a far better read.

[Narrator] "A month, we have given them!" Namion stood impressive atop the platform overlooking the underground valley now uncomfortably housing the majority of the guild's remaining members. "Are you angry? Do you hunger for vengeful reprisal? Long enough, we have spent lulling them into a false sense of confidence. I want all of you to seek out any who have collected bounty in regard to our dead brothers." A roar of approval echoed from the valley's walls at near-painful volume. "I do not only want them killed. I want their friends, families, and loved ones to be made to answer for their crimes. Soon, my colleagues, very soon. I will return within the next few evenings to release you all to purpose. For now, gather arms and prepare yourselves for what proves to be a glorious conquer."

Soon after his conclusion, the Avians sat assembled for orders. Namion casually stood at the head of a square dining table, looking upon his elite. "Previously, the city has only experienced hints of your presence. Small tastes of what could be delivered. This was obviously not enough to achieve purpose. Owl, Eagle, I have for you three names, unimpressive nobles of minor weight who spoke in approval of the bounty. I want them slain, and I want it known that the Avians did it. Afford these self-righteous asses the knowledge that even in the safety of their home district, they are vulnerable.

"Vulture, Sparrow, I have for you three names, nobles of low regard who have yet to gain entry to the sanctuary of the noble district. I want them untouched, but I want their families and loved ones to experience the nightmare that is your crafts. Let it be known—not only will those who speak against us suffer, but their families and loved ones as well.

"Raven, Falcon, I have for you, Alliander. I want him to inexplicably disappear. I do not want evidence or outside witness to Talon involvement. I want him gone in such a way that the people of Lados will believe that even the gods are behind our efforts and against their nobles. Before this disappearance, I want you"—he pointed to Falcon—"to take the names of our other six targets to your contacts. Let them know who is marked for death. Lend rise to their fear, and see it come to life. I want them to try and prepare themselves for us. I want them to watch their petty attempts fall to pieces before them. I want this concluded by nightfall tomorrow, upon which time I will unleash the guild. It is time to prove your positions and worth to me, time to unleash unholy fury, time to sing such a song of death that the gods will cry."

[Callahan] Ah, fuck all. Alliander, Kaville's next in line for position of governor. Yep, we will just make this man disappear. Second most influential man in all of Lados and we'll just up and make him not exist. Where's the level 64 mage ninja when ye need him, eh?

Now is as good a time as any to divulge what I spent my fortune of a reward on during that prior month of downtime. With all necessities covered by guild allegiance, my reward was left free to be spent on entertainment and toys. Nothing says toy to me quite like magically enhanced items.

I went to a gambling hall to break a couple of the platinum down to gold. I took that gold and gave a few coins to both Horuce and Hemrick for their loyalty and service. While delivering payment, I also inquired as to the whereabouts of any discreet black market merchants peddling magic wares. Why not just go to a public magic shop since my coin is valid? Well, mate, aside from only carrying trivial, near-useless items, their large sales are monitored by both the Lados nobles and the crown. Items of a useful magical nature are not overly common throughout the world of Calarr. I had never even considered the possibility of purchasing such items until I had held that fortune in my hand.

I detest the temple district and all that it stands for, but there I was led to the temple of Vertigo. A few whispered passwords and I was ushered to an underground shop with toys aplenty. Brunt of my fortune later, I was equipped with a necklace that would warn of any possible impact as well as turn any nonmagical missiles from the wearer. I also gained a ring that allowed its wearer elven night vision and gloves that afforded their wearer a normal body temperature regardless of external conditions. In retrospect, it's a shame they didn't carry any cloaks for vanishing a well-guarded, never-alone holy-shit influential noble.

During that month of downtime, I also pursued the book of Entearra Gharu. Much to my dismay, the priests of Malaki were a tight-lipped lot. The coin I spent toward the end of obtaining information turned up little more than rumor and hearsay. At this point, I was left with a suspicion that the priests had secreted the book away in an attempt to permanently hide its secrets.

[Narrator] Mind racing to find a solution to the puzzle that was the contract on Alliander, Callahan left Raven hard-pressed to keep pace. Leaping lithely from one rooftop to another, he heard a loud groan. Turning, he saw Raven roll from her rough landing to stand glaring at him.

"Don't look so sour there, darling. I could help hold yer skirt tails if ye feel ye can't keep up." Callahan found himself impressed by the natural-looking manner in which his necklace caused the thrown chunk of stone to pass harmlessly by his head. "Hmm, slow to run and yer aim is off. It's that time of month, eh?"

"Such witty comic relief may impress loose brothel denizens and fat barmaids, but I am no more impressed by it than I am with the dumb-luck manner in which you've accomplished your prior tests and jobs." Collecting herself, Raven pushed even harder to maintain Callahan's pace.

"I'd hate to bungle us into another amazing success, so I would appreciate any ideas you may have in regard to our target." Purposely slowing his pace, the two were now traversing side by side.

"If you can remember lessons of mine, I have the necessary clothing and insignia to pass us as visiting nobles of the crown from the capital city, Stockard. Once in their district, I can provide distraction, but at best, we will find him with six bodyguards." Raven found herself looking at the location of Callahan's old homestead. "That's your—"

"No, it's Callahan's old house. For Falcon, it is merely the residence of a contact. Wait here." Leaping to the street, he didn't hesitate to walk right into the house.

Moments later, Horuce rushed off in the direction of the noble district. Raven watched for Callahan's approach until she heard a whisper in her ear. "So my place or yours?"

Ducking then sidestepping, Callahan couldn't help but look approvingly at the ease with which she drew and wielded her cutlass. "As I was saying, where should we get in character?"

Smiling despite Callahan's nearly constant demeaning nature, Raven suppressed a chuckle. "Not many get a jump on me. Follow, I will take you to where I keep them stored."

"Bah, I look like a fucking poof." Callahan looked in the mirror at his ridiculously oversized puffed-up noble outfit. Large enough that he was able to wear his normal ensemble underneath it, he felt that the whole getup made him look ridiculous. In an odd way, he found himself ashamedly impressed that his earring and necklace fit well with the getup.

"Get over yourself. We do a lot of things in our line of work that are less than comfortable. I would hope that this is far less uncomfortable than having to slay grieving mothers." Raven, though not the most beautiful of women, wore her getup well. Callahan found himself slightly smitten yet again.

"Floozies and loose beauties are a dime a dozen, but women of strength and character—now they provide the delight of conquest. You're quite drawing, me dear." Flashing his half smile, Callahan sought an opening.

"Really? You're gonna go there. I'm not a streetwalker to be swayed by a few half-assed compliments thrown out by a heartless con man. Now come on, and keep your mind to task." Leading out of her storehouse, Raven carried herself in her dress like a haughty, self-important noblewoman.

"Hold! Ooh. I've a brilliant idea. So unless ye've come up with something yerself, come back in yer house here, and let me explain." Looking to the ominous dusk sky as he exited, Callahan had come upon an interesting plan.

[Callahan] You may have noted that throughout the course of our story thus far, the narrator and I have neglected flowered speeches about weather, foliage, wildlife, and the many visual aspects that would be abundantly available to uselessly expend brain cells on. For the most part, I find such discourse to be draining and cumbersome. That being said, I find it now a pertinent point to illustrate that Lados, being an oceanside city, found itself prone to many a storm. In particular, lightning storms were a frequent and troublesome occurrence.

In the earlier days of Lados, lightning accounted for a great deal of damage and natural deaths. A lot of trial and error found that certain metals attracted its attention more than others. Further study found that if rods crafted of these metals were fashioned above the rooftops and ran into the ground, it would prevent much of the damage caused. Mages and metallurgists crafted such rods and placed them throughout the whole of Lados, diminishing the danger. Lightning came to be a welcomed and sometimes worshipped sight as it danced from rod to rod throughout the city, often lighting the night sky in a beautiful display.

The worship and celebration of lightning in our world had led street performers and entertainers to find a metallic dust that when put to charge would burst in a multicolored display. As a child, I watched a few such acts and delighted in them. Being me, I couldn't suffice with just watching. So I inevitably studied and broke down the process. During such study, I found that even slight static buildup would release enough energy to light the dust which, in turn, would multiply the charge and conduct it, consuming said dust in the process.

One might ask themselves what an assassin occupies his mind with in his off time. For me, I have often pondered new and ridiculous methods of death. One such pondering led me to the study of these rods and the currents of energy provided by lightning. I envisioned disabling one such rod and running its charge to a concealed metal plate for the purpose of, as you would call it in your world, electrocution. Not being privy to knowledge of electricity as in your world, my imaginings seemed far-fetched and risky at best.

With a limited time frame and a seemingly impossible goal at hand, far-fetched and risky plans seemed a lot more feasible than normal. When I had stepped out to follow Raven, I saw that the ominous clouds moving into place above the city on that night appeared to be ones holding promise of a great deal of such lightning. In Raven's storehouse, I outlined an elaborate plan that she begrudgingly agreed to.

An hour or so of material gathering later found us both carrying a bit more concealed weight toward one of the gates leading into the noble district. Before the rest of my elaborate plan could flourish, we would first have to secure entrance to the district while carrying a fairly large amount of questionable items. The ridiculously oversized outfit Raven had placed me in no longer seemed like such a bad idea. Remember the armorsmith plates I spoke of earlier? Well, now they come to use. For what I had in mind, it took three of the plates and a lot of thin metallic wiring. I had to smuggle the wiring in my pants, which left me rather burdened. I was burdened to such an extent that I was forced to walk in an odd manner. A manner that resembled what one would imagine a man who had recently been sodomized by a horse would walk in.

[Narrator] Approaching one of the nobles' gates, Callahan noted that the level of security was greatly heightened since the time of his youth. One of the two attentive guards stepped forward to challenge the apparent nobles approaching. "Halt. Passes or invites." The guard held out his hand.

"Go ahead. Show him the invite, dear." Raven passed an annoyed and impatient look Callahan's way as she spoke.

"No, you brought them." Callahan returned her look with mounting frustration.

"Oh, you blithering moron. Why my father paid his enormous dowry to the lowly Delrose family, I'll never understand." Thrusting her nose into the air, Raven turned away from Callahan.

"Delrose? As in Lord Hubert Delrose?" The guard seemed to be takenaback.

"Do I look that old to you? Buffoon." Callahan shook his head as though this were all beneath him. "I am Lord Richard Delrose, son to Lord Hubert Delrose."

"Wow, if it's an inherited trait, she must be one resilient woman." The second guard had leaned into the first to whisper.

"I'm not deaf, you lowly peons!" A shocked expression on her face, Raven took a step back from the guards toward Callahan. "But if you all must know, my father's dowry needed to purchase at least one useful trait now, didn't it?"

Snickering, the guards fought to keep their laughter hidden. Callahan stepped forward. "Enough of this folderol. Let us by. We are late for Kaville's dinner."

"Not our fault you forgot your passes, and the noble's orders are very specific about no one passing these gates without notarized pass or invite. I think we may be able to work something out in that we might choose to look the other way for a minute." The guard leaned over to his buddy and whispered, "Five silver says it's not nearly as big as they say it is."

"You're on," the other guard responded.

"OK, if Lord Delrose will show us his supposed mammoth asset to clear a bet, we will turn the other way so you can get to your dinner." The guards seemed to delight in this exchange.

"Bah, what a ridiculous prospect." It was Callahan's turn to push his nose skyward.

"You left the invites. You insisted on dragging us out here. You housed us in the merchant district instead of the comforts provided in the nobles' district. You . . ." Raven started pointing her finger at Callahan's chest.

Having taken the time during Raven's short rant to adjust his smuggled gear and clothing appropriately, Callahan produced his genitalia for the guards' viewing. The first guard turned to the second and said, "Not that big, bah, fucking told ye."

The second guard reached into his pouch and produced the promised bet. "Fine, here ye are."

"Be damned with ye both. I may not be huge, but I'm more than large enough to put a bit of wobble in her hobble, if ye know what I mean." Callahan popped himself back in his pants. Raven then led the way through the gate, leaving the guards howling with laughter.

When out of earshot, Callahan leaned in toward Raven. "The fucking Longhammer? Really?"

"The Longhammer?" Raven burst into laughter. "Never heard him called that."

"Lord Delrose was talked about by a bunch of the streetwalkers when I was younger. Supposedly, that guy was packing 'bout a foot and a half. They all called him the Longhammer." Callahan's face lit up with a wry grin.

"I never thought your pecker would gain entry to anything in my presence. Guess I was wrong. You did break character a bit at the end, though." Raven couldn't help but smile as she fought to suppress laughter.

"Break character? Yer lucky I didn't just fucking 'lose me shit completely when ye told 'em I was Delrose's son. I thought I kept it together pretty good, given the circumstances." Callahan chuckled then started muttering under his breath, "You'll be amazed by what my pecker will gain entry to, given time."

"What's that?" Still suppressing laughter, Raven shot a glare at Callahan.

"I said you play being a nagging shrew quite well, must be all that practice ye put in." With that, Callahan took to a nearby alley to unload some of his encumbering contraband.

For the next hour, Callahan went to work in the noble district while Raven kept a lookout. He concealed plates near three separate lightning rods between Alliander's and Kaville's residences. He ran wire from the plates to right next to the rods, and then he tested one using the powder he carried. Discovering its success, he fixed the rod back up to avoid a hapless passerby ruining his scheme and then prepared his flask of dwarven spirits with the same powder. He fixed the drink following the logical course that if this dust were so effective under a direct charge then entered into one's bloodstream, it may well help to ensure death, thus alleviating the threat of Alliander surviving the shock.

Dusting off his noble attire, Callahan pondered aloud to Raven, saying, "So how exactly do ye intend on getting us into Kaville's manor?"

"Well, Lord and Lady Delrose are in the merchant's district. They're here in support of one of the lower-renowned district reps. We'll waltz right into the manor as such and mingle in support of the up-and-coming rep that is Harmod Flarg." Raven set to adjusting her dress.

"Just a second, they're not going to notice that we don't look anything like young Lord and Lady Delrose? I mean, I don't even know what the fucking Delroses look like." Callahan gave a frustrated look to Raven.

"Young Richard and his wife have never been to the city before. Flarg used to frequent the capital for his education and, in such, befriended the Delrose boy. Rising in status, Flarg recently sent for the support of his friend to help expedite said rise. That is why I chose them. Vulture and Sparrow will be dealing with them in their fashion due to Flarg being one of their targets." Raven gave Callahan a mock version of his own half smile.

"This is all mighty fucking convenient, isn't it?" Callahan didn't like coincidences.

"My father chooses his assignments very carefully. He doesn't send us out to fail. He just doesn't like giving out information, so he enjoys making us piece it together ourselves." Raven started walking on to the luxurious governor's mansion.

[Callahan] Just like with the Bradier job. I hate going into things lacking knowledge. Namion, knowing that about me, delighted in sending me in blindfolded. He wanted me to succeed, but he definitely made it clear that he didn't want to make it comfortable for me.

I had fashioned a small metal strip that could be inserted through the sole of a shoe in such a manner as to lend no discomfort to the wearer while allowing the metal to sit inside against one's foot as well as outside in contact with the heel.

Like I said, assassins have downtime too, and when I do, I craft off-the-wall things. I try to think of every eventuality.

Making our way inand mingling with the nobles at Kaville's ball was an easier task than I had imagined. For the most part, it consisted of introducing oneself and letting the other self-righteous tit blather on about whatever they wanted. Again, yet another coincidence being that on the night we, as a guild, are to assassinate a collective of nobles, they would be gathered together in one place, throwing a ball. Well, in explanation, if ye had all the wealth and power, what would ye do with yer weekend? Or if ye prefer, we can refer back to the fact that knowing Owl and Eagle were in line to plug three of these pompous assholes, Namion had selected this particular night due to the existence of a gathering such as this.

Seeing Alliander disappointed me due to the fact that my shoe piece would be ineffective. All that planning and the man had decided to wear his ceremonial armor to the event, turning him into a delightfully giant tin can.

Raven moved about the nobles in an artful dance of deceit. She seemed at peace with the role. I took my time as I watched her move from one group of gossipers to the next. Aye, physically beautiful women were as easy as a spot of quick charm and a dashing smile, but she was so much more. A mind such as hers was not an easy trait to come by.

[Narrator] Moving to where Alliander was seated, Callahan pulled up a chair. "Sorry to impose, good sir. Your reputation precedes you, and I was curious to see if you would let me share of my dear friend Harmod Flarg. Perhaps in doing so, I could give you a pull or two of these fine dwarven spirits I brought with me from Stockard."

"I'll humor you a bit, lord." Reaching out, Alliander took down half the flask in one steady drink. Gritting his teeth through the strong drink's bite, he then sat with obvious disinterest as Callahan spouted about Harmod's wonderful traits and skill sets, all of which he made up as he went along. After polishing off the flask then listening a few more minutes,

Alliander then rose. "Sorry to cut you short, lord, but I really must be on with my evening. You know how wives get when one stays away too long." Signaling to his guards, they began preparations to leave.

"Yes, nagging wenches just don't know when to keep their place, do they? Thank you for your time, and may the gods bless your trip home." Callahan signaled Raven, who politely parted from her gossip session. Heading out the entrance, Callahan and Raven rushed to their previously plotted hiding spots.

[Callahan] We had three chances at this. After we watched Alliander's departure to ensure that he took his usual route, Raven would wait for me at each of the three points we had set up. If the lightning strikes were lining up and things were looking promising, I would then signal her. She would rush in to distract and shift his position over the plate, while I would disable the ground and connect the plate to the rod. Yes, I was well aware of the possibility of lighting myself up, but such a risk seemed minor to the delight I would have if this succeeded.

Out came Alliander, and all my plans fell to shit. I couldn't believe my eyes. I thanked the gods I didn't hold faith in for all the following noise that covered my outburst of laughter. I watched as Alliander, in his glorious armor, strode out of the mansion like the arrogant ass he was. I watched as a lightning strike lit the rod above the mansion. A rod that was far too visible to have been tampered with. I watched as that bolt jumped from the rod to Alliander. I watched oozelike blood and flesh seep from the armor's creases and listened to the popping and crackling sounds made from his burning flesh.

Apparently, the powder had a far more potent effect in the bloodstream than I'd anticipated. It was by far the most horrifyingly beautiful act of chaos I'd ever witnessed. What did remain of his body that hadn't exploded, melted, or been otherwise burned was soon being pawed and cried over by his guards and the party guests. Looking to where Raven hid, I gave signal to leave. Guessing from her delayed response and slow departure, she had found herself in as much awe of the scene as had I.

In the time it took us to gather all evidence of our presence from the three sites that had been intended, the whole of the district had jumped to arms. People were shouting and blundering about all over the place. Owl and Eagle had accomplished their jobs. With three assassinations and one inexplicable liquefaction, the nobles were running scared. Using the confusion, Raven and I quickly hurried on to her storehouse.

[Narrator] Dropping the tools and gear, Callahan shirked off his noble attire. "Have ye ever seen anything like that?"

"Not in a hundred years. It isn't possible. How do you do it?" Raven pulled her dress above her head, revealing to Callahan's eyes her complete lack of undergarments.

Most would think it would take a direct act from the gods themselves to silence Callahan, but that purpose was accomplished by the simple revelation of Raven's body. Taking advantage of his slack-jawed silence, Raven rushed in, tearing at Callahan's clothes.

[Callahan] Aye, apparently, men popping like water balloons cause women to percolate. Who would've guessed that such an event would get her so hot and bothered, but I definitely didn't complain. I wasn't a virgin by any means, but up to that night, it had always just been physical satiation. With Raven, I experienced a ferocity and passion that lit my spirit in a manner that had only been accomplished previously through the act of murder.

Writhing about in an animalistic fashion in her storehouse, I found myself at peace. In a life where most everything I did, I did because I had to, it was a breath of fresh and exhilarating air to do one thing just because I wanted to. What to her was nothing more than a celebration of success was to me the rebirth of hope for more. I found life in her arms. I existed in a world of survival and presence, unfulfilling and dark. With her embrace, I could feel imaginings of more arise within my mind. That lost ember of humanity could be felt pushing itself to the surface.

Oh, what? Ye didn't think I'd describe it like that, did ye? Ye were probably waiting for me to go into a lengthy spiel on her nipples, ass, or vagina. Bet ye wanted me to talk about how we went from standing to missionary, to spooning, to doggy style, back to missionary then finishing it up in doggy style with a donkey punch. Maybe ye even wanted me to talk 'bout her back door or some props and restraints. Well, bugger off, ye perverted twerps, 'cause it wasn't like that at all. As far as I'm concerned, Raven is off the joke market. So, Reader 1, count yerself forewarned.

[Narrator] Chaos and panic greeted Raven and Callahan as they reentered the city the next morning. The citizens were all aflutter with news of death, uprising, and turmoil. Nodding to each other, Raven and Callahan took in the sounds of pain and tragedy. They drew those sounds in and reveled in them as tangible evidence of the guild's successful evening.

Callahan found himself gravitating toward the sound of a man speaking from atop a makeshift podium. The man was saying, "The events of last night only go to further display how stifled our voice has become. Nobles are now raining their sins down upon our heads. It's our city that burns, not just theirs. Rise up, dear friends and neighbors. Rise up, and help me to throw off the bounds of enslavement placed upon us by our own nobles and by the criminal Talons. Let us spread the word and unite again as did the brave men who founded this dear city. Lados was the city of the free. It can be so again, if we just make it such."

A good crowd of individuals gathered before the speaker eating up his words, while still, others passed with groans and shaking heads. "As evil as the Talons are, they have opened up an opportunity for us to voice our frustration. They crafted an opening, showing us and the nobles that noble law is not untouchable. They can be put down. Take

Alliander, for example. Do you think it coincidence that even the gods conspire with criminals against this treasonous lot of oppressors? This city can, once again, rise in glorious unity."

Callahan watched a contingent of Lados guards burst through the crowd toward the speaker. A reluctant Horuce stood at the forefront of the guards. "Insurrection and inciting riot is a crime punishable by death. Disperse now, and we will forget what we saw and heard here."

"See, here they are to yet again oppress the true voice of the people. Representatives, bah. Who do they represent? Not I." The speaker continued until a guard forcibly pulled him to the ground.

The guard raised a drawn blade prepared to strike down the criminal speaker until a voice pushing through the crowd rose up. "That man is most likely a raging lunatic. That does not negate the validity of his statements, though. Your voices, the voices of freedom long forgotten in this feudalistic society, have gone soft and unheard for far too long." Callahan was given wide berth as he fearlessly strode toward the contingent of guards. Finding himself so engrossed in the ideals expressed and lost in his desire to see their fruition, Callahan had failed to notice Raven's hasty departure from her place at his side.

Cursing the gods, Horuce turned to look into his dangerous friend's icy blue eyes. "This is no affair of yours. Like everyone else, you should avoid trouble and disperse. We are humans too. We don't want bloodshed any more than you do."

"Then raise your voice. Stand beside that man instead of on top of him. Everyone wants to shy from the terrifying state of the city because it's beyond their control. Well, it's not beyond my control, is it?" Callahan leapt atop the makeshift podium and turned to the crowd, revealing his tattoo. A shocked gasp and then a low roar of disgust shot through the masses. "Hear me! I speak not as representation of the guild but only as representation of the Falcon. This city is what it is not because it has to be but because we sit idly and quietly by, letting it be such." The guards stood prepared with weapons drawn, waiting for Horuce's order. Mouthing the words "Go ahead," Callahan winked at his friend. "I don't do what I want to do. I do what I must do. Apathetic indifference to crime is a crime. So don't look upon me in judgment. Instead, know that my hands and the hands of my guild mates are forced by your inaction." Sliding back to the edge of the podium, Callahan waited until the first of the guards got within reach before he violently threw himself into a backflip. The action thrust the podium forward into the closest guard, throwing him back into several of his fellows.

Having drawn two throwing knives in midflip, Callahan crouched at the ready. A quick scan of the scene before him caused Callahan to sheath his throwing daggers. Twenty-plus guards were coming from nearly all directions. The crowd of citizens were gathering makeshift weaponry and joining the guards.

[Callahan] Fucking figures, eh? I get a wild hair up my arse and decide to try to be human, most likely because of my recent spiritual experience through copulation. I found, in doing so, a horde of merciless and pissed guards and citizens, who would have been at each other's throats until I stepped in to unify them against a singular enemy. Having spilled more than enough blood and being outside of any guild order, I decided to attempt a nonfatal approach. I sought the crowd for escape options and /or allies but found only a nearby alley that would act to funnel my opponents.

[Narrator] Lurching into the group of men between himself and the alley, Callahan delved back into a world of familiarity. With his left hand, he caught the wrist of an overhead diagonal sword swipe; twisting the wrist, Callahan drove the blade's hilt into the side of the owner's face. His right hand slid in, removing the blade from the guard's loosened grasp, and tossed it lightly into the chest of the next closest man. Clumsily dropping his sword, the man awkwardly caught the tossed weapon just before Callahan's right foot smashed into his chest, launching him to the ground. Twisting that kick into a low sweep, Callahan launched another one of the mob from his feet.

Getting a sense of doom, Callahan started to feel a bit claustrophobic as more and more people crowded in on him. A knife hand to a throat, a jumping kick to another's collarbone, and a straight kick into yet another's kneecap, Callahan's smile spread from ear to ear. A sweeping sword nicked his shirtsleeve, a punch grazed his cheek, and then a makeshift two-by-four club clipped his shin. Reaching down, Callahan prepared to draw his blades, but a barked order split the crowd, and Horuce approached, armed with sword and shield. "Surrender, and you'll be brought to proper trial."

Laughing boisterously, Callahan shook his head. "Proper trial, what a joke. Public execution is more the term I think ye sought. Look well upon me, Lados! Fear me! I am the Falcon!" Rolling under Horuce's haphazard swipe, Callahan brought his body behind Horuce's reach as he shot to his feet. Smashing his head forward, Callahan felt Horuce's nose crumple under the impact. Seeing an opening as Horuce's body slumped to its knees, Callahan pushed him out of the way and ran through the gap in the crowd. Darting into the alley, he then spun back around just in time to duck a spear thrust.

Rising under the spear, he grabbed a hold on it. Jerking it from its owner's grasp, he spun it then thrust it through his opponent's shoulder. Callahan shoved the skewered man back into the crowd, trying to find an opening where he stood. A quick glance down the alley showed the mob closing in from both sides. Hopping up, Callahan grabbed a ledge on the side of a building and, in doing so, dodged an incoming thrust. Pulling his feet up to his handholds, Callahan caused yet another passing swipe to miss. Flipping back off the wall, Callahan landed behind a man thrusting a spear to where he had been. Kicking the man forward into the wall, Callahan grinned as the staggering man dropped his spear.

[Callahan] Yep, I knew I was in a tight spot. Both sides of the alley were closing up on me, and at this point, any self-respecting man with a regard for life would have surrendered. So I reached to pull my blades in an attempt to take as many of those bastards with me as I could. Fortunately, this was the point when Raven lowered a rope to me from the rooftop.

I know, I know. What is more cliché than constant near-death miraculous rescues? Well, when yer the one whose ass is getting pulled out of the fire, ye'll be thankful for a rescue, even if it is cliché. After we had managed to clear some rooftops and break free from the mob, Raven chewed me up one side and down the other.

[Narrator] Her voice heightened in anger, Raven asked, "Why would you ever think to do something so blatantly stupid? Why would you put your life at risk for some lowly protester?"

"It wasn't the messenger I was upholding, it was the message. Wouldn't ye like, just once, to be welcomed instead of feared and run off? Just one fucking time, wouldn't it be nice to have people celebrate our arrival? The nobles are as tyrannical as the founders of this city had feared the crown of becoming. We, as a city, have digressed. We lost all those values fought and died for. Let's give the people back their say. Why should we be feared as criminals? When we could just as easily be hailed as gods incarnate?" Callahan's eyes twisted and lit with a depth of emotion Raven had not seen before.

"That boy I once knew. That boy I once saw. I see him before me." Raven's voice softened, and moments later, the two were wrapped in each other's embrace. Sunlight beamed across the rooftop, where the two shed clothing.

[Callahan] Before you ask, yes, we had an angry mob after us. Yes, we were in mortal danger. When the fuck have I not been in mortal danger? If ye get a chance to rack it out on the one you love, to fuck with the consequences, ye get down to doing it. I'm a damned assassin; every day I get to wake up is a miracle. Knowing full well that I should die each day, I'm able to see a beauty in all things. A child's laughter, a ray of sunlight, the embrace of Raven—these things all held significant purity in the effect that every time I experienced them, it should have been my last.

Throughout all the courses, the twists and turns of my life, those moments with Raven were the ones I always longed to have back. All the pain and neglect of my childhood; all the violence, gore, and death of my adulthood; all the tension provided by the insatiable void of chaos within my mind—it all accounted for nil when Raven touched me.

Did I lock myself in a room for months on end, thus ensuring the absence of any poor decisions brought on by the afterglow of good cooch like any self-respecting sane man should do when he feels that he is in love? Nope. I went and did what most men tend to do in that circumstance; I took the most blatantly ignorant route of action I could conceive of. I hunted down Namion.

In the lower-class district, there were streets that all knew not to walk. The streets where men would skewer ye just for having a crooked smile; dreary and dark were those streets. That was just the kind of place where ye would suspect a man of Namion's repute to reign.

Nope, he had a quaint little shanty in the middle-class district. Not far from the very gate Raven and I had used to gain entry to the noble district just the night before.

[Narrator] "I'm asking ye to not let the men loose on the city tonight. We can be so much more." Callahan looked pitiable and almost begging as he sat alone with Namion amidst the humble furnishings.

"Why would you care? Vicious deliverer of death, who leaves tragedy in the wake of his every motion, what could motivate such a sudden pull of morality?" Namion seemed frustrated and amused at the same time.

"It's not a matter of morality. It's a matter of profit. Yer putting us at risk of turning the very people we depend upon against us. The guild has no power and no pull without profit. If the people of Lados see us as evil, if they turn completely against us, then we will disperse like the fading of fog." Becoming more animated, Callahan wafted his hands about as he spoke.

"Calm yourself, boy. I will not stand for such insubordination, not even from you, young Callahan." The use of his given name brought grave attention back to the danger that was Namion.

"Lend voice back to the people. Ye have the power to. Free these people from the suffocating grip of the nobles, and they won't just tolerate ye for it, they won't just like ye for it. They'll fucking worship ye for it. They'll worship us." Scrambling to avoid Namion's rush, Callahan attempted to roll over the back of the lightly cushioned chair he sat in.

Pinning Callahan motionless to the chair, Namion pressed his face in close. "I do not care about profit. Look around you. Do you see wealth abounding? Do you see me making public speeches and showings? Do I look like a man who needs adulation? No, little Falcon, I am a nightmare. I want them to want me inactive. I want them to want to not see me. I want them to think of me as they do that fluttering dark thought that skims the back of their mind. That thought that they pretend they did not have. That thought that brings to light the holes in their self-imagined morality. I want to drain not just this city but this entire gods-be-damned world of every last drop of hope. I want to drink in every last drop of peace until even the great walls crumble from the despair of it all. I want to draw forth the gods from their respective heavens in attempt to deal with me personally."

Loosening his hold and returning to his plain chair, Namion continued, "Take your youthful ideologies, and do with them whatever the fuck you want. Do what I tell you when I tell you to do it. Jump whenever I say jump. Do not seek to instruct me. Do not deign to be my equal. You are not. You never will be. You yet live because I allow it. If I wanted, your life would be forfeit before the sun exited our vision this night. Correct yourself, Falcon. Do so quickly. In the midst

CHRIS CURTIN

of this evening's festivities, you will take Vulture with you to Tellian's mansion. You will let him do what he does best, and you will wait at the well behind Tellian's home. It is the exit for his underground escape. You will kill him however you see fit. When you are finished, you will go about your life however you see fit until next I call upon you. You will never come to ask favor of me again. Am I clear enough for you? Is that put simply enough to be fully understood?"

Nodding in silence, Callahan took his leave and headed off to where he and Raven had planned to meet back up. A few minutes after Callahan's departure, Namion pushed the false wall next to his fireplace aside and ordered, "Raven, get closer to him. Distract him. Keep him reeling. I want no uncertainties. I want no avenue unguided. You are doing splendidly thus far."

After arriving at Raven's storehouse, Callahan did not wait long before she entered the front door. Shaking his head, he sounded almost mournful. "It's no use, Raven. He's inhuman. There'll be no reasoning with 'im. There can be only obedience."

"I know. I was there behind his false wall. He teamed us under the order that I was to get close to you. He wanted my presence to unsettle you. He fears you, Callahan. I have never seen him fear anything, but he fears you. I cannot understand the draw, but regardless of my understanding, I am drawn to you, and I don't want to see you die." Raven embraced Callahan, resting her head upon his chest.

Even without the benefit of his earring, Callahan would have eaten up every word from her lips. "I cannot stand against him. We are bound, he and I. I cannot stand against him."

[Callahan] OK, most that enjoy this particular genre of story are probably baffled by the sudden changes being seen within my character. I'll let ye know that yer virginity is a leading factor to yer current confusion. Any man who has ever felt the pangs of love knows the complete breach of cognitive function that follows it. I usually delight in the similarities between a nervous breakdown and love, but seeing as this is the retelling of my experienceof it, it's not so fucking funny to me now, is it?

[Narrator] "You must stand. A large chunk of the guild would stand with you if you did. Not all of us think like Namion, do we? Most of us, deep down, want exactly what you want. Most join due to the weight of their helplessness. They bare the tattoo because it's the only force with weight to lend them an outlet to their rage at life's futility." Raven's eyes now expressed a look of longing.

"It's not yet time, I fear. I fear because it's gonna get much worse before it can get better. Whatever light remains of your humanity, hide it well. This night and many to follow are going to cast this city into a living nightmare the likes of which only Vulture could dream of." Resting his head upon Raven's, Callahan did all he could to stretch out the following moment. A quiet embrace with words unspoken, it was the embrace given by those looking upon their own mortality. This would be the memory in which he would lose himself when all around him became unbearable.

Carving out an imposing image against the dwarven stone walls, Namion stood atop the platform entrance to the underground valley. "As promised, you will soon be unleashed." The cramped mass of Talons, filling the valley base, cheered their approval. "Here in this underground prison, you have too long suffered. I am sure you heard of last night's triumphs. Nobles outside the safety of their district scramble even as I speak to find sanctuary behind its walls. Nobles in their district know the futility of such. They know their own vulnerability even in their imagined sanctuary. All fear the anger of the gods themselves, who seemingly rise to our cause—the very gods that wrecked vengeance upon Alliander before the eyes of his guards and friends. Vertigo himself paves the path for us in respect to our strength. Kaville, his family, and any who are contained in his mansion are not to be harmed. Other than that, let blood flow in rivers through Lados's streets this night. Let the echoes of this moment be heard through all the generations of Calarr." Turning, Namion exited the underground valley and watched the pestilent plague that was his guild belch forth from the bowels of the city.

[Callahan] Life during wartime is not but the absence of death. I walked, a hollowed shell devoid of a soul, as I listened to the orchestra of death. Weeping cries sung lullabies to the night air as men I would call comrades raped and pillaged any and all unfortunate enough to be present.

"Falcon, hey, come 'ere. Get a piece of this while she's still fresh." Vulture, defiling the corpse of a young woman with no thought to the moral complications it could present, smiled at me with his gnarled and yellowed teeth.

I may have had to console with the fact that I could count meself amidst the ranks of the damned, but even as such, there were acts I wouldn't undertake nor tolerate. "On with ye. We haven't time for ye to be getting yer rocks off on corpses. Yer to be making more corpses, aren't ye?"

"Ruining me fun, are ye? I haven't a clue what Namion sees in ye? Yer soft and weak." Vulture was about to continue his actions until the flat of my rapier lashed solidly across his back.

"Our mission is to enter Tellian's manor and allow ye yer luxuries. That doesn't mean I need to be tolerating yer dishonor the whole way through it." I prepared myself for his response with a readied stance.

Glaring menacingly, Vulture returned his pants to their proper place and pulled his dual-handed axes from the body. Licking the blood from one of his axe blades, he snarled toward me, saying, "Ye ever strike me or even think of striking me again and—"

A quick thrust placed the tip of my blade at Vulture's throat while I simultaneously drew forth my short sword with my off hand, stepping forward and sliding the short sword none too gently sidelong across Vulture's gut. Callahan wore his wry half smile as he spoke. "Weak and soft though I may be, I'm quick enough to open ye a new hole for breathing while decorating this street with yer innards. So mind yer tongue and yer place. Do what ye were told to do, and don't let me catch ye straying from task again."

That being sorted, Vulture reluctantly entered the nearby mansion. Dispatching a few undertrained and unprepared guards, I also entered the final stages of this night's endeavor. I could hear the cries of horror Vulture was inspiring within the mansion as I waited for my mark to appear. The rockery around the well I was perched upon shifted as the secret exit from the mansion revealed itself. Tellian, cousin to Kaville, crawled out, glancing nervously from side to side, never suspecting to look up.

As death's deliverer, I longed for these moments. That breach in the fabric of time where all slows to a crawl while you recognize your own power of divinity over the life before ye. Just as I prepared to finish my mission, I heard further scuffling in the secret passage. Tellian pulled forth his daughter and wife.

I've done much that taints the fabric of my soul, but in that moment, I knew I was losing my edge for serving Namion. The thought of making this child an orphan while having her watch turned my insides.

Tellian, releasing some kind of growl, finally witnessed my presence. Skill and experience backing him, he tested my footing with a few thrusts. Dancing lightly, I inwardly cursed my earlier hesitation. Leaping from the well and easily batting aside his overly aggressive onslaught, I couldn't help but think that maybe Vulture was right. Maybe I was getting soft.

Then he presented an opening, raising his blade for an overhand sweep. I thrust forward with my rapier, and it found its mark. "Please . . . my child." Hitting his knees, the gurgled plea left his lips as his punctured lung collapsed upon itself.

Dodging lithely, I instinctively swung my short sword as his wife attempted to take advantage of my distraction. Parted open from shoulder to hip, her life's blood rushed forward, showering me. Her dagger fell to the grass from her already lifeless hand.

Gurgling blood with his attempted pleas, Tellian stretched his hand toward his little daughter. Who, with tearless eyes, watched in shocked horror as her life disappeared before her eyes. Another thrust of my blade ended his attempts, and a solid hack with short sword parted head from body. "Yer going to live, little one. I was supposed to allow Vulture some time with ye, but ye've more than enough image to spread the message we desire. I'm Falcon of the Talons, and my hands did this act under order of Namion. Grow big, healthy, and strong. Train well. Someday, perhaps ye'll be the one to send me on to the judgment of the gods, but today, I fear, my dear, is not your day." Tossing her mother's dagger to her feet and collecting her father's head, I looked once more as I departed into the night. "Go and do not look back." I uttered those parting words as much to myself as to her.

The following days were such that even the priests in their temple district barred their doors and shuttered their windows. None but the bravest dared the streets. The guards tried to quell the rise, but so quick, so mercilessly vicious, so widespread was the Talon reprisal that all attempts fell to disorder. I managed to make my way to Horuce's residence. There, I found Horuce, his family, and Hemrick huddled inside on high alert.

[Narrator] Callahan scratched a Talon symbol on the front door as Horuce uttered in protest, "Hey, that mark will group us with the lot of you. When this city comes back to order, we'll be hung."

Callahan, emphasizing his first word, responded, "*If* this city comes back to order, it'll never again be as it was. This mark'll save ye when the rest of the guild get yer name. They've more than likely already marked ye for dead. Hemrick as well. I told ye—I don't forget those who don't forget me. This may not be yer desired salvation, but it's the best I can offer ye."

"Salvation? Take another look outside. Look, Falcon!" Horuce pointed to the multiple fires bursting to life around the city. "I think ye'd be best to choose another word."

A solid right cross further mangled Horuce's already broken nose. "Raise yer voice to me again, and I'll feed ye to the fucking wolves. Live and redefine yer lives, or I can walk away now and ye can take yer chances with my fellows."

Sputtering through his pain, Horuce looked ashamed. "Forgive me, Falcon, I'm scared for my family. I've a lot to lose today, and I really don't want to lose it."

"Then leave Falcon to do what he must." Raven dropped from the home's roof and walked to join the group as she closed the marked front door behind her. Turning her attention to Callahan, she continued, "This is out of control. The very survival of this city hangs in the balance. We must do something. I've arranged a meet with Owl at my storehouse. We need to go. You've done all you can for this lot. We'll figure out what we can do for them, if and when this all stops."

Unable to offer any consolation, Callahan just turned and followed Raven on to her storehouse. Lamenting innocents, crazed looters, and bloodthirsty mobs were the visions playing out below them as they traversed the rooftops. "There's inciting chaos, then there's this. The gods really have abandoned this city, haven't they?" Callahan muttered to himself and then maintained a morbid silence for the duration of their trip.

"Is this what it has to be? Is this what we represent? This is tragedy born of aimless ambition, not an act of one looking to lead." Callahan paced the storehouse nervously as he talked to Owl.

Sitting calmly, Owl looked forlorn. "This is not what it always was. Namion's slipped from sanity's grasp. Even with that reality, he is not one to be trifled with. Someone within the guild would need to rise up and challenge him as is our

103

law. Who contains the skill necessary to stand against him? You?"

"If Falcon were to challenge, I would back him." Raven kept vigilant watch through the only window in the small storehouse while listening to the conversation.

"That sentiment pulls at one's heartstrings—it really does—but it does not change the fact that loving supporters cheering from the side are not what you need when standing against Namion. You speak of mutiny as though its accomplishment is as easy as its utterance. I would gladly follow another who could usurp Namion. The reality is I do not foresee such an act. Even with magic and wit, you are no challenge to the likes of Namion, dear Falcon." Owl shook his head and continued, "No, the cold reality is we will see this through to its conclusion. A conclusion that only Namion is privy to."

"What laws does Namion honor? What rules does he uphold? None. If he can't be bested in fair challenge, then it falls upon us to remove him in our own fashion. Are we not assassins? Have we not carved out our very existences upon the unfair deaths of many?" Raven turned to face the two men.

"Owl is right, Raven. We need to weather this storm awhile longer. Actions such as the one we conspire toward cannot be rushed, even in necessity. We must allow this to play its course and bide our time, waiting for an appropriate time. Logic and intellect must win out over emotion this day. No. Ever the plotting type, Owl, as I, knows that hasty plans and dumb luck will not suffice in regard to Namion." Slumping against a wall, Callahan released an exaggerated sigh. "Can we count ye with us when the time does call, Owl?"

"Of course." Owl nodded to the two, and then as if heading out for an evening stroll, he casually walked out the front door.

"We're to sit idle. We're to do nothing as all that we've ever known goes to shit. Terrific, it's moments like these when I really treasure my heritage. Mother was a strong and influential royal heir to the island of Dennai. Namion found information he needed to ruin their family via sharing her bed. He kept her locked in the hull of his ship through her pregnancy. He kept her locked there through my youth. He released her, broken spirit and all, on to some rocky outcrops off the coast. At the age of eight, I watched my mother's body break against the rocks. I watched the waves bounce in seemingly endless succession against her corpse. He later told me that the only reason I didn't join her that night was because of that tearless viewing. He let me live because, apparently, my heartlessness gave evidence that his blood ran my veins." Raven's eyes visibly clouded as she looked upon Callahan. "How much longer must I stand idle and watch my soul die?"

Real sorrow behind his blue eyes, Callahan looked longingly into the hazel tone of Raven's. He recognized the similarities to his most recent job and felt even deeper pity for the girl he had released. "I choose my words carefully as I must. There are factors that I cannot disclose, even to you. It's not that I will not act against Namion. It's that I cannot." Wrapping Raven into a tight embrace, he did all he could to impart his sincerity. In that embrace, he imagined sweeping aside all her pain; he imagined battling away her demons. In that embrace, he wished he could be more than he was.

The two remained in that hold, which allowed them to block out the rest of Calarr, until the sun broke on another day. In silence, they both found a union in their mental escape. Sleep was fitful and unrewarding. The next morning dawned on Owl's return.

"The Avians are being called for orders. Sounds like there is a planned conclusion to this after all. Come, let us be on with it." Owl led the sullen march through the wreckage that had been a bustling and beautiful city.

Namion's plan disclosed, the Avians set to purpose; everything returned to its usual rapid pattern of organized chaos.

[Callahan] Images of those nights are still among my fiercest nightmares. Not much scares me, not much bothers me, but those nights tore irreparable holes in the fabric of my being. The guards had eventually gotten their shit together enough to secure the temple district and the noble district. They offered solace there to any seeking it that could, in one way or another, prove they held no connection to the guild. Kaville had sent out word that he would speak to the remaining people of Lados, sent out word that any who would seek an end to the uprising should stand present at his rally. I would've looked forward to hearing what rubbish he would spew, except being privy to Namion's plans, I had very different anticipations.

[Narrator] The grand amphitheater and its surrounding fields in the temple district proved to be the perfect locale for Kaville's speech. Usually set aside for some of the more elaborate religious ceremonies, the amphitheater proved to be the only area adequate to hold the vast number of people gathering to hear what was to be said. Guards abounded on high alert throughout the area. Kaville stood center stage, pacing off his inability to contain his rage. The large oval half roof provided cover from the sun so that those upon the stage were allowed a clear view of the packed stadium seats as well as the massive overflow in the surrounding fields. Straining to see and hear the stage, the mass of onlookers was a staggering yet encouraging sight in light of prior events.

Satisfied with the presence, Kaville stepped forward and, with practiced art, projected forth his voice. "My people. My friends, my colleagues—" The speech's introduction was cut short as a body dropped, hanging not but a few feet from where Kaville stood. Horror lit Kaville's face as he came to recognize the bouncing and swinging body to be that of his wife's.

Shooting off a couple of darts, Sparrow entered from stage left. Preceded by an arrow, Eagle entered stage right. Owl to his left and Raven to his right, Namion walked from the back to the front of the stage and down the center to stand right behind Kaville. Sliding from the rafters down the rope hanging Kaville's wife, Callahan casually sat at the edge of the stage's front, dangling his legs over like a bored child.

In a harsh whisper, Namion leaned toward Kaville. "Do not fret, my friend. Vulture will provide your childcare for our peace announcement." Tears openly ran down Kaville's face as wave after wave of emotions crashed within him. Stepping aside, he made room for Namion while waving away what remained of his personal guard.

Namion smiled as he projected himself to the gathered crowd. "This transition was difficult. For that, you have Kaville's apologies. He has come to see the err of his way. Bounty on my men is abolished that we may live in peace, profit, and progression. In return for such kindness, I have offered forth my services toward the end of Lados's future protection. My men are to be treated with but not limited to the same amount of respect shown the guard. My men will aid in maintaining city order. You may look to me as Kaville's new stand-in. I will act as advisor and guide that we can rebuild Lados and put you all back to the courses that were your pathetic existences. Look upon the city, look upon this stage. Do you really wish to continue your efforts against me? Do you really wish to see more?"

Stunned silence, abject horror, and shaking heads were the crowd's response. Leaning back, Callahan flashed his wry half smile upon Kaville and said, "This is the part where ye confirm what was just said. 'Less, of course, ye'd care to think 'bout what yer children would experience prior to death. Trust me, Vulture has ways that make even the hardest of us want to cry."

Stepping forward, Kaville again addressed the people. "This day forward marks a new allegiance." Pausing to clear the shakiness in his voice, Kaville looked solidly beaten. "Do not lament, but celebrate such a hasty close to bloodshed. That our miscommunications cost us so dearly, we must redouble our efforts toward a new and brighter future. A future that marks solid union between the republic and the Talons' guild. With such strength, we needn't fear."

"Good, now give them a wave and exit stage left. Yer children will be evidence enough of the wisdom held in your decisions today." Smiling broadly, Namion exited the same way he entered.

[Callahan] It's been a good long while since Reader 1 has tested my patience. He finally upped and buggered off?

[Narrator] He had a few things that needed to be taken care of.

[Callahan] Oh, the incessant howling from his mother calling for him to do his chores finally pulled him away, eh?

[Narrator] That's all right. I've seen fit to bring in a new voice.

[Reader 2] Hello.

[Callahan] My goodness, this one's female. How are ye, lovely?

[Reader 2] Isn't that a bit bold now that you're with Raven?

[Callahan] My dear, monogamy is the crutch of the insecure. No one holds ownership over me.

[Reader 2] I think Namion would argue that last point.

[Callahan] A sharp-tongued lass, eh? Let me guess. Ye bedded down with the narrator to do yer kind deed for the year, and he wrangled ye into making comment in his book?

[Reader 2] A lady wouldn't speak of such things.

[Callahan] A lady wouldn't hang out with my narrator.

[Narrator] A little harsh there, isn't that?

[Callahan] Fair price, I'd say, for constantly interrupting my wonderful life story. Besides, I wasn't looking to insult. I was just asking for scientific purposes.

[Reader 2] Scientific purposes?

[Callahan] Aye, I'm looking to do a study as to whether or not intelligence can be sexually transmitted. Ye seem far more intelligent than our verbal punching bag, Reader 1. So I sought to discover if ye were getting better lines due to sleeping with the narrator or if it were due to intellect born of sexual congress with the narrator. If it were such, then it would go to further evidence why the narrator and I should endeavor to share the gift that is our sexual prowess with as many women as is possible.

[Reader 2] You're incorrigible.

[Callahan] And that, my dear, would account for why yer panties moisten at the thought of me.

[Narrator] OK, so killing that argument before it can begin, where do we go from here, my love-struck rogue?

[Callahan] The years following those dreadful days of Talon uprising were deemed by the populace to be the "aftermath," so . . .

Chapter 4

AFTERMATH AND WANDERINGS

[CALLAHAN] NAMION MOVED OUR base of operations into what had previously been Kaville's mansion. He no longer needed such vast, wide open spaces, did he? I mean, in lieu of his newly condensed family dynamic, Namion figured he could suffice with Tellian's old dwelling. Namion's citywide terror sweep had accomplished its purpose. People met all Talon presence and activities with a subdued and respectful fear. With the majority of the city present to see the taming of Kaville, little doubt existed as to who truly ran Lados now.

Things calmed for a bit in the reconstruction following those days of battle. It was nice to settle my mind and nerves after the near-constant action that had been my recent life. With all the chaos that had occurred, no one had taken notice of Horuce and Hemrick's protection. Horuce's nose, though permanently crooked, did heal in time.

The nobles, having been decimated, were hard-pressed to reorganize and found more and more of their powers and responsibilities falling into Namion's hands. Purpose accomplished or not, I couldn't help but lament the vast and seemingly unnecessary cost of it all. Entire city blocks burned to the ground, thousands left dead, and a destruction of morale throughout the populace. Yes, our purpose was met. I refused to let it go quietly and unanswered. Raven and I started putting out our feelers for any and all who would be sympathetic to the cause of usurping Namion's rule. That being said, we were both well aware that most would love nothing more than to be able to turn traitors over to Namion. The process of Namion's downfall would have to be a war of attrition.

Vulture seemed to take more interest in my activities after our last outing. I believe he and Sparrow suspected Raven and I to be treasonous. Eagle distanced himself even more than was his usual. He refrained from contact with any of the other Avians. Owl would plot with Raven and me on occasion but was always quick to find fault in any plans against Namion.

The next few months were tense about the city as reconstruction took place. As humans tend to do, quick was the fading of memory. People adapted to the new leadership imposed by the Talons in the same quiet and subdued fashion that had allowed the nobles to previously steal their freedoms. Slowly, trade routes that had closed in response to the Talon rise reopened, and the city came to the leveled plain that would be their new normal.

The crown, having caught wind of the activities in Lados, was not sitting idle. Recognizing the puppet system now in place, the king declared that peace had never been established with the Talons. The king, seeing Namion as the leadership in Lados, absolved the peace between Lados and Stockard. Mobilizing the northern armies, the king had begun the process of war preparations. Envoys sent from Kaville requesting time to get the city back under proper order worked to cease the offensive, but it was quickly evident that those attempts were at best going to delay the conquest.

Given my inability to directly oppose Namion, I utilized Horuce and Hemrick's aid in helping to finance, supply, and organize some of the more militant citizens. The ones who wanted to lend more than just whispered words toward the achievement of their freedoms. I remained the silent benefactor. When Namion caught wind of these men standing against him in rebellion, he would probably send me to kill them. So many difficulties arose in my existence due to that cumbersome pact made to garner survival.

Spending every possible moment I could with Raven, I came to notice a direct correlation present in my reality. The correlation I made was that the more time I spent with her, the more I seemed to care about my fellow humans. The plight of Lados and its populace of mindless bleating sheep never occurred to me to be anything more than a bad punch line—that is, until Raven. In her presence, I felt as though my life could serve a purpose and that all around me could ascend their own ignorance and powerlessness.

As I've said previously, I'm well aware that love bit me hard. A mind usually consumed with plotting escapes, backups, manipulations, and deaths was instead consumed with ideology. In retrospect, I was becoming that asshole that constantly spews forth an eternal ray of sunshine from his rectum. Spitting butterflies and pissing rainbows, there I was, off to save the fucking world.

[Narrator] Despite the base of operations being moved to the governor's mansion, Namion still chose to reside in his humble middle-class dwelling. It was here that Callahan had been summoned. Sitting in the same seat Namion had previously assaulted him in, Callahan questioned his employer. "Am I to guess what ye have for me to do? I've been sitting here looking at ye looking at me for damn near an hour now."

"Can you not shut up? This last hour has been the most peaceful one I have ever spent with you. Your extracurricular activities in regard to your attempt at insurrection amuse me and have future purpose. That is why I have not brought about your death." Namion, seated calmly near the warm glow of an evening fire, looked almost approving in his demeanor toward Callahan.

Smiling with his wry half smile, Callahan kept his gaze steady upon Namion, preparing himself for another attack. "Denial at this stage in the game would be pointless and ignorant, wouldn't it? So congratulations on yer approval."

Letting forth a frustrated sigh, Namion lightly shook his head. "Ever the wiseass, you are. The envoys sent out by Kaville to the crown have bought us more time than I originally thought they would. The king agreed to prolong peace for two years' time. I cannot abide by you having two years to stir rebellion, but I do have future use for you. What would you propose I do with this problematic equation?"

His smile spreading to its full breadth, Callahan responded, "I'd suggest ye write it in triplicate on real thick paper. Take that paper, fold it twice. Crumple that paper, and then cram it right up your self-important arse."

"Like father, like son. Even in the face of death, you find the presence of mind to crack a joke. Your mother did have a penchant for us sailor types, did she not?" Callahan's jaw dropped at Namion's declaration.

[Reader 1] Hmm, cliché with the added touch of incest, that's a new one.

[Callahan] To say that I haven't been missing the pleasure of belittling ye would be a lie. Welcome back, and don't be jealous because I'm actually able to accomplish your dearest wet dream, even if I did accomplish it by accident.

[Reader 1] She's only a half sister so that doesn't quite account for my dream, does it?

[Callahan] That, my friend, is delightfully disgusting.

[Reader 1] You both share a love for killing and a complete indifference to mankind, so I figured that secret out by the end of chapter 1.

[Callahan] He's black, and I'm white.

[Reader 1] Ah fuck.

[Callahan] Yep, for a split second there, I even considered allowing ye to think yerself intelligent, but no, that blatantly obvious disillusionment needed to be disclosed.

[Narrator] Collecting his jaw after a quick second of thought, Callahan burst into laughter. Following his laughing spree, he found enough voice to say, "Ye had me going for a second there. Not like yer dark skin tone vice my albino skin tone wouldn't be enough evidence, but both you and I know yer just jerking me round. Way to speak in muddled suppositions so as to avoid my earrings' detection, though. Touché, ye've my respect for that joke."

"I know of your tryst with Raven, and I care not. I did delight in that moment of confusion and disgust you just portrayed. Regardless of all factors, I want you alive to serve my purpose. I cannot allow that here in Lados. So you will pursue my knowledge of your old book." The room gained a quieter ambiance as Namion spoke. "I have heard tell of it being secreted away to the mage tower of Calleigh. You will travel there and retrieve it if you can. You will then travel to the northern barbarian tribes and gain allegiance in case war does erupt with the crown."

"Should I pull the stars down while I'm at it?" Callahan was becoming more and more frustrated.

"You shall do all that I order, and you shall excel at it. When finished with the barbarians, head west, and locate the orc tribes. Secure their aid as well. While you are accomplishing these tasks, take some time to acquaint yourself with our world. Return here in one and a half years, and before you even think to ask, no, you will not take company with you. You will do this alone. I am not unrewarding, though, and you did a splendid job with recent events. So you may have this night to spend however you choose before I expect to hear of your departure in the morning." Namion smiled wickedly at the disgust he saw present in Callahan's eyes. "Good luck, my dear, dear Falcon."

A short time later, Callahan held Raven in his arms. Looking about the storehouse that had become like a home for Raven and himself, Callahan felt a depth of anger at his circumstances.

"I'll go with you, fuck him. We don't need to return. We can go out and craft a new life for ourselves, one free from the disgrace of this place." Raven looked at Callahan with anger and sorrow mixed into one within her eyes.

"He would kill ye for yer disobedience. I must do as he commanded. Eighteen months is not so long a time, and we both know I'll find me way into accomplishing the allegiances he seeks. When I pull off yet another miracle, he won't be able to turn down my request to marry ye, will he?" Callahan looked to Raven prepared for laughter and insult but longing for approval.

Stepping back from Callahan, Raven looked stunned. "Marriage? Not only marriage, but you intend to make that a request of Namion?"

"Damn right. If ye'd but have me, my life would be one of purpose. I could feel accomplished. I'd be willing to sacrifice all my freedoms and imagined futures for yer presence in my life." Callahan looked nervously to the floor.

"You make it back alive, and I will go against all sense and reason with you. Return, and I will marry you." Raven wrapped Callahan back in her arms as they collapsed upon the bare floor. One last lengthy session of lovemaking before Callahan went out gathering necessary supplies in a knapsack. Just before the sun rose on the next morn, Callahan found himself looking longingly over his shoulder at the west gate of Lados.

Before Callahan can even pop out a smart-ass interjection, I will have you all know that I purposely left the gathered supplies vague and undeclared. My intention is to use such a nondescript fashion to explain off his future use of items he would have no way of gaining out in the wilderness. Cheesy and unimaginative as that is, you can all blow a rhino dick if you don't like it.

[Callahan] BAH! HA HA HA!

[Narrator] Having stopped by Horuce's house on his way out, Callahan let Horuce know of his departure and of the compromised nature of the rebellion. Reluctantly leaving it in Horuce's hands, Callahan had to shrug off the worry of their success or failure. Focusing upon his own course, Callahan once again cursed his luck.

Walking the road through the outlying farmlands, Callahan paused a minute to take in the sights. Being the first time he had ever traveled outside the city walls, he couldn't help but feel some trepidation toward the unknown that was the outside world.

[Callahan] Goblins, orcs, and ogres, oh my. Follow, follow, follow. Follow the shit dirt road, eh? No place like home.

[Narrator] Come on, you are making a mockery of a piece of art that is of treasured value to many people's youth.

[Callahan] Countlessmasturbation, pedophilia, necrophilia, blasphemous, unpatriotic, incest, calloused, and cold jokes later, you choose this particular joke to interject upon.

[Narrator] I don't recall any pedophile or necrophilia jokes.

[Callahan] Well, then I missed out because nothing is more bothersome than the chafing hair brought on by puberty, and there is no better way to keep them still than to wait till they've already passed on.

[Callahan, interjecting his own interjection] So everyone knows, that last line caused me to puke in my own mouth a little.

[Narrator] Can we please pretend that never happened?

[Reader 3] This is the part where you pick up an upbeat halfling sidekick for the purpose of comic relief, isn't it?

[Callahan] What about our story catches ye as upbeat? Should I now also bust into delightful song calling upon the arrival of the local wildlife? Perhaps I should skip merrily about my way as I progress on my wondrous journey to see the wizards, eh?

[Reader 3] Don't all medieval fantasies have cheery halflings?

[Callahan] Well, we do have dwarves, but *surly* is a more apt descriptive for them than *cheery*. Aside from that, they worship Drakin, the god of labor, and they don't tend to bathe much. So they smell of something fiercely awful. You know, like those short people your world has—the ones that pick apples or do gardening and lawn care. Wonderfully hard workers humble enough to work for cheap and do those terrible shit jobs no one else wants to do.

[Reader 3] You mean those illegal Mexicans who steal our jobs, don't you?

[Callahan] Steal yer jobs? When was the last time ye were chomping at the bit to pick apples? Steal yer jobs? Bah, if yer such a person that an individual who is illegally present and can't speak the language can take yer job, then isn't it high time ye reevaluated yer course in life? Don't be pissed because they're humble enough to take crap pay to do crap work ye'd never want to do.

[Reader 3] I bet you'd support equal rights for blacks too, wouldn't ye?

[Callahan] Ye do recognize the narrator is Irish, right? What are the Irish but the European breed of nigger? The only reason they weren't picking cotton next to the blacks is because they burned up in the sun, so instead, they were put to building railroads with the Chinese.

[Reader 3] You sure know a lot about our history for being from a world of make-believe.

[Callahan] I know what the narrator knows, remember. Difference is since I'm fictional, I'm allowed to cross boundaries of race and other touchy subjects. I'm not racist. I don't think I'm better than any one person or race; I know I'm superior to the whole lot of them. Namion is of a darker persuasion, and I've all the hatred and respect for him that one should hold for an archnemesis.

[Reader 3] Oh, make the black guy out to be the villain, brilliant under-the-surface way to establish their natural tendencies toward crime.

[Callahan] His daughter would also be black, and she is my lead love interest, so plug it up yer arse, ye dolt. Who the fuck are ye anyway? When did we get a Reader 3?

[Reader 3] I'm your average white Christian, who is patriotic and Republican.

[Callahan] Come off it! So everyone is aware, the narrator is trying to push his political and ideological views through me using the mocked voice of Reader 3 to goad me into ranting, and he's screwing my story trying to do so. If it isn't bad enough that Lados's whole political history is based off the American government, we have to blather on 'bout it in our interjections as well?

[Narrator] I can neither confirm nor deny the possibility that there is a chance that that may or may not be somewhat kind of accurate. Leaving it in that fashion would not properly express the full scope of my views, though. Considering I've no more respect for bleeding heart liberal vegetarian pussies that'd have everyone be mindless lazy zombies leeching off the state.

[Callahan] We've got necromancers that can raise zombies, absolutely dreadful-smelling creatures those are.

[Narrator] We as humans are crafted by design or evolution, depending on your views, to consume.

[Callahan] All religious people are not stupid, but all stupid people should be religious. Stupid people left to their own designs without strict guidelines and rules tend to do stupid things, thus your liberals.

[Narrator] Right, now enough of that.

[Callahan] Moving on in our story, I was excited and worried about the prospect of the outside world. I'd grown up under rough circumstances and thus became rough, but most in the city were soft and untrained. In the outlands, skill and strength were necessary for survival. A high level of prowess was not as uncommon a thing in the world at large as it'd been within the city's walls, granted not as high a level of prowess as to provide challenge to a level 64 ninja mage.

As I came to the northern hillcrest beyond the farmlands outside of Lados, it was already late afternoon, and the sun was starting its descent, lighting the fields in a golden glow. I looked longingly off toward the vast city I had and would always call home. Whispering one more goodbye to Raven upon the night air, I turned to the tree line on the other side of the hillcrest and plunged into that forest ready to face anything to get back to her arms.

118

[Narrator] As darkness overtook the forest, Callahan pulled forth flint and steel to start a nighttime fire.

[Callahan] The fuck I did.

[Narrator] What's that supposed to mean? How else are you supposed to keep warm? See? Cook food?

[Callahan] OK . . . wait for it . . . that should be sufficient pause for the reader to wonder what the fuck happened to yer brain. Since when did Reader 1 become the fucking narrator? Now to yer questions, answered in the order asked. It means I didn't start a fire. I've gloves that maintain body temperature. I've a ring that allows me night vision. Finally, I'd have fucking packed rations, wouldn't I? Who the fuck wants to go on an adventure to have to pluck bird feathers or skin and gut defenseless animals? Not that I give a shit about defenseless animals, but that's a lot of bloody work for very little reward, if ye ask me?

[Narrator] Then you lit it for ambiance.

[Callahan] Ooh, if I were sitting next to ye instead of in yer mind, I'd pop ye right in the back of the head. I mean, who doesn't like an orc hunting party, stray ogre, or other random nefarious beastly creature to come raining devastation upon them? Nothing screams ambiance to me better than an unnecessary struggle to survive.

[Narrator] Now that that is clarified, I'll be taking over my story again, thank you.

Smoking some of the ambion, the herb that Namion had introduced him to for the purpose of resting one's body, Callahan was able to traverse the night through.

[Callahan] Ye just made that name up due to our use of the word *ambiance*, didn't ye?

[Narrator] So?

[Callahan] That is wretchedly horrible and absolutely pathetically hilarious. Comes to mind that we tend to prattle on like we have been anytime yer having difficulty piecing the story line together; I told ye it'd be a good idea to dual narrate it 'cause here, where yer drowning, I can jump in to save the day.

A few days into the woods, I found a cave. Before ye think it, I'm not in the habit of wandering into random caves; that's a horridly stupid idea. No, this cave had a door of human design at its entrance. Earlier, I said I had packed rations. Well, I also packed some coin. Coin that had vastly multiplied after my packing of it; that, I'd suspect, I could thank Raven for. Rations tend to wear on a person after even just a few days of consumption. Might I add that these rations are crafted of foods that the narrator has yet to imagine, so the gods only know what bland and ridiculously stupid things I was being forced to consume. In light of these facts, I figured that coin plus humans could easily equal food, so I knocked on the door.

[Narrator] As the door opened, Callahan found himself greeted by the most delightfully upbeat little man he had ever seen.

[Callahan] Fuck you. Just fuck you.

[Narrator] All jokes aside. Knocking on the door, Callahan kept his senses perked. Something wasn't right. *Click.*

Callahan turned to see a man aiming a crossbow from around a nearby tree. Holding steady aim, the man addressed his would-be intruder. "What do you want? I could sense the magic on you from miles away. Your appearance screams death and danger. Any quick movements and I'll plug this bolt right into your heart."

His wry half smile lighting his features, Callahan kept his hands in plain view. "Rations are crap. I've got coin. Ye look to be the type who could use some renovations. Renovations cost coin. Ye look to be the hunting type. So logically, I want cooked meat, and ye should fix yer fucking house. We can help each other."

"Risky talk for a man staring down death." The outlander still remained steadfast.

"What's risky is pointing that thing at the Falcon." Drawing two throwing daggers, Callahan watched the crossbow bolt fly harmlessly over his left shoulder. The first dagger stuck into the crossbow's slide mechanism, causing the whole bow to be knocked out the man's hands to the ground. The second dagger stuck in the tree next to the man's head. "I didn't miss. How did ye sense me magic? How much do ye want for a week's worth of meat? Are ye satisfied that I don't want to kill ye?"

Nodding in respect, the man picked up his crossbow, removed both daggers from their locations, and walked toward Callahan, offering forward said daggers. "I'm Ferris. Sorry about the warm reception. Not as though I get that many visitors."

Callahan replaced his daggers then nodded back to the man. "No worries. As said, I'm the Falcon."

"Falcon is a bird, not a name." Ferris's appearance gave no hint to whether his statement was said in an earnest or jesting manner.

"Guess inner workings of Lados aren't as widely spoken of as I'd thought. I'm Falcon, member of the Avian assassins, which are a subset of the Talon's guild in Lados." Callahan lent view to his tat.

"I've heard of Namion and the Talons. Avian assassins, eh? Couldn't come up with something more terrifying than bird names?" Ferris still maintained an aloof persona.

Laughing, Callahan grinned. "Guess not."

Opening the door to his cave, Ferris bade Callahan to enter. "If my much-needed renovations and lacking décor are too much for you, we could always just stay outside." As Callahan followed him into the oddly cozy interior, Ferris continued, "Not very characteristic of an assassin to tell me he's an assassin, is it? 'Less, of course, you intend on offing me. In which case, I've bared witness to your ability to do so, and I'd just ask the chance to have one more smoke before you do." Retrieving his pipe from a fireplace, Ferris took a seat in a cushioned chair atop a rug next to the fire.

"Nice setup for a cave dweller. I'm not here to kill ye, and in Lados, we're no longer a secret, so I've just gotten used to proclaiming it out loud." Callahan took a cushioned seat opposite Ferris across the fire.

[Callahan] I bet when ye heard that I was going to see a man who lived in a cave, you prepped yourself for a horrible Islamic extremist joke. But no, when did ye ever see those cave-dwelling towel heads sitting in cushioned chairs atop a rug in front of a cozy fire?

[Narrator] Callahan felt strangely at ease speaking with Ferris. "Back to me pertinent questions at hand, though. How—"

"I remember your questions, and I'm satisfied ye don't want to kill me. I don't care for coin, being that I don't often find occasion to seek other people, and I'm not about to tell a self-confessed murderer how I could tell he was coming without first getting something worthwhile. You don't look the type to be willing to part with magic items or weaponry, so I've a task to ask of you. In return for its completion, I'll give ye a week of fresh meat, as much dried meat as you can carry, and I'll disclose how I could tell you were coming." Ferris puffed calmly on his pipe as he spoke.

"Ye've piqued me interest." Callahan gave his wry half grin.

"There is an elf of infamous renown in these parts. Not that any elves are friendly, but this one has taken a real liking to hunting any humans who have the misfortune of straying into this area." Still puffing his pipe, Ferris looked toward the fire as though he were seeking something very personal within its dancing flames. "He took someone special to me, but being a man of intellect and reason, I'm aware that I'm no match for him."

[Callahan] For the reader's edification, elves in our world are six to eight foot tall on average. Not tiny winged tree lovers. They have a severe disdain for any who would seek to, as they say, taint nature. Laintell, god of nature and elves, calls upon his people to purge any who would do such. Most elves calmed their natural instincts toward such an end, at least enough to be peaceable with humans, but some zealots took to slaughtering the unnatural with a lustful pleasure, much like your hippies and animal rights activists.

I've seen a few elves in my life, but they were so humanized they may as well not have been elves. That or there were three different occasions in my youth when I'd watched as scouts captured scouting too close to the city's borders were brought to public execution. Upon the creation of the great walls, a few tribes of races were not fully segregated in explanation of why dwarves and elves could be found within the human realm. The ones who remained in the human realm had found peaceable solace in avoiding the more "civilized" human lands. Some found sanctuary with the founding men of Lados, and for a good long time, they grew and prospered as well as integrated members of the city. As the time passed and popular opinion gave way to noble rule, the nonhuman races were segregated and subjugated until they moved on or fell into positions of indentured servitude.

In studying the history and traditions of Calarr as a youth, I quite often found myself strongly sympathizing with the so-called lesser races' hatred for humanity. All of these facts taken into perspective, I had no more reservation in killing them than I had when set to kill humans.

[Narrator] As nonchalant as though he were ordering a meal, Callahan popped off, "How would ye like me to evidence the act? A finger, his whole bloody head, maybe just an ear?"

Waving his hand lightly, Ferris chuckled and replied, "No, I full well intend on tagging along to witness the deed. I understand this is most likely not the usual course with you, and that is why I didn't ask. If you want what I offered, then you'll accept my terms, liked or disliked."

"I'm not a babysitter, and on the grounds that ye seem to be a man of education, I would hope you'd already understood that. That being established, yer allowed to put yer ass at risk whenever ye want. That and I don't know me way around these woods for fuck all." Callahan lightly nodded his agreement to the terms as he spoke.

[Callahan] We sat for a while longer in that comfortable cave before we moved on. It was a half-day trek through the woods before we would reach the area in which the elf was prone to camp. That left plenty of time to get to know Ferris.

Ferris was an unusual sort, at least as far as I was concerned. His burly lumberjack stature, full brown beard, and shaggy hair portrayed him as the outdoorsy type. For such a gruff-looking man, I found his tendency to stop to chat with each small animal he saw as odd. When there were no animals present, he would, on occasion, exchange single-sided banter with flowers, oddly colored mosses, or other vegetation. He spent little time in regard to meself. He seemed to find far more pleasure in his own company.

After a considerable amount of prodding in the form of me incessantly telling him stories of my childhood, Ferris relinquished a bit of his story. "I was once a farmer in the southlands. Well regarded throughout the kingdom. Individuals came from far and wide to partake in the harvest from my blessed fields. The gods granted me much prosperity in those days."

"Good thing the gods had enough time to tend yer fields. Too bad, in doing so, they neglected the thousands of others who're starving." I did little to hide my disdain.

"Doubt all you want. The gods work in mysterious ways and never give us more than we can handle, only more than we want to handle." Ferris seemed undisturbed by my blasphemy.

"I'm starting to seriously reconsider my earlier abstaining in regard to yer sudden demise." Shaking my head, I continued, "Don't mind me. It's yer story. Tell it however ye care to imagine it being."

"I imagine nothing, but there is no sense in arguing the color of the sky with the blind now, is there? Your persistent prodding is why I even started to speak to you. If you didn't want to hear what I had to say, you should have just left well enough alone." Ferris still seemed unaffected emotionally.

"This is turning into a long trek, and I could use for a fairy tale to pass the time. Please continue. I'll withhold further insult until you've finished." I was enjoying the company, even if it were that of a delusional psychotic.

"Laintell came to me in a vision. He showed me the error of human ways. Showed me the pain felt by our intrusions into nature. I abandoned my lands, moved to the wilderness, and here have I remained in peace with nature. In my visions, I see that peace, though preferred, is not always possible. As disgusting as man's acts against nature are, it gives no one the right to hunt innocent families and passersby. I went to speak to the elf of such matters as were spoken to me by our patron god, Laintell. He killed my canine companion and told me that no matter how elflike I pretended to be, I would always be a tainted one." Ferris stopped to wish good luck and fair journeys to a passing squirrel.

"Holy shit. Whoa. I'll kill the elf. Ye give me what's promised, and we'll part friends. I apologize for asking ye to speak and will refrain from making that mistake again. Promise to never unleash that level of crazy on me again, and I'll promise to keep my spoken words specific to our mission." At that point, I recognized further discourse would only work to split my brain. This man wandering beside me not only spoke to animals and plants but also conversed directly with gods. In our world, that isn't entirely out of sorts but is still more than enough to make me cringe. On top of communions with the divine ones, he was enlisting the services of an assassin to kill in the name of vengeance for a dog. I understand some people have a creepy and all-too-connected relationship with their pets, but come on, an assassin? In yer world, that would be much akin to squashing a fly with an atom bomb—effective yet ridiculously counterbalanced in regard to necessity.

[Narrator] Approaching the area, Ferris had indicated Callahan could see a visible change come over Ferris. He no longer stopped to speak with wildlife or vegetation, his smile faded to a grimace, and what had been a light cheerful stride turned into a purposeful march. Ferris almost growled as he spoke, saying, "Just as I knew of your approach, I can sense the heathen. Through this next copse, we will find his camp."

That peaceful, easy feeling he'd experienced earlier was replaced by a cautious unease as Callahan observed Ferris's changes. "Anything I should know 'bout his armaments, skill sets, or companions before I go ignorantly bounding into the midst of a contingent of soldiers?"

"He is alone. The gods will not allow such a trespasser companionship. Kill him swiftly that the lands can be purged of his sacrilegious ways." Ferris's eyes gleamed with the light that can only be delivered by a man in the grips of fanaticism.

[Callahan] I always thought religious folk were off their rockers, but this gent took the cake. Unfamiliar with climbing trees, I found myself thankful for my ring as it silenced what otherwise would have been multiple devastating blunders. Skirting to the edge of a branch, I surveyed the site before me. A humble little camp with a small fire and a tentlike structure built of refuse branches. Sitting next to the fire was my target, whose slender build and hideously oversized pointed ears betrayed his race as that of an elf. Thinking to draw my throwing knives and end this whole thing from a distance, I was brought to a pause.

Dusk was approaching, and the moon had been nearing its full cycle the night before. This was brought to my line of thought by the multiple wards painted upon rocks placed in a circle around the elf's campsite. Wards that, had I not been so well read, could have easily been overlooked. Wards designed to keep lycanthropes at bay. Lycanthropes, for those unfamiliar with this genre of story, are men who transform into beasts in the moonlight—some in any moonlight, but others like the more traditionally known werewolves required the moon to shine in its full glory.

Unlike other stories currently popular in your world, in our world, vampires and werewolves don't tend to find themselves in odd love triangles by sleeping with underage girls. They're harbingers of death with bestial and insatiable hungers, and for fuck's sake, vampires don't bloody well glitter in the sun; no, they burst much like Alliander in a lightning storm. By the way, can ye imagine what it must be like to be a guy trying to bed a gal who has odd bestial tendencies that cause her to sleep with random mythological beings? First, a vampire, then a werewolf. Fuck, it'd take a horse to please that gal.

[Narrator] Springing awkwardly from the branch into the circle provided by the wards, Callahan rolled to his feet, nodded at the shocked elf, then shouted, "Bah, ye blimey shit! Almost had me, ye did. Get me to kill this elf who was on to yer truth, then ye would've eaten me. The whole time, I couldn't detect lie because the wolf in ye would've committed the crime, not the human."

Callahan noticed the elf chanting as he pulled his blades and clumsily chopped at the thorn-covered vines bursting from the ground, entangling him from the waist down. "Come on, mate, I'm not here to kill you . . . anymore. Tanith branch, yer poisoning me? Fuck all, and fuck you. Why does everyone on this gods-be-damned planet want to kill me?" Cursing his luck, Callahan took a deep breath, dropped his swords, drew two throwing daggers, and then sent them to purpose. The first blade shot through the elf's right thigh, breaking his concentration. The second pierced the underside of the elf's left forearm.

With a shocked expression, the pain-wrecked elf sputtered, "How—"

The third and fourth daggers pierced the elf's chest, ending the conversation. "Sorry, mate, I'm not one for lengthy explanations that lend time for opponents to craft my death." Kicking himself free of the tangled mass of poisonous vegetation, he found himself thankful for the many Sparrow-induced sessions of Tanith oil doses. Sending a tormenting firelike sensation through one's arteries in small doses, it would cause the heart to flutter and equate to lengthy hours of exhaustion and pain. Heavy doses would stop a man's heart dead cold. His body, acclimated to the toxin, yielded little more than a slight nausea.

Scouring the campsite for anything silver, Callahan found himself coming up empty-handed. "Right, fuck the gods! This is bullshit! Course the bloody elf wouldn't have gathered anything to actually kill the beast. Nope, probably intended to tame it and keep itfor a pet."

Ferris stood outside the ward circle and said, "You've accomplished my request. Stay the night within that circle, and I'll deliver your fresh meat. The dried meat, you will have to return to my home to retrieve."

Callahan flashed his half grin and responded, "If I exit this circle, it'll be to claim yer head, mate."

Ferris smiled. "No need to turn this unfriendly. To this point, I have not misled or betrayed you, have I? That elf killed my wolf guide." The last sentence turned his smile into a look of longing. "She was the only love I ever knew. Just because I hold within my veins a different breed of blood does not mean that you need to seek my extermination."

"Ye would've gone at me like a fat kid in a sweetshop, so don't give me this 'why can't we all just get along' rubbish." Callahan continued to scour the camp for anything of use. He came upon an emblem fashioned in the form of a brooch, a cast-iron pan, and a small notebook inscribed in elven. The few words he recognized in the book indicated that it was a description of some nature magic incantations. The brooch was fashioned in the image of Calleigh's crest, so he tossed it in his knapsack. While tossing the brooch in his pack, he paused for a second then grinned wide.

"You're making this personal when it needn't be. I thought that someone of your persuasion would understand my position and stick to purpose. I was going to disclose my secret in honor of our agreement being that it was not your magic that attracted my attention, it was your flesh." Ferris, finishing his statement in an animalistic growl, then twisted and contorted as his form shifted.

"Come on, the sun hasn't even set all the way yet. What the fuck?" Throwing his hands up in frustration, Callahan then undertook the task of bringing the campfire to life.

[Callahan] Ugly buggers, lycanthropes are. Hair didn't quite completely cover the body, leaving patches of torn-looking flesh, large sharp teeth sticking awkwardly from a poorly formed underbite maw, and yellowed jaundiced-looking eyes; yep, I could see why that gal would hop on one of these. My readings had been incorrect at one crucial point; the moon didn't have a fucking thing to do with their ability to transition. Lycanthropes hadthe ability to shift at will in so long as they fed on a daily basis. Myth in regard to the full moon began due to the fact that if left unfulfilled, their hunger would then be at its greatest height.

I stoked the fire well into the night, getting it as hot as I could while Ferris, in feral form, stalked constantly and unyieldingly around the ward circle. When I felt it was sufficiently hot, I set the cast-iron pan on the coals and dropped a couple of my silver coins in. Melting the coins down, I poured the remains upon the tip of one of my throwing daggers. From what I had read, silver had a vastly detrimental effect upon the lycanthrope species. Figuring that it didn't matter if it were sturdy or not, I just wanted to get the silver set in a way to achieve injection. My complete lack of forging experience made no difference.

Second myth I discovered discovered: The dagger pierced Ferris's hide where his heart should have been but apparently didn't achieve that level of depth. The only difference the silver seemed to make was in the fact that it had thrown my aim off by at least an inch. It seemed as though Ferris was laughing at me in a growling manner as he removed the dagger and tossed it back into the ward circle. At this point, recognizing that I really didn't know shit about werewolves, I sat to ponder. It never once occurred to me that with the elven nature mage deceased that perhaps the wards he had crafted would have a shelf life, but lo and behold, well into the night, as I puffed ambion herb, Ferris kicked one of the ward rocks aside and charged in.

Instinctually, I pulled my swords, ducked the swiping claw, and seeing an opportunity, made an upward swing with my short sword. Ferris's maw and face removed, his body transformed back into its very naked human form. Rather disgusting, actually. Who wants to see the hairy naked form of a burly fat guy with or without the front half of his head? Apparently, silver or no silver, killing a werewolf proved to be the most effective method of killing a werewolf.

A few uneventful weeks later found me gratefully at the edge of Void Lake. Void Lake is a massive crater of unknown origin and depth, in the middle of which sits a large floating island, the length and breadth of which is covered by the immense mage tower of Calleigh. On each directional location of the void sat large marble orbs atop stone bases. In the bases were slots for the different kinds of keys provided to students, residents, and visitors of Calleigh. Having read so much in regard to the tower, I stood in awe for at least five minutes. I'm not really the idling type now, am I?

How is it that I so easily navigated the landscape of Calarr never having left the comforts of Lados? I brought a fucking map now, didn't I, and to top that off, Owl had gone over geography with me in greatdepth. Eagle's instructions had also lent some aid in knowing how to traverse the varying terrains.

Before further investigation of the nearest orb I assumed would be my entry, I just had to check out the void. Tossing a copper, I silently counted. When I reached one hundred, I got bored and decided to do what any self-respecting visitor to Calleigh should do—I relieved myself into the void. Feeling smugly satisfied, I returned to investigate the orb.

Removing the brooch from my pouch, I attached it to the base into the slot it fit in. To relate that in terms ye might understand, imagine those toddler toys designed to teach shapes. Even at that young age, ye should have the capacity to recognize that if something is the same shape or smaller, it fits; if not, it does not. Upon its attachment, the echo of a voice emanated from the orb. At this point, I made a mental note that when availability arose, I would really like to take the time to learn elven. Staring blankly at the orb, listening to words I hadn't the foggiest clue about, I started to become frustrated.

Kicking the orb—it's marble, all right, and hurts like a motherfucker—I shouted, "How in the fuck do ye bring in new mages when ye haven't any defined methods of allowing an individual to speak to ye?"

A soft, alluring voice responded, "Did you try speaking to us?"

"Touché, don't I feel fucking stupid?" Shaking my head, I watched as stones appeared from the depth of the void, colliding together, until before me was a solid bridge crossing the void.

"It shouldn't be a needed warning, but if you exact any violence within the grounds of our tower, you will be granted intimate knowledge as to the depth of Void Lake." The soft voice issued forth from the stone again.

Pulling the brooch, I hesitantly walked the bridge. There was something wonderfully fright-inspiring about the unknown of Void Lake. I just couldn't help but eagerly wait for the day I would have the chance to toss someone in it.

[Narrator] The tower of Calleigh had originally been fashioned to house the council of the gods when Calarr first came to be created. Upon discovering that their immortality could only be sustained if housed in outside realms, the gods gifted the tower to mages. Mages are individuals who can channel energy of the gods through the use of components and incantations. Some rare individuals are blessed with the ability to spawn forth magical energies free from the use of encumbering components; those individuals were known as sorcerers.

Susceptibility to the funneling of the gods' powers depended upon many variables, such as faith, genetics, favor in the eyes of the gods, and so forth. A few individuals found themselves such apt receptacles for such power that they could become fully ingrained with the essence of their deity or, if you prefer, become possessed. These individuals were known as the god-touched.

[Callahan] Getting ahead of ourselves there, aren't we? That, my friend, is best left for a much later tale. Suffice it to say that during the time of this story, people by and large just weren't that loved by the gods, and I, for one, shared their sentiment in like kind.

[Narrator] Reaching the grand doors leading into the tower, Callahan watched as the bridge collapsed behind him, falling back into Void Lake. Turning back to the doors, Callahan took a moment to respect the ornate artistry on their face. One door held the image of a proud unicorn upon which sat a middle-aged paladin with shoulder-length hair; the other contained the image of a Hydra-like creature known as the Kahllorgh upon which rode three scantily dressed women known as the daughters of Janel. Janel, being the handmaiden of Vertigo and the goddess of seduction, had daughters who held a semblance to our myths of what nymphs or sirens were.

The doors opened of their own accord which, after the show put on by the void's bridge, left Callahan rather unimpressed. Greeting his vision was a woman with pale white skin in a full-length sheer black dress, long black hair reaching down to the small of her back.

[Callahan] That was mistakenly stated as though I were actually paying any attention to her hair.

[Narrator] "Welcome, Falcon, your reputation actually does you justice in this case." Hers was the soft alluring voice he had heard through the orb.

His wry half smile lighting his face, Callahan responded, "Unfortunately, though, ye've obviously heard tell of me. I've not been afforded the same luxury on yer accord. I would've recalled a telling of such heart-stopping beauty. To say yer the most gorgeous gal I'd ever seen wouldn't be entirely true, but yer damned close."

Shaking her head, she gave a seductive smile. "I'm Veracliff, your envoy for the length of your stay here in Calleigh. I've benefitted greatly from my many dealings with Namion and the Talons, so I hope to continue to do so. You've a particular item of interest to look into while here, but that doesn't mean you can't enjoy our vast hospitality while you're present." With that, Veracliff bade Callahan to follow. Walking through the halls of Calleigh, Callahan watched curiously as the side corridors shifted and changed before his eyes. "You needn't worry about where you should or should not go here in Calleigh. The tower allows passage as the gods will it. You will only be granted access to areas the gods see fit for you to access."

"I see access I wouldn't mind making." Callahan's smile grew as Veracliff caught his gaze lingering on her backside.

[Callahan] Wow, that really sounds like a bad anal reference, doesn't it? I'm not really a back door kind of guy, but hey, I'll rarely turn down the opportunity to explore previously unexplored terrain. Before one of the readers comes out of the woodwork, I'm not homosexual, so get over it. That being said, I must admit that I have some pseudohomoerotic tendencies. In that if I were to say, "I like dick," it wouldn't be inaccurate due to my love of my own dick; and let's face it, I must admit that if I were not me, I would turn gay to try and be with me.

Oh, and before any of ye numb nut fantasy nerds out there decide to go try that line in the regard of getting laid, recognize that taking romance/pickup advice from fantasy novels is most likely a leading factor to yer continued virginity. This woman was a priestess/mage of Janel, and as such, random sex was considered prayer to her goddess. I would've had the gal in bed the second she saw me regardless of what I would've said.

[Narrator] The next morning, the sun beamed pleasantly upon Callahan as he awoke alone in Veracliff's plush and comfortable bed. During the wee hours of the morning, Veracliff had donned her dress and departed, leaving Callahan to ponder where his envoy snuck off to. Callahan dressed and looked out the ornate window to view the northern plains leading in seemingly near-endless waves to the frozen tundra. Pondering his next moves, Callahan knew that in this tower of mages, he was well beyond the borders of his comfort zone. Not holding any favor for or from the gods, magic was found to be a highly elusive concept within Callahan's mind.

Glancing around the room, Callahan was reveling in the luxury of it all when he laid eyes on a note sitting on top of a bedside nightstand. "If further access to the tower is desired in my absence, you must ask in prayer that one of the council be your patron. If accepted, they will lend access to you in accord to what they wish for you to see." Cursing his luck, Callahan continued looking about the room. At this point, he noticed that all of the walls were solid and inaccessible, excepting the north-facing window of which he had earlier looked out.

Soon, boredom got the better of him, and Callahan stated aloud as though talking to someone present, "Fuck the lot of ye arrogant buggers. I don't want yer patronage, so unless one of the lot of ye has interest in me seeing something in this place, I'll be taking back to sleep." Heading back to the bed, Callahan wasn't even going to bother with trying to find a hidden door or passage after what he had seen of the shifting corridors.

Climbing on to the bed, he looked to the ceiling and noticed a slightly out-of-place-looking stone. Climbing the bed's sturdy canopy edge, Callahan pushed at the stone. It shifted easily, uncovering an opening in the ceiling. Pulling himself up, Callahan found himself amidst the shifting corridors again. "Oh, fuck this childish nightmare. I don't care that much about anything ye all have to show me. I'm going back to bed." Turning to drop back into the room, Callahan was unsurprised by the fact that his recent entry point was no longer present. "Note to self: never return to this tower."

Wandering for what seemed like hours, Callahan's frustration mounted as he started to recognize the futility of traveling inside the tower. Preparing himself for a lengthy rant directed toward the mages he assumed were watching his every move and then thinking better of it, he produced his pipe. Sitting against a wall, he smoked some of the ambion herb and relaxed. Several more hours passed with his quiet reflection, so he produced some rations from his pack and set to eating. Finishing a light meal, he pulled forth several of his copper coins, and using the corridor's wall, he started to play a game he enjoyed as a child. Tossing one coin then the next, whichever coin ended closest to the wall was deemed the winner. Usually, this game would be played with a companion at which time the owner of the winning coin would pick up all the coins from the field that had been thrown during that round.

Quietly playing, Callahan chuckled imagining the what-the-fuck look that must be spreading on the faces of any observers. After two more small meals and enough coin-tossing practice, Callahan found that he could lean one out of every three coins against the wall, which would pay double the bet if and when he could get another to play.

"If you do not pick a patron, then your welcome in this tower is expended, dear Callahan." Veracliff entered the corridor that had become Callahan's playing field.

"Hey, watch yer step there. If ye scuff the floor, the coins won't slide properly." Callahan showed a complete lack of interest in Veracliff's presence.

"Don't you want to enjoy more than just the hallways? With patronage, there is no end to the delights this tower could provide." Veracliff softly rested her hand upon his shoulder and then seductively rubbed the back of his neck.

A wry half grin spread across his face as Callahan shrugged. "This is the first time in as long as I can remember when everything around me wasn't in an immediate race to take my life. At first, I was frustrated, but now I'm absolutely delighted.

This is wonderful." Sloughing off Veracliff's hand, his grin widened. "Been there, done that. So before ye ask me if I want to put it in your wet spot or your tight spot . . ."

Her hands shuffled in a frantic fashion, and Veracliff began a slow chant. Callahan could feel his earring emanate light warmth into his body. Maintaining his grin, Callahan stood and pushed Veracliff against the wall. Leaning in close, he spoke in what was only slightly above a whisper. "Regardless the rules of Calleigh, I take unwanted magical intrusions upon me as an act of violence. If ye ever try something like that again, I'll break every one of yer fingers. Then I'll, in less than surgical fashion, remove yer vocal cords. Take me to the book I seek, or I'll inject my rapier so deeply into yer cooch it'll tickle yer nostrils from the inside."

Grinning softly, Veracliff kissed Callahan's cheek. "You are delightfully full of surprises. That charm should have had you dancing to my tune. Namion wasn't wrong about you."

"Ye keep referencing Namion as though ye speak to him on a regular. Mind imparting knowledge of how that's possible?" Callahan released his hold on Veracliff and picked up his straggling coins.

"I do mind. Suffice it to say we have ways of sharing words. I'll take you to the book because I adore you, but know that you'll be unable to do anything with it. The tower's mages placed it upon an altar to the council. Only those most beloved by our gods could remove an item from that altar." Veracliff walked down the hall, beckoning to Callahan to follow.

Giving an exasperated sigh, Callahan launched into a rant. "Terrific. I'm so wonderfully excited. Let me guess. In order to gain favor of the gods so that I can remove the book, I need to go on some ridiculous lengthy quest into the depths of some monster-infested cavernous dungeon in the attempt of retrieving some underdescribed useless trinket of value only to you. You will then take said trinket and try to exact some overblown and exaggerated plan to enact world domination. I'll have to go on yet another ridiculous journey to locate the only item in the world capable of destroying the first item and will, as such, become hero of Calarr despite my nefarious character traits."

Laughing, Veracliff smiled as she responded, "No, my dear lovely and imaginative man, you needn't do anything extravagant. Even if you were to pick the book up, it has been enchanted by Calleigh's head mages. Much like the halls and corridors of this tower, its words will forever be shifting and changing to any unwelcome eyes."

Smiling, Callahan cheered aloud, "HA! Yes! Finally, of all the bungled tragic acts of the gods, they do me a massive favor. I'll have no reluctance in passing such a book on to Namion. Fuck him, and more immediately pertinent, fuck ye too."

Entering a vast hall, Callahan took a quick moment to reflect on the beauty of it all. Massive portraits lending visuals of the gods lined the walls; jewels and vases of worth encased behind glass on pedestals lined the red carpeted center of the hall, leading to an altar upon which sat the opened book of Entearra Gharu. Walking up to stand before the altar, Callahan looked again to Veracliff. "So if I try to lift this thing, am I going to be assaulted by a vast army of magically enchanted golems? Perhaps I'll just be evaporated or blown up, much like my ole friend Alliander."

"Nothing so dramatic. The altar will just refuse to yield the book to any hands the gods have not favored to such end." A shocked expression lit Veracliff's face as Callahan nonchalantly picked the book up.

Closing it, Callahan dropped it in his bag. "Hmm, well, that turned out to be easy. How 'bout ye craft me up a portal or something so I don't have to walk all the way to the northern tundra."

"You are an amazing specimen of manhood. I would ask that you share a few more nights with me before departing, and sorry to inform you, but you will be stuck undertaking usual methods of travel." Veracliff seductively loosened the top of her dress.

"Tempting as that offer is, I must decline due to my overwhelming desire to be free of this strangling tower. So if ye would be as kind as to show me out, I'll be putting this den of horror behind me and hopefully never returning." Callahan eagerly urged Veracliff to lead on.

"Exit is availed before you." Veracliff pointed to the same door they had entered. "You are such a delightful breath of fresh air, dear Falcon. We could accomplish much together. I'm sure as the days turn to years, I will be seeing you again. You will come around to the benefits of magic, and someday, you will be mine."

"Well, on that exceedingly creepy note, I take my leave." Opening the door, Callahan found himself outside the northern face of Calleigh. Crossing Void Lake's odd bridge system once more, he watched as it collapsed back into the void. "Glad to leave that fun house behind me." Setting himself for the next arduous leg of his journey, Callahan took one more occasion to relieve himself into the void.

[Callahan] Though a bit anticlimactic, I was really pleased with the tower's outcome. Not everything ends in bloodshed, and honestly, with the life I've lived as ye've read it, the rare moments I managed to get where I didn't have to end a life were quite pleasant.

Unbeknownst to meself, back in Lados, things were getting pretty rough for my friends and acquaintances. Namion, securing his solitary leadership of Lados, set the remaining Avians to the purpose of putting down my rebellion. Pockets of people who sought to rise against the nobles or the Talons were being put down in holocaust proportions.

Horuce lost his position with the guard on promptings from Namion to Kaville. Hemrick's house was repossessed. All in all, Namion was doing a terrific job of ensuring his position. Unfortunately, the crown was well aware of the activities being undertaken in Lados and, in response, continued their unifying mobilization of their military forces. Honoring their time frame, they were maintaining said forces well outside the boundaries of Lados, lending a slight hope that Kaville and the republic might regain control.

Raven found Hemrick swinging from the main rafter within his home the night before he was to have vacated it. Returning to the streets was just too dreary a concept for the poor ole bastard to wrap his mind around. Cowards escape, if ye ask me. Hopefully, he gained his rest; the gods know he earned it. Other than wishing him his rest, he was deserving of no pity; pity should be held for those of us poor sods who still have to carry on.

Horuce and his family secreted away to the outlying farmlands to stay with family friends. He continued to aid in lighting fire to people's desire for change. Despite their dire circumstances, many objectors refused to give up the fight.

[Reader 1] Having the book again brings to mind the question "Can you even fucking read it?"

[Callahan] No more or less than before. I did find occasion before venturing far from Calleigh to cross-reference the elven book of nature magic I'd picked up with the book of Entearra Gharu. If I'd had a month or two in a quiet environment, I'm sure I could've unlocked the key I needed to be able to read the elven language, but that wasn't much a possibility now, was it? As for the shifting and changing words, apparently, I was one of the chosen ones who didn't experience that. That fact led me to fear the possibility of Namion having a similar result, which led me once again to salute the heavens with my one-fingered respect.

Taking that last thought in mind, I remembered Namion's exact words: "You will travel there and retrieve it if you can." Nowhere in his orders did he state I was to return the cursed fucking thing, so I did what I do best. I fucked everyone and threw the book in the void.

[Reader 1] Do you mind running that by me one more time?

[Callahan] Yep, I tossed that bitch of a book right on in; it fluttered and flapped in the wind of its descent much like a wounded bird. Didn't know that, in doing so, the gods saw fit to intervene. The book was returned in an unknown fashion back to its altar in Calleigh. Upon seeing its return, Veracliff succeeded in picking it up; apparently, my disturbance there had dispelled the wards that prevented its handling. Upon picking it up, she took a trip back to Lados and delivered it personally to Namion. All of this is getting way ahead of our current point in the story, though.

At our current point in the story, I continued my endeavors toward securing allegiances with "the tribes."

Chapter 5

THE TRIBES

[CALLAHAN] As I PROGRESSED across the seemingly endless plains leading to the tundra that housed the odd warlike barbarians of the north, I managed to find a small lake. The locating of a lake, though good for replenishing my water supply, was far more celebrated for the much-needed washing of my socks. Have ye ever tried to wear the same socks for weeks on end? They get stale, crusty, and horribly uncomfortable. I can suffice with dirty shirts, pants, even dirty underwear, but even after having brought five pairs, I couldn't stand the discomfort brought on by dirty socks.

At this point, I found it appropriate to light a campfire.

[Narrator] So now it's OK, after all that bitching.

[Callahan] I had to sterilize the water for drinking somehow, didn't I? Potable water sources that were openly available became housing and resting sites for a variety of creatures. Bears to reason that with that many creatures frequenting an area, there would be a lot of urinating and defecating. Some may find it acceptable to drink urine; I'm not such a person. Even with such medieval minds as those of our world, by and large, we recognized the benefits provided by boiling water before keeping it for drinking.

This also leads us to my next puzzle. Being in a place where creatures should be in abundance, I was oddly alone. My senses piqued, I kept myself on alert for any incoming intrusions. As I finished my washing and water preparations, I drew my silver-tainted dagger and began the process of cleaning it of my unwanted addition. As I completed my

CHRIS CURTIN

self-appointed chores, I noted that there had still been no activity around the lake, and dusk was fast approaching. Holding a throwing dagger in each hand, I prepared myself for any eventuality and walked to the water's edge.

[Narrator] "All right, come on out. We can wait until I pretend to go to sleep for ye to pop out and get killed, or we can just avoid wasting yer time and mine. Come on out, and meet the Falcon." Waiting calmly, Callahan listened carefully, but nothing broke the silence. "Really, come on now. Let me guess. Yer a spirit from beyond the grave, and ye were betrayed by someone ye thought loved ye. They drowned ye in this lake, and now until someone frees ye of yer curse, yer forced to reside here, pulling hapless passersby in and drowning them with ye. Well, let's have at it 'cause if yer substantial enough to hurt me, then bears to reason yer substantial enough to be hurt by me."

With silence the response, Callahan turned to finish gathering his gear for what he hoped to be a hasty departure. Daggers still held in his hands, he proceeded two steps then turned suddenly, releasing them both. Both blades harmlessly soared through the enchantingly beautiful incorporeal young woman at the water's edge to splash into the lake. "How did such a handsome, powerful young man come to know of my plight?" The ghost's voice was soft and alluring.

"I would say that flattery and ego-boosting comments will only get ye so far with me, but no one has yet to reach that limit, so please keep pouring 'em on." As Callahan responded, he felt warmth spreading from his earring yet again. Somehow, he was able to see a small bluish tendril stretching from the woman's spirit down the water's edge to a rock outcropping, where due to his magical night vision, he was looking upon an aquatic humanoid holding a wand, kneeling upon the rocks, and blending in nicely.

"So long it has been since I have shared company. Please come sit by the water with me, and share your story that I might break the torture that is my solitude, if only for one night." The spirit beckoned to him seductively. Watching the

142

shaman, Callahan could see his mouth move in time with the words. Scanning quickly as he seemed to be heading toward the ghost, Callahan noted at least three more of the fish men hidden skillfully around the tall grasses and shrubs of the water's surrounding landscape.

"If I had a nagging shrew half as ugly as ye and dumb enough to get into deep water near me, I'd have drowned her too. So why do I want to waste me time listening to that shrill voice of yers for a moment longer?" Sliding two more daggers out, he kept his eyes on the illusion while watching the aquatic creatures through his peripheral vision.

The beautiful ghost's image gained a shocked and hurt expression. "Hmm? What could you possibly—" Cut off in midsentence, the spirit dissolved while the aquatic shaman choked upon the two blades lodged through its neck.

"One of ye fish-faced fuckers is gonna go get me daggers out of the water. Yer gonna cease any further effort toward the end of eating me and suffice yerselves with the meat that bloke will provide." Drawing his last two daggers, he kneeled in preparation.

"Peace, land walker. We apologize for underestimating your abilities." A fish man he had not noticed stood from behind him, adorned with a belt of multicolored feathers. "I am Chief Yerglarix. That was my lead shaman, Moninferix."

"Whoa! Just stop with the names already. For fuck's sake. I'm not about to try to pronounce that, and regardless, I really, really don't care. Five seconds ago, ye all wanted to turn me into a dinner, and now ye want to shake hands and exchange names. Go deep-fry yerself, ye oversized fish stick." Callahan shook his head in frustration as he watched six other fish people wielding spears circle around him. "I'm about to have meself a fish fry to end all fish fries if any of ye come one step closer."

Holding his webbed hand up, Yerglarix spoke again. "Halt. Porthinuisx, retrieve the man's blades from the water. Gerphliknamix, get the body of Moninferix and return him to the lake that we may honor his body. Tireolnm—"

"Enough is enough! Told ye to stop with bloody names now, didn't I?" Callahan launched one of his remaining blades into the chief's right eye and the second into the throat of one of the nearby spear wielders. Drawing both swords, he plunged his rapier through the heart of one more. Spinning and slashing with his short sword, he cleaved another's head down the middle while simultaneously pulling his rapier free from the other. Leaping forward, he performed an inward dual-crossing slash with his blades, forcing another fish man's spear down while splitting his chest in an X.

Looking to the bewildered remaining two, Callahan stuck his tongue out and roared. They dropped their spears and fell to their knees before him. "Which one of the two of ye wants to be the new chief?"

One of the two stood up, looking hopeful. "I'll honor the position." Callahan attempted to cut its head off but found it a more difficult task than with normal humans. Their bodies were oddly shaped and considerably thicker than the human form, so misgauging the distance, the blade slid easily through but did not reach the back of its neck.

[Callahan] Aye, to relate that in terms of understanding for those of yer reality, it was much like a child's candy dispenser, but instead of containing candy, it contained a lot of sushi.

[Narrator] "Return my daggers, and I'll let ye live." Callahan watched the last surviving creature splash into the lake. Thinking twice about that decision, Callahan grabbed the shaman's wand, the chief's belt, and the rest of his gear, including the four daggers not in the water. Putting a fair bit of distance between himself and the water, Callahan didn't find a bit of surprise as countless fish men poured forth.

An hour later, along the plains, Callahan had yet to slow his running pace. Thankful for the lengthy stamina training he had performed under Eagle's instruction, Callahan couldn't help but laugh about his last encounter.

[Callahan] In retrospect, they would have probably shown respect to me due to the loss of their shaman. I might have even wrangled up some supplies, but there is just something about someone trying to eat me that seems to cause me to take a natural dislike toward them. The rest of the trek across the plains was fairly uneventful despite being obnoxiously long. As plain transitioned into tundra, I found myself thankful for my gloves. Why anyone would subject themselves to such fierce weather conditions baffled me.

Nomadic people, the barbarians would spend the warmer seasons hunting on the plains then muscle into the tundra at the foot of the mountains which, though harshly cold, protected them from the worst of the winter storms. Arriving during the close of the warmer seasons, I caught the tribes while they remained spaced apart. During the winter, the tribes were forced to camp uncomfortably close to each other at the foot ofthe mountains, so they delighted in near-constant warfare to break the monotony of it.

Still turbulent and warlike during the warmer seasons, they broke the wars only on account of having enough room to spread far apart into their prospective territories so as not to tread on each other's toes. Rivers divided much of the plains in this region, making the territory boundaries considerably easier to assess. Crossing one such river on a wooden bridge, I caught glimpse of someone combating more of those fish people up the river.

[Narrator] Jogging up the riverbank, Callahan gained perspective of the battle as he drew closer. A man in bearskin attire was doing his best to hold four of the fish creatures at bay, wielding a massive double-sided battle axe. Chuckling lightly, Callahan found it humorous to watch a man of no larger stature than himself attempting to wield such an ill-proportioned weapon. The four spear-wielding fish men were playing the obvious game of tiring the young man out. Unleashing his four throwing daggers and then finishing the remnants up with his two blades, Callahan collected his weaponry and gave a wry half smile to the young man before him. "That giant hunk of shit would be better used by an ogre for chopping down trees."

"In strong hands, these axes work to fell city folk by the dozens." Attempting to stand proudly, the thin man did little in the way of cutting an imposing figure.

"Don't ruffle yer feathers, mate. Let me see that thing." Callahan extended his hand.

"A tribesman is not to give up his weapon unless in surrender." Grasping tightly to the axe's haft, the man stepped back as though preparing for battle.

"I just saved yer arse. Really, do I have to now go and pummel ye?" Shaking his head, Callahan darted quickly inside the man's reach. His left hand grasped the axe haft, twisting until his right hand pushed the flat of the axe's dual blades into the man's face, dropping him.

Groaning, the man tried to gather his feet. "That was dishonorable."

"Not my fault yer slow and overburdened. What the fuck ye mean dishonorable? Ye hunkered up like ye wanted a fight. I obliged ye. Where is the dishonor?" Stepping back, Callahan dropped the massive axe and drew forth his short sword.

"Men of honor meet face-to-face in a show of strength." The man's words petered off as he watched Callahan cut his axe haft in half. "What are . . . ?" He silenced himself when Callahan next chopped one side of the dual head off.

Sheathing his sword, Callahan then picked up the now-manageable axe and tested its balance. "Hmm, a bit off, but it's a hundred times better than what it was. Standing toe to toe with a larger, stronger opponent isn't a show of honor. It's an act of sheer fucking stupidity. A real swordsman knows that the victor is the one who strikes first, strikes true, and gets the fuck out of the way." Tossing the newly trimmed axe to the man, Callahan drew his blades.

Dancing in and feinting, Callahan watched the man smile with delight as he instinctually parried. The next several minutes were spent in this fashion. Callahan would lead an attack, while the man would defend, then vice versa.

"So ye still want to die in honorable combat, or would ye rather keep that and stand as victor?" Callahan flashed his wry half grin.

"The tribe would not approve of such a thing, but you have shown me its benefits. Thank you, I am Yurin." Yurin brought the axe up in salute.

"Fuck, really? Yer bloody parents named ye Urine. Wow, they must really hate ye. What the fuck are ye doing out here? Ye obviously shouldn't be out here alone. Oh yeah, I'm Falcon, here to find the tribes and secure allegiance." Callahan continued grinning.

"I am son to Oreeck of the Ooreethra tribe. I've been exiled to prove myself. I am small and weak. The tribes do not harbor the small and weak. I was sent to prove myself against the Narcin." Yurin looked disgusted by Callahan's questions.

Laughing uproariously, Callahan shook his head while smiling from ear to ear. "They called ye Urine from the Urethra tribe. That's so beyond fucked it's hilarious. Yer parents took cruelty to a whole new level of demented wit."

"Enough!" Yurin lurched forward with an overhand swing. Stepping lithely to the side, Callahan grasped the haft of the axe above Yurin's grasp with his right hand and punched Yurin's wrist with his left.

Gaining control of the axe, Callahan jerked it into a quick sideswipe using the back end to smash the side of Yurin's head. Dazed and looking up at Callahan, Yurin cringed as Callahan whipped his ribs a few times with the axe's haft.

"Saving yer life and giving ye a functional weapon bought me the right to insult ye as much as I want." Callahan dropped the axe next to him, then seated himself a few feet away. "If ye don't like that, I can always chop ye into little bits so that I can use yer remains as chum to fish out some of these Narcin. One way or the other, someone is going to answer my questions.

They exiled ye because yer small? Well, as ye can see, size doesn't make someone weak."

"We live in a different world than you, outsider." Yurin sat up, spit a bit of blood, and then pulled his axe close. "The dwarves expanded their underground territories and took a few of the lakes that used to house the Narcin. Seeking new feeding grounds, the Narcin followed the underground river systems and are popping up all over the plains. They are a plague upon my people. They consume and disrupt the herds that provide us food stores for the winter. My father sent me to prove my worth against them so that I could gain some respect in the tribe."

Reaching into his pack, Callahan produced the shaman's wand and the chief's belt, tossing them in front of Yurin. "Would something like that be enough to secure yer respect?"

"That is a shaman's wand and a chief's—" Yurin sputtered in surprise.

"Well, I rightly know what the fuck they are, don't I, master of the obvious? Else, I wouldn't have fucking tossed 'em to ye." Losing his smile, Callahan's patience was waning. "Wise up, boy. I have crafted my existence to date by killing many a man more powerful and intelligent than yerself. Yer gonna take these gifts and regain yer position in yer tribe. Yer gonna use said position to endear me to yer father, and yer gonna do it all with a smile."

"That would be a lie and, therefore—" Yurin's look of disgust returned.

"If ye say 'dishonorable' one more time, I'll kill ye. If you state the obvious one more time, I'll kill ye. If ye so much as burp in a manner that displeases me, I'll kill ye. I'm done playing games. I saved yer ass, and now it's time ye chock up a bit of dishonor in the name of repayment." Callahan's wry half grin returned.

"What is fair, is fair." Yurin thought about what he said then continued, "Please, that wasn't meant to state the obvious. It's been an odd day, and a lot has just happened."

"Granted, so please shut up. Just walk me back to yer tribe, celebrate yer slaughter of the chief and shaman. Think of whatever ye have to, to make it work and endear me to yer tribe. Agreed?" Callahan stood and prepared himself to leave.

"Yes, I will honor such a pact." Slowly picking himself up and rubbing his bruised ribs, Yurin started to lead Callahan on. Callahan cringed at Yurin's use of the word *honor*.

[Callahan] By some miracle, Yurin was actually able to guide me back to his tribe without me killing him. Before we arrived, we camped down for a day, and I did my best to instruct Yurin on some of the finer tactics he could use with his newly fashioned axe. As we approached the camp, we came upon a couple of barbarian youths. At least I assumed they were youths. The smallest of the males I saw on the outskirts of the camp and within the camp as I could see were at least twice our size.

[Narrator] "Ha, look, little Yurin brought us yet another tiny man to help with the woman's work." The first of the approaching two chuckled to his companion.

"Little Yurin's now carrying half an axe. Ha, he can't even manage the weight of a real man's weapon," the second barbarian responded.

"OK, no killing. Ye take the one on the right, and I've the one on the left, but hold off till I start," Callahan whispered to Yurin, who looked like he wanted to argue, but the approaching barbarians were getting too close. In his usual volume, Callahan addressed the two barbarians, and his wry half grin lit his face as he spoke. "Speaking of womenfolk, the two of ye are a bit too rotund for my liking, so how about sending us a couple of those thin little blonde gals?"

Observing Callahan's odd clothing and mannerisms, the first barbarian stood stoically before Callahan. "Outsiders are not welcome. Weak city folk are wise to stay behind their walls. Turn, leave, and take the whelp with you."

Looking to Yurin, Callahan chuckled lightly. "If I'm not gathering this wrong, that young punk there is challenging us.

If only he knew that ye just finished up slaying a Narcin chief and his shaman."

"Aye, I return to show trophiesof my triumphs. I return with the belt of a Narcin chief and the wand of a Narcin shaman." Yurin held the items before him with pride as he spoke.

Reaching forward, the first barbarian looked as though he intended to snag the items from Yurin. Ducking under the man's arm, Callahan shot a left knife hand to his throat. Spinning, he then delivered a right backhand to the man's temple. The barbarian collapsed to his knees, and Callahan drove a right knee to his nose, delighting in the cracking sound.

Turning, Callahan smiled as he watched the now-armed Yurin ducking a swipe being delivered by an oversized axe; coming up under the swing, Yurin smashed the head of his smaller axe under the behemoth's chin, dropping him. Using the haft, he whipped at the man's ribs as he spoke. "Take us to Oreeck. Do not be slow."

Begrudgingly, the two men collected themselves and led Callahan and Yurin to the center of the camp. As they traversed through the encampment, Callahan found a good deal of pleasure in the numerous looks of curiosity that lined the residents' faces. The two guides bowed their heads then stepped aside when the group reached the large bone-crafted throne at the camp's center. Adorned in paint and an animal skin loincloth, the chieftain stood from the throne as he laid eyes on Yurin and Callahan.

"What is the meaning of this? I sent you to find an honorable death." Oreeck glared at his son.

"I have found honorable strength." Holding forth the wand and the belt, Yurin stood as proudly as he could. "I killed a Narcin chief and his shaman. I saved this man beside me as he was in honorable combat against overwhelming odds. I havenow returned to regain my place as your son in the tribe."

Callahan did all he could not to snort aloud when he heard that Yurin had apparently saved him. "Good chief, I have come in an attempt to forge allegiance between the City of Lados and yerselves."

"Tiny men like you are suited for no more than washing, cleaning, and gathering. You are suited for women's work, and I do not render negotiation with women." Oreeck's glare turned in Callahan's direction.

"Father, this man—" Yurin had set the items before the throne and stood again beside Callahan.

"Speak not to me of men, you whelp. I cannot believe such a useless whelp as you left my loins." The chieftain waved to the nearby men, who gathered in a large circle around the conversation.

"Hey, chiefy, what do ye tell a woman with two black eyes?" A wry half smile spread across Callahan's face as he figured he had nothing to lose. Giving sufficient time for the chief's puzzled look to be shared by many of the barbarians, Callahan continued, "Nothing, ye've already done and told the bitch twice now, haven't ye?"

Caught completely off guard, the chief chuckled and paused. Callahan rolled with the momentum. "Aye, don't trust anything that can bleed for seven days and not die."

Laughing, the chief returned to his throne. "OK, little man, I will humor your presence. If you can best Tarlack in honorable contest, we will discuss terms of your allegiance." The chief waved his hand again, and a man, massive even among the barbarians, stepped forward.

Yurin groaned and stepped aside as he whispered quickly to Callahan, "It's to the death. No rules."

The circle cheered as the massive man drew forth a two-handed sword from his back. The sword was at least five feet in length and about a foot and a half wide. Callahan found his curiosity piqued as to how anyone could even think to wield such a large blade. Lightly swinging the blade from side to side before him, Tarlack smiled. "Come, little man. See the meaning of strength."

Picking up a palm-sized rock, Callahan tossed it lightly into the air. Catching it, he smiled his wry half grin and said, "Ye don't want to dance with me, mate. This isn't gonna end well for ye."

"Silence, mini man." Tarlack stepped forward to advance on his much smaller opponent.

Tossing the rock, Callahan laughed as it made an odd echoing thud bouncing off the barbarian's forehead. Stumbling and losing hold on his giant sword, Tarlack dropped to his knees. Darting forward, Callahan grasped the hilt of the giant blade, lifting it just enough to smash its base into Tarlack's jawline. A loud cracking sound was his reward as Callahan watched the immense man topple to his side, half of his jaw hanging in such a way that it grotesquely stretched his cheek. Dragging the blade over, Callahan used its hilt to repeatedly smash Tarlack's face. Smiling from ear to ear, Callahan absentmindedly hummed a working tune as he methodically mashed the man's head. Nodding to the onlookers, Callahan found a good deal of satisfaction in the soft squishy sound now emitted by his work.

Three times, the chief called for him to halt before the request actually registered. "Look here, chief. I did that without even touching my favored weapons. I'll burn this village and every one of its people without losing my smile. I'll make ye watch while tied upon a giant anal spike slowly splitting ye in half. I'll do all of this and still concede to ye the fact that yer stronger."

Sputtering, the chief fought to collect himself. "Listen, one lucky dishonorable show does not afford ye the right—"

"If I want any lip off of ye, I'll peel it off my dick!" Picking up the stone that had dropped Tarlack, Callahan winged it to the throne, very near Oreeck's head. Ducking in shock, Oreeck could feel pieces of his bone throne bounce off the back of his head and neck. "Garble, garble, garble. Clear the shit out yer throat, and speak to me as an equal, ye overblown pomp ass."

An old and hunched man wearing a bear skull hat stepped out from behind the throne. "Hold, chief, this man does not lie or exaggerate. His is strength we should show proper respect. I feel the presence of a god upon him."

"Oh blimey, really, this is all fucking bollocks. I'd sooner slaughter the lot of ye than be saved on the misconception of godliness." Callahan produced two of his throwing daggers and prepared for what could be a lengthy fight.

"Calm yourself. As word of the shaman states, I have shown you a great deal of disrespect. A meal and warm lodging will be provided. Eat, rest, and then we shall sit to negotiate. Yurin, you will accompany our guest and ensure his comfort. Please accept my apologies, outsider." The chief then turned to the crowd of onlookers. "Hold fast, and show this man all the honors we bestow upon one held as guest in our village."

The shaman stepped through the crowd, drawing near Callahan. "You may hold no credit in the gods, but at least one of the gods holds credit in you."

[Callahan] If I hadn't desired some cooked food and the chance at a warm bed, I'd have gutted that bastard and used his intestines as a jump rope. The barbarians treated me as they were demanded to, but there was still an obvious disdain for my newest companion. It was a nice change of pace to eat meat and a full cooked meal, not to mention that despite being subjugated and treated like material possessions, by and large, the barbarian females were very attractive and friendly. One particular well-endowed thin little blond-haired gal was paying a bit of extra attention to my presence.

Just as I was preparing to have that gal show me back to me bed for the night, Yurin tromped in to wreck the evening. "A woman's place is not one to be pestering a man while he eats. Even the daughter of the chief should know that. Get on with yourself, sis, and clean some of the evening's mess."

"Yer bloody sister, bollocks. Well, lovely, it was nice chatting with ye, but nothing puts a hamper in the negation process quite like racking it out with a man's daughter." Shaking my head, I looked longingly as the blonde girl reluctantly meandered off.

"She is promised to another. It would be unwise to bed a barbarian gal, my friend. Our people tend to get overly jealous, and any further killing would make your position for negotiation precarious." Yurin stayed near me the rest of the evening running a few of their traditions by me so I would be better prepared for negotiations.

"Remember, most likely, there will be a test of large proportions before Oreeck will agree to send any of the barbarians away from the territories. We don't traditionally craft alliances with outsiders," Yurin warned as he led me back to where I would spend my evening.

"Then we beat them to the punch," I said as Yurin looked confused. "You and I will offer to investigate the spreading influence of the dwarves and, thus, the cause for yer Narcin invaders. We'll do what we can to dissuade further Narcin incursion and, inso doing, purchase yer position back in the tribe and mine as a solid ally. Ye'll enjoy a newfound respect around here, and I'll ensure a spokesperson on my behalf remains behind."

Nodding, Yurin consented to my plan, saying something 'bout great honor and yada yada. Who really cares what the ill-fashioned barbarian runt had to say. I just wanted some kind of allegiance secured and an excuse to go meet dwarves. Shit, by this time, I'd killed all kinds of things but had yet to kill a dwarf; I figured why the fuck not do so while playing the part of a barbarian hero.

[Narrator] The next day found Callahan and Yurin proposing that very idea to the tribe's shaman and the chief. They agreed that if the two were to succeed in quelling the Narcin uprising, then the tribe would not only offer its allegiance but would petition the other tribes, out of a debt of honor, to hold allegiance to him as well.

Pleased with himself, Callahan let his mind wander as Yurin guided them to the mountain cave entrances that would lead down into the dwarves' vast mining circuit. His personal meditations were destroyed when Yurin spoke, saying, "If you thought we were an unwelcoming people, just wait until you meet dwarves. They may be short, but they are sturdy and a well-respected lot from the tribes. Many a war has been forged between us. They are worthy opponents."

The caverns started as rough and natural-looking but soon gained a very similar structure to the Talons' underground training valley. As they moved beyond natural light, they noticed an occasional torch on the wall utilized in a similar fashion to those in the Lados underground. It wasn't long before the two rounded a bend in the well-fashioned stone corridors to be greeted by two armored dwarves as wide as they were tall. "Halt, uplander. State your name and the purpose for this intrusion."

Yurin spoke with pride. "I am Yurin of the Ooreethra tribe. We come to discover—"

Cutting off his companion, with his wry half grin, Callahan stepped forward. "Yes, he did just say he's Urine from the Urethra tribe. Please feel free to laugh as much as ye would like. I'm the Falcon, emissary of the Talons' guild from Lados." Reaching into his pouch, Callahan watched the two dwarves prepare their axes for combat. Producing two platinum pieces from his bag, he felt edified in their immediately calming personas. Tossing one to each, he chuckled. "This jack bag is my guide. I'm here to meet with yer head brewer. I would like to set up a mutually profiting endeavor to trade coin for fine dwarven spirits. The shipping lines will run from yer breweries to Lados itself."

"Humph, well, yer coin is good, so come on. Just make sure that numb nuts guiding ye stays shut up." One of the dwarves remained on post, while the other guided them through a few more series of twisting corridors.

Yurin leaned in, about to say something to Callahan. Callahan stopped him before he could say anything. "This fine gent requested that ye stay silent. So unless ye've ever wondered what a rapier tastes like, I suggest ye adhere to that request." Grunting in disdain, Yurin reluctantly obliged.

[Callahan] Dwarves are a race renowned for greed, above all else. Greed and whiskey. I figured the best way to get in their good graces was to appeal to both of those sentiments. Besides, wouldn't I be awfully remiss if I didn't take a valid opportunity to set up a solid stream of dwarven spirits into the city of Lados? Gem and precious metal mines existed all around the human realm, and almost every one of them was run and inhabited by dwarves. I couldn't help but have a solid respect for their work ethic and architectural genius, but beyond that, the foul-smelling cave-dwelling drunkards were no more pleasant than orcs, if ye asked me.

Dwarves governed themselves under a monarchy that existed in the depths of the northern mountains. Clans existed throughout the human realm under the guidance of nobles who answered to the king. Having much longer life spans than humans and being of a generally more ordered nature, their monarchy was far less prone to corruption. Sturdy and unafraid of war, they, despite all appearances and rumors, much preferred calm lives of mining, forging, and brewing ales, which happened to be their profession of highest esteem. In camps or colonies set away from nobility, their leadership fell to the head brewer.

[Narrator] Taken to their head brewer, Callahan and Yurin listened as he spoke. "Aye, the reason we've been expanding so far into old Narcin stomping grounds is because the Narcin have been goading us to war. These bloody warmongering morons"—the head brewer pointed at Yurin as he spoke—"have been blaming us for their surface activities. The whole while we've been down here trying to fight back a seemingly endless array of assaults from all directions, it's as though those blighters have come upon new leadership. Whoever this new leadership is, they are not happy with just scavenging the underground waterways. Ye put an end to those pesky Narcin raiding us, and we'll oblige yer trade proposal.

The proposal will be at triple the cost per barrel until ye can supply yer own transportation for it. I can't stand going to the city, and neither can me boys."

"Despite being utterly predictable and a serious pain in my arse, I'm on it, and I find yer prices fair. 'Tis a long trek to Lados, and it's not easy. I'll have ye know, though—I expect my product shipped on time and of proper quantity. If it comes up short or late, I'll only pay half the price for what is there. As long as it's delivered appropriately, I'll pay appropriately." Callahan shook the dwarf's hand. "By the way, ye couldn't possibly point me in the direction of these Narcin, would ye?"

[Callahan] BAH! Ye wound up doing it to me anyway. I did my best to avoid ye dumping me into the cliché situations of quest leading to quest leading to quest, but no. Through the course of my existence, ye insisted on forcing me into yer rehashed medieval fantasy bullshit.

[Narrator] Well, I could've just had ye grow up a stable hand until, one day, ye became a riding instructor, but I felt this story line to be considerably more gripping for a reader.

[Callahan] Shovel horseshit or become badass assassin who can say and do pretty much whatever the fuck he wants? Hmm, guess I'm glad ye went with the latter.

[Narrator] Traveling deeper into the mountain, Yurin carried a torch to light their way. Callahan kept his ability to see in the dark to himself. The tunnels transitioned from dwarven fashion back into natural outcroppings. An odd glowing moss grew in abundance along the cave walls, which alluded to the fact that they were nearing one of the underground lakes/water systems.

Yurin's voice uncomfortably broke the silence of the cave. "I do not like how you make me appear subservient before the dwarves. I am a proud—"

"Ye are subservient as is evidenced by the fact that I'm about to tell ye to shut the fuck up, and yer gonna do it without further question. Yer gonna do it 'cause I'm willing to wager ye like yer organs to remain free from the influence of cave air." Flashing his wry half grin, Callahan unthreateningly drew his blades. "All this dirt and moss—shit, ye'd be prone to pick up an infection dragging yer intestines back to the surface."

Axe at the ready, Yurin continued by Callahan's side in silence while they entered an open area containing a large underground lake. On one side, an endless waterfall poured forth, churning the lake, and Callahan imagined that a similar outflow existed under the surface of the lake on the opposite side. A small whirlpool further evidenced Callahan's thoughts on the water's flow.

At this point, Callahan noted several points of unnatural waves heading toward the water's edge. "All right, boyo, looks like yer about to get yer shot at earning some respect from me. Prep that axe. Looks to be at least four of 'em coming on quick." Torch in his left hand, axe in his right, Yurin did as Callahan had said and prepared himself for combat.

Crouching and moving toward the water's edge, Callahan was not in the least surprised when the four he had predicted burst forth, launching a net toward the two intruders. Rolling easily under the net, Callahan found himself impressed as a well-placed axe swipe opened enough of the net that Yurin quickly pulled himself free of its grasp. Thrust, swipe, thrust, sidestep. The first of the intruders did not drop quickly as Callahan danced about it. Succumbing to the wounds Callahan had inflicted, it did collapse, at which time a rapier thrust through the top of its head and ensured it would stay down.

Breaking free from the net, Yurin sidestepped a spear thrust, and with quick slashing, cross motions brought his axe to rip through his first Narcin opponent's shoulder and chest. Turning to face the next, he noticed the multitude of reinforcements now pouring from the lake. "Alert, friend, we have company!"

"Bah, the more the merrier." Callahan's smile had grown full as he settled into his dance of dodging, spinning, thrusting, and slashing. Three more of the aquatic attackers were laid to their rest at his feet. "Come, dance. For this is the dance for which I was born. It is the very reason I draw breath."

"OK, my psychotic friend, you may be fine, but I could sure use a hand." Dropping one more Narcin, Yurin shoved his torch into the face of another. Three more attackers were bearing down on him, and he knew he could only hold pace for so long.

Stabbing both blades into an opponent's chest, Callahan sent all four of his throwing daggers, one after another, into the crowd gathering around Yurin. Drawing his blades back out of the collapsing creature's chest, he spun, slicing through another's midsection with his short sword while simultaneously ducking a spear thrust. "Aye, 'tis getting a wee bit heavy, I'll admit. Just hang in there another minute or so, and I'll work my way to ye."

Watching three of the four targets Callahan had chosen drop before him, Yurin pressed the advantage, dropping a couple more. Glancing back to the water, Yurin felt gripped with fear as he watched masses of Narcin still exiting the water.

A low rumble, almost inaudible amidst the combat, alerted Callahan's senses. Garbled calls for retreat lit the air in the Narcin's native tongue, and they started fleeing back to the water in droves. "Ha, that's right. Flee, and do not dare to incur our wrath again!" Yurin celebrated as the Narcin fled into the water.

"Oh, shut up, ye complete tit! A whole contingent of warriors just ran from two tiring quarry. They lost more than a dozen of their fellows trying to bring us down, and just as it appeared they had us, they decided to flee. Fuck me, ye really are retarded, aren't ye? Prepare to swim, dipshit, 'cause I'm willing to bet something big and mighty unfriendly is about to say hi." Callahan gathered his throwing daggers and held his blades ready as he ranted at his companion.

Rocks burst forth, showering the two, as a sixteen-foot-tall armored-looking creature with apelike claws reaching to its feet pushed itself into the lake cavern. Its insectlike feelers twitched awkwardly above two tiny beady black eyes. A cavernous toothy maw displayed a multilayered array of fangs coupled with pincerlike outcroppings from its jawline.

"Piss! A fucking umber hulk." Having read about the creatures of the underground that crafted caves in their wake, Callahan knew he was in for a good one. Thinking about taking to the water, Callahan ran some quick calculations through his head. *Swim, possibly escape the umber hulk to be drowned by fish people. Fight the umber hulk, wind up its next meal. Run, the giant thing, now on myscent, would not relent until sated. Feed it Yurin, tempting but counterproductive.*

Cursing his luck, Callahan released his throwing daggers; three bounced harmlessly from the creature's armored hide, and the fourth found hold in one of its beady black eyes. "Yurin, do everything ye can just to stay out of the way, would ye? That petty axe of yours isn't going to equate to shit. Watch the water, and make sure the fish fuckers don't mess me up." Keeping his rapier sheathed, Callahan swapped his short sword to his right hand in hopes that its magical ability to cut through armor and weapons extended to umber hulk hide.

[Callahan] Apparently, my subconscious mind had bought into the barbarian shaman's bullshit about me being chosen by the gods because, against all reason, I charged that massive creature. I'm a pretty slick guy; there are very few people who could've even imagined standing against me, but to this creature, I wasn't but a mosquito trying to bite its ass.

The magic silencing provided by my earliest ring didn't extend to quelling the slight vibrations createdwithin the ground. Umber hulks accustomed to subterranean travel use vibrations as their means of sight. My balls-out charge toward the creature was met by a full-on swipe of its right claw. I tried to jump out of its way, but it was much akin to a suicide jumper trying to dodge the ground.

Crumpled on the ground, struggling to breathe, I tried to collect my thoughts after my impromptu flight that ended suddenly against the cave wall. My wits returned in time to see the umber hulk's claws closing in from either side. I knew that once this thing got a hold of me, I was going to be squashed flatter than a whoopee cushion under a fat woman. Grabbing my fallen sword, I knew I was done.

That bloody moron of a barbarian thankfully ignored my orders. He bounced the torch off the creature's head. Little did we know that fire worked to completely scramble its senses. Rolling out between its legs, I could tell I had, at the very least, bruised some ribs because pain lit my senses from the movement. Gritting my teeth through the surges, I leapt atop the behemoth's back and stabbed. The blade sank in, true to its enchantments. I propelled myself further up the creature as I withdrew the blade.

Retelling this part, I really wish I could have watched from Yurin's perspective as I soared above its head then, with a dual-handed stab through its skull, rode its writhing and dying body back to the cavern floor. As we crashed to the ground, I rolled back to my feet, short sword withdrawing in the process, and roared for all my worth. Turning back, I proceeded to kick and stab the creature's body as I laughed and roared again.

"It's dead, and we have more company, friend." Yurin's voice pulled me back to reality as I turned to see the Narcin returning from the water.

[Narrator] "Fuck me, won't ye all give five fucking minutes to celebrate one of the most awesome things I've ever accomplished before ye force me to slaughter half yer population in what appears to be my last hoorah." Callahan switched his short sword back to his left hand and drew his rapier with his right.

"You killed the great hunter." One of the Narcin stepped forward, pointing at the umber hulk's body.

"Oh shit, fuck yeah. Now ye all are going to bow and worship me, aren't ye?" Callahan still held his blades at the ready.

"You kill without mercy and thought. You are cursed by the gods. Gather what you must. Leave, never return. We will not bother the surface anymore now that the great hunter is gone. Return here, and we will kill." The Narcin turned, returning to the water.

"Yer welcome, fuckers." With that, Callahan gathered his throwing daggers. Yurin grabbed the torch then watched with horrified puzzlement as Callahan used his short sword to carve several panels of the umber hulk's hide away. After gathering several large chunks of its armored hide, he chopped out its mandibles from inside the jawline.

"You are an odd person, Falcon. What, may I ask, are you doing?" Yurin couldn't hold his curiosity in check any longer.

"I would degrade ye and belittle ye, but shit, ye just saved me arse. I'm gathering some materials to craft what I'm hoping will be some really cool bracers for ye. Ye can't kill something like this and walk away without some kind of trophy." Gathering up the removed creature pieces, Callahan painfully followed Yurin back to the dwarves.

[Callahan] The dwarves were shocked by our story and wouldn't have believed it if it weren't for the chunks I brought back. I had the dwarves aid me in shaping the hide down. I punched slits in two such pieces with my short sword. The dwarves then attached the mandibles using metallic wire and soldered them into place. Upon completion, Yurin was adorned with two bracers that had foot-and-a-half-long umber hulk mandibles spiking off of them. I would have kept them for meself, but they clashed with my fighting style, and I really did owe the scrawny fucker my life. On top of the bracers, we had the dwarves fashion chest, back, and leg plates as well. By the time we finished, Yurin was looking to be a rather formidable warrior.

Dwarven spirit shipments having been arranged to begin when the brewer received message from me, Yurin and meself returned to the barbarian encampment. Upon our return, we told our story, once again unbelievable if not for the very real existence of Yurin's new bracers.

"You have honored us, outsider. You have our pledge that anything we can do to aid you will be done when you call upon us. You have brought great honor to my son as well. If it is his choice, we would like to offer his aid to you that he may act as our eyes and voice in your city," the chief said as we stood before his slightly chipped bone throne.

"I accept that honor, Father. I will travel with Falcon, and I will represent our fellows in the city to the south." Yurin bowed respectfully.

"Whoa, what the fuck? Thank you and all, but, um, well. Shit. All right, I owe ye one, so it would be my pleasure to have ye accompany me." I was a bit put off by the prospect of having a tagalong but knew that at least the long days of walking would be accompanied now.

We remained at the camp for a few weeks until my ribs felt adequately healed. During those weeks, I did find several occasions to sneak off with the chief's daughter and even more occasions to tell the shaman how dumb I thought he was. Replenishing rations and supplies, Yurin and I left the camp none too soon. I could tell my welcome was starting to wear thin with the other residents.

A few miles out of the camp, I turned to Yurin and said, "The first thing that has got to go is that horrendous fucking name of yers. From here on in, we're gonna call ye Hawk. Ye'll be my unofficial recruit into the Avian assassins." After a few seconds of looking offended, Yurin grinned and nodded his consent.

So there, Narrator, I notice that interjections are becoming few and far between. Starting to get a bit of confidence in yer writing, are ye?

[Narrator] Oh, come off it, are you really about to psychoanalyze me? Let me guess. This whole manuscript is nothing but some Freudian breakdown of an oedipal complex in which I really just want to sleep with my mother, and I express that through writing about your struggles.

[Callahan] Actually, no, I was going to speak more about how yer schizophrenia has managed to find a somewhat healthy form of expression before ye crossed the bridge to being a serial killer.

[Narrator] Either way, there is a reason I didn't choose to go into psychology. It's all a bunch of hogwash trying to explain why people aren't all alike and why some people are what other people perceive as crazy.

[Callahan] Ye don't have to justify yerself to me, mate. I'm a figment of yer own mind, remember? Besides, ye didn't just choose not to go into psychology; ye pretty well chose not to go into anything.

[Narrator] Thanks for that astute observation. Now can we return to the story?

[Callahan] Not quite yet. Before we close out this chapter, I did want to ask one more question. Did Reader 2 get so put off by yer crazy nerdish nature that she fled, or are ye just hiding her in the wings? Because that whole bit about barbarians being chauvinistic pigs really did leave room for feminine objection.

[Narrator] Naw, she was just too busy doing my laundry and dishes because she knows what's good for her.

[Callahan] Budda dum dumb. OK, now that we were able to allow ye a bad joke, I do believe we are prepared to launch into the next leg of our journey.

Chapter 6

UN NAGA FRUEH

[NARRATOR] "YOU WOULD DISHONOR our newly founded allegiance by attempting to bring orcs into it." Hawk was quite frustrated when Callahan explained their next course of action.

"What inspires more fear in southern humans than orcs? A contingent of orcs at our side, and the enemy will be convinced that Vertigo himself backs us." Callahan smiled his wry half grin knowing that answer would make no difference. The thought of forging an alliancewith orcs was as disagreeable with him as it was with his companion.

"Orcs know no loyalty. At what price would you seek to win your war, Falcon?" Yurin sneered at the idea of it all.

"We do what we must. Please suffice it at that. The quicker we secure this said allegiance, the quicker we can depart their company." Callahan did enjoy having his newly named companion with him. Conversation, even if mind-numbingly ignorant, helped to break the monotony of the journey. He was forced to drastically slow his pace due to Hawk's lack of training and magical enhancements, but even in spite of that, he still enjoyed having a victim to receive his many pointless rants.

Orcs were a tribal people of the western jungles and plains. They had, at the crafting of the realms, been much like the barbarian tribes of the north. As time progressed and they evolved, their cannibalistic ways and darker allegiance with Vertigo warped their bodies. Their skin became a grayish green hue, their teeth pointed and enlarged. Naturally hairless, they adorned themselves with tattoos to distinguish between themselves. The tattoos also held meaning in regard to tribal allegiances. They primarily stayed housed in the west, leaving the borders of their territories to lay at the swamp's edge in the south, mountains in the north, great wall in the west, and the point where jungle turned to forest in east.

Some orcs would extend beyond these borders, but such creatures usually fell away from tribal influence, traveling in small packs scavenging the land. Orcs held a tendency toward enslaving their weaker smaller kin known as goblins. Goblins were, on average, three to four foot tall with a similar appearance to orcs. Far more cowardly in nature, they tended to adhere themselves in servitude to creatures of greater power.

Some of the more powerful orc tribes delighted in locating and controlling their much larger ogre kin. Ogres averaged twelve to sixteen feet in height and also shared physical traits of the orcs. War was bread and butter to all of the goblinoid races.

[Callahan] To put their kind into proper perspective, just think of Vulture and what his offspring, if given generations, would evolve into. I had no desire to have to deal with these creatures but, at the same time, was rather enjoying my sightseeing venture of the world. Despite the treacherous climbs and horrid weather we faced, I had talked Hawk into a detour that allowed me to lay eyes on the northern great wall.

I found it rather awe-inspiring. It stood as tall as the mountains themselves and thicker yet. It stretched on beyond sight in both directions and almost left one with a respect for the gods. Almost, as I've said many a time—fuck those blighters.

As we traversed the rougher climate of the mountain passes, I would occasionally lend use of my gloves to Hawk so as to avoid any encumbering issues like hypothermia. At one point, we came across a wide cave that was tempting in regard to its contents.

No, we didn't get so retarded as to explore it. Ye've read my track record with caves, so we did the sensible thing and gave it a wide berth. As we returned to the tundra, we noted some very large humanoid tracks and followed them, in the opposite direction of their travel, for a while. All in all, the journey into the more tolerable weather of the western plains was uneventful. We spent much of our time familiarizing Hawk with the use of his new bracers.

Who would have thought it, but Hawk actually had an uncanny knack for hand-to-hand combat. Add to that the fatal nature of his new bracers, and he was actually becoming a formidable ally. He maintained his obnoxious overuse of the word *honor*, but in light of the entertainment provided by his ever-present tolerance of my verbal abuse, I learned to forgive him his minor quirks.

[Narrator] Entering the western plains, Callahan and Hawk came upon a small farming community of human outlanders. Each of the random farmers had an odd assortment of requests to make of the two companions, ranging from the purging of goblins and wolves who were poaching the flocks to the random spleen and eyeball gathering from orcs in the forest.

[Callahan] What the fuck? Are ye taking a piss? Yer fucking with me again, right?

[Narrator] Yes, actually, I am. If this ever does become a video game, then that is most likely what would occur, so we may as well get ye prepped for it, eh?

[Callahan] No. No, we shouldn't. I think it's a wretched and pointless idea now. Later, I'm sure I'll just think it's even worse. Pointless grinding sessions toward the end of gathering singular organs seems extremely wasteful and mind-shatteringly retarded. Besides, in this time in the history of Calarr, humans had yet to try to establish any set societies this far from civilized lands. Any homesteaders in these parts knew how to survive in the wilds, hated visitors of any kind, and reproduced in a much similar manner to yer Appalachian people. Yes, that was an incest joke.

Actually, as I stated earlier, our trip into the western plains was uneventful. After a bit of traveling, we did come across some tracks that appeared to be made by goblins. Following the tracks, we came upon a small encampment of six goblins all huddled around a foul-smelling cauldron containing an undefined stew. The creatures squeaked and grunted in their goblinoid tongue. This brought to memory my failure in the regard to speaking elven. I came to the recognition that negotiations on this leg of the journey were most likely going to run into some slight communication hiccups. So I decided to communicate as I best knew how. Four throwing daggers and a rapier thrust later, Hawk had pinned the last surviving goblin to the dirt using his umber hulk mandible bracers crossed above its neck.

"You no kill. Please. Mercy." The squeaky voice grated on my ears, but it was a necessary evil. At least, with that small bit of speech, I knew it had a rudimentary understanding of the common language. In other words, "it speak a good Engrish." For those equal rights nazis out there that would get up in arms because I refer to English as the common tongue, get over yerselves. In Calarr, humans held a primary language, and being that we existed in the human realm, it was called the common language. Many of the different factions of humans had secondary tribal languages, but what you would call English was the primary. On top of that, my narrator only speaks English, so if ye don't like it, get a translator.

[Narrator] "Listen, ye smelly little blighter, yer gonna find the nearest tribe of orcs and establish a meeting for me." Callahan stood over the goblin's head, watching it squirm uncomfortably under Hawk.

"Want to meet orc?" The goblin stopped its squirming to give a puzzled look at the apparently crazy human above him.

"Holy crap, this isn't gonna be easy, is it? Yes, I want to meet orc. You bring me to orc. You no speak no more. I like smashing dumb things like this." Callahan, stomping on the face of one of the deceased goblins, displayed his wry half grin.

Nodding vigorously, the goblin pointed at the umber hulk mandibles holding him down. Callahan chuckled aloud. "Hmm, for being world-renowned morons, this little blighter catches on quick."

Hawk shrugged. "Surprising, if you ask me." Letting the little guy up, Hawk and Callahan watched him cautiously.

Gathering his throwing daggers, Callahan smiled at his newest little companion and said, "All right, wee one, though I'll most likely quickly regret this, I'm retracting the silence bit from our arrangement." The goblin looked puzzled. "Ah, fuck all. Means ye can speak as long as yer quiet about it. What's yer name?"

"Name is Hull." The creature made an attempt at a smile that lent sight to his six remaining blackened teeth.

"Let me guess—from the tribe sphincter or some other term alluding to a rectum." Callahan shook his head. "That's neither here nor there, Hull. Take us to see the orcs. I wish to secure alliance with them."

Hull prattled on and on about orcs not liking humans. He spoke of being an escaped orc slave, and he spoke about other things, but Callahan lost all interest and blocked out the obnoxious little thing's squeaky voice. As evening moved in, the clouds grew ominous, and Callahan could see Hull getting highly uncomfortable. Seeing a thick copse of trees, the group settled in.

Hawk understood far more of Hull's gibberish and translated as much as he could. They sat around a campfire discussing orc habits, while Callahan watched the lightning storm around them. Laughing internally, he couldn't help but reminisce about Alliander's demise when a bolt of lightning struck nearby. A bush was struck, set alight, and emitted a high-pitched squeal as it burned, with occasional pops and whistles. The process amused Callahan until Hull shrieked in terror and started chanting, "Un naga frueh, un naga frueh."

Shrugging his shoulders, he looked to Hawk. Hawk responded, "The end times. It's an old prophecy that Vertigo's child on Calarr will arrive upon the call of a burning bush. Plagues will then follow, and the followers of Vertigo will be called to war."

A wry half grin lit Callahan's face. "How much do ye know of these plagues?"

"Considering the prophecy is shared by our people as warning of an orc uprising, I'm pretty well versed in them." Hawk looked puzzled.

Smashing his fist against his chest, Callahan shouted at the sky as loud as he could. "Yes, Father, I hear yer call, and it shall be answered. The soldiers will heed my call or bear witness to yer wrath. Hull, run as fast as ye can, and tell the orcs of our approach. Father calls me, and I must speak. We shall heed his call."

Without question, Hull took off on a sprint, watching well his direction of travel. Callahan couldn't stop his smile from spreading. "OK there, Hawk, we've some planning to lay out."

[Callahan] The tribe's encampment was near a forest's edge. From our vantage point, we could see a vast gathering of the green skins berating and laughing at Hull, who was tied to a post in the camp's center. Two days had passed in travel that, thanks to the ambion herb, we were able to make faster than our little friend. During the dark of the night, I entered the orc camp, stole several sacks and a few other necessary items, then went about gathering some things from the forest. After undertaking some preparations, I watched Hull's arrival and the subsequent ridicule that followed. Not feeling particularly merciful, I waited idly for the signal smoke in the sky, indicating Hawk's initiation of our plan.

Being a bit lacking in divine power, I had to rely on my ingenuity and hoped that my bluff would be sufficient. Striding confidently from the tree line, I walked straight on toward the orc camp's front entry through the surrounding palisades. "Release my herald! Ye dare to mettle in the fulfillment of Vertigo's promise."

"Ha, a human, our warrior guide. That is a joke." One of the guards pulled a hefty axe, and the other pulled a darkened sword, not that it mattered when they both dropped due to my daggers adding an uncomfortable depth to their eye sockets. Gathering my daggers, I cleaned them on their bodies and threw them again at the next two orcs that came into sight.

"Hear me, all! For every one of ye that stands against me, three others will die. I'm Vertigo's son and will be hailed as such, or as yer own shamans prophesize, I'll unleash the plagues upon ye!" Walking on to the center of the camp, I released Hull.

[Narrator] The chief, in elaborate war paint, approached carrying a large scythe. Flanking him was another orc dressed in feathers and different animals skeletal parts. The chief growled in a rough common tongue. "Human, you trespass. You die!" The orcs from the camp started to close in when shouts from the camp's edge arose.

In their growling orc tongue, the mass shouted and slowed their advance. Looking to Hull, Callahan sharply ordered, "Translate, ye turd. I want to know what they are shouting."

"The river runs blood." Hull looked to Callahan with awe.

"See, as it is foretold, I have delivered. Yield, or I shall continue." Callahan smiled his wry half grin. Drawing his swords, he cut down two orcs who came too close for his liking, then surging forward into a small group, he roared. Three more orcs down, Callahan found that he barely ducked a fourth's sword swing. Still acclimating his muscles' motions to the lack of his long-present ring, he found difficulty staying ahead of the orcs' movements. Hopping another swing, he delivered a solid kick to one orc's neck. Listening to the snap, he landed lightly and then thrust his blades forward and spun the orc, now skewered into another. Withdraw, thrust, withdraw, and thrust. "As promised, six dead on behalf of the two aggressors. Now bow to the prophecy."

The orc chief, infuriated by the human's display, raised his scythe and shouted, "Onward! Week's double ration to the orc that brings me his head."

Yelling as loud as he could, Callahan looked at the chief. "Behold! I unleash the second plague." Three scattered masses of frogs soared ungracefully into the camp, one after another, in about one-minute intervals.

Shocked and frightened, the crowd of orcs stepped away from the man in the center of the camp. Shouting at the chief, Hull hopped up and down. "See, I says, he come. See, I told you. See, Hull not an idgit."

Callahan overheard the shaman saying to the chief, "Un naga frueh."

Excited whispers rushed throughout the crowd, but none dared to approach Callahan. The chief, enraged, pointed his scythe at his people. "Cowards, every one of you!" Stepping forward, he looked as though he were going to personally attack when one of the crowd pointed and shouted. Looking to his legs, the chief saw several leeches. Many of the crowd shouted about havingthe same.

"Need I continue? I have unleashed three of the plagues upon ye. Bow in service to *un naga frueh*! Yield lest I continue." Callahan smiled his wry half grin.

Brushing the leeches from his legs, the chief dropped his scythe and kneeled before Callahan. The camp followed suit. "Lord, please forgive my doubt."

Walking forward and looking to the crowd, Callahan used his short sword to swiftly behead the chief. "With his blood, ye all have purchased freedom from the remaining plagues. Shaman, now ye shall unite the hordes."

Nodding reverently, the shaman grunted his assent. "Aye, lord. I shall do as ye ask. But, lord, the prophecy calls that we rise against your own kind with yer arrival."

"And ye all shall do just that. The arrogant men of the southlands are already amassing their armies in preparation to take the hordes' lands. Send scouts, and see truth of my words. Gather the hordes, and in one year's time, yer all to assault the southlands, showing those puny men the meaning of real strength. Orcs are the chosen, orcs are strong. Remind these infidels who ye are. Remind these humans why they fear ye. Rain death upon the weak!" Callahan smiled with delight as the bloodthirsty mass riled in cheer. Lowering his voice, Callahan turned to Hull. "Yer my messenger. Make sure they stay on task."

"Yes, lord. Yes. Lord, don't forget your sword. The plague bringer is yours by rights." Hull bowed ridiculously before Callahan.

"Hull is to be my voice in my absence. He has brought message of my sword, the plague bringer. Where is it?" Callahan no longer had any idea what he was talking about but figured he may as well strike while the iron was hot.

Throwing himself prone, the shaman sobbed, saying, "Oh, lord, we tried. Ssarrin raided us years ago and took it from us. They stole it away to their swamps. We do not risk the swamps so know not where they secreted it to."

"I shall retrieve it. Worry not, unless ye fail in raising the hordes. Then ye should fear the remaining plagues." Turning, Callahan sheathed his swords and marched unchallenged from the camp.

[Callahan] People joke frequently of orc stupidity, but as far as I can see, they are reportedly more intelligent than yer ancient Egyptians. At least they got the point within three plagues. Now to further explain, Gypian root is a plant that shady merchants in the know frequently use to darken their wines. It is aptly known as the blood root. It grows in abundance in these woods, and a smashed sack full of said root is enough to darken a river's flow for about an hour's time.

Fashioning makeshift slingshots in the woods was a bit tricky, thus the delay to our launched sacks of frogs being that finding the right distance between trees for proper launch took effort. The real fun came in having Hawk strip down to go bog diving in order to collect the leeches.

Hawk had vehemently objected to my plan on grounds of the severity of its blasphemy—that is, until I told him of the amassed southern armies. And with a little colorful exaggeration toward the effect of the army looking to move north to the barbarian lands, he found himself open to a bit of blasphemy. Lending him the use of my ring and acclimating him to its use over the course of our two-day travel, he used it to quickly move from where he placed the sack of Gypian root in the river to the slingshots. At the slingshots, he unloaded a sack of frogs and then rushed to the next one in line to repeat the process. After launching all three sacks, he sped on to where we hid the sack of leeches. Utilizing the silenced movement provided by the ring in conjunction with the distraction provided by my showmanship, he spread the leeches throughout the back ranks of the crowd. I never thought he would actually get the chief, but that did turn out to be a beautiful addition.

[Narrator] Walking on out of the camp, Callahan met Hawk at their predetermined place after he had cleaned up the evidence of their tampering. "Ha, beautifully done, my friend."

Hawk extended Callahan's ring to him. "That is an amazing ring, my friend. Thank you for affording me its use. So where to from here?"

"South to the Ssarrin swamps. They have a blade I want." Callahan smiled in the face of Hawk's disgust.

"You know, I'm not as surprised as I should be and definitely not as afraid as I should be. Do you have a plan for this one?" Hawk started walking into the woods as if heading for an evening walk.

Smiling at his barbarian friend's newfound confidence, Callahan walked beside him. "Aye, the plan is to—"

"Kill any who get in our way." Hawk chuckled at Callahan's shock when he finished his sentence. "Delightful, hear that? Anytime I can finish one of your sentences, if you listen carefully, you can hear a small piece of my soul die."

Laughing uproariously, Callahan clapped Hawk on the back and set a rough pace through the woods on toward the southern Ssarrin swamps.

Back in Lados, Namion intercepted a letter meant for Kaville from one of the king's head advisors.

Dear Kaville,

We do not want to see war with Lados. It is only our intent to rectify our mistake. We unleashed this monster upon Calarr, so the king sees fit to put an end to his rise. We have heard tell of some slight insurrection rising within the people. If the people can be brought to full-scale rebellion against the brigand Namion, the king is willing to stem off the war. We would send aid to such a rebellion if and when we could. If such an uprising does not occur, the king will march his armies against the city. Please stay well, my dear friend; we understand your hands are tied. Good luck, and may the gods bless you and the people of Lados.

Sincerely,
Lord Rodiford

The letter's discovery put further plot to action within Namion's mind. He knew that full-scale war with the crown would burn the city to the ground. With the city razed, Namion would be forced back to the seas. His pirating days were at an end, and he would see Lados remain under his control.

Back in the jungles to the west, Callahan was warming up to his companion, Hawk. Lessons in combat, stealth, and other assassin traits occupied their lengthy travel. Callahan knew that his time for this side quest was limited in that he refused to spend a day longer than necessary away from his beloved and ever-thought-about Raven.

With Raven in mind, Callahan was wading through the thick beginnings of the swamp when a drawing and beautiful song drifted by, carriedon a light breeze. Breaking through the thick vegetation, Callahan and Hawk emerged on the edge of a spring. On large green petals atop the spring's waters, three naked women with beauty unsurpassed sat singing a song that soothed even the most chaotic mind.

Callahan could feel the warming glow of his earring and knew that something was amiss. So powerful was the draw that even knowing it to be a charm spell, Callahan took a few tentative steps toward the spring's edge. His actions were brought to full pause as he watched Hawk wading knee-deep toward the beauties.

[Callahan] Referencing back to the tower of Calleigh, anyone who didn't see the whole Kahllorgh shooting tentacles out of the water to grasp Hawk hasn't really been paying attention, have they? Don't get yer jollies up too much, though. Being that the narrator is not Japanese nor is he much of a Japanimation fan, there unfortunately will not be a random tentacle orgy despite the appearance of what could be aptly described as a tentacle plant monster. Of course, watching my newest trainee/companion grabbed up by a beast of world renown immediately gave me a desire to beat feet. As I turned to run, a moral twinge struck me, and I turned back. I couldn't rightly let those excessively awesome bracers go to waste without getting to see them in real action at least once now, could I?

Knowing that any honorable warrior would rush in and hack the vines, freeing Hawk, and as such, leave himself susceptible to the immediate reprisal of hundreds of other unseen tentacles, I opted for the wiser route. Pulling a throwing dagger, I took aim at one of the naked beauties. Their draw and beauty, despite my earring, were still enough to cause my hand to twitch as I released. Some might call it a premature ejection.

[Narrator] The dagger grazed the neck of one of the daughters of Janel. The scene immediately came to a halt as the tentacles stopped drawing Hawk's still-entranced form into the gaping plant maw prepared to devour him. A soft and soothing voice spoke in surprise. "How? So long has it been since we have fed upon a human. How do you resist our draw?"

"Uh, maybe it could just possibly have a little to do with the massive carnivorous plant about to consume me mate." Callahan, free from any mental draw due to the last blade's distraction, prepared another throw.

"Hold." All three of the women spoke at once. The Kahllorgh stayed in a state of stasis, not moving Hawk any closer to his impendingconsumption.

"What's yer offer? 'Cause far as I see it, me mate's screwed. But I'll take at least one of ye binks in price for my umber hulk trophies." A wry half grin lit Callahan's face as, against his better judgment, he withheld his throw.

"Never has a human been able to speak with us. We delight in the company. Please, come be more comfortable that we may speak in length." The sisters seductively smiled as a fourth petal appeared at the spring's edge.

Laughing aloud, Callahan took a second before he could respond. "I'm fairly new to the whole monster-slaying business, but um, no. I'm not fucking retarded. I'll not climb up there to be sucked into that plant's mouth, or worse yet, if yer telling the truth, I'd be stuck here for the gods only know how long, listening to the three of ye dawdle on 'bout how great it is to see a man and be able to talk to him. Inevitably, as what could possibly turn into years passed, ye all would bore of me, then I would feed that great green beast."

"You are wise, even if you are rude. Ssarrin are the only ones we have met that can resist our charms. Yet here you are, seemingly unaffected. For such entertainment as you have provided, we offer a bargain. The plague bringer will be yours in return for allowing us to feast upon this human. So long has it been since we have tasted human." The three voices still spoke in unison.

Pausing a second, Callahan then responded, "That is very tempting, but no. And how, by chance, do ye even know I was looking for the plague bringer?"

"Your mind is clouded from us, but his is wide open. You are an impressive man, Falcon." The Kahllorgh released Hawk outside the spring. Sitting in a daze, Hawk was still unable to collect himself before the presence of the daughters.

Sheathing his dagger, Callahan nodded. "Thank ye, ladies. I appreciate ye releasing hold on my bracers. So how is it ye all came to be in the possession of what I seek?"

The daughters' petals shifted to sit at the spring's edge, adding a bit of peace to the discussion—that is, until anytime Callahan looked over their shoulders at the ever-present hungry giant plant. "The Ssarrin are the only meat of substance in this swamp. So though they are resistant to our charms, they are not resistant to the strength of the Kahllorgh. In bargain to contain us to this spring, they offered us several items of magical nature, not least of which is the sword."

"Hmm, well, aside from feeding ye me mate, can I have that sword?" Callahan batted his icy blue eyes in a mockery of their mannerisms.

"What do you offer in trade?" The daughters looked intrigued.

"Aside from the reward of being graced with my presence?" Callahan's grin did not abate.

"What would you seek to do with such a weapon of power if we were to bestow it upon you?" The sisters posed seductively as they continued the discourse.

"Hmm, good question. Well, being that ye seem the intuitive type, I guess telling ye that I would look to unite the world in worship of Janel is out the picture, isn't it? No, the truth is that I will most likely use the blade to rain chaos and death upon any and all who stand between me and whatever half-cocked goal I come up with." Callahan shrugged his shoulders lightly.

"Take it, and do not disappoint, favored one. Someone is looking out for you, whether you believe in them or not." With that, the Kahllorgh withdrew into the spring. The petals swirled up, swallowing the sisters in what appeared to be flower buds before descending into the spring. As they disappeared from sight, the spring belched forth a rapier of pristine quality. Feeling the blade out, Callahan found himself absolutely delighted despite yet another reference to him being chosen by the gods.

Slapping the back of Hawk's head and tossing his old rapier to the ground, Callahan spoke. "Come on, lover boy, we need to get the fuck out of here before those ladies change their mind and, more particularly, the mind of that giant tentacle man-eater."

"Huh?" Hawk's daze was just beginning to fade as Callahan drug him roughly through the brush.

[Callahan] Gives me a newfound respect for vegetarians. The next leg of our journey was spent skirting a few scouting parties of Ssarrin. My goal having been met, I saw no need for unnecessary risk. Well ahead of my desired time schedule, we pushed further east into the calmer woodlands. In our spare moments of rest, we would continue Hawk's training.

This went on for a good while before just a few weeks' travel from Lados itself, we came upon a small budding township of humans. Being three months from my arrival date, we decided to try our hand at taking it easy for a bit, so we approached the town. A spokesman greeted us as we openly approached. "Greetings, adventurers. We don't get many visitors, especially from the west." Looking rather skeptical and put off by our armaments, the man continued, "We have more than enough trouble with roving orcs and goblins. We don't want any from you."

"Well, aren't ye just the cult of fucking personality. We don't want to cause trouble, and we don't want to do yer orc and goblin hunting. We want some warm lodging and food, and we've plenty of coin to pay a fair rate. Stay out of our way, and we'll stay out of yours." I was tired and in no mood to powder the man's ass.

"Wouldn't last long out here if we depended upon jeweled fairy types to come in and protect us now, would we? If your coin is good, then so is your welcome." The man waved his hand toward their small town.

Veridan was the small town's name. After some getting used to, it was a welcoming community. Staying there a few months, we trained regularly, paid with my coin, and occasionally, just for practice, did aid in stemming off their orc and goblin problems. The umber hulk bracers proved, as I suspected them to be, sturdy, effective, and a really cool method of death.

Hawk was shaping up to be of Avian caliber, but I had other plans for him. I gave him a rundown on some of the Lados dynamic, and he quickly fell on board with wanting to aid the people's uprising in an attempt to bring down my employer. I, of course, neglected to mention the pact and my inability to disobey Namion.

While in the town of Veridan, my attention was drawn to a tall lanky young man named Pellith. Pellith was a universally disliked, arrogant bowman. He had lived with his father, the town bowyer, until his passing. The people whispered rumor of his heritage being half elven. I just had to investigate the young man when I discovered that he paid for all his needs with trophies collected from his many kills.

[Narrator] Approaching him, Callahan could see a grin spread on his face as he greeted his town's guest. "Come for a bow lesson, eh? Well, I might find time, but how much are you willing to pay?"

Callahan met the boy's grin with his own signature half smile. "That good, eh? Well, let's test this skill of yours. Two gold says that I'll best ye in a target shoot."

"You've got yourself a wager." Pellith took Callahan behind his house that doubled as the town's bowyer shop. Four targets were set at varying distances. "You shoot, I follow. Best two out of three wins. Call your intended target, and fire when you will."

"I'll need to borrow a bow. It's been awhile since I've wasted time with such bulky and cumbersome weaponry." Callahan picked one off a rack that Pellith pointed to.

"You break or damage it, and you pay for it." Pellith seemed bored waiting as Callahan tested the bow's quality.

Deeming the bow fit for use, Callahan gave his half smile again. "Farthest target." With little hesitation of his aim, Callahan let an arrow loose, striking the target just off center. Callahan was impressed as Pellith released his shot before Callahan's even found its mark. Pellith's arrow found its mark right beside Callahan's.

"We can call that a draw, though mine is slightly more centered." Pellith smirked.

"Same target but how about, to add fun, we say any arrow that touches another is disqualified. You shoot first, and as ye did, I will immediately follow." Smiling, Callahan was enjoying what appeared to be fair competition.

Letting the next shots fly, both nodded as they hit the center target, again leaving little room to spare. Pellith nodded to Callahan. "Your shot first, same rules."

Again, both arrows seemed to find impossibly small targets, missing the other arrow but still landing in the center. "I can do this all day as I assume ye can do as well. So I'll stand before that same target. Ye take one shot at me, and I'll take one using my throwing dagger. First to draw blood wins double or nothing."

"You're on. That's an impossible distance with a dagger." Pellith waited until Callahan took his place. Firing his shot, he watched Callahan release a dagger. The arrow skimmed harmlessly over Callahan's shoulder after turning sharply when it neared its mark. The dagger, with only minimal velocity, barely made a scratch as it bounced off the top of Pellith's head. Reaching up, Pellith cursed aloud when he saw a small dab of blood upon his fingers.

"Leave nothing to chance, boy." Callahan was flashing his wry half grin as he retrieved his dagger and replaced the bow he had used. "You're good. Why do ye stick around here? Ye could make a fortune in the southlands or even in Lados."

"Is that a job offer?" Pellith almost looked hopeful.

"Well, we'll see about that." Callahan looked again at the target, nodding in approval.

[Callahan] From that day on, Pellith joined Hawk and meself in our training. He was a remarkable bowman, agile and stealthy. He couldn't wield a sword worth a shit, but I saw potential with some work. Hawk seemed resistant at first but warmed up to him after our first orc-hunting party. I explained that if he were to join us, he would more than likely be dead within the year, but he blew that off as an exaggeration, and I found meself with another follower.

The townsfolk seemed sincerely disappointed to see us depart. I must admit it was as I suspected it would be—a really nice change of pace to have my presence celebrated instead of met with terror. I was almost a little sad to leave, but as quickly as those thoughts arose, so did the memory of Raven. *Perhaps someday, I would secret her out to a place just like this*, I thought to meself, but that thought too quickly vanished in lieu of Entearra Gharu.

Now came the task of reintegrating meself into Lados. I wasn't about to barge on home without first knowing what I was walking into. Fashioning a letter and sealing it, I gave Pellith directions to Raven's storehouse. I told him to wait a block away and watch people, especially females. The way I saw it, Raven would either interrogate the boy, at which time my message would get through, or she would kill him and find my letter on him. Win-win situation, if ye ask me. I would hate to lose such a promising young ally, but if it came to it, I really wouldn't have lost anything I was overly attached to.

So Hawk and meself waited at the edge of the woods, outside the farmlands. It didn't take long before a slightly worse-for-wear Pellith returned with a message about Horuce's whereabouts. Raven was unable to get away due to being frequently observed by Talons under the order of Namion. Meeting up with Horuce, he caught me up with the happenings in Lados. At this point, any resistance members that still remained in the city were laying low, awaiting opportunity, for fear of Talon reprisal. Namion had solidly secured his position. Hearing of Hemrick's end was disheartening but, at this point in my life, was not shocking. What did bring me concern was news that a dark-haired female mage had been seen mingling with the Talons.

Not wanting to lend evidence of my newest allies, I got Horuce to agree to secret them into the city. Believing meself as prepared as I could be, I waited till eighteen months to the day of my departure and headed on toward the gates.

While entering the gates to the only place I had ever and would ever know as home, I couldn't help but reflect upon the last eighteen months. Eighteen months of travel, fighting, and struggle, but eighteen months free from the manipulative plotting of Lados. The stress of it all gripped my mind and laid a crushing weight upon it as I tried desperately to shift back into that world of dark mind-sets. I almost found myself jealous of the farmers, peasants, and merchants. Sheep that could so easily close their eyes, plug their ears, and wish all the darkness away by pretending it didn't exist. They justified their plight as being the plan of the gods and could endure untold amounts of suffering simply by imagining reward after death.

To Namion, Kaville, the crown, and even meself, these unfortunate sheep were made to be nothing but tools. The reality is that they were people. People who have been so downtrodden, so absent hope, so lost that they could no longer harbor imagining of more; they couldn't find the strength to resist their tyrants. They didn't stay quiet because they wanted to; they stayed quiet because they didn't know another way.

I wanted to hate these sheep. I wanted to continue on using them as I had without reserve, but I found that I had a need to inspire them. I wanted them to see as the founders of Lados saw; I wanted them to know that they didn't have to tolerate what they had. That they could rise up and be what they wanted to be instead of just being stuck being what they were forced to be. I

Perhaps it's all just rubbish, and this is just the meanderings of one criminal. Only time can tell, eh? Walking through those gates, I should have felt uplifted. I should have felt empowered. Instead, I just felt the crushing weight of the stress of it all. I knew what was to come. My war with Namion and its depths of collateral cost, yet so much darkness to come before this city could ever hope to see the light of peace again.

[Narrator] Getting deep there, eh, Callahan?

[Callahan] Oh, bugger off. I was human, wasn't I? Journeying that long with Hawk, I couldn't help but start to get a twinge of feeling toward his constantly celebrated honor. Honor is a self-defined thing now, isn't it? So all in all, just as anyone does, I was trying to find out who I really was. That ember of my humanity, long hidden, had been given life once again by thoughts of a life with Raven. A life always just outside the reach of my fingertips driving me ever onward.

[Narrator] Back to the city—you married Raven, had children, and lived happily ever after, right?

[Callahan] Fuck ye, just fuck ye. No different than the gods, ye are in my eyes. If I'd the capability, I'd hold ye to account for all the atrocities I had seen and the ones I would see.

[Narrator] Thankfully, you do not, and with that, we will move on.

Chapter 7

HOMECOMING

[NARRATOR] CALLAHAN ENTERED NAMION'S small house to see Namion seated by his fire across from Veracliff. "Welcome back, young wanderer. The important part of your journey has been explained to me by Veracliff. She speaks very highly of you and has decided to join the Talons in your regard." With Namion's declaration, Veracliff gave witness to her tattoo. "Worry not. As promised, she delivered the book on your behalf. As far as the other tasks, did you succeed?"

Covering his shock, Callahan shot out his wry half grin. "Aye, I did, and it's good to see I wasn't wrong about her. Ye see, someone that sad in the sack has to have at least one redeeming quality now, don't they?"

"Ah, you sharp-tongued young man. It is always such a delight." Veracliff winked at Callahan.

"The adults have some further discussions to hold, so feel free to hunt down Raven. She should be more than happy to fill you in on what you have missed. I will call for you soon." Namion didn't seem to have the slightest interest in what Callahan had been up to for the past year and a half.

Upon his departure, Callahan eagerly hurried on to Raven's storehouse. She was there, seeming burdened and jumpy. A weight lifted from her demeanor when she laid eyes upon Callahan, and before any word of worry or woe could be expressed, the two collapsed in a lovers' embrace.

[Reader 1] So is this when you saw your kid?

[Callahan] Do what?

[Reader 1] You're medieval people who fucked like rabbits, and you were gone for eighteen months. You should have had a nine-month-old kid by now, shouldn't you?

[Callahan] Oh bollocks, really? I mean, you're not entirely wrong, are ye? Not like we can go pick up contraceptives at the corner merchant now, can we? Fair question. Suffice it to say that those in the know can utilize certain herb combinations to prevent lasting damage while lending a strong chance at preventing conception. So no, she hadn't gotten pregnant.

[Narrator] Rapier and short sword in hand, a naked Callahan bolted to attention as Owl walked casually through the front door. "Welcome home, Falcon."

"What?!" Astonishment spread across Callahan's face as he lowered his weapons. Raven dropped her sword and stepped out from the shadows against the wall where she had taken position, also still in a complete state of undress.

"We should discuss expediting your plans for Namion's fall. He is going to launch this city into an unwinnable war with the southlands." Owl took a seat across the room from the makeshift bed that had previously held the lovers.

"This is really going on?" Callahan's expression had changed very little as he stood in the middle of the storeroom.

"Eagle may turn, but I cannot be the one to approach him." Owl looked casually to Callahan for a response.

"I'm fucking naked now, aren't I? In what fucking world is this OK? When do you barge in on naked people and hold a secretive life-or-death conversation? My sack is swaying in the wind, I'm staring at my wizened elderly assassin mentor, and the worst part is I'm strangely OK with this." Callahan pulled a chair. "I can approach him. Not as though it'll raise shock from Namion if I'm turned in trying to betray him."

"I'll tell my contacts to be on the ready." Raven sat casually on the makeshift bed.

"The sooner we can figure out a plan, the better. War is imminent." With that, Owl stood up and left as quickly as he had entered.

"Aside from that being amazingly awkward, did anything else about that alert your curiosity?" Callahan turned to admire Raven's form while he spoke.

"Namion sent his best assassin away in the face of war. The guild is alight with whispers and questions. Owl is here on your first night back because I'd assume he sees that Namion is not absentmindedly sending the guild into war. No, he is purposefully bringing about destruction to Lados that will never heal. As much as we are painted the villains, profit as opposed to mass slaughter is the majority's goal." Raven began dressing.

"I know we're in a hurry and all, but it's not like I'm gonna find Eagle tonight now, is it?" Callahan looked to the bed suggestively. Raven, continuing to dress, chuckled. "Ah piss, all right. Something needs to shake Namion up a bit and throw him off his track of mind. Who better to do that than me? I'll seek him out after I meet with Eagle." Callahan smiled his wry half grin.

[Callahan] No rest for the wicked, eh? My peaceful night of copulation blown to shit by the sudden entrance of a deadly old man wanting to talk of a revolution. I sought out Eagle's usual points of interest until I managed to find him atop a building, observing the gate to the noble district.

[Narrator] "Evening, old friend. Long time no see." Callahan announced his presence as he approached.

"I taught you well. Too well, if you ask me." Lowering his drawn bow, Eagle nodded respectfully to Callahan.

"Heavy order awaits this city, and little has been done to prevent it in my absence." Kneeling near Eagle, Callahan pondered what Eagle may have been observing.

"Cut straight to the chase. I've always respected that about you, Falcon. Such talk removes question of your loyalty." Eagle's muscles slightly twitched, alerting Callahan to the bow's readiness.

"You are a highly skilled man and a valuable asset." Callahan maintained a peaceful demeanor.

"I am in it for the money, Falcon. Money follows power, and the power is held by Namion. In so long as that remains fact, my loyalty is solid. That said, I respect you and, as such, will make no action against you or your followers by choice. Know that if I am ordered, I will do what I must." Eagle stayed at the ready.

"Easy mate. I understand and accept your position. You were a valued mentor, and I sincerely hope I never see the day whenwe are enemies." Callahan nodded one more time then departed again into the night.

[Callahan] No more money to be had than could be had by turning in a traitor. My mind was scrambled. Namion had the book and was driving the city to war. Veracliff was an unknown variable in the equation of the game. Owl was pushing for immediate revolution. Eagle was most likely going to turn on me. Yep, it was so nice to be home and at it again.

[Narrator] Entering Namion's house, Callahan announced, "I would like your permission to marry your daughter."

"What?! You just barged uninvited into my home to say that? What the fuck did you get into? What the fuck are you all about? Where the fuck did that even come from?" Namion, seated by his fire, seemed more disturbed and on edge than Callahan had ever seen him.

"I have followed orders and not only survived but have excelled in all that ye've asked of me. Ye know Raven, and I've grown close. Please allow me this favor. Allow me to marry your daughter." Callahan gave a sincere look of pleading.

"You have got to be fucking with me? You, who does not believe in the gods and their power. You, who does not hold loyalty to any but yourself. What suddenly made you think that this is some kind of friendly family environment?" Namion's anger turned to amusement.

"I'm not crafting pact before the gods. As I've said before and will say again, fuck the gods! I'm also aware that marriage isn't but a self-imposed pact of slavery. Raven isn't most people now, is she? I don't craft pact of ignorant monogamy before celestial beings. I craft a solitary offer of friendship and loyalty eternal. I do not wish to envision a life without Raven." Callahan found himself impassioned as he spoke.

Shaking his head, Namion chuckled lightly. "I do not understand you, boy. Right when I am sure I have you pegged, you blindside me with some off-the-wall act. You have probably been thinking about this since you left. You probably ran this conversation through your head a hundred times. What am I supposed to say, Falcon? Am I supposed to play the role of loving father? Young Falcon, I would be honored to call you my son only if you agree to protect my dearest daughter against any and all harm. If harm comes to her, then I want you to wreck unholy vengeance upon any who harm her. Kill them all, Falcon. Kill any who would dare attack my dearest and most beloved daughter. Is that what I am to fucking say, Falcon?"

"Well, is that what you say?" Callahan still looked with pleading.

Long moments passed as the two stared at each other. An evil smile spread across Namion's face as he spoke again. "Yes, Falcon. That is what I say. I order you to seek fatal reprisal upon any who would bring harm to my daughter. I will make the arrangements. Your wedding will be the talk of the whole city through. Leave. I will have details sent to you. Oh, and, Falcon, son or not, pact or not, if you ever barge into my home uninvited again, I will unleash all the horror of Vulture upon you and yours."

[Callahan] That went a lot better than I'd expected. The next few days were bustling with activity inside the guild and out. Namion set up a wedding inside the temple district to be conducted and overseen by Kaville himself. Puzzlement and confusion were abundant throughout the guild. Outside the guild, Hawk and Pellith were getting integrated, with Horuce's help, into the underground revolution. Horuce began jokingly referring to the rebels as Falcons. His intent was to have the rebellion rise up with me in the lead. Once we put down Namion and ended the threat of war to the city, we would then bring down the nobles and lend power back to the people.

[Narrator] After a day filled with meetings and talks, Callahan found himself gratefully back en route to Raven's storehouse. Walking casually, Callahan pondered the uncharacteristic ease with which all of this was coming to pass. As his mind crawled uncomfortably beneath his skin, he heard a call. Focusing his attention, he saw Veracliff walking toward him.

"Ah shit, what can I help ye with, mage?" Callahan looked at her with obvious distrust.

"You should be happy to see me. You still haven't thanked me properly for returning the book." Sliding next to Callahan, Veracliff seductively ran her hand up the side of his leg.

"Thank ye? I should fucking kill ye." Pulling away, Callahan placed his hands on the hilts of his swords.

"Ooh, such hostility toward an old friend. Tread lightly, Callahan. Janel has promised you to me in return for my service. As I said before, you will be mine. I know you now marry Namion's daughter to curry favor with him. When she is out of the picture, you will see my many benefits." Veracliff smiled softly as she spoke.

As his blades started to leave their sheaths, he heard the end of an incantation and felt the dark bolt strike him in the chest. Slamming back into the wall of a nearby building, Callahan slumped to the ground. Energy coursed his body and clouded his mind, draining his energy to stand. "See, I've learned a bit since our last dance, dear Falcon. You may be resistant to my magical charms, but you are not resistant to the other varied multitude of magics I possess. Do not think me some acolyte to be bested by blade. I am a sorceress of Janel and not one to absentmindedly be trifled with. I purchased your freedom from Namion's wrath by delivering the book to him, and I want to be treated accordingly. I know that you like to play hard to get, so please do. Know that, as I have said, you will be mine, dear Falcon. Take this. I would hate for another like myself to get to you. It will ward against magic assaults. Its protection is limited, so do not think it a fail-safe." With that, she dropped a brooch upon Callahan's lap and walked casually away.

[Callahan] Yep, what prestigious man doesn't get wrangled up with at least one die-hard stalker? Mine just so happens to be one of the lead followers of the goddess of seduction and deceit with untold vast powers of magic well beyond my understanding. Gifts from magic users are often tainted, but I could feel the energy from it while it stayed in contact with me, so I took it to the temple district. After spending far more coin than I would have liked, I was able to get reliable information in regard to its legitimacy. As well as had it checked for any kind of tracking or monitoring aspects, which it was found to be free of.

That time out of Lados had slowed my mind and put me behind my game. I knew there were aspects I'd left improperly planned, and I knew there were plots I was yet to fully see, but for some reason, I found myself unable to fit the pieces together. Namion wasted no time, and within the week, the wedding was set to be held. A large gathering hall just within the temple district and it was to be overseen and administered by Kaville himself.

The day of the wedding arrived, and the hall was filled with members of the Talons. I didn't feel the least bit nervous as I watched Raven walk up the aisle to stand beside me. Kaville issued a slightly irregular ceremony in that he specifically cut any mention of the gods or monogamy from it.

Yes, I'm that much of a blasphemous, arrogant arse that I'd make him change the vows. Namion had refused to play any part as had the rest of our associates. Namion had chosen a seat in the front row, which had surprised me and raised my curiosity. Namion is not the type to have a packed hall of people unwatched at his back.

Raven and I stood before Kaville not in wedding attire but armed to the teeth in our usual fashion. We were assassins, not dandy noble people. Ours was not a wedding of show but a wedding of love. Leave the tuxes, dresses, flowers, and so forth for the morons needing to prove their worth and love. For us, all we needed was us.

I felt human. As I stated my personally crafted vows, I felt every word. All the noise, all the thoughts—they all faded to nothing as I looked in her eyes. I hadn't lied when I said I couldn't imagine a life without her. All the other chaos of my existence, the vast insatiable void that caused me so much self-destruction—it all quieted when I looked in her eyes. I knew I was damned. I knew I was evil. I knew meself to be well and beyond redemption, but in her eyes, I found my salvation. That hidden ember of my humanity lit a bonfire. With Raven by my side, I could find the strength and compassion necessary to be Lados's savior.

Then as with the rest of my life, Namion strolled right up at the completion of the service and took a large steaming shit on everything.

[Narrator] As the ceremony concluded and Callahan kissed Raven in matrimony, Namion rose from his seat and stepped before the newlyweds. "Time for a father's speech."

Offering his left hand to Callahan, Namion nodded at him. "My brothers-in-arms, behold, two of our greatest become one." Callahan accepted Namion's gesture, and his left arm was raised to the view of the crowd as Namion continued, "In unorthodox fashion, this tattoo came to be. This young man impressed us all with his training. He impressed us further when he brought down Bradier. He has preformed many acts that have astonished and impressed. Not the least of which, capturing my daughter's heart. So I bestow upon them a wedding gift and dowry." Callahan dropped to his knees, writhing in excruciating pain, as Namion's dagger split Callahan's tattoo.

"I allow these traitors to live." Namion drew his rapier, holding its point to Raven's throat. "Aye, in return for their positions, in return for their glory, they have both sided with the rebel forces. I thought a year and a half would clear Falcon's addled mind, but obviously, it has not. Upon his return, he immediately sparked his betrayal yet again. The whole time, my daughter aided him in doing so." Positioning Raven near Callahan, Namion lowered his weapon and continued, "War beckons from the south, and we need unity, not division. We need strength and prowess, not indecision and question. I offer, as gift of dowry, one week. For one week, these traitors are to be left to flee. If they do not, they are to be treated as would any who would betray us. They are fallen, disgraced, and exiled from the Talons."

Owl rose from the side of the crowd and, drawing his sword, moved to stand near Callahan and Raven. "Who would rise against the whip of a madman? He drives us into an unwinnable war. He leaves death and sorrow in his wake like a plague upon this world. For too long, I have sat idle and watched. Now Falcon has shown a better way. Stand with me, stand with Falcon, and see an end to the madness."

"He has twisted loyal minds. This upstart has spat upon our guild since his arrival. Would you have us return to sailing about as fugitives? I, for one, will no longer slink in the shadows, not when I can stand feared and respected. Look, my men, have I not delivered you to a life where you walk about as though noble? Your presence is now feared and respected wherever you go. Any who do not hold value in that, stay here with the Falcon. Any who would seek to continue their rise under my leadership, let us depart this disgraced company." Turning, Namion left the hall with Kaville in tow.

Vulture, Eagle, Sparrow, and the majority of the hall stood and departed with Namion, leaving a handful of members in their wake. Callahan, regaining his senses, shook his head and, as he often found himself doing, cursed his luck and the heavens. "Owl, what have you done?"

"What do you mean what have I done? As promised, I stood at your side." Owl sheathed his blade and looked to the men who had remained behind. "He promised a week for Falcon and Raven. The rest of us will be greeted with death if we leave this hall, and that is why I prompted his decision toward this very hall. I suspected he would make an attempt against Falcon. In the back of this hall, there is a privy drain that will allow access to the sewers. We can use those tunnels to make our escape."

Looking to Raven, Callahan's eyes welled up with frustrated tears. "This could have been a new life, but instead, it looks to be a new death."

"We will win, my love. It is time for the Falcons to become more than a whisper and a dream of Horuce's. It is time for the Falcons to gain name and presence. It is the end of my father's time and the beginning of ours." Raven looked hopeful.

As the group followed Owl, they noticed flames starting about the hall. "See, they already seek to smoke us out. Quick, friends. Namion is, despite his faults, not a dumb man. He will know I have something up my sleeve, so we must make our leave quickly." Owl opened the drain to the sewers, and the group dropped in one at a time.

As Raven dropped in, leaving only Callahan and Owl behind, Callahan turned to Owl. "Had you left it alone, we could have left. You just condemned us to war. I appreciate your loyalty, but yer timing is fucked."

[Callahan] Swimming in shit, literally and figuratively. Had Owl remained silent, Raven and meself could've been on our way to a new life in Veridan. Now, though, even if we fled, we would be hunted to the ends of the world. Namion didn't directly order my death, so he remained within the pact. He was within his rights to kill me for my betrayal but chose not to. Instead, he was weeding out disloyalty in one fell swoop. He had cut my bonds, releasing me from my hold to the Talons, but that didn't break our stronger bond of Entearra Gharu.

Having used his dagger to break the tattoo, I knew that anything I had known at the time was now suspect to having been read. As we left the sewers, I issued a quick litany of assignments seeking to protect Horuce, Pellith, Hawk, and the rest of what would now be called the Falcons. Raven and I sought out Horuce directly outside the city, where he was staying.

[Narrator] "What do you mean he could know everything?" Horuce was confused as he held his toddler son, while Callahan wrecked through the home, grabbing whatever looked immediately important.

"I mean, get yer previously fat ass moving. He'll be sending a none-too-pretty death here in short order. I'm no longer a Talon. I can afford ye no protection here. We need ye in the city. We need to breathe life into the Falcons. It's time, my friend, the time ye've long awaited. It's time that I lead these people to the downfall of that tyrant." Callahan watched Raven entering with Horuce's wife in tow from the upstairs of the house. "Anyone else here?"

"No." Horuce still looked shaken and confused as he gathered some things for his son.

"Get down, stay quiet." Looking to Raven, Callahan signaled three fingers and pointed upstairs.

Raven drew her sword and headed silently back up the stairs. Callahan drew two of his throwing daggers and flashed his wry half grin at Horuce. "Being that these are old friends, I'll greet them."

Leaping through a front window, Callahan released his throwing daggers, rolled into a kick that busted the front porch's railing, and landed lightly onto the yard, drawing his next two daggers. The first dagger shot into the side of a Talon's neck as he prepared to kick in the front door, and the second sunk into the chest of a man beside the first. Releasing the next two, Callahan brought down the man who was crouched below the window he had leapt out of and finished the injured man. The last two daggers found home in the man leaping from the roof toward Callahan. Stepping aside, Callahan laughed aloud as he heard the thud and crack of the dying body.

Drawing his blades, he chuckled again as a man split from groin to shoulder soared out of a second-story window. Circling the home then meeting Raven inside near Horuce and his family, they left using the darkness of the night for cover.

Elsewhere, back in the city, Hawk and Pellith were playing cards with a few members of the rebellion in one of their safe houses. The front door burst open, and a crossbow bolt buried itself in the rebel sitting between Hawk and Pellith. Diving from the table to the wall, Pellith retrieved his bow and quiver. Spinning from his seat, Hawk followed suit, slipping his bracers on with practiced ease, and brought his shortened axe to bear in his right hand. Several rebels rushed the front door but foundthemselves outmatched by the experienced and superiorly trained Talons.

"Front door's a bit crowded. Let's cover the back." Pellith peeked around the wall then released a shot across the room, lodging his arrow through the eye of one trespasser. "Looks like we're not gonna miss out on the wedding reception after all, eh?"

Hawk had already broken cover of the wall, upturned the card table from his path, and was moving like a juggernaut toward the other two Talons who had infiltrated the back door. Raising his right bracer, he deflected an overhead swing from one attacker while, punching out with his left, he pushed an umber hulk mandible through the chest of the second. Withdrawing and continuing his rush forward, he pushed the remaining Talon off balance. Hawk's right-handed sweep raised the man's sword in a parry, blocking the axe. Hawk was about to release his grip on the axe to punch the bracer forward, but Pellith's arrow through the man's neck beat him to it.

A quick assessment found the front of the house compromised, so the two bolted out the back door. Punching both bracers forward, Hawk then swept them aside, skewering then launching another Talon who was seeking entry.

"Dishonorable wretches, you need cover of night and surprise. Well, come and see what a barbarian is made of." Crossing the mandibles, he pushed an incoming sword thrust harmlessly down then followed with a backswing of his axe, nearly beheading the man.

Clearing the path of obstructions as the two prepared to flee into the night, they were greeted by a gray-haired older man wielding a long sword. Pellith watched as the man easily batted his arrow aside and held his hand up to pause. "Hold, I am Owl. I'm a friend of Falcon's. If you want to survive this night, follow me. No time to explain." Reluctantly, the two followed the man and listened as he filled them in.

[Callahan] Half the remaining rebellion was put down that night, and I suspect it was all because of that fucking dagger. I couldn't tell anyone how he knew, and so many emotions were washing over me I almost lost touch with reality. Keeping my calm and directing the remaining men to the shady streets of the poor district, I secured us a place to hole up for the night in the underground cellar of an old gambling hall that was large enough to hold well over a hundred men. Unfortunately, we were but twenty or so.

I wanted to give a rousing speech to inspire and light a fire of hope, but instead, I kicked a wall and cursed incessantly. I was relieved to see that Hawk and Pellith were among the men who survived. Skilled men were going to be needed if we were to pull something together out of the absolute wreckage that was my life.

"Glad you roused me from the boredom of Veridan, Falcon. Shit is by far more interesting here." That plucky little fuck, Pellith, actually made me smile as he walked about looking as happy as a pig in shit.

"Ye lanky fucking bird neck, can't believe yer among the living. Guess ye earned a moniker, eh? We'll call ye the Pelican." I took a deep breath and let it out as a sigh then made the best we'll-be-OK speech I could muster under the circumstances. "We may not number up. We may be beaten down. We may be straight fucked. But one thing stands to order, and that's that we're not dead yet, are we? Namion has beaten me down from day 1, and every time he's had me with me back against the wall, I've come back with a vengeance. Stand by me, brothers, and we'll do no less this time. Or worst case, we'll fuck their world up on our way out."

"Rest, my friend. I'll go see if I can find any further survivors and check the integrity of a few old contacts." Owl nodded respectfully to me before making his exit. I still couldn't get over a selfish anger toward him casting us to war. Had he just shut up, Raven and I would be well on our way to Veridan already, but then again, I knew Namion wouldn't let me go that easily. Even if Owl hadn't spoken up, Namion would have eventually had me hunted down. No, I would find no peace until Namion was staring at the wrong side of a grave.

[Narrator] Later that night, Owl walked casually into Namion's new home within Kaville's old mansion. "So the pieces are in play."

"Good, I will hold the guild in check. We need his little rebellion to raise some ruckus. As much as it pains me to let him slip through my grasp unchecked, I need him to appease Kaville and the crown. We need his little group of followers to stir things up. Once we have the crown off our backs, we'll finish this once and for all." Namion smiled as he watched the flames dance in his fireplace.

"Those friends of his from the outlands could prove troublesome. They are not the unskilled, disorganized sort as are the rest of the rebels." Owl took a seat opposite Namion.

"No worries, my old friend. I'll put Vulture and Sparrow to task." Still watching the fire, Namion leaned back, satisfied with the turn of events. "The best sheep are those that think themselves wolves."

[Callahan] And where was the great narrator when this shit was going down? Don't ye think I could've used a spot of information like that? Blinded by love and ideology, mind distracted from my wanderings outside the city, I fell right into the trap Namion had planned from the beginning.

[Narrator] Well, seeing that as far as you're concerned, I'm God, I would answer that question by saying I work in mysterious ways.

[Callahan] I really do hate ye. I know that all that is good in my existence as well as my existence itself is due to ye, and for that, I thank ye. But the opposite holds true in that all that is evil, painful, and ugly within my existence is also due to ye. So I reiterate—I wish I could kill ye. Be glad I'm but a figment of yer twistedimagination.

[Narrator] Yep, I know you're angry, I know you're a badass, but most importantly, I know you're not real, so why don't ye just stop threatening me and accept your plight as an unalterable reality. Continued threat against me is much like a dog chasing its tail, all kinds of fun for no practical purpose, and if you do catch it, it just hurts like a motherfucker.

[Callahan] Aye, so next order of business was giving image to the Falcons, and well, being me and knowing that I had at least a week of immunity, I hit the streets in plain view. The others plotted and planned; they stayed low, hoping to outlast the current storm, but I knew better. Namion was not going to let this rest until all who stood against him faded in death.

Telling the others I needed time to think and that I would be gone a few days, I left that next morning. Plans, bah, who needs plans? For too long, I had planned and to what avail? Namion one-upped me at every turn. The only times I managed to gain ground on him were from acts of sheer random chaotic luck. So that in mind, I fully intended on wrecking out some luck.

Many heads turned to regard me as I passed, but few did more than offer hushed whispers. I walked on to stand before my childhood home that had turned into Horuce's family home. It was now filled with Talons milling about it. In a state of disrepair, one drunken Talon who had not quite made it inside during the celebrations of the night before sat slumped near the front door. Hope the poor bastard enjoyed his revelry.

[Narrator] Callahan approached his old home, kneeled before the passed-out man, and grabbed a handful of his hair. Smashing his head into the siding of the home until the siding burst, Callahan then stuck the man's head into the splintered wood, creating quite the mess. The front door burst open as a hungover Talon started growling, "What the fuck are ye doing now?"

Before the man could grasp the situation, he gurgled blood as Callahan's rapier withdrew from his gut. Callahan's smile was one born of pure madness. Pushing the dying man off his blade and drawing his short sword, Callahan walked into the home. A thrust ended the passed-out member near the front door. A groggy man exiting the kitchen gave a shout to raise alarm before Callahan skewered both blades through his chest.

Swipe, thrust, leaping stab. Callahan moved through the house, leaving none alive in his wake. As he entered the master bedroom of the house, he recognized the Talon who had a long sword at the ready. Attempting to surprise from just behind the door, the man thrust his sword toward Callahan as Callahan entered. Stepping back and wrapping his left arm under the man's arm, Callahan pushed violently upward, listening as bone snapped, with a smile still wide upon his features. The prostitutes on the bed screamed in horror.

"Ah fuck, Falcon. Why don't ye just leave?" The confused and broken Talon looked up at the visage of death before him.

"Ha flee? No. Be glad you don't have to watch as I burn everything." With the hilt of his swords, he smashed the man's face until his death spasms ceased. Looking to the women on the bed, he laid warning: "Leave now, or burn."

Walking down the street with a bonfire growing behind him, Callahan got a feeling of déjà vu. A smile still spread on his face, he kept his swords at the ready as, blood-soaked, he walked proudly and openly. Three Talons receiving word of trouble burst around a corner, running toward the house. Ducking, Callahan took two legs at the knees then brought his blades forward, and up he lifted the third into the air, blades lodged under his ribs. Pulling apart and pushing forward, the man dropped to the ground, opened for the world to see. Turning and finishing off the other two as they tried to crawl their way to safety, Callahan noticed the gathering mass of spectators.

"For too long, I bore their mark and had atrocities forced upon me! Now it is time that the Falcon returns the favor!" Fevered madness gripped his countenance, and the onlookers took a step back, horrified by the man before them.

The gathering grew larger as he neared the cliff stairs descending to the docks. "I'll return shortly for those who do not care to follow." A bowman waited at the stairs' base, launching an arrow at the sight of Callahan. Laughing wickedly as the arrow passed harmlessly by, Callahan leapt over the remaining stairs. His feet landed roughly on the man's shoulders as Callahan ungracefully rode the man's fall to the ground. Spinning, Callahan slashed his short sword across the man's gut and walked casually away, leaving the man fighting to keep his insides inside.

The inn closest to the underground training valley was active as was its usual course since the Talons transferred ownership. Sheathing his swords, Callahan set his daggers to purpose as he hardly slowed his pace entering the inn. Few civilians and sailors would go near the inn since it had become a known Talon gathering place, so Callahan felt no moral resistance as he killed anything that moved. In his current mind-set, little moral resistance would have arisen in any circumstance.

Covered from head to toe in gore, the inn burning in his wake, Callahan walked toward the noble gate with a massive crowd of citizens following at safe distance behind him. Approaching Namion's home just outside the noble district's gate, Callahan noted the resistance to be lightening as he traveled. Despite the rage, Callahan kept his mind and vision clear. He noted two men preparing a net on a nearby roof. Grasping a gutter drain and flipping himself easily up, he charged, leaping the distance between the roofs.

Rolling through his landing, he kicked one man off the roof. Turning, the other Talon barely gained a look of terror before two blades wrecked their purpose upon him. Grasping the net, Callahan spun, releasing it down into the next alley, where he was rewarded with cursing. Dropping into the alley onto one of the would-be ambushers, he continued those blades' purpose. Three more dead in his wake, he set to burning Namion's house.

Standing atop a nearby roof and watching the home burn, he turned to the mass of onlookers and said, "No longer. No longer will we yield to tyrants and bullies. Lend rise to your anger. Let us burn them out as they did to ye all but a few short years ago. This city burned once in the name of subjugation. Let it burn now with the flames of redemption."

Dropping from the roof, Callahan was met by a contingent of the Lados guard. The captain stepped forward. "Lower your arms, Falcon. Do not make these people feel the penalty for your crimes."

"My crimes! My crimes! No, we haven't begun to scratch the surface of my crimes. Instead, ye'd have them all suffer the penalty of yer corruption. No, for once, I offer them more than penalty! I offer them vengeance!" Daggers lodged unerringly into the guard's neck and face.

Ducking, dodging, thrusting, and swinging, Callahan came to the realization that even he suffered fatigue if pushed hard enough long enough. A blade cut deep across his ribs as he found himself slightly delayed by a side step. As the forces started to overwhelm him, Callahan watched a rock bounce off the side of a guard's head. The onlookers gathered makeshift weapons as they tore into the guards. Callahan pushed his charge with the mob aiding him. They killed any who found themselves too dimwitted to flee.

"The Falcons will rise under my leadership, dear people. Blood will flow these streets as a flooding river. Sit idle no longer. Pain and tragedy are the price, regardless of your actions.

So rise up, and ensure your reward for prices paid." Callahan wiped blood from his face as he spoke.

The frenzied mass pushed into the noble district, killing any who would stand in opposition and adding a multitude of followers as they marched toward Kaville's old mansion. Rushing up to Callahan's side, Owl approached, saying, "Whoa, what the fuck are you doing, Falcon? Now is not the time for outright war."

"That is exactly why I'm doing it. Fuck letting him prepare. Fuck gathering traitors and amassing more collateral bloodshed. Let's just speed up the process and get shit kicked off right. So grab a torch. Let's burn this city, or get out of my way." Callahan's eyes still gleamed with madness.

"These are not untrained town guard or brigands you march against, Callahan. Currently, there are at least one-hundred-plus skilled and experienced murderers at that mansion. You march this crowd of civilians to their deaths." Owl reached his hand out to grasp Callahan in an attempt to slow his advance.

Spinning the arm off, Callahan pointed his short sword at Owl. "I do not jest when I say stay out of my way. I'll kill ye no less than any other. Aid me, or leave now. I want no further word on the matter."

Callahan watched from his peripheral vision as Owl disappeared into the crowd. Passing another known Talon safe house, Callahan kicked the door in. As he entered to wreck out more vengeance, Callahan laughed uproariously. He found himself unable to do anything but back out the front door as the home flooded with an angry mob busting every door and window to make entry. The few Talons left inside found themselves drowned in a flood of angry citizens.

Moments later, with yet another home burning in his wake, Callahan smiled wide as the mansion's grounds came to view. Having been warned of the uprising, Namion had chosen to withdraw the majority of the Talons from the mansion. Within the hour, the grounds and the mansion burned while, in the shadows, Namion watched from a distance. "Welcome home, dear Falcon. You never cease to amaze me." Walking calmly away, Namion delighted in the chaotic wreckage of it all.

More and more of the city's masses gathered before the mansion's fire when Raven, Hawk, and Pelican caught up to Callahan. "Callahan, what is the meaning of all this? Are you purposely reenacting the terror of just a few years ago?" Raven seemed sincerely concerned.

Caked in blood and calmly smoking from his pipe while watching the masses writhe in fanatical celebration, Callahan turned to his allies. "Look. Look, and see what I see. See a mass of broken people displaying strength through chaos. The bodies in our wake bear the mark of Namion. A few have died to bring this to pass, but we've yet to draw this to conclusion."

"You've done and lost your sense, friend." Hawk looked around him as still more Lados citizens came to celebrate near the burning mansion.

"Or perhaps we've just finally stumbled upon some sense." Callahan climbed atop a nearby building with a bit of difficulty in light of his wounds and fatigue. "People! Are we mad? Have we breached that gate into insanity?" The people turned to attention and seemed confused by his words. "Or is it that we finally recognized that men who do not speak can never know that their voices have been stolen? Is it that you, like I, have grown so tired of oppression that burning all who would stand before you no longer seems evil? It has been brought to my attention that today resembles nearly two years ago when Namion ordered the Talons to set fire to Lados. Does it? 'Cause if I remember, two years ago, invaders burned their way in, pushing us into despair, and today, we start fire to reclaim what is ours. Are we done?!"

A resounding no split the air. Pelican leaned in to Hawk and Raven and said, "I wasn't here two years ago, but looking at the amassing army before us, this is looking to be less like madness and more like prudent planning."

Shrugging, Raven and Hawk could not disagree that the citizens seemed to be more than happy to jump on the bandwagon in regard to overthrowing Namion. Callahan's voice split the air again. "I'm the Falcon. The Falcon is no longer a person but an idea. It's the hunter, it's the warrior, and it's the citizen who is willing to say, 'No longer. No more!' March again, and be one of the Falcons but for one day. Let Namion know his error in abusing ye. Let us storm his underground safe haven and push him out in the open that he can burn in the light of day. As ye see, I'm no demon to need darkness to cover my acts. No. I walk, stains and all, in the light of day. March with me, brothers, and let us reclaim what is ours." Leaping from the rooftop, he smiled at his friends. "Let's secure a solid place from which we can birth the Falcons. Take to the sewers with our skilled men. I'll lead this horde in the front entrance. Flank them when I've got them thoroughly entrenched. Today, we take the valley."

The crowd was riled into fervor. Marching on toward the docks, still more citizens, emboldened by the number, joined ranks with any makeshift weapon they could find. Running full tilt, his three companions went to rally any and all skilled supporters they could find. Having witnessed the scene in person, they could see that not only was this actually happening but there was actually a sliver of hope toward its success.

[Callahan] My wounds were starting to take hold at this point. Delirium had fully gripped me by the time I reached the docks again. It would have been nice had I passed out from blood loss or just been so weakened I found myself unable to continue. But no, the delirium I spoke of was that I believed that I really was a god-chosen savior of the city. I can't remember much of what I ranted while we walked that beach to the cave entrance, but what I do remember makes me cringe.

Whatever bullshit rhetoric was coming out my mouth appeared to have worked, though. Hundreds if not thousands of Lados citizens stormed into the caves from behind me From my time in the caves, I knew there to be only one functional entry and exit, which was the one we were entering. That being said, small air shafts did run near the sewage river, and at one juncture, it could be used for entry if one were willing to swim in a river of shit to get there. I had laid faith that my friends would be willing to do just that.

The valley entrance was barricaded, and as we rounded the bend before it, a multitude of arrows and crossbow bolts peppered the cave. This is when I learned that my ability to divert missile objects did not extend to predicting my erratic motions. Jerking sideways, I placed myself in line with a bolt that otherwise would have missed. It lodged itself deep into the meat of my right bicep. Charging forward, I sliced through wood and armor alike with my short sword then kicked forward, splitting the makeshift barricade.

The crowd swirled around me with such frenzy that many fell off the platform or were pushed from it or the stairwell as they tried to dodge the multitude of arrows raining upon them. Many stumbled over fallen comrades, and with what little sanity remained in me, I called a retreat. Holding in the cavern, I could tell many were quickly losing their lust for the fight. Mobs make terrific shock troops, but I find them rather lacking in the realm of strategy. Short of the few arrows we could return fire with, it became a waiting game. I needed Raven and the others to pull through on their end.

[Narrator] Pulling himself from the river, Hawk shook his head, replaying his life since having met Falcon. He had battled an umber hulk, aided in unifying orc hordes, survived the Kahllorgh, and now participated in a civil war. Prior to having met Falcon, his greatest accomplishment had been not dying at birth. Falcon had given him a new definition of honor, a new sense of purpose, a whole new identity. Hawk nodded his respect at the tumultuous life he now led then aided in pulling Pelican from the river.

Pelican's thoughts upon exiting the river and puking violently were more akin to hatred. He could not care less about the people and their struggle. He thought Falcon's ideological war to be nothing more than an overly perpetuated joke. His allegiance was to himself, and as was current, that ran course with the only people of power he knew.

Raven drew herself from the water, collected her senses, and prepared herself. Whispering sharply, she turned to the others who were now trying to help the prior Talons and random men of skill gathered for the flanking mission. "We need to hurry." Leaving a few men to help the rest out of the water, Hawk, Pelican, and Raven took to the nearest air shaft.

Slightly confined, it was an interesting descent, leading to a fifteen-foot drop to the top of the chow hall. Dropping to the roof first, Raven led the entry. Not waiting for the others, she surveyed what she could see from her vantage point. A good majority of the Talons were positioned under the entry platform, raining death upon its steps. Hawk and Pelican dropped down shortly after her.

"What, ye want to bet at least one jackass will topple down that tunnel behind us, blowing this motherfucker up? Let's get this party started already." Drawing his bow, Pelican watched Hawk and Raven drop from the roof, taking off toward the archers. Letting loose his first shot, he watched it enter a man's back. He was able to drop two more before the Talons even knew that anything was amiss.

Chaos erupted. Men dropping from the air shaft ran to aid Hawk and Raven, who were cutting into an isolated section of archers. Talons scattered in the confusion. Callahan, seeing an opening, surged forward, followed by the multitude. Vulture was the last of the elite fleeing through a tunnel that had always been present under the wood flooring of Callahan's old room. He took a minute to mentally wrestle with his orders. He knew they could have held the valley if Namion hadn't ordered all the elite and trained men to flee before combat, leaving prospects to hold the lines. Doing as told, he entered the tunnel, and as he neared its end, he smashed the support, causing the tunnel to collapse behind him.

[Callahan] In short order, we swept up what had remained of the Talons in the valley. The people, despite their losses, rejoiced in victory. Raven and Hawk greeted me as a champion. Pelican looked quite pleased with himself. All in all, I just got pissed.

Talking to Raven, Hawk, and Pelican, I shook my head. "Something's amiss. Namion allowed this. Why? He had more than enough skilled men to put this down long before it grew into what it did. He's up to something."

"Quiet. You want these people to think that their friends just died for nothing? Turn, give them hope. They need to have hope. We'll figure out the rest later." Raven also shook her head, not at the questions raised but at the multitude of wounds I had about my body.

"Aye, Falcon. I agree with Raven. Whether or not we really gained victory this day, we need these people to believe we did." Hawk stood proudly looking at the underground valley filled with voices of victory. A hollow victory, if ye asked me.

The wounds were weighing heavily upon me as the adrenaline faded. Climbing my way to the entry platform, I addressed the people who had followed. I addressed them from the same spot I'd watched the Talons addressed by Namion so many times. "Citizens, friends, neighbors, we have only scratched the surface of an iceberg this day. Namion will seek retribution. Fierce retribution that will crush this city, retribution that need not occur if we stay vigilant. From this very valley, I'll lend birth to the voice of the people. The Falcons will not shadow their actions or hide from ye. We'll walk side by side as yer force. Let the people run Lados again. This will once more be Lados, the city of the free."

Wounds got the better of me, and I was forced to allow Raven and Hawk to aid me in finding rest. As I lay down, I could hear the celebration continuing. These morons were the blind being guided by the deaf, who listened to directions from the mute. My mind raced at a fevered pace, trying to calculate all possibilities, until I succumbed to my wounds and passed out.

[Reader 2] At this point, you had to at least be grateful that you no longer worked for Namion and you were married to your one true love.

[Callahan] Yep, who doesn't dream of a honeymoon spent without their bride, slaughtering multitudes of men who were colleagues and coworkers just the day before? Oh, and not to mention doing so by starting a civil war in their own hometown, burning places that had been safe havens that same day before. No, the last thing I'd call this situation is something to be grateful for.

[Reader 2] But love will always find a way. True love beats all evil.

[Callahan] Seriously, someone gag her and beat her with a blunt object. Ye blimey bink. Next, you'll tell me that Namion is really just a scared child who needs a hug and some tender loving care. No, sometimes things really are just shit, then they get worse, then just when ye think they're getting better, they get even worse. Ye grit yer teeth, ye buckle down, ye shovel the shit, ye delight in the few moments of life when ye can manage a breath of fresh air, then ye shovel more shit.

[Reader 2] That's a horrible viewpoint. You need to let go and let God.

[Callahan] Henceforth, Reader 2 is no longer allowed to speak. Someone go eat excessively spicy and greasy food, take a laxative, let loose, then drown her in that privy. A mastermind of evil is not only plotting my demise but the destruction of all ordered society as we know it, and yer advice is to just let it be. To any that think that just letting go and letting God is a good idea, please come be my friend. I'm always in need of new puppets.

[Narrator] All right, enough of that. On to the next chapter of our tale.

[Callahan] Aye, let the war continue as we forged the . . .

Chapter 8

FALCONS

[CALLAHAN] THE NEXT FEW days were frantic, and despite needing rest to recoup from my wounds, I knew that time was of the essence. The people calmed after that first day and yet again set to repairing their city. Ramifications from my riling could be seen in the deaths of several Lados guards. Namion was holed up in the gods only knew where. Kaville had barricaded the area of the noble district where he now resided and offered sanctuary to the guards. People citywide were claiming freedom while looting stores, ransacking houses, and killing any who would object.

I'd succeeded in stirring my rebellion but was unable to maintain its harness. People free to do what they want do as people do. They fuck everything up. Securing the underground valley, my allies brought in any promising rebels to bolster our numbers. One such member stopped me and asked, "Falcon, this anarchy? This is what ye'd have us endure instead of tyranny?"

Not disagreeing with his disgust, I could only respond, "Growing pains. Change is difficult in the best of circumstances. They will calm. In the meantime, we need to capitalize on the distraction they provide. They've locked Kaville in the noble district. They've locked Namion in hiding. We need to rise like the phoenix from these ashes and gain our ground and power while we can."

Assembling my closest allies, I held a meeting. No one was to travel alone; Namion would put what remained of the Avians to purpose, and knowing him, they would seek out our head people and their families. Horuce was given a residence in the valley to house his family and was set to task organizing the village's transition to Falcon control. Hawk and Pelican were set to recruit more promising sword arms. Owl and Raven were set to find out as much as they could on Namion's actions.

Ignoring the first of my orders, I headed out that next day to the temple district. People cheered me as I passed—cheered me, despite the fact that once again, I'd aided in burning all that they knew. Reaching the temple of Vertigo, I sought the man who administered the Talon tattoos. A few acolytes approached as I barged in. "Falcon, you are not welcome through these doors." Both of those men went to meet their patron with my daggers in their throats.

[Narrator] As the acolytes fell, Callahan could feel a surge of energy course through the tower. Ignoring it, he gathered his daggers and prepared himself for further assault as he moved down a staircase toward the lower floor wherehe had received his tattoo and once shopped for magical items. "Falcon, ye've spilt blood on Vertigo's holy ground." A dark robed man greeted him by brushing his hand lightly through the air, sending Callahan's released daggers to the wall. "We do not participate in the struggles of your kind. We stay reverent and idle through the turbulence. You risk awakening a force you cannot hope to defeat."

"No. I only seek to end your aid to Namion and his men. Ye don't sit as idle as ye'd like for me to believe. The tattoos are ingrained with power. Power I too wish to harness." Callahan drew his blades and marched toward the priest. A half smile spreading on his face, Callahan prepared himself.

The priest uttered chants and released dust into the air, forcing all around them to turn black. Darkness enveloped the hall—a darkness that would blind any man. Any man not wearing a charm that allows sight in the dark, that is. Walking undeterred, Callahan raised his blades in a crossed fashion, set to pin the priest's neck to the wall. Uttering another chant intended to melt the blades, the priest found himself racked with terrifying pain as the plague bringer reflected the magic. Pinned to the wall, the priest uttered one more chant meant to blast Callahan's body with dark energies.

Feeling the brooch from Veracliff warm as it warded away the attack, Callahan leaned in close. "One more utterance and ye'll be singing yer disappointment directly to Vertigo. Now that we've established that I'm no altar boy for ye to bend over, let's fashion a mutually beneficial business arrangement."

[Callahan] Several hours later, I left with my new tattoo. On my right arm, just above the elbow, there were two black armbands representing my initiation status into the Falcons. Those black bars were separated by a silver one representing rookie status. Above the arm bars, a perched falcon, covering the meat of my bicep, representing full membership, and above the falcon, five golden stars representing different degrees of leadership within the guild. The fifth would only ever be worn by meself.

The lack of regard for his members was one of the things I'd disliked aboutNamion's guild. The Falcons would give credit to achievements through a ranking system. Yes, I'm aware that the structure was exactly the same, being that my say was the only real say. But men with the illusion of hope still have hope, do they not?

As well as the tattoo, I left the temple with a priest in tow. The priest carried all the equipment necessary to perform the tattoo rite for any others who would seek it. I also left with the order to never step foot within a temple of Vertigo again. Killing acolytes and threatening the life of a priest drew the attention of Vertigo's high priest. Wards or not, the high priest let me know, in no uncertain terms, that my presence would never again be tolerated.

My general course of life was one in which most of the things I did should have gotten me killed. I don't know how I got away with marching into a temple of the dark god, killing his followers, and issuing demands, but I did. Much of my life was this way. While I guided the priest back to the underground valley, he informed me of yet another of the tattoo's finer points. With it being a pact between guild leader and member, it could only be broken by the guild leader. As such, it was though the bearer were purchasing the tattoo at the price of a small portion of their soul—a portion of the soul that could not have joint ownership—so any who bore the Talon mark could not also bear the Falcon mark.

Returning to the underground valley, I saw that the cleanup was going quite well. Nothing ruins a good décor like rotting corpses, ye know. As my fellows-in-arms received their tattoos, starting with my lovely bride, I settled in to let my wounds rest. Owl handed me a letter that he and Raven had been given.

[Narrator] Owl looked pleased as he passed Callahan the letter from Kaville. The letter spoke of allegiance between the guard and the Falcons. An allegiance that would be set to cleanse Lados of Talon presence while restoring the nobles, thus restoring the city to how it had been prior to Namion's arrival. Snorting derisively, Callahan crumpled the letter. "He'd have us shirk new tyranny for old. How could I look at these people with any pride if I accepted such a bargain?"

Owl shook his head. "War is on the horizon with an unbeatable army. Do you not recognize that little fact? Now is not the time for pride and pomp. Now is the time to prevent absolute destruction."

Raven spoke through gritted teeth as she endured the tattooing process. "He speaks true. We can't hope to fight all at once. Sometimes the enemy of your enemy must be your friend."

Hawk looked as though he wanted to add something to the conversation, but shaking his head, Callahan waved him to silence. "Other times, the enemy of your enemy is also your enemy. I'll not promise these people voice and deliver further enslavement." Standing, Callahan marched with purpose toward the platform at the valley's entrance despite his friends' protests. As he departed, Callahan looked to Owl. "Let's see what the people say to such allegiance."

Owl turned to Raven after Callahan's departure. "He's going to bring about destruction no less than Namion."

Following Callahan as he took to the stairwell leading to the platform, Hawk asked with a puzzled expression, "Why not tell them of the orcs? Why not assure them that you are not taking the potential war with the crown lightly?"

Shaking his head, Callahan smiled his wry half smile. "We don't play our high cards till endgame, mate. Owl lied to me."

Still puzzled, Hawk continued his questioning. "What do you mean Owl lied? He gave you a sealed letter. Other than that, he spoke of known truths. What did he lie about?"

"I was too fired up at the time. I didn't recognize the warmth of my charm. When I led the masses toward the mansion in the noble district, he told me it housed hundreds of Talons. He was lying. Why and how? The why, I could play off for being an attempt to prevent mass death. The how is what puzzles me. We all thought that Namion had hundreds of trained Talons in the mansion. We didn't know he had withdrawn them. Yet Owl did know they had been withdrawn. That is why it rang a lie when he told me they were there. In short, friend, I no longer trust Owl. I haven't enough to think him a traitor, but I've more than enough to raise question. So I don't want him privy to my endgame." Callahan nodded respectfully to his friend as he made it to the platform.

Turning to the valley, Callahan held up the crumpled letter. "Fellows. Look upon this. It is offer from Kaville. Offer for ye all to return his yolk to yer necks. He would have ye return to bowing before the nobles. This would avert war with the crown. It would aid in keeping Namion at bay. It is a convenient answer that solves our problems." Callahan looked at the crowd's varying attitudes. Some were nodding in approval, while others spat at the ground in disgust. "How should we respond? Should we yield to convenience and ease? Should we recognize that even with such aid, the cost for such an existence will be high? Or should we say, like those who founded this city, 'Fuck yer costs! Fuck yer imagined authority!' Should we rise up, continuing our course to lend real freedom to the people of Lados? I say yes, but I'm but one."

"Fuck the nobles!" a random citizen aiding the in cleanup shouted out. Quickly, the people gathered in the valley shouting disdain for the crown, the nobles, the Talons, the gods, and pretty much anything that had ever been held in authority over them.

"Go forth, my friends. Let the city know. Let our answer sing to the very heavens themselves. Steep will be the price for our insolence, but know that anything worth having is worth fighting for. I'd rather die because I voice freedom than live a slave." Callahan nodded to Hawk with a wry half grin on his face as the two stepped aside, letting a flood of men out the tunnel.

"This is going to restart the rioting up top." Hawk looked a little dejected.

"Aye, and so long as the people are in riot, Kaville and Namion will lie low. We need time, my friend. Unfortunately, there are times like this when purchasing time costs lives. I'd ask ye to return to yer northern brothers." Callahan started back down the stairs.

"At this point, I'm committed, mate. Where ye go, I go. I'll not turn my back on you." Hawk walked the stairs at Callahan's side.

"Ye misunderstand, mate. Get yer tattoo, then seek out aid. Any barbarians who would like to carve a new life, bring them back with ye. The remaining Avians are most likely already on course to kill yerself, Owl, Pelican, and Horuce. Aside from Raven, yer the closest thing I've got to a real friend. That's not a good thing in the course of my life. Ye'll be their primary target. With ye out of the city getting allies, it'll lend me peace of mind as well as I'm sure ye won't fail. A force of barbarians moving in the city will aid in stirring all kinds of beautiful chaos. We need all the allies we can get. In addition, all armies need funds, so secure the shipment of spirits from the dwarves." Callahan clapped his friend on the back lightly.

As they reached the valley's base, Hawk nodded to Callahan. "Well, I'm gonna get right on that. For their sake, let's hope the Avians don't find me on my way out. They might find that you've trained me a bit better than they'd planned on."

"No rush. Rest, then get supplies for the trip." Callahan headed back to where Owl and Raven were still at.

"Do you have an inkling of a clue as to what the fuck you're doing?" Owl looked irate as he glared at Callahan upon his entrance.

"I've been real nice lately. Maybe I've been a bit too nice. Mind yer tongue, ye geriatric git. Talk to me in such a way again, and I'll make public show of yer lengthy death." Throwing his dagger purposely high, Callahan bolted across the room, crossed both of his sword blades, and pressed them forcefully under Owl's arm as he caught the dagger. Lowering his swords, Callahan kicked forward, sending Owl against a nearby wall.

"Have you lost your mind?" Raven paused the tattooing priest who maintained his quiet during the whole drama.

"No, I'm just a bit unnerved. Owl, I've no bloody clue what I'm doing. Same as when I killed my parents and Selfin. Same as when I killed Bradier and the poor mother. Same as when I watched Alliander pop. So on and so on. My lack of knowing, as always, led to an adaptive process of successful thought. I shine my brightest when my world meets sheer chaos. If this isn't to yer liking, then ye shouldn't have opened yer fucking mouth at the wedding, should ye?" Callahan stood at the ready, prepared to end Owl at the first sign of aggression.

"Your intent is just and worthy of following. I merely question your means. Mind that you don't become that which you hate, dear Falcon." Hands in plain sight, Owl shifted toward the room's door.

"Pelican!" Callahan called out loudly over his shoulder. A few moments later, the lanky young man rushed into the room.

Pelican stopped as he saw the scene before him. "Whoa, having fun again without inviting me?"

"No one is to travel alone. I would hate for the Avians to catch ye unaware. Travel with Owl. He'll show ye the ropes. Introduce ye to a few contacts and so forth. Stick to him as if ye were his shadow." Callahan, sheathing his blades, gave Owl a dismissive scowl.

After the two departed, Raven's look bore through Callahan as he spread a wry half grin. "Fear not. This too will pass. Owl is to be watched. I no longer trust him. Pelican's just as likely to turn, so I may as well group them. Any transition is turbulent. It's not as though we are changing the gate guard, is it? We're changing the whole governmental structure and mind-set of a long-subjected people. It's gonna cost a very dear price. We need to continue to sow seeds of doubt and fear into our enemies. Make them question my plans and motives. The more off guard and confused they are, the more they will doubt themselves. The greatest weapon against any enemy is that enemy themselves. Turn them against themselves, and win not by force but by insidious infection of the mind. I do to them no more or less than has been done to me."

Raven still looked skeptical. "You doubt Owl yet speak of strategy before a priest we do not know?"

"Ha, I've crafted pact with the high priest. He'll keep his tongue." Callahan smiled wickedly at the priest, who looked more than a little uneasy.

"I don't know nor do I want to know what it is to crawl in that mind of yours." Raven looked almost apologetic.

"Too much to get done, far too little time. Just be glad this mind sets itself to purpose on yer side of the field." Callahan motioned the priest to continue, gathered his dagger from where Owl had dropped it, kissed his wife lightly, and then departed.

[Callahan] The rebellion rose to paramount levels, gained their voice, and deemed me king. All was perfect, and we lived happily ever after.

[Narrator] Pretty sure that's not true.

[Callahan] Well, it should have been.

[Narrator] Anticlimactic, wouldn't ye say? And it leaves thousands of unanswered questions.

[Callahan] I don't really care for the answers to those questions, so as far as I'm concerned, the ending I outlined is just fine.

[Narrator] Get off it already, mate, and get on with it.

[Callahan] Bah, fine. The narrator's not lying. That's fucking bollocks now, isn't it? Nope, like just about every other plan of mine, it all went to shit. People—by *people*, I mean humanity as a whole—are fucking stupid. They didn't go into the noble district and steal from people who had shit worth stealing. No, they stayed in the poorer districts. They stole from each other, they killed each other, and in short order, I was turned from hero into villain. With the anarchy I gifted to them, did they revel in the beauty of pure freedom? No, these mongoloids gathered around people who exhibited strength, forming, within only a few days, a pseudofeudal system. The city of Lados, instead of becoming a city of the free, turned into a plethora of small gangs.

At this point, I did what any good man should do. What any good husband should do. I left it all up to my wife to clean up now, didn't I? Fuck, I mean, a husband's job is to cause chaos and turbulence, while the woman behind him cleans up his wreckage. Isn't it?

Now this next part gets a bit confusing. Calarr's histories would tell ye that I went to the city surface and observed for the next day. Then under my guidance, the Falcons forged an alliance with Kaville. My mind, being changed by the above, outlined chaos. Namion's Talons rose back in force, and soon, the nobles, the Falcons, and the Talons forged a turbulent triangular power struggle. This was the state of affairs that existed when an envoy from the crown came to investigate the city. The envoy's report would decide whether or not the king would go through with his declaration of war against Lados.

As I said, that is how history is told. The truth is that after a day of observing the surface, I felt a terrible fever gripping me—a fever of hatred toward humanity. I returned to the entry platform of the underground valley and called attention to all who would listen. Being that it was the wee hours of the morning, about three people heard my weak shout, one of whom was Horuce, who was having difficulty sleeping. Now my memory is real foggy about the next part, but apparently, my fever was not of hatred but of infection. My wounds, left untreated, had festered and had infected me, damn near causing my death.

Under the influence of the near-fatal infection, I apparently waited till about four in the morning to shout out to the whole underground. When I was satisfied that people could hear me, I said something to the effect of being the illegitimate son of Zen, the god of chaos. I then said that my father was burning his way through my flesh to wreck death on all the unbelievers. I stripped off my clothes and equipment. Then I urinated off the platform, stating that I must purge the human from me, and proceeded to attack Horuce with my genitalia when he attempted to calm me. Waving my genitalia viciously at all we passed, Horuce had to drag me bodily to where Raven was staying.

Raven and Horuce secreted me away to some healers. The healers strapped me to a bed. That bed and a room set up for those who are mentally unstable became my home for the next few months. The healers had a fuck of a time with my infection and said that they had never seen anyone that sick recover. They made the mistake of telling me the gods must be watching over me, and even when my full cognitive capabilities returned, I still found myself strapped to a bed.

During that time, Hawk made the journey to the north, secured the dwarven ale shipments, and gathered some of his barbarian brothers. Unfortunately, they only numbered twenty-eight in total—a solid addition to the Falcons, no doubt, but not a real solution to any problems that existed.

While I was under the constant watch of the healers, Raven took control of the Falcons, telling everyone else that I was with Hawk in the north, securing aid. In my absence, Raven, with aid from Owl, accepted the treaty with Kaville. They did so because the feudal gangs I spoke of earlier quickly turned to using the Falcons as a scapegoat for the problems of the city. They were going to march on the underground valley until under the treaty, the guard and Falcons rose up together, reestablishing some semblance of order.

The Talons rose again from the merchant's district, and the fight for territory and following was on. With Falcon aid, Namion's men were held in check by the guard. Within two short months, Lados came under the guide of their own noble system—a noble system being contested and guided from two sides, the Falcons and the Talons.

This was in no way what I had envisioned or what I wanted. Thankfully, I had been locked away because, to top off the infectious insanity, I had a nervous breakdown. Despair and hopelessness gripped me because I realized Namion was right. My ideology of true freedom would never be more than a whisper in the wind. People didn't want freedom. They wanted the illusion of freedom. Freedom came at far too steep a cost. Freedom took compassion, hope, love, and responsibility in the form of personal accountability. That, unfortunately, was beyond the capacity of most mortal men. Most mortal men needed great imagined celestial janitors to absolve them of all personal accountability.

I was jaded and near broken. Horuce and Raven would come visit me whenever they could to give me vague updates. When I pressed for more information, they would tell me that I couldn't be upset. Upon Hawk's return, he too started visiting me. Being brought up to date by Raven, he played into the story of my absence by saying that I'd taken a side trip with a promise to return soon. It was all a weak story, but they didn't really leave room for people to question.

During such a visit from Hawk, he informed me of the crown's envoy.

[Narrator] Hawk paced the room in which Callahan was being held. "Envoy arrived from the crown today. Under pact of truce, he is meeting with Kaville, Namion, and asked to meet with you, but Owl intends to speak in your stead. I understand the decisions they have made thus far, but isn't it about time we get back on track? They're speaking of a citywide truce in which territorial lines would be drawn. They intend to make Namion and yourself nobles. Representatives within Kaville's government. Are you about done playing dead? Are you going to continue to sit here whining like a child pulled from tit? Or can we hold out hope that we might see Falcon rise again?"

"Does anyone know about the orcs, and more importantly, do we know about the orcs?" Callahan shook his head as though trying to clear the fog.

"My brothers in the north have heard tell that the orcs are massing in record numbers. No one is sure why yet, and no, no one here has heard of their rise." Hawk looked hopeful.

"I need to find a way out of here and grab my gear." Callahan stood up, assessing the room. "OK, ye'll call out to the healers. I'll hide behind the door. No, I'll call, ye'll hide. No, I'll play dead, and ye—"

"Gear's in the hall. I paid the healers. Raven knows I'm coming to wake your ass up. Owl still doesn't even know where you buggered off to, and the meeting is in only a few hours. So you don't have time to think. You don't have time to second-guess. You only have time to get your gear on and make a Falcon-worthy appearance." Hawk smiled and opened the door as Callahan hurriedly donned his gear.

After donning his gear, Callahan gave Hawk his wry half grin. "I need directions to this meeting." Defeating Hawk's questioning look before a word could be formed, Callahan continued, "Ye'll need to organize the guild and quickly. Set the underground valley's entrance to collapse, secure passage through the sewers till we can craft a better way. If they were unhappy with me before, they're going to be out for blood with a vengeance in record numbers after today."

Hawk's look of approval turned to one of worry. "You're still not all there, are you, mate?"

"Have I ever been? Don't worry, mate, I've a horrible plan that'll go all wrong, and we'll come out the better for it in the end. Let's make these fuckers sweat, eh, mate?" His wry half grin spread to a full-blown smile.

Hawk gave directions, then rushed to task. Callahan covered the distance to the meeting as quickly as he could. Reaching a few blocks from his destination, Callahan ripped the right sleeve from his shirt, proudly displaying his tattoo. He cautiously watched all angles in case of an ambush but was met with no resistance until he made it to the front entrance.

"Halt, no one's to enter until . . . Falcon. Well, fuck me. Go on." The guard at the entrance stood aside in shocked admiration as Callahan passed. "Um, sorry to be a bother. I almost forgot. No one's to carry weapon into the meeting."

"Tell them I killed ye. That's why ye couldn't take 'em." With a wry half grin, Callahan carefully watched the guard's confused reaction. "They're coming in with me. I'm going to put them to purpose. I don't want to hurt either of ye guards. Despite all appearances, I really do want peace for Lados. So craft a quick story, step forward so I can knock ye out, or die trying to raise alarm."

"Uh . . ." Both guards looked very close to urinating themselves.

"Really. They set the two of ye jabbering morons to guard something this important. Looks to me like they wanted someone to get in." Giving another few seconds, Callahan leaned forward and, in a harsh whisper, exclaimed, "BOO!" The two men scrambled over each other as they fled. Drawing a throwing dagger in each hand, Callahan slid them up, concealing them with his palms.

Walking proudly into a large dining hall with a long square table, Callahan took a quick assessment of all present. The envoy was at the head of the table, Namion at the far end of the table, and on either side, Kaville and Owl. No guards were seen present.

"Wow, ye blighters actually respected a no-arms pact." Callahan nodded to the room.

"Falcon . . ." Owl looked puzzled. Namion grinned, Kaville cringed, and the envoy turned with an infuriated look.

"Shame I didn't think to do this sooner. But, Owl, have ye been conspiring with Namion?" A wry half grin lit Callahan's face.

"Yes." Owl didn't hesitate.

"Good, at least I know where we stand. Pleasure to see ye as always, Namion." Callahan shook his head slightly.

"Who do you think you are? Stand down and give those weapons to the front guards. Wait till the king hears of this affront. Do you want open war?" The envoy, still flustered, shook his head angrily at Callahan's impertinence.

"Believe it or not, the Falcons will honor our treaty with ye, Kaville." Callahan stepped forward behind the envoy. "To answer yer question, little man, yes, I do want war." Thrusting a throwing knife through the back of the envoy's skull and waggling its tip out his mouth at Namion, Callahan launched the second at Owl and dove headlong out the nearest window.

Running full tilt, he could hear shouts of alarm rising behind him. Laughing aloud, Callahan couldn't believe the ease of it all until an arrow struck the ground just before him, tripping him up. Rolling through the fall, Callahan came to his feet with two daggers in hand. Scanning the rooftops, he found that his target was concealed. Preparing to bolt for a nearby alley, Callahan thought of the bolt that had nearly cost him his life. He instead stood frozen in place. A second arrow soared by right where his head would have been had he moved.

"Ha, you sneaky bastard." A voice called out to him from the second shooter's location.

"Pelican, and we had just started to become such good friends." Callahan, calming down, walked to the nearby sheltering alley. "Eagle, I presume yer up there too, eh, mate?" Cursing his luck, Callahan knew it had been too easy.

The darkness of the alley's shadows shifted ever so slightly before Callahan. Looking, Callahan could see nothing, even with his night vision. "Quiet, Vulture and Sparrow wait on the other side of this alley. You must trust me. Remove the brooch I gave you, and step into the shadow."

Stepping into the enveloping darkness, Callahan removed the brooch then phased through the wall. Following Veracliff's lead in silence, Callahan spewed a whole litany of obscenities within his mind. Eagle, Pelican, Vulture, Sparrow, and Veracliff—Namion really had expended no shortage of effort on this one. "The mistress promised you to me. I'll lead you out of this, and in return, you'll accept me as a new ally." Veracliff, in her sheer gown, would be a vision of beauty to any but Callahan.

"Fuck, just fuck, and another double dose of fuck. OK." Shaking his head and glaring at the ground, Callahan then nodded at Veracliff. Veracliff chanted and sprinkled Callahan with dust. On he followed as she weaved spells to conceal them and phase them through solid walls until, a few streets over, they were once again able to run.

"Its yer turn to follow if ye want me to hold my end of the bargain. Keep up because they're going to raid the underground, and we have to beat them there." Callahan was running as fast as he could go, and due to some magic, Veracliff kept pace right behind him.

Back in the meeting hall, Namion laughed aloud as Callahan burst out the window. "He is gone. If he does show

224

up, even he will see the prudence in a temporary treaty to forego open war. He is under control. Owl, my dear friend, did I not tell you? You cannot control chaos. You can merely hope to guide it." Namion's expression went cold as he drew his dagger and rapier.

"Namion, how could I plan that? It's suicide." Owl shuffled back across the floor from where he had dove to dodge Callahan's dagger, not even daring to reach for his sheathed long sword.

"You could not. I sympathize with your position. You know how I take failure. What is done is done. Get up. It is beneath a man of your caliber to grovel." Sheathing his blades, Namion turned his glare on the still stunned and motionless Kaville. "You are lucky that you may still serve my purpose. Prepare your people for war." Waving dismissal, Namion delighted in the noble's scrambled flight from the room.

"Owl, prepare six ships. Have them wait off the northern coast. If war cannot be averted, we will use them to return to the old life." Namion waved dismissal toward Owl. Standing alone in the hall, Namion spoke out loud to himself as if addressing Callahan. "Falcon, my boy, you still amaze. Though it would destroy everything, you risk it just to put me in a bind. There might be hope for you yet. The game has once again come to life, eh, Falcon?"

[Reader 1] Whoa! What the fuck, man? You said everyone was unarmed, yet Namion drew his weapons, and you made mention of Owl's long sword being sheathed.

[Callahan] They're assassins. At least they appeared unarmed, but in my defense, the envoy and Kaville were unarmed.

[Narrator] Arriving on the beach, Callahan could hear the rallying cry of anger echoing from the city. Rushing onto the entry platform, Callahan and Veracliff found Raven, Hawk, and Horuce waiting. "Who's this?" Raven looked at Veracliff.

"Veracliff. Not to be trusted. Hurry. Secondary passage?" Short of breath, Callahan frantically fought to collect his thoughts.

"What did you do?" Horuce looked horrified.

"Shut up. Collapse the tunnel now. Secondary passage? Have you secured the sewage tunnel?" Callahan grabbed Hawk.

"No, we sealed it. Ran a rope ladder to the top of the air shaft instead. It comes out amidst the cliffs. Its location will be unknown to the old Talons. We left the old escape route sealed. The air vent will be the only way in and out." Hawk shook off Callahan's grasp.

"Owl and Pelican have yet to return." Raven looked at Callahan as though seeking an answer.

"They betrayed us. Collapse the cave!" Callahan watched as Veracliff turned and chanted. Throwing a black dust into the cavern, Veracliff and the group watched as a swirling darkness worked itself into the cracks of the weakened tunnel, then a rumbling shook the valley.

Running to the valley's base, the group, now being joined by the entire valley's populace, watched the main entrance crumble closed in a mass of rubble. Horuce looked to Callahan with surprise. "They betrayed us?"

"Come on now. Really! They don't call us a fucking thief's guild because of our philanthropy. Anyone here who is shocked by Owl and Pelican's betrayal, please do me a favor, and sit upon a full-sized spear. Now I want a full-time watch on the top of that air shaft starting ten minutes ago." Callahan started marching toward the armory to replenish his daggers.

"Hey, I think we all deserve a little explanation." Raven looked frustrated.

"Owl spoke out at our wedding to force us into war against Namion. He did so on Namion's request. Falcons allied with Kaville's guard would lend show to the crown that there was sufficient force to keep Namion in check. With Namion in check, the crown would be forced to honor its old alliances with the people of Lados, thus no war. Pelican is a shifty shit, and he's been so since the beginning. I knew he would turn on me the first chance he got. Veracliff is a random dark priestess whore from Calleigh that I racked it out on to gain aid in the tower. She is now lead stalker number 1, but she did just save my ass from the entire collective of the new Avian assassins. I killed the crown's envoy to ensure war with the crown." Callahan spoke in such a tone that all present could hear his words.

"You're still mad?" Horuce spoke in a low tone so as not to be heard by any but Callahan himself.

"Any who attempt to leave without my permission will die! I want Lados to thrive. I want Lados to see functional freedom. I want a lot of things, but for right now, I just want a few minutes of fucking peace. Fear not, friends. As I always have, I'll get us through this. I'm not without my own tricks." Lowering his voice, Callahan turned to his close friends. "Hawk, give Veracliff a tour, and keep a close eye on her. Raven, Horuce, join me, please."

Callahan looked at his friends. "I'm sorry I haven't had a single moment to collect meself, more or less catch ye all up. When I did have time, I was a bit preoccupied with madness. *Un naga frueh.* The orc hordes are amassing in record number prepared for an all-out raid of the southlands. We need only maintain the city's security until the armies are withdrawn inthat regard. I'm a bringer of chaos, death, and destruction. Every time I've tried to lead, people have died in mass numbers. Leadership is best left to those with the heart for it. I'm a hunter, so on the morrow, I'm gonna go catch me a few birds. Care to join me, dear? Horuce, you lead the Falcons. They're your men. Ye'll yield to me, but in all matters not commanded by myself or Raven, you've the say." Callahan gave his wry half grin. "Now let's find that witch before she turns Hawk into some kind of amphibian."

Horuce stayed behind, shocked by the course his life had taken. Lazy fat guard to renowned captain to disgraced outcast to a general in a pseudomilitaristic thief's guild. Horuce chuckled as he quietly whispered, "Still love the shit out of ye, mate."

Raven leaned in to Callahan as they walked. "So she is a looker. You cheated on me with her while you were gone, eh?"

"Oh, get off it. How many did ye rack up doing what ye had to do while I was gone?" Still grinning, Callahan shook his head.

"Eight." Raven shrugged her response.

"Bah, far as I see it, that makes us even. I did two. One just won't stop following me. So we'll call that even for yer other six, how 'bout that?" Callahan playfully pushed Raven.

"You push a hard bargain, but sure." Raven dove onto Callahan, wrestling with him.

A light faked cough alerted them to company as they prepared to go full market on each other. "Sorry, mate, wanted you to know that watch is set. One of my brothers. No offense, but until we figure who we can trust, I put more faith in barbarian honor than guild loyalty." Hawk nodded respectfully toward Callahan.

"Leave it to a barbarian to interrupt a performance just as it's getting good." Veracliff stood with a longing gaze placed upon Raven.

"Mm, well, perhaps we can speak, you and me? Callahan may continue said performance later, and since we must keep you under watch, where better to do so?" Raven gave Callahan one more playful shove as she escorted Veracliff away. "The room you so gently took from Hadrick is now our residence, dear. You can join us if and when you're ready."

"Something 'bout this rings all wrong. Not good in the least." Callahan glared at Veracliff from a distance.

"What do you intend to do?" Hawk asked, offering a hand to Callahan.

Accepting the help to his feet, Callahan grinned at his companion. "Well, it's all bad. Nothing good can come from it. So I fully intend to do them both and love every second of it."

[Callahan] Any man who has ever had a hard-on recognizes that the blood that fills the penis is directly diverted from his brain, thus the reason why, no matter how brilliant it seems at the time, one should never trust his own decisions while horny.

[Narrator] "That's not what I meant, and you know it." Chuckling lightly, Hawk shook his head. "We aren't really just going to sit down here waiting for if and when the orcs save our asses. Are we?"

"No, I suppose not. We are going to occupy the next few weeks making sure the people here are well fed and supplied. We are going to put them to work clearing the entrance tunnel in a few days. All of that can be handled by Horuce, though. You, Raven, and I are going to go bird hunting. I want Pelican. I want Sparrow. I want Owl. Most of all, I want Vulture. Eagle will be left at peace unless he deems otherwise. Oh, and worry not, my friend. The orcs will come through for us." Callahan smiled as he finished.

"How do you know that?" Hawk still looked concerned.

"Because if they don't, we're all fucked." With a laugh, Callahan darted off toward the room containing the two women.

"Why don't I find that as funny as you do, mate?" Hawk, shaking his head, chuckled despite his fear.

[Callahan] I may have laughed, but I did recognize the severity of our situation. That is why, despite knowing the dangers of it, I did so delight in my following ménage à trois. Upon our impassioned completion, I lay there with the love of my life on one side and a demon spawned of the goddess of seduction and deceit on the other side.

Veracliff sighed and uttered, "Ah, I do believe we can make this work."

To which I responded, "What the fuck do ye mean by we?"

"Janel may have promised you to me, but that does not mean that I'm beyond sharing." She sounded so nonchalant with her insanity it caused me to leap from the bed.

Looking at Raven with sincere concern, I queried, "Can I kill her now? I mean, did ye just hear that shit?"

Raven chuckled lightly as though it were all a lighthearted laugh. "Veracliff, my dear, it would be me who would be sharing, but you may be right. I could use a magic touch keeping this one in tow."

"I'm delighted that you're not as difficult to communicate with as our loving Falcon." Veracliff leaned in to snuggle with Raven.

"You have got to be fucking kidding me. This is a nightmare, right?" Then it clicked. Ye have to remember, I'm not overly familiar with the workings of magic. "Veracliff, have ye placed a magical charm upon Raven?"

"No, of course not, my dear." There we had it. Obvious though it may have been to anyone reading our fine story, as I stated earlier, erections cause a temporary state of retardation. Oh, and before ye ask, yes, I do make habit of keeping my jewelry on at all times. Unfortunately, though, my brooch was upon my shirt, so as it sat, I had no defense against any potential magical assault.

"Good, well, I need a breather. Ye all ladies don't get started again without me, eh." I started donning my clothing. "Think I'll check on the air duct and make sure our entry is still secured."

"Stop moving now. I would hate to have something unfortunate occur to your wife." Looking right through my feigned surprise, she continued, "You are not the only one adept at catching deception. I told you, you would be mine. I'm willing to share, but you need to be a whole lot nicer to receive such a gift from me."

My hand upon one of my throwing daggers, I paused. "One slight hiccup that sounds like chanting and I'll have me dagger through yer windpipe."

"Calm yourself, Callahan. Veracliff has done business with my father for years. I'm well aware of her dusts and charms. She tried to weave a charm on me, but we nipped that in the bud. I didn't survive all these years because I needed a man to protect me now, did I?" Raven chuckled a bit. "You are right. Veracliff can't be fully trusted and she isn't completely harmless, even without her spell components, but for the meantime, I'm confident she means us no harm."

"Is she under yer charm now, Veracliff?" I didn't know what to believe.

"No." Veracliff's simple response rang true but did little to ease my distress. A viper was loose in our midst, one that I had no hope of controlling.

"As I said, calm yourself. I'll watch Veracliff. In the meantime, know that Veracliff and I are not unfamiliar with each other's company." Raven gave me a wink.

I guess I shouldn't have been so bloody shocked. Par for my course, isn't it? Complete chaotic insanity wrapped up in a delightfully horrible package. Needless to say, I didn't sleep much that night. Ha, double meaning there, eh?

The next morning, I went and mingled with the others imprisoned inside the valley. Eighty-plus men and women locked underground below a city that had been home. A home that now represented death to any bearing the Falcon mark. I tried to ease the tension with kind words of inspiration, but it wasn't long before small crowds of less-than-approving individuals were gathering around me.

[Narrator] "What say we just turn you over to them? That's all they want, isn't it?" A man stepped forward, rallying support from the gathering crowd.

Callahan calmly held his hands up and walked toward the man. "I understand yer frustrations. I understand that ye all are scared. I understand that my leadership hasn't been of the most compassionate caliber." Lunging forward, Callahan grasped the man's head and twisted it brutally. A loud snapping sound split the air as the crowd went silent. "But since when is this a fucking democracy! Ye all don't need to understand my leadership or actions. I'm far nicer than Namion, and I really want us to have a say and work together as a team. I don't want to lead ye as a tyrant and a slave master, but at the same time, recognize that this guild was crafted by the act of me slaughtering any who stood in my way. I'm not to be questioned. I'm not to be disobeyed." The crowd started fading back, looking defeated. "Stress is high, and I'm in the midst of enacting processes that will either doom this city or provide an opening for this guild to become a leading power within Lados. I need ye all hardened. I need ye all ready. Walk beside me and see glory, or stand before me and die with the rest."

"Ye can push around these little city folk. Why don't ye try a stunt like that on a real man?" One of the recruits Hawk had returned from the north with stepped forward in challenge.

"HAHA! This is what we need. Ye all want to blow off steam. Ye all want to see some sport. To the arena!" Callahan led the crowd to the center of the valley.

Rushing to Callahan's side, Hawk issued quite the question. "Falcon, now is not the time for further death. Would you mind telling me what you're up to?"

"These people are scared shitless. Justifiably so, if I do say so myself. So what better way to alleviate stress than through friendly gladiatorial competition?" Callahan gave his wry half smile.

"The barbarians will be uncontrollable if you do anything they perceive to be dishonorable while in fair competition." Hawk looked concerned when he glanced from the massive barbarian to Callahan.

Once in the arena, the barbarian shouted to the crowd, "I, Tagrisk, from the tribe of Orridith, challenge this small human called Falcon for leadership of this rabble."

"Seriously. Ooh, this is gonna be delightful." A wry half grin spread across Callahan's features as he handed his vest and swords to Hawk. "To the death, then, ye giant knuckle-dragging numb nuts. Bring to bear whatever weapon ye so choose."

"You come unarmed?" Tagrisk, withdrawing his large double-sided battle axe, looked curious.

"Aye, I'm gonna use yer axe to kill ye." By this time, everyone except the one barbarian on entry guard duty was present around the arena. A light chuckle gripped the crowd in light of Callahan's seemingly absurd proclamation. Passing Callahan's equipment to Raven as she arrived, Hawk moved into the crowd, prepared to take action if things deteriorated.

In usual barbarian fashion, Callahan's large opponent turned to face his comrades and held his arms up as though in victory. "Behold, real strength and honor."

[Callahan] Further déjà vu struck me as I contemplated killing the man with his back turned. It always pisses me off when someone underestimates their opponent, especially when that opponent is me. This was not about victory, though. This was about entertainment and rallying the crowd's support again.

[Narrator] "I've really got a lot of shit to do. So do ye mind hurrying up a bit?" A wry half grin spread across Callahan's features as he watched the hulking man turn and dip his right shoulder ever so slightly, indicating a low sweep. Springing straight into the air, Callahan dropped his left foot onto the passing axe handle while spinning his right into the side of the barbarian's face.

Having lost his grip on his axe, the barbarian staggered back from the blow. Tap-dancing awkwardly while landing, Callahan quickly regained his balance and moved in on the far larger man. Ducking the man's arms as they reached to grapple, Callahan drove two quick uppercuts, one left and one right, into the man's diaphragm. An overhand right to the man's sternum sent him gasping for air to his back. Not unfamiliar with combat, the barbarian rolled away from Callahan, gaining his knees in an attempt to stand despite his difficulty breathing.

Sticking out his tongue and shaking his head, Callahan smiled wickedly. "Come now, friend, let us continue this dance."

Roaring, the barbarian charged. Dropping low, Callahan delivered a sharp right kick to the barbarian's left inner thigh. Momentum carried the off-balance barbarian's body into Callahan, who used the momentum and a backward roll to launch the man into a flip that once again left him winded and on his back. The crowd was on its feet shouting and cheering at this point. Following the roll back to his feet, Callahan spun, lurched forward, and ducked above the barbarian, delivering a sharp knife hand to his throat.

Sapped of all oxygen and strength, the barbarian writhed, nearly helpless on the ground as Callahan calmly walked to retrieve his battle axe. Debate raged within Callahan; every instinct he had lived by told him to kill the barbarian as he had stated, but the lingering ember of humanity within was telling him to show mercy. Mercy would inspire compassion and lend proof to the fact that Callahan wanted his men to feel like equals.

[Callahan] No one's my equal. That's why I dropped that hulking tree sweeper of an axe right into that bastard's forehead then proceeded to stomp his genitalia despite his absence of life. The crowd's amusement turned to horror, and two of the barbarian's closest friends saw my disrespect of the fallen man as cause to rile. They drew their weapons and were about to charge me when a leaping Hawk skewered an umber hulk mandible through each of the men's necks. Riding their falling bodies to the arena floor, Hawk rolled to his feet to stand beside me.

"I lead. Hawk is a four-star Falcon as is Raven. Horuce is a three-star. Ye'll do what we say. If ye don't like that, step forward now and offer challenge, but know that each death is putting us at further risk. When the Talons are weakened and frightened as I intend to make them, we will need all here to be at full strength. Ye want blood, ye want freedom, ye want redemption? Well then, for fuck's sake, steel yerselves to such resolve. Follow, and I'll lead. Question, and I'll kill." With that, I walked over, grabbed my gear, and ordered a few people to clean up the aftermath.

Hawk was one fuck of a find. Ha, hard to imagine when I found him, he'd been outcast for being a sissy. He was about to be fish food for unskilled, awkward fish men. Now he effortlessly hacked through two skilled barbarians and stood respected at my side. Chants of "Falcon!" followed me as I walked to a meeting with my closest companions and, unfortunately, Veracliff.

[Reader 1] So now that you had a bunch of loyal and contented followers, where did you all go from here?

[Callahan] Loyal and contented? I'm not sure what reality looks like in the haze of yer stupidity, but in my world, killing a man's coworkers/friends and pushing them on toward what all perceived to be assured death did little to inspire loyalty and contentment. Now slaughtering skilled men with ease brought about reluctant obedience, but it was far from loyalty. Do ye blame 'em?

To everyone's perception, I'd single-handedly invited the absolute destruction of Lados and imprisoned them underground with little to no hope for a brighter future. Not being one to enjoy hypocrisy, I didn't fault them one little iota for wanting to kill me. If I were to break yer nose, would ye feel sorry for me on account of my sore knuckles?

[Reader 1] No, I'd—

[Callahan] Damn right ye wouldn't. Being someone who doesn't believe in accepting sodomy with a smile and a thank-you, I didn't expect them to. I stood on the brink of losing my fledgling guild, I stood on the brink of losing my life, and I stood on the brink of losing my mind in the stress of it all. My success was dependent upon a whole lot of questionable and uncontrollable variables.

[Reader 1] How—

[Callahan] I needed the orcs to hold off long enough for the armies of the south to march upon the walls of Lados, thus forcing Namion into a tactical retreat, and then just as the crown would endeavor to choke the city's supply lines, I needed the orcs to rise, causing the crown to back down in protection of its own lands. Then I needed to rally people who had no faith or trust in me to my cause of securing hold in the short time of Namion's absence. Aye, it was all a far stretch, if ye asked me. So if I were a member, I'd be really pissed at me too.

[Reader 1] So—

[Callahan] And furthermore—

[Reader 1] Hey, shut the fuck up. You've interrupted me three times in a row now.

[Callahan] Ha! The nutless wonder bares teeth. By all means, mate, please enlighten me.

[Reader 1] How do you intend to keep up the illusion of a hierarchy while locked in that rat-infested shithole?

[Callahan] One plus one equals five, my friend. That is how. I intend to keep them distressed and on the brink of revolt controlled through stress-laden endeavor while showing them one and one equals five. Perception defines reality. Write one plus one equals two. Now turn it upside down, and place it against a mirror. Ye'll have a poorly scripted five equals one plus one. If five equals one plus one, then the inverse must be true, so one plus one equals five. Smoke and mirrors—it's the manner in which any religion or government controls it populace. They state facts in such a convoluted and twisted manner that those who hear it see other than what they should. The fact that ye see a falsity in the form of one and one equaling five does not alter the very real truth that it breaks no mathematical law. The only lie is yer perception of it. So, my friend, I tell them the truth in that manner until the time comes to remove said equation from the mirror and shine light on the full scope of its truth.

But on to functional conversation. What is yer name? I'll warn ye ahead of time. If ye pop off with one hint of stupidity, I'll put ye on the same banned-from-speaking list as Reader 2.

[Reader 1] Sean. Not Sean the master, the third, or Sir Sean. Just Sean. I have seen the result of trying in any way to glorify my name.

[Callahan] Good. Well, Sean, thank ye for aiding the narrator and meself in the retelling of my illustrious and uplifting life story. Do ye want to be known for more than just yer first name, or are ye sated with just being called Sean? Oh, and do please recognize that this little blip is the narrator's acknowledgment of yer aid. Don't expect any further fanfare, promotion, or celebration.

[Sean] Fair enough. I think, with what is contained in this book, it would be best to keep a glimmer of anonymity. The fact that I find so much pleasure in this book disturbs even me.

[Callahan] Not everyone can be blessed with balls of steel in combination with a complete lack of care toward the world's opinions and sensibilities, such as the narrator and meself. Thank ye once more, mate. Feel free to count yerself a Falcon.

Chapter 9

AVIANS

[NARRATOR] SUMMONED TO A gathering of the Avians, Pelican sat at the bar drinking strong ale as he looked at the various beauties who would be available for use after the meeting. Pelican jumped as a hand clapped him lightly on the back. "Hey, mind yourself. Lay your hands off me." Pelican growled as he turned to look at the dark-skinned scarred man taking a stool next to him at the bar.

Displaying his tattoo, the man nodded. "I am a brother, fear not. Sorry if I startled you. I could not rightly pass up opportunity to sit awhile with the Pelican, though, could I?"

"Bah. Pelican is a horrible name. The Falcon gave me that. My name is Pellith." Pelican snorted derisively at the man interrupting his evening.

"That is right. You worked with the Falcon and turned on him. You knew him back when he was exiled for a bit. Am I right?" The man was presented a glass of water from the tavern's proprietor while he spoke.

"More profit was offered in work for the Talons. Falcon gave me a way out of my pathetic life in the outlands, and I found my skills to be highly sought after here. Let him and the few that would follow him stir revolution for all I care. I just want coin." Pelican sat up and looked around the room as though disinterested in the conversation.

"Falcon was supposed to be seeking aid from barbarians and orcs. Any idea on how many allies he may have secured in his travels?" Sipping lightly at the water, the man maintained a stoic expression.

"Ha, who knows? Does it matter? The crown will wipe this place off the map regardless of outside aid. Namion and the Falcon condemned this place to doom either way. It's just on us to get as much coin in pocket as possible before it occurs. Problem with people like Falcon and Namion is that, much like most smart people, they think far too highly of themselves. Falcon always nipped at Namion's heels, and Namion thought himself so superior he didn't think to keep tab on Falcon's actions. Rookie error, if you ask me. One should never underestimate their opponent or friend." Pelican turned, annoyed expression toward the man interviewing him. "I'm not in the mood for twenty questions, so if ye don't mind, I think I'm going to partake in some more of this establishment's delights."

"I do mind. I hear you are quite something with a bow in your hand, but how are you in close-quarter combat?" The man set the water back on the bar.

"Are you threatening me? I'll have you know that Owl himself enlisted my aid. I'll—" Pelican's words were cut short as the stool shot out from under him, bouncing the side of his head off the bar.

"You should know who you work for, at least enough to recognize them when you see them." Namion spoke calmly as he stood, pushing his stool back.

Rolling back, Pelican pulled his bow with one hand, pulling an arrow from his quiver with the other. Drawing the weapon, he gulped as he attempted to draw cut string. "I don't know what they did. All I know is they killed an umber hulk, tricked some orcs, and then found me. They didn't talk about it much."

"So you really do not know what Falcon intends with his latest stunt?" Namion stalked forward, drawing his dagger.

Pulling his sword, Pelican stood ready for attack. "No, I haven't the foggiest fucking clue. I just know that he's lost his fucking mind and condemned everyone here to death."

Namion nodded toward a back corner of the tavern. Turning, Pelican raised his sword to defend himself and felt fire erupt throughout his body as the dagger, plunged into his side from behind, siphoned out his life. "As you said, it is a horrible rookie mistake to underestimate an opponent. One that I must regrettably admit I did make in regard to Falcon." Namion's words fell on deaf ears as he let the Pelican's body drop.

Delighting in the energy siphoned, he shook his head. "Well, he was telling the truth. He really did not know anything of use." The tavern's patrons who had not already fled did so as soon as the ruckus started. Looking about the empty tavern, Namion again found himself respectfully pondering the plight Falcon had forced upon them. Walking back to the bar, he pulled his stool back to its place and continued to drink his water.

A short time later, Vulture and Sparrow entered, followed promptly by Eagle. The three men stood respectfully by until Namion finished his water and turned to regard them. "If you cannot bring me Falcon, find me the one they call Hawk. Do not bother returning to me if you fail. I will find you."

[Callahan] Pleasant bastard when he's pissed, isn't he? Really wish I could've seen the look on his face. Bet he was just stewing over the fact that he thought so little of my actions outside the city that he never even questioned what I'd done. So assured was he of his own plans that he never thought any action of mine could have lasting consequence. Aye, even the smartest men can make stupid mistakes.

[Narrator] "Sometimes the wisest course of action is inaction. I need the crown to make their move before any more of my plan can come to fruition. Problem is we've a whole crowd of frustrated and scared people locked down here, and we've got to keep them sated till the appointed hour." Callahan paced as he spoke to his closest friends and Veracliff.

Hawk nodded. "Well, that latest stunt of yours will go a long way in keeping my brethren in line. They've no doubt of your prowess."

Horuce smiled weakly. "It'll take some effort, but I think given some time without any more death or chaotic happenings, I can keep things under control down here, at least for a while. We're well stocked on provisions and weapons, thanks to the previous residents."

Raven placed her hand on Callahan's shoulder. "The uncontrollable variable that could set this place to disorder will be topside in attempt to crush Talon morale. Won't you?"

Displaying his wry half grin, Callahan chuckled. "Aye, I will. First, I want those few remaining who still bear the Talon tattoo to be brought to me. I want to ensure that we are leaving no loose ends."

After questioning those men and a few more bodies later, Veracliff, Hawk, Raven, and Callahan prepared to ascend the air shaft using the makeshift rope ladder, leaving Horuce in control of the valley. Waiting until they were the last two on the meal hall's roof, Callahan grasped Raven's shoulder and looked to the ground with tear-filled eyes as he said, "Raven, I love ye. Please, recognize that the man I display is not the man I am. We are on the brink of our life. We're almost there. We need only be rid of Namion, and we'll find that peace. We'll find our life—a life where we can be together in peace without the constant contests, a life where we'll no longer have to scrape and fight for mere survival."

"Callahan, our life is not on the brink. It's not something that will come when we triumph. It's not something we will attain. It's not something we have to strive toward. Our life is right now. Our life is this moment of strife and stress during the in-between. I'm not ashamed that I married you, even if we haven't had a day of peace." Her smooth dark features caressed Callahan's spirit with their compassion as she spoke.

"But, Raven, it's all been struggle. It all looks bleak and dark. I haven't a clue as to how all this will turn out, and I brought ye into this." Still welling with tears, Callahan shook his head.

Forcing Callahan's blue eyes to meet her own, Raven smiled. "You didn't bring me into it. I was born into it. You've been the one bright spot in it all. It's at these moments when you shine your brightest. When all goes wrong and everything is against us, you run headlong into it with a half smile and a snarky comment. You show me the definition of strength and lend me the courage to carry forward. Don't apologize for being who you are. That is who I married."

"I stand . . . I stand on the brink of madness, dear Raven. Unlike my fellow humans, I see . . . I see so many who think that life is OK because they step back from that brink. Yet watching them, I still . . . I choose to leap forward into the mouth of that madness knowing full well the pain it will bring. And I don't know why. When we're rid of Namion, I'll find some peace. I'll be a better man. We'll be free of him, and when free of him . . . I'll be better." The stress of it all hit his shoulders as he spoke, uncharacteristically lending him slight pauses in his speech.

"No, dear Callahan. No, you won't. Namion isn't your problem. You're your problem. You dive into that madness because it's who you are. You needn't be the rest of them. I didn't marry them, did I? I don't care about them, do I? I care about you, and I care about you because you are that crazy son of a bitch that'll jump into the madness, that would fight opposition despite overwhelming odds. That's the boy I fell in love with. That's the boy I married, and that's the man I see before me. I am honored to call you mine." Raven wrapped Callahan into a tight embrace.

Chuckling lightly, Callahan spoke again. "Someday, someday, we'll look back on these days . . . but today, I just don't see an out. I don't see the sunshine."

"You don't have to see it for it to be there, Callahan." Raven stepped back, looking concerned at her husband's demeanor.

"Oh, don't start with that rubbish faith speech. I don't wanna fucking hear it. Ye know how I take to that." Raising his voice in a snarky ridiculous tone, Callahan continued, "Just because you don't believe in the gods doesn't mean they don't believe in you." Returning his voice to normal, he stated, "Fuck the gods. Fuck the eternal ray of sunshine that flows forth from believers' asses. Life's crap, isn't it? It's just on us to fight on. But if the world's all shit, then I'll take my brand of shit over anyone else's any day."

Harshness entered Raven's voice. "Callahan, put your mind to task. Leave your battles with theology and ideology for another time. Tonight, we go to do what you've wanted to do for a long time. Tonight, we go to hunt the Avians, and we need your mind in order. We need you on task. We need you to be the Falcon. We don't need you to be worried about what you should be. We need you to be what you are. You've said it many a time to me—you are what you are because you have to be—and right now, you have to be that. We need you collected."

"Damn right. Enough of this warbling and crying, this bemoaning of my poor existence. Sorry, even I have times in which I just feel all too human. You're right, though. Now is once again about survival, not about life. So I'll grit my teeth, lower my head, and I'll shovel some more shit. Come the conclusion of this night, the city will once again know why I am at once feared and loved." His countenance shifting with near immediacy, Callahan displayed his wry half grin.

"Just remember, dear Callahan, honor is not what you do when everyone is watching and life is easy, contented, and going your way. Honor is what you do when no one is watching, the world hates you, and nothing is going your way. Honor is how you conduct yourself in your darkest moments. It doesn't matter how the world perceives you. It just matters how you perceive you. The only thing you need to have peace with when you close your eyes to rest, when all is quiet, is you. You're all that need approve of your actions." With that, Raven started up the rope ladder, quickly followed by Callahan.

[Callahan] I just wanted to be human. I just wanted a life. I eventually maybe even wanted children. Horrifying as that concept is. I grew tired of always having to fight and scrape. I didn't want to have to always kill people. I didn't want to be the bringer of death. I wanted to be the bringer of life and freedom. I wanted to give what I wanted to everyone else. I wanted everyone to have the opportunity to be who they wanted to be. It wasn't real, though, was it? It was all just a fucking fantasy. So I'd fight and I'd scrape, and I wouldn't give up. That night, I went forward while the world hated me. On that night, I went forward in that hate, and I sought to cleanse them of a terror, whether or not they approved or appreciated it. I would take what I saw to be an honorable course and remove the threat from the city, even though I still proved to be perceived as the greatest threat to the city in their eyes.

[Narrator] The next morning, the sun broke over the city's oceanside cliffs to light the tower of Sintell in the temple district. That tower's bells rang in the new day joined by the tormented screams of Sparrow, whose body was intricately fixated just below the tower's bellhouse. The first bell released a counterweight, pulling free Sparrow's gag. The second bell dropped a counterweight, causing the chains holding Sparrow's right arm and leg to wrench out. The third bell dropped the final counterweight, wrenching out the chains on Sparrow's left arm and leg. As the process came to fruition, Sparrow's dismembered torso bounced with sickening thuds down the length of the tower, finally meeting its brutal end before the temple's immense front doors, displaying the poorly drawn Falcon upon his back.

[Callahan] I had a lot of spare time with a less-than-sane demeanor while locked away with the healers. In retrospect, a quicker, less dramatic end would have sufficed, but shit, it left me feeling warm and fuzzy. Unable to access the temple itself, I had to secure a rope to ole boy's body and make the climb up the treacherously sheer walls of the tower, carrying a backpack full of chains and weights. Then thankfully, being a skinny little puke, I was able to pull him up to the bellhouse.

The hardest part was holding his unconscious body still while suspended to attach the chains and fix the whole system together. It all took a good portion of the night so I was real glad that the first part of our plan went swimmingly.

Raven divulged the fact that Sparrow had an odd fetish for assertive women. He frequented the brothels and streets that commonly teemed with ladies of ill repute seeking special dominating women. Being an assassin, he had the obnoxious habit of changing up his locations with random frequency, so it did take a little work to find the particular brothel he would be in.

Not being overly familiar with Veracliff, we changed her look a bit and, much to her chagrin, placed her in a dark blue gown instead of her usual black. A little magical alteration and she fit right in with the brothel denizens. A little coin exchanged between Veracliff and the proprietor ensured Veracliff a room and freedom from question. Sparrow was in the midst of chatting up a gal he had previously held arrangement with when Veracliff interrupted by slapping him across the face.

"What's the meaning of this?" Sparrow's hand shot to the handle of his poisoned dagger.

Grasping his crotch, Veracliff leaned in. "Silence, boy, you'll speak only when your mistress allows it."

Grinning sheepishly, Sparrow licked his lips. "Yes, mistress." Easy as that, Sparrow followed her up to her room.

Raven had begun to tell me how she knew of Sparrow's weakness in that regard, but before she could get into it, I just said that whatever she had done prior to me was none of my business, just as what she did on her own time after our marriage was none of my business. I really just didn't want to hear the details because no shit like that was ever gonna go down in my bedroom.

When Sparrow was stripped and in the process of a spanking, I walked into the room and placed myself between Sparrow and his gear. "Ye've been a bad boy, eh, Sparrow?" Laughing, I enjoyed his shocked look as he turned to regard me. I laughed even harder when Veracliff stabbed him with the Ssarrin-saliva-coated needle I'd given her. "As ye taught me, there's no antidote or preparation that can be made in regard to the temporary paralysis brought on by Ssarrin saliva."

"One of our city's darkest nightmares brought down because he likes it rough. Isn't it a bitch to know that despite all of yer devious assassinations and skills, ye'll forever be remembered as that one guy who met his end because he stripped down and bent over for a spanking? Wow, I really hope I leave a better legacy behind me than that one." With that, I smashed the side of Sparrow's head, ensuring a decent night's sleep. I wanted him well rested for the morning to come.

Veracliff preformed some kind of chant then pointed me in the direction of target number 2 shortly after I watched the bell tower incident. Moving silently with ease on account of my trusty old ring, I came up behind Eagle on his rooftop vantage point. "Old friend, one twitch toward yer bow and I will turn ye into my personal dagger sheath. Yer not all that shit a guy, are ye? I mean, ye kill people for profit, but fuck, I just killed a man while he was trying to get his jollies off, so who am I to judge? Ye want profit and I'm sure ye want to live, so tell me where I can find Vulture, and then yer gonna deliver this sealed letter to the first lord in the crown's army ye find while ye travel south to forge a new life. I'm going to give ye mine and Raven's life savings to fund yer journey and yer own retirement if ye so choose, and the letter will most likely get yer life spared if ye get caught by the crown."

"You and Namion can have your war. Between the two of you, the city is ashes anyway. I accept your offer and will be slowly turning around now." As he said, Eagle slowly turned, accepted the letter and coin pouch I offered him, and gave me Vulture's whereabouts to the best of his knowledge.

To clarify, I didn't forget about Owl. I just know that aside from Namion, the only individual ever aware of Owl's whereabouts and actions was Owl. He was an issue that would need to be addressed at a later time.

I returned to the meeting place my companions and I had set in one of the middle-class district parks, detailed the next part of our plan, and then watched as Hawk and Raven went off to start their parts. Delighting in the ease of the whole event, I smiled at Veracliff and said, "Good to have ye on board, Veracliff. Things are starting to look up for the Falcons, and in part, yer to thank." Who doesn't foresee this going south at this point? I didn't because no, I'd closed my eyes, plugged my ears, and fallen into that whole life-is-wonderful, things-are-working-out-for-me, let's-just-get-completely-fucking-retarded mode and forgot that the individual I was speaking to was one of Calarr's leading forces in dark magic. Oh, and did I mention my number 1 stalker—I mean, fan.

"Yes, our guild will flourish, you will have your desired power, and we can finally rid ourselves of that obstructive woman, Raven. Must be difficult having to grit and bear your teeth married to Namion's ugly bastard daughter." Veracliff said this as though it were a well-known fact. She said this as though I should laugh and say, "Yep, it's a real bitch." So of course, I met her jaw with my right fist as hard as I could. The pop of her jaw dislocating brought vast quantities of relief and, dare I say, joy.

She attempted to curse and chant some spell, but apparently, both of those are nigh impossible when attempting to do them with a freshly broken jaw. Her expression was probably still one of shock long after I left her ass sitting in the park. Why didn't I kill her? Well, terrific fucking question. I don't know, but I sure would like to go back in time and torture myself until I could answer that question. Yes, I really just left her there.

Having arrived at an old contact of Raven's, Hawk stood in the entry to the tavern, blatantly watching every move Raven made so as to appear a bodyguard. Raven approached the barkeep that had once been her informant and talked to him about possibly moving shipments of untaxed dwarven ale. The barkeep feigned interest, and moments after Raven and Hawk's departure, I watched him run off in an obvious rush.

Knowing he had bought it, I rushed back to my appointed place at a low point of the cliffside rock folds above our air vent entry. Raven and Hawk greeted the barbarian on guard, and Raven not-so-quietly stated, "Good job, friend. If anyone were to cut this ladder, we'd all be screwed down there." Raven and Hawk then climbed down.

I did tell ye all earlier that Vulture had no business being an assassin, right? This man was as smart as my left nut removed, set on fire, ran over by a herd of animals, eaten, digested, shit out, and ran over again. He lurched onto the scene, planting both of his axes into the barbarian from behind. One of which had found its way through the back of the barbarian's neck, choking off any alarm. Vulture cut the rope ladder, roared a laugh into the air vent, then hooked his axes to the back of his belt as he started dragging a large stone to cover the vent.

Letting him drag the hulking stone until it was mere inches from the hole, I then exited my hiding place and dropped down next to him. "This is gonna suck." I got to watch his eyes widen with shock just before he disappeared down the shaft. I blissfully listened to the dull, sickening pops and thuds of his descent. Lowering the spare rope ladder I'd set aside, I climbed down to see a gagged and bound Vulture being held by Hawk.

After tying him up to my long unused crucifix, I attempted to question him. "Vulture, what I most love about finally getting to see ye go is that I feel as though I'm cleansing a stain from my very soul by partaking in yer removal from this world. Furthermore—"

"Of all the imaginable torture, having to listen to a speech from you is far worse than anything I could've thought of." Several incidences of spitting and screamed obscenities later, it was well illustrated that further questioning would be futile, so I regagged him and started a betting pool on how long he would last. That took care of Vulture and temporarily solved our morale problem.

Now many of ye who read this retelling of my story probably find disappointment in Vulture's less-than-extravagant death, but come on now, give me a bit of credit. I had a beautifully constructed and functional plan, and I played it through. Besides, one amazingly twisted death planned and exacted within a twenty-four-hour period as well as solving my personnel dissention issues is no small accomplishment now, is it? That being said, I recognize that it was not as glorious and twisted a demise as I would've liked, and the evening as a whole did leave a few inconvenient loose ends. I say inconvenient like the forcible removal of one's genitalia would be inconvenient or perhapswaking up to discover that the blonde ye had drunkenly gone to bed with was actually a hideous troll not genetically far removed from a whale.

Telling Raven of the Veracliff incident, the rush was on to find new entry and exit from what could easily become our tomb. So we set the newly invigorated and inspired men of the Falcons to work clearing our old main passageways. Leaving the men in higher spirits, I departed again.

Hours later, after dodging several guards and watching eyes, I found myself waiting patiently in Kaville's study.

[Narrator] "The crown thinks they are getting exactly what they paid for with Namion's old bargain of amnesty, don't they?" Exiting the shadows, Callahan watched Kaville jump and grip the edge of his table tightly enough to cause his knuckles to whiten. "If I wanted ye dead, ye can be assured I would've already done it."

"I know. You, like Namion, are not kind enough to let me die. Instead, you take every possible opportunity you can to torture me and my fellows." Kaville shook his head. "The word has gone out. The troops will be at the city gates within the month. The stunts you've pulled this last day have sent half the populace to rage and the other half to celebration. You are far more detrimental than you are beneficial, Falcon."

"I did not lie. Our allegiance holds fast. Don't worry yerself about the crown. I'll handle that problem. Bring the farmers inside the walls for safety, and prepare to have all shipping routes blockaded for a month or two. They'll lay siege and wait for us to turn upon ourselves. Survive that and keep the guard and public under control, and we'll not only survive this but come out the other side of it free from Namion's terror. After that time, you will turn a blind eye to me and my guild. We will reap profit but, henceforth, remove ourselves from political aspirations. The Falcons no longer seek to dissolve the nobility. Fuck the sheep. They can fend for themselves. I, like yerself, just want some peace. I want to settle in and live." Callahan smiled his wry half smile as he prepared to leave.

"Why should I trust you, Falcon? You have killed my wife, my cousin, my friends, and have sent my beloved city into madness and destruction on several occasions." Kaville still held tight to the table, not wanting to make any aggressive movements.

"Ye make a real good case for hating me, don't ye? I have done those things, and I would do them again if ye stand against me. Namion seeks power and ambition beyond these walls and thinks little for the destruction within those walls. I seek life free from oppression. I want no kingdom, I want no army, I want to make my living and not be bothered by anyone. Ye do have to choose one or the other, ye know that? So looking at things from yer perspective, I'd choose me. I'm the Falcon. Fuck yer city, fuck yerself, I'm an asshole, and you can too." Callahan chuckled lightly and made his exit.

Kaville shook his head at the table. "What in the fuck is that even supposed to mean? I've been overrun by madmen and suicide cases. Worst part is I can't do fuck all about it." Soon after, Kaville called to order his advisors, and the process of moving the outland residents inside the city walls began as well as pulling in as many provisions and stores as could be found.

Namion stared into the flames dancing within the fireplace. He sat alone in a safe house on the outskirts of the temple district. Never had he anticipated that young boy he had met to become the greatest adversary of his entire life. Namion smiled wide in recollection of it all. He could not recall why he had spared that boy's life, why he had entered into pact, but the times of his life he had enjoyed most were the times leading to his current stalemate.

Owl was the last of his Avians. Word had reached Namion that the crown's forces were moving toward the city and would have it besieged within the month. Groups of his members were already deserting and fleeing for the outlands. How quickly the balance of power can shift. The sea had long called to him, but Namion enjoyed the chaos of the city and the Falcon far too much to want to depart.

"You look strangely calm for someone on the brink of losing everything." Veracliff's speech was slurred and muddled.

Looking up to see Veracliff's puffed up and discolored face, Namion burst into laughter. "I take it your goddess has yet to deliver you your promised prize?"

"He will come around when the distraction your daughter provides is removed." Veracliff's angered expression further distorted her damaged features, causing Namion another chuckle.

"The Falcon cast you aside after you turned from me to his aid, and now you return. Takes a lot of courage to risk my company again." Namion returned to watching the flames dance. "I've always had a kinship with flame. Just like the kinship I feel for the sea. I am a man of chaos. Fire has no compassion, no sympathy or empathy. It consumes. It keeps nothing, consumes all it needs, and leaves nothing but ash in its wake. I lose nothing, mage. I have gained a worthy foe that has even yet to fully recognize the scope of his capabilities. I will return to the seas until the time arises if and when I can face the Falcon again. I concede this round of contest that I can live to combat him again."

"A bit of magical intervention disclosed to me the contents of the letter being delivered to the crown's forces as we speak." Veracliff sat opposite the fireplace from Namion.

"You would not have dared my presence with any less. Speak, and earn your breath." Namion maintained a calm demeanor. Veracliff was many things, but suicidal was not among them. Namion knew she had information worth her life, and that is what had, thus far, stayed his hand.

"Eagle accepted a bargain fromFalcon. He delivers information about ship movements from the harbor and tells the crown to watch the seas for you to flee. I would suspect that within the week, ships will be moving into place to intercept your escape." Veracliff shifted back in her chair and prepared a spell in defense as Namion unexpectedly burst into a raucous laugh.

"You shifty little fucker. Brilliant. Sheer fucking brilliance. Hmm, he intends on surviving this. I know he has an out, something hidden. He does not just intend to survive, but he intends to steal my position once and for all. What else do you know?" Namion returned to calmly pondering the fire.

"I know little more than you already suspect. He has no fear of the crown's armies and dismisses any talk of the impending destruction to Lados. What puzzles me is how he knew your intention to escape?" Veracliff kept her vigilant watch of Namion.

"That does not puzzle me. He knows me, and he knows that his pattern of thought is almost identical to my own. Most likely, he just planned what he would do in my position and set to motion counterplans. Letting him live has proven to be the highlight and excitement of my elder years. Same as this fire before us, I suspect far more to be consumed before we are finished." Namion tossed another small log into the fire as a wicked smile spread across his face. "Veracliff, have you ever awoken to find an undeniable urge to watch the world burn? Awoken to find that you want to stir revolution to such a cause? I eagerly await the coming of the gods. Not because they will whisk me away to some wonderland by magical means, no. I do not qualify for such. I await the coming of the gods because it marks the burning of this world. It marks the destruction and end to all. I delight in such thought. Do you know why I delight in it? I delight because in that instance when I am left behind and the world is in turmoil and everything is death and torment, I will watch as others externally exhibit the signs of how I feel within. They will feel, in very real fashion, the pain that eats at my senses every moment I draw breath. They too will know what I know. I will love it. I will eat up every moment of it. I wish to expedite the ushering of this era unto humanity."

Veracliff shied back from Namion as he continued his smile unabated. "The Falcon aids in this endeavor. Whether it is what he desires or not, those are the actions he puts into play. I will not run, not as all suspect I will. I will put into play the courses that make it appear such. But no, I will not run. I will stay. I want to delight in this destruction. I want to invite this destruction. This is how the Falcon and I are alike. Our motives and means may differ, but our result is very similar. I eagerly await its fruition." A gleam as though born of joy lit Namion's eyes as he again tossed a log to the fire. The fire's heat increased to an uncomfortable level as Veracliff fought to maintain her calm in the face of Namion's madness-fueled rant.

"Veracliff, take, for example, a bloated and rotting corpse. Think of the corpse as Calarr. It is passed and it lays there, and it will spread disease and cause the other realities and worlds that exist to also catch said disease. Just as maggots have their beautiful dance of collective consumption upon the bloated corpse, we are the maggots of Calarr. Our design is to consume, our purpose to devour, we leave nothing in our wake to spread the disease. That is what we are. We are the universe's maggots. Set to consumption, thinking nothing of the cost. It's our purpose. The Falcon and I, we only seek to perpetuate said cycle. We, unlike most, recognize what we are, and instead of shedding tear over it, instead of wallowing in guilt, we delight in it. We accept our position in the universe, and we do all we can to aid in expediting the process of natural design." The gleam dissipated and smile faded as Namion leaned back to savor the discomfort brought by the excessive heat.

"The Falcon is my greatest accomplishment. I do not want his death. He is the greatest villain ever known to Calarr, and he thinks himself a hero. Better yet, he inspires others to believe likewise. I do not want any harm to him. He is the embodiment of Entearra Gharu. I cannot hope to defeat him, and I do not want to. I want to further him. I want to aid him. I want to support him. I want the Falcon to rise. So much potential remains untapped within him. I want to see him attain the pinnacle of his potential. He accomplishes everything I have ever desired, and my hands are clean. Let us work together in this, Veracliff. That you can have your promised reward, and I can have the embodiment of chaos unleashed upon Calarr." Namion grinned as Veracliff solemnly nodded.

[Callahan] So pretty safe to assume ye'll be trying to market this book in the self-help section, eh?

[Narrator] Well, my friend, though it is therapeutic to write and though it does help me to keep myself better collected in my life, I'm pretty sure that anyone who reads this and not only enjoys it but agrees with it has, in my imagining, condemned their soul to an eternity of hell. So I think I'll keep it in the fantasy genre and try to sell it as such.

[Callahan] Wise endeavor, if ye ask me. I'd have to agree with yer assessment. Doesn't seem like the warm and cheery, uplifting kind of document now, does it? But it's my life, isn't it? And ye scripted it such. I notice the pages are getting thin, and we are moving on toward the conclusion of our saga of inspiration. Not much for length, is it?

[Narrator] I don't have to be the next fucking Tolstoy for it to be a good read now, do I?

[Callahan] Touché. Besides, people will be so fucking confused the first time they read this they'll have to read it a second time, eh?

[Narrator] If this inspires interest and people want more, I guess they'll purchase a copy and tell others to do likewise, won't they? Turning this into a financially beneficial accomplishment would be the quickest way to get me to write more.

[Callahan] Did ye really just plug the sale of yer book within yer book? Come on, how fucking sheisty can ye get?

[Narrator] I like to write. I like to entertain. But enjoyment does not always equate to money now, does it? So bears to reason that unless I can find a way to make money, yer gonna be stuck as nothing but a personal imagining now, aren't ye?

[Callahan] I can get on board with that logic. So to those who love the blessing that is my ever warm and cheery disposition, do yer damndest to spread the word so I can return in untold numbers of sequels. I want to take yer money as many times as is possible and offer ye nothing but snarky, cynical pessimism in return.

[Narrator] Enough of this mindless drivel, though. Let us continue the story.

[Callahan] Aye, nothing inspires me more than chaos, so on to chapter 10 . . .

Chapter 10

THE ORDER OF CHAOS

[Narrator] The next few weeks were held in quiet reservation. Anger, hate, and fear boiled just beneath the surface of it all, but none dared to whisper of the impending doom. None dared whisper of the armies starting to amass around the outside walls of Lados. None dared to whisper of the death calling to them.

As the armies came into view of Lados, ships graced the harbor. Many of the Talons made an exodus upon those ships. Namion, Veracliff, and Owl boarded the fleet's second ship, leaving the flagship for lesser members as a method of disguise. Upon boarding the ship, Namion looked to his followers and delivered a speech. "What kind of captain would I be if I fled? No, my men, I give to you this escape. Take it. Take these ships, and go on about your courses. If and when the turmoil turns to calm, return, and we will again take up the cause. We will again force Lados to bow before us. In the meantime, we are met with temporary defeat. So take your leave and save your lives, and I, as captain, will go down with the ship that is Lados."

With that, Namion, Veracliff, and Owl boarded a small rowboat and set it on the water. Owl rowed them to a quiet place upon the shore where they could maintain a view of the harbor while being unseen themselves. Callahan also watched the fleet's departure from the cliffs above the air shaft's entry.

They watched as the ships pulled away from the dock and began sailing from the harbor. They watched a flag rise upon a small merchant vessel outside the harbor. Then they watched as a fleet of the crown's navy came into view. The fleet closed in on the six ships and, with little challenge, set all six ablaze to sink into the ocean outside of Lados. Callahan smiled with delight, as did Namion, while watching the burning ships sink just outside the harbor's shores.

A few days later, Callahan traversed the city. Keeping in disguise with the use of a heavy cloak, he listened to feel out the populace, but as was stated, quiet reservation was the voice throughout Lados. That is, until he reached the southern gate late in the morning, where a mass was gathering. They were calling for the gate to be opened. One such man proclaimed, "Argh, let them in. Let them cleanse us of the evils that exist within this city. Let them purge us of these Talons and these Falcons. Let them bring us back to the order we once knew. Let the crown come in here and restore peace to our city. Let them come. Let them have the city. Perhaps they can bring us to a new order."

Callahan lithely sprung to the walls atop the southern gate. Pulling off his cloak, he clapped his right arm, where his tattoo existed. "Hey, my people, greetings and salutations, and before ye all rile up and start throwing things at me or doing something stupid, I'd ask if anyone here has ever held presence at one of my prior speaking engagements? Because ye can let everyone else know how well it works out for those who interrupt me. So yer gonna stand there and hear what I've to say. Yer gonna do so by choice, or yer gonna do so by force. Ye have no idea how many of my members exist amidst ye. So rise up, fight me, and die, or sit idle and listen to what I've to say."

Callahan found himself slightly surprised by the lack of a response, so he continued, "Yer citizens of Lados. They imprison us within our city walls. They besiege us. They take our food and cut our supply lines, and they think that we will break within the month, turn onourselves. But again I say, 'Yer citizens of Lados.' Yer born and bred of pain. That's yer bread and butter. Pain, dismissal, oppression—these are the things ye've grown knowing. They don't know that. They think ye'll break under the easy strain of a siege. Bah! I know better. We do worse to ourselves on regular occasion. Those men know nothing of pain. They know nothing of what we are. They think they can break us? Ha, I laugh in the face of the crown's army. Have they ever weathered a Lados thunderstorm? Have they ever weathered the pain that is our existence? Have they ever had to live in daily threat of their own brother slitting their throat? No, they don't know what pain is. They don't know the meaning of torment. Let us show them how strong we are. 'Cause the lives we live may not be ones of glory, ones of presence, or ones that bring us to the all-holy Sintell and his ideals of heaven. No, the life we live—it brings us to strength. It brings us to honor. Honor that is self-defined. Hold fast that honor. Hold fast that strength. I assure ye this army will not break us. This army will not walk away peacefully and happily from this occurrence. This army will know what it is to challenge the people of Lados. This army will meet such destructive chaos that they will whine, whimper, and cry as they crawl themselves all the way back home to their mothers. This is what I promise ye. Lend me yer patience. I ask nothing of ye. Ye don't need to rise. Ye don't need to fight. All ye need do is remain calm. Remain peaceful. If ye can do such, I'll cleanse ye of this current turmoil. Give me time—just a little time."

With that, Callahan slipped from the wall into the shadows of a nearby alley. Donning his cloak, he prepared to make a mad dash for the underground sanctuary but heard a ruckus in the crowd outside the alley. A man shouted out, "The northern plains! They crawl with thousands of barbarians!" Smiling broadly, Callahan changed his course and headed for the northern walls.

Reaching the northern gate in the temple district just before dusk, Callahan scanned the mass of people trying to get to the wall to see the barbarian hordes setting up camp on the northern plains. As he scanned the crowds, he smiled at Hawk trying to hide his umber hulk bracers beneath a cloak. Moving to Hawk's side, Callahan whispered, "Ye stick out worse than a whore in church, mate."

"Ah, Falcon, so have you seen my friends. Right on cue, they sent an envoy in, but he refuses to speak to anyone but the Falcon." Hawk couldn't suppress his smile.

"Ye shifty blighter, how'd ye manage this?" Callahan reciprocated Hawk's smile with his own wry half grin.

"Well, we don't play our high cards till endgame, do we, mate? Know that I'm loyal and count ye my closest friend and ally. Ye've better shit to worry about. They're on our side, and they'll not act unless ye give them the call to. They're not enough to beat the crown or even put a dent in them, but they are enough to slow the process down a bit and give us the time we need for the orcs to do their thing." Hawk's smile widened as Callahan nodded his respect.

"Yer a damn good friend and an even better four-star. If and when the time comes for me to leave the guild in another's hands, be it temporary or permanent, ye'd make a damn fine Falcon. Now where is this envoy so we can properly greet our northern brothers? By the way, I like how ye stole my words on that one." Callahan followed as Hawk led him to the area of wall closest to where the envoy had set up camp on the other side of the wall.

Hawk clapped Callahan on the shoulder just before Callahan ascended the wall. "What's wisdom but other people's rehashed bullshit anyway, eh?"

Smiling, Callahan pushed his way through the crowd and waited until he was at the wall's edge to drop his cloak. "Brother, what the fuck are ye doing? There is more than enough time for rest once yer dead. Stand, make noise, drive some serious fear into those sissy southlanders who dare to call themselves men."

"Hail Falcon. The tribes have united to the cause of repaying our debt to you. We stand at the ready to answer your call." Callahan recognized the envoy as a member of Hawk's tribe.

"Well, hang in there, and try to keep yer men calm. I don't want any premature fighting. Hold off, and I'll send word if and when we need anything more than just yer visible presence." Turning to the people within the city, Callahan smiled. "I didn't abandon ye. I didn't cast ye to the wolves. No, I pulled ye from the brink of enslavement. So stay calm, go home, live yer lives. Let the Falcon worry about the king's men."

Walking away free of harassment from the crowd of people, Callahan nodded to Hawk and tapped his right arm. Catching the hint, Hawk removed his cloak, joined Callahan, and the two walked on toward the underground valley. A rough entry had been reopened beneath the outflow river. "So 'bout time our boys got some fresh air, isn't it? Chomping at the bit and stir-crazy, I say we send them on the hunt for any who still bear the Talon mark, eh? Reservedly, of course. We don't need to go my usual course of city-burning revolution. Even I've had about enough of that shit. Maybe next week." Callahan gave his wry half grin.

"Sounds like a good plan to me." Hawk grinned at the wonderful change being brought about as Callahan's plans fell into place.

Upon hearing the order, the Falcons who had so long been imprisoned underground shouted with celebration and quickly set to task with a lustlike joy. Callahan informed them to keep their activities collected so as not to prematurely stir the populace. The Falcons, so eager to be free of their dungeon, would have agreed to any stipulations if it meant breathing fresh surface air once more.

Lying next to Raven later that evening, Callahan spoke with a resigned sigh. "In light of Namion's ships going down in the harbor and the arrival of the barbarians, everything is going swimmingly. It's going better than I could've anticipated or planned. I'm just waiting for the other shoe to drop, eh, Raven? I'm unsettled. I'm almost more upset now than I was a week ago when all was wrong."

Raven looked at him in her sympathetic manner. "Why do you always preplan destruction, Callahan?"

Callahan sat up in the bed. "It's not preplanning destruction. It's preparation for the inevitable collapse. My life is not one of success and glory. My life is one of really good plans going to shit. I keep waiting for this one to go to shit. I don't think Namion's dead."

Raven sat up and looked curiously at Callahan as he continued. "I really don't. If it were me, I would've constructed that fleet. I would've sent out a bunch of nobodies on those ships. I would've reserved my best men and kept them in hiding. Then I would've made a show of getting on that ship, and I would've found a way to get right the fuck back off. I wouldn't have thought that plan to go through. So I don't think he would've. I'm pretty sure he's still alive. I feel it. What frightens me is that he's quiet now. He could easily stir shit up on me. He could easily upset all the plans I have in action just by showing his presence. He can completely shatter everything I have going for us, and I'm waiting for it. I'm trying to plan it, but I don't know. I don't know where the holes are."

Raven smiled and lightly shook her head. "For once, why don't you just let the inevitable be the inevitable? Just enjoy the moment you have. You're succeeding, you're winning—leave it at that. These are the moments that we should treasure. When it all goes to shit, we'll deal with it then. We don't need to deal with that before it occurs. All we're doing is lengthening that moment of pain if we do."

Callahan flashed his wry half smile. "Aye, I suppose yer right. No need to kick me own arse. There are plenty of other people willing and ready to do that for me. So why don't we get to the more important matter of further celebrating this moment?" Leaning in to Raven, Callahan felt one of those rare moments in which everything was just as he felt it was supposed to be.

[Callahan] She was right. Life is crap, but there are moments, and they should not be tainted.

[Narrator] Frustrated with the reopened trade routes through the northern gate, the crown allowed a few days for observation then sent forth an envoy to meet with the barbarians before the gates. The crown's envoy announced his presence to the north gate, requesting representation from Lados to meet with them for negotiations.

After assembling a group of his best guards, Kaville donned his ceremonial armor and prepared to depart for negotiations. He was tired of allowing others to run his city, so he decided that, instead of an envoy, he himself would meet for negotiations. Standing before the gate in his armor, surrounded by his guard, Kaville gave the order and watched the northern gate open before him.

As they started to step forward, Kaville's nearest guard leaned in, saying, "I think I'll join ye. Make sure ye barter us a good deal." Pulling up the visor, Callahan flashed Kaville his wry half grin. "I'd hate to have ye put me out at the last second, eh, mate."

"Falcon, please. Please do not kill this one. Please don't force us to war. There is still room for negotiation. There is still room to end this without bloodshed." Kaville kicked himself for not seeing Falcon's telltale weapons.

Stripping the helm and chest plate, Callahan displayed his usual clothes underneath. "No, mate, that time has done and passed. Ye can take these metal prisons ye use to display all yer pride and prestige, and ye can fuck off. I'll not have this city condemned to the tyranny of the crown. Not after all I've done. All I need is some time. Just a little more time and they'll leave on their own. Trust in me. I'm not sending ye to the wolves, Kaville. I've got this under handle."

His frustration building, Kaville responded, "I seriously doubt that, Falcon. I've seen how you and Namion handle situations. I really don't want that kind of order in the city."

Callahan continued to grin. "It doesn't much matter what ye want, does it, mate? 'Cause if ye get in my fucking way, I'll end ye no more or less than I have many others who tried to stand in opposition to me. So mind yer tongue, mind yer place, and I'll give ye back yer governorship."

Stopping in his tracks, Kaville looked to Callahan. "How can I hope to get you to stop bringing endless suffering to the people of our city?"

Callahan paused with Kaville. "I'm not endeavoring to bring suffering to the people. I'm endeavoring to bring freedom. I will bring freedom."

Kaville pointed wildly at the sky and said, "Even the threat of the gods and eternal torment does nothing to slow you. Is there nothing you believe in?"

Callahan responded after a derisive snort. "Eternal torment. Fuck the gods. Fuck their threats. How can ye hope to illicit obedience via threatening torment to a life of torment? There's no threat there. Fuck them. What are they gonna do to me that they don't already? I hold no presence for the gods. The gods can hold their own. No great imaginations are gonna make it all OK for us. Nah, they're not gonna come down and wash us clean of all our sins. Look. Look around you. There's torment, there's pain—why do we have to wait for eternity to experience it? The threat is very real in the present. We don't have to wait for them to deliver it after our death. They give of it freely while we yet live. Nah, Kaville, I do believe. I believe in God. Not the gods, not even a being of definable essence, but God—everything that is and everything that isn't and the interconnectivity there between. So when I look at ye, I see God. As when I look at myself, I see God. I don't need a great overseer of spiritual nature to come down and preside over me because I am that is, as are you. That is why I carry myself as though I'm divine because I am. So grab a hold of yer nuts, recognize yer own divinity, and start saying what ye want to say. Not what yer supposed to say. Start being the individual deity that ye want to be. Stop being the sheep that is presented for ye to be, though it is convenient to be. Convenience is not self-awareness. Convenience is not what gets us to where we want to be. Convenience is what we allow ourselves to be because we just can't handle the struggles. Grab yer nuts! Be a man! Grasp yer divinity, and utilize it."

Callahan paused a second before continuing. "People don't like what they don't understand, and they don't understand those like me. Those who say what they want to say, not what they're supposed to say. Those who are what they want to be, not what they're supposed to be. People try to stomp that out. People try to quell it. People try to crush it, but don't let them. Don't let them crush what ye need to be, what is you, just because they don't understand. So many—so many—bow to an existence they can't stand just because they fear that others won't approve. 'Cause others won't like them. Bullshit! Bullshit. It's all fucking bullshit. Stand up, be who ye are. Now that comes at cost, and it may be a steep price. It may put ye on the outs. It may brand ye treasonous. It may make ye a revolutionary. It may not make ye desired and liked. But when ye look in a mirror, ye'll know the truth of it all. When ye feel that deep-seated pride when yer actually what ye want to be. When yer not just a sheep to be guided and forced along their path. When ye craft yer own way and grasp yer own divinity, recognizing that God is not separated from ye but that God is you. In that drive, in that desire, in that goal, not even the council themselves can stand in opposition before me lest they fall."

Pausing a moment more, Callahan displayed his wry half smile yet again. "Life is like a child's toy, Kaville. It's like a kaleidoscope, and we are but the chaotic broken shards within that kaleidoscope. Complete chaos and disorder with no semblance of system but if ye hold that child's toy to the light and ye just let it be, ye let the light shine through. The beauty can be beheld in the proximity between those pieces. So, Kaville, life and existence is beautiful. Chaos is beautiful. We need only let it be what it is. We needn't try to fix it. We needn't try to get our hands in it, shifting it about. All that accomplishes is to further separate the pieces. Let us bring those pieces together. Let me organize us. Let me bring order to the chaos."

Kaville looked a bit taken aback as he responded, "You're a madman no less than Namion. You're completely out of your mind, but there is hope in what you say. There's a lot of hope in what you say. I want to believe you. I want to follow you, but I just don't see the results. I don't see the light at the end of your tunnel. I just can't see any proper conclusion."

"Ye needn't see my conclusion. Yer one-tenth my intellect. I don't expect ye or anyone else to see my conclusion. I don't want ye to see it. That ruins the surprise. Just sit back and enjoy the show, my friend." Extending his hand in an invite to leave, Callahan ended their discourse.

The two headed out to meet the envoy. The crown's envoy, the barbarian envoy, Kaville, and Callahan sat in tense silence, waiting for each other to open the talk. The tent in which the gathering was being held was surrounded by the crown's and Kaville's guards.

Tension grew while Callahan joked with the barbarian and greeted him with friendly handshake. Kaville sat in silence, knowing that any word from him would only spur the Falcon to action. The crown's envoy sat there, confused by the obvious disdain held between Kaville and the Falcon. Before anyone dared break the ice, word called out from a guard. A courier was riding hard from the south.

Arriving, the courier, not even pausing to request entry, burst into the tent to kneel beside the crown's envoy. The barbarian reached for his axe but stayed the action from gesture of the Falcon. Smiling wide, Callahan watched carefully. Attempting to read the hushed courier's lips, he found difficulty due to the courier's hand attempting to cover the conversation. "Naga frueh" was all Callahan needed to discern. He turned his face to the barbarian, displaying his full and undeniably joyous smile.

The envoy waved off the courier as he finished. Sitting in obvious contemplation for a second, the envoy then spoke.

"We can negotiate peace now, in which you will open the southern gate and allow a contingent of our armed forces to reside within. They will restore peace and stability while reporting directly to the crown. Or this very night, we will open combat and bleed this city dry. We will leave you in ashes and rebuild from the ashes a city properly honoring our true king."

Callahan turned his smile on the envoy. "If it weren't for the fact that I need ye to tell yer employers to fuck themselves, I'd kill ye right now." The guard could be heard stirring with readiness outside the tent. "But I think I'll give ye a pass. I'll let ye go so ye can go and tell them I showed ye my scrotum." Much to the dismay of all present, Callahan did just that. "Tell them that I told ye to shave it with yer teeth and floss with the remnants. 'Cause that's the best yer gonna receive from the citizens of Lados. Yer nothing but a scab—a bothersome scab soon to be removed. A quick sharp tug with a little pain, then ye'll be gone. So go. Go back to yer employers. Tell them what I told ye. Stuff it up yer ass."

Kaville stammered and stuttered. "Wha . . . huh . . . no . . . uh . . ."

Having replaced his lower extremities in his pants, Callahan snarled at Kaville. "Silence yerself. The people of Lados have spoken through me. If you or any of the guard attempt to open that southern gate in response, I'll kill ye. I'll kill the whole fucking lot of ye, and I'll laugh as I do it." Turning his snarl to the envoy, he continued, "Go about yer merry fucking way, and let's see this city burn. Let's see ye put us to ashes. Come on, then, let's see what yer made of."

The barbarian smiled and let loose a guttural laugh as the envoy stormed out in frustration and anger. Looking at Callahan, he asked, "Shall I let my men know that we play tonight?"

With a look of respect, Callahan calmed his voice. "Ye know, I respect ye all, friend, and I'm grateful ye have come to our aid. Ye answered my call. I'll not forget this, so consider our debt squared. Tell yer men to leave the field. Tell yer men to return home. There is no need for yer honorable people to endure complete loss. We cannot come out of the city to aid ye. We need to shelter in like a turtle hiding within its shell. Ye all would die. Every man and we can't come out to aid ye. Their forces are well trained, and they greatly outnumber ye. Yer tribes and people would rip a solid dent through them, but even with that, I cannot see yer people go to slaughter. Not for nothing. So, my barbarian friend, in all honor, tell yer men to take their leave. Let the crown gain hope for but a moment, and trust in the Falcon. Ye've honored me well. I've got Lados."

The barbarian nodded solemnly. "It has been an honor, Falcon. I wish we could bleed together upon the same field. I wish we could show the crown what real warriors can accomplish, but we'll honor your request. My men will pack up, and we'll be gone before the morning sun."

"Aye, friend, may fair weather guide ye and yer people. Survive this winter as last, and enjoy what battles ye'll be graced between now and when we meet again." Callahan gave a nod of respect then departed, taking Kaville with him.

Upon leaving the tent, Kaville, nearly in tears, turned to Callahan. "When will enough be enough? When will enough of our citizens have died to sate ye? When—"

Frustrated, Callahan snapped out in retort, "Shut up, Kaville. Stop yer pissing and whining. I told ye I got this, didn't I? I'm not going to cast our people to death. Silence yerself. Stop this whining. Ye sound like a menopausal old woman. I'm tired of it. I'm gonna fucking end ye if ye keep annoying me. Get yer fucking men, and start setting up some defenses along the southern wall. My men will undertake the taxing endeavor of evacuating the innocents and useless people from the district. Get to fucking work. We haven't got long now, have we?"

Entering through the northern gate, Callahan left Kaville's side to meet with Raven and Hawk. Delivering orders to set the men toward the end of evacuation, Callahan also gave a quick supply-gathering task to Hawk. The Falcons did as they were told, greatly minimizing the potential for collateral damage.

Later, as evening fell upon the city, Callahan came upon the southern gate to view the absolute disorder present there. Lacking any confident leadership, the guards lazily milled about, cowered in fear, or crazily bounced from one place to another, not knowing what to do.

Observing the complete clusterfuck that greeted his vision, Callahan approached the southern gate and searched out the head captain. "How in the fuck did ye get this position?" The man huffed up proudly as though he were going to argue when Callahan continued, "I mean, who did ye have to bend over and take it from? Ye obviously haven't a fucking clue as to what yer doing? Tell yer men to stand to attention. Tell yer men to listen well."

Turning red with anger, the captain started to snarl back at Callahan. "Who . . . who do you think—"

A quick knife hand to his throat turned any further argument to nothing but choked gurgles. "I'm really getting sick of getting questioned today. I'm really sick of having people tell me what needs be done. I'm really sick of morons running this city." Climbing to the top of the city walls, Callahan could see the crown's trebuchets being pushed into position. Shouting off the wall to the guard, he commanded, "Gain some order! Collect yerselves! Cowards! Steel yerselves! Bunch of fucking fools, ye are. You!" Callahan pointed to a random captain. "Those trebuchets and catapults—why are they out in the open, and why aren't they firing upon our enemy?"

Sheepishly responding, the captain shouted up at the wall, "Well, Falcon, uh . . . uh . . . uh . . . they just don't reach."

Looking at the nearest trebuchet, Callahan shook his head. "That's because ye have the tension all wrong, don't ye? Look at the thing. I mean, fucking look at it. I'm no fucking engineer, but even I can tell that's loose fitted. Tighten that up, and move it two blocks to the east. Shelter it up behind that alley. Use the buildings as protection. Move the other ones likewise. Get these fuckers up and rolling." Smiling, Callahan watched a group of Falcons arriving with Hawk in their lead. "Yeah. See those men just now arriving? They're now yer leadership. Ye want to survive, do what the fuck they tell ye to do. See those bags my men carry? I want those loaded on the trebuchets and catapults. Those will be our first shots. Look to the skies, my friends. See the clouds that have been amassing since yesterday. There is looking to be another lightning storm. Let it aid us. Let's use it to our advantage. They don't know the fury of a Lados lightning storm now, do they? They don't know the fury of the people of Lados. Steel yerselves. I mean, when did ye all become whimpering little boys crying fer yer mom's tit? So get the fuck off it, and get the fuck to work!" Barking orders, Callahan ran up and down the walls. Any sitting idle were quickly sparked to action.

The night sky lit with fire as the crown unleashed shot after shot into and over Lados's city walls. In response, the city lobbed the bags Callahan had ordered placed. They landed just shy of the enemy's lines. Shouts went up from the crown's men as they laughed at the ignorance of the city dwellers. Shouts went up mocking Lados for not lighting their shots. Some of the crown's men ran out, dragging the bags back to their lines.

A few of the bags burst open, revealing nothing but dust inside. Six of the bags were launched; two had burst open, and the other four were being loaded to return fire when the sky opened with its lightning. Tongue out and shaking his head, Callahan roared his delight as the bags burst with multicolored light blasting energy on and through any unfortunate enough to be standing near them. The explosions of the sealed bags blew apart the siege weapons upon which they had been placed and wrecked havoc in the lines. Disorder and chaos shot through the masses.

Chaos remained rampant for several minutes after, but the crown's men were not untrained. Jumping to action, a few of the crown's present nobles pulled the army back into a state of order. Shot after shot again rained in upon the city. Callahan did all he could to run about, keeping spirits up as the shots continued well into the night. Seeing the men tiring and their spirits dampening, Callahan scrambled to think of a new ploy. Raven and the remainder of the Falcons had joined the force, placing pots of heated oil atop the campfires present for the use of the archers on top of the walls.

A lucky shot smashed one of the gate's hinges, almost breaking it down. Scrambling, Callahan put many men to the task of shoring the gate as he watched the outside lines begin their full assault. Ballistae fired from Lados's walls but did little to thin or slow the mass of troops approaching. Leading the line's charge was a contingent of men carrying a battering ram.

Boiling oil poured over the battering ram and those carrying it. Flesh bubbled, much like the liquid poured over it. The men that survived fell away from the ram only to be replaced shortly by more men, and so the cycle went until the defenders ran out of oil. Siege ladders and grappling hooks were taking hold upon the wall in mass number. Callahan called to the men inside the wall to aid in their removal. Raven and Hawk watched in horror as they took to the wall, joining Callahan at its top, just as he lobbed a lit torch down into the oil.

Fire erupted across the battering ram and troops assuming position on it. The tormented screams of pain answering his action led Callahan to grin wickedly. The men on fire dropped into rolls, trying to douse the painful flames, but the action just furthered the cause of spreading the flames. Flames spread from the battering ram, men, and the ground to the gate itself.

Raven shouted at Callahan, shaking her head. "What are you thinking? The gate is made of wood as well. Did you lose your mind?"

Shrugging, Callahan looked to Raven and Hawk sheepishly. "Well, in retrospect, that may not have been the wisest course of action, but it did prove to be quite entertaining."

Hawk chuckled lightly. "I often ponder whether meeting you was the best or the worst thing that ever happened to me. As is your usual, what brilliant near-suicidal plan are you concocting this time?"

Callahan laughed at his friend. "Well, um . . . um . . ." Callahan looked up and down the wall then burst into a smile. "Grab a hold of some of those grappling hooks. Shake off their owners. Tie yourselves off around the waist. We'll rappel down before the gate and hold it while the men get some shoring up. When we're done, we'll climb back up, pulling the ropes with us as we go."

Hawk shook his head again. "Yep, that sounds very Falcon-like. Drop down off a wall into the midst of the crown's army. In essence, let's smile and commit suicide via guards. Sounds pretty good to me. I've been growing bored. Let's get to bleeding some of these fuckers, eh?"

While tying themselves off, Callahan barked orders to get the guard's archers prepped for his plan. The three quickly dropped down the wall and moved to an area lacking fire near the gate.

[Callahan] Watching Raven draw her cutlass, I recognized I'd never actually seen Raven in combat. I trained with her and watched her train with others. I knew she could fight, but as we faced that crowd of opponents, I'd never seen her in functional combat. I was excited for the opportunity to do so.

As we initiated our combat with the crown's men, I noted for the first time that Hawk had assumed possession of Vulture's hand axes. Swinging his axes and piercing with his bracers, Hawk moved with chaotic awkward beauty as he carved his way through the multitude of attackers. He had an unusual fighting style which was both offensive and defensive. His arms seemed to move of their own accord, almost independently of each other.

I was pondering all of this as I put my own blades to purpose. The plague bringer was proving to be a rather worthwhile find. The iridescent green glow of the blade was accented by the illumination provided by the burning shots flying through the air from the crown's trebuchets as well as the occasional flash of lightning. I really did appreciate the beauty of the whole scene as we stood in triangular formation before the fire provided by the oil on the gate. Wave upon wave rushed us, much to their detriment, as we fell into the artful dance of death's delivery. The main difficulty we found ourselves with was the cumbersome distraction provided by the ropes tethered to our waists.

Slicing a man's throat while simultaneously piercing another's heart, I found an opening from which to see Raven. Carving masterful circular dancelike movements, Raven rolled in and out of the enemy's guards, turning their blades then irreparably carving through them in fluid singular motions. The enemies dropped before her without a wasted motion.

My distraction proved to be nearly problematic as, barely ducking a wild swing, I watched a blade cut my favorite shirt's sleeve. Further exacting our dance, we watched the bodies piling around us. This was my art. This is what empowered, emboldened, vitalized, animated, bolstered, and encouraged me. This was my essence delivered in tangible form. This was my reality, for I am the Falcon.

[Narrator] Atop the walls, Owl, covered in full guard armor, approached the tethering ropes while firing arrows into the crown's men to maintain his disguise. Callahan signaled the walls, and the three began their ascent under the cover of guard arrows. Ensuring freedom from witness, Owl cut the nearest rope, dropping Hawk into the fire before the gate. Hawk's descent caused the guard on the wall to huddle near the other two ropes, causing Owl to take his much-needed leave before being able to cause any further disorder.

Rolling from the fire, Hawk leapt back into the fray with a group of the crown's soldiers while simultaneously doing his best to pat out the flames. Reaching the top of the wall, Callahan noticed Hawk's plight as Raven pulled herself up, joining him. Turning to look at Raven, Callahan lightlyshouted, "Watch my rope. Ensure it doesn't go the same course as Hawk's. I'll not see another of my dearest friends fade to pay price for my decisions. Selfin was enough."

Callahan hardly slowed his descent as he rapelled back down before the gate. Landing roughly, Callahan felt his ankle twist painfully. Rolling through the landing, he hobbled awkwardly as he again entered combat at Hawk's side. Despite their injuries, Hawk and Callahan fought in perfect unison, holding the crown's men at bay.

The situation looking bleak and overwhelming when Hawk gave a raucous laugh. "Can't believe you actually came back for me. Kind of heroic, isn't it?"

With his wry half smile, Callahan gave a quick nod. "I put way too much effort into getting those bracers to let them go to waste in the crown's hands."

Laughing together, the two prepared themselves for the next rush. An arrow split through a nearby soldier's helm, then another, and yet another. Confused, Hawk and Callahan both noticed that the arrows were not coming from above but were coming from behind the soldiers on the ground.

Throwing off his helm, letting loose one more arrow, then strapping his bow to his back, Eagle drew forth his long sword. "You were right. Profit is not enough to live for. It is better to die with a purpose than to live without one. It was a bit of a tough haul to get back here. The crown is not very forgiving to our kind. They took the letter, and you were right. They spared my life on its regard. Shipped me off to be imprisoned in the capital of Stockard, so I slaughtered the group transporting me, and I decided it was time to give these people a piece of your medicine."

Raven tossed a second rope. Eagle nodded to the two and held the forces back while they ascended. When guard arrows rained down, providing distraction, Eagle followed behind Hawk on the spare rope. Falling under a rain of arrows, stumbling upon the obstruction provided by the burnt battering ram and multiple bodies, the crown's men found themselves losing heart and quickly tiring.

After half an hour or so of more failed attempts, the crown's nobles called a strategic retreat to collect their forces. As the crown fell back, the Lados guard began cheering in victory. Callahan shouted at the top of his lungs, "Hey! What've ye to cheer about? We're not finished yet. Get to putting the flames out on that gate. Shore it up, clean up these bodies, and let us get our shit in order. This isn't the last run of it. Look out there. It's a veritable fucking sea of men. We're not finished by a long shot, mates. Don't celebrate till the fight is done. Get to work, and set yer minds to purpose. We will see tomorrow's light but only if we maintain our vigilance."

The men rushed to order, immediately ceasing all celebration. They did just as they were told. Flames were extinguished, shoring rose to solidify the gate, and bodies were being removed. Only a few moments passed when an envoy rode forward from the crown's lines. "Falcon, what is your answer now? We have multitudes yet to throw against you. We will rain them down upon you with continuance if you do not peaceably lay down arms."

Falcon turned to his men behind the walls. "What's our answer, mates? What do ye say to such an offer of tyranny?"

One guard turned and, in a low shout, said, "Well, this is kinda rough." A dagger stuck in his throat, the guard fell back with no further response.

Turning again to the guards and people within the walls, Callahan reiterated his question. "Aside from that jackass, what is our answer?"

[Sean] A strangely familiar voice from one of the men clearing corpses from below shouted out, "Fuck the crown!"

[Callahan] BAH! HA HA HA HA HA!

[Narrator] A puzzled-but-amused expression crossed Callahan's face as he again spoke. "Yes, random . . . citizen. Damn right. Fuck the crown!"

A chant broke out across the wall and into the city itself as all the men took up the shout. "Fuck the crown. Fuck the crown. Fuck you, and fuck your crown." Laughter burst out, replacing the chant. The entirety of the defenders seemed to joyously celebrate as they cursed the crown.

The envoy, confused and puzzled, rode away almost smiling as he pondered to himself, *What the fuck do they have up their sleeves that they have nerve enough to shout so?* Slight fear gripped him at the prospect of having to continue a charge against walls filled with madmen.

Quiet fell upon the crown's lines. Behind the Lados walls, the men did not fall idle but continued their work in preparation for another assault. Callahan sat atop the wall in vigilant watch of the crown's lines. Just as dawn broke, Callahan smiled as he watched the crown's men setting the trebuchets and catapults for travel. Morning light broke over the cliffs, shining upon an army departing.

Another envoy rode up before the wall. "Men of Lados, we offer you temporary reprieve. Take this as warning. We shall return if you do not find the strength to correct yourselves. Kaville is to reassume command of this city. We will—"

Callahan cut the envoy off in midsentence as he shouted his retort. "Bah, ye blowhard! Pack it up. Ye haven't shit else to say to us. Ye come here to lay threat after ye just received a solid spanking at our gate. Ye arrogant, pompous moron, with what ground do ye think ye have to threaten us from? There is no ground for yer threats to find foundation. Yer no threat to Lados, and yer not packing up because ye've laid yer warning. Yer packing up because, if I haven't missed my guess, ye've got umpteen thousand orcs crawling up yer arse from the south. Yep, orcs fucking yer lands all to shit, possibly even risking the sanctity of Stockard itself."

The confused and flustered envoy shouted back, "How could you . . . ?"

Callahan laughed before continuing. "Well, I am *un naga frueh*. I inspired those orcs. I set them to purpose, and if ye, yer crown, or any of yer yolk ever threatens my city again, I'll rain such death upon ye that even Stockard will run with rivers of blood. Don't stand against the Falcon. Stand in opposition before me, and fall." Pointing out to the departing troops, Callahan addressed the men inside Lados. "Look, citizens and guards of Lados, this is their recognition of our strength." The envoy departed, thankful to put the crazed city behind him.

[Callahan] That, my friends, is how to manage a proper siege. Confidence, assurance, and a solid I'll-take-no-shit-from-anyone attitude. Granted, it really helps to know that there is a massive horde of orcs rolling up their back end. Considerable damage was done to the appearance and structure of the southern merchant district, but loss of life was minimal. The crown suffered a grave loss in their bluff. They had attempted to surge-attack us into surrender while knowing full well that they needed to march on to stop orcs, and that plan blew up in their face.

The crown's army made it to the south and crushed the orc uprising with little difficulty. Their delay in quelling it caused untold amounts of death and damage throughout the southern lands but no real lasting damage of permanence. Restorative work in regard to the lands and people would be years in the undertaking. With the immediate necessity to rectify his own problems, the king lost all desire for Lados.

So the reader is aware, it isn't arrogance when you really are just this fucking good. As is the course of any life, the afterglow of victory only holds for so long, so on to chapter 11 . . .

Chapter 11

THE CHAOS OF ORDER

[CALLAHAN] I SHINE MY brightest when chaos is in full swing. It had been for so long in my life that I simply didn't know how to exist without it. That is why the six months of celebration that followed the siege brought me to near mental breakdown.

After the siege, the populace of Lados celebrated the Falcons' presence as saviors. I reveled in it; everywhere I went, people showered me with praise and gifts. Raven and I were granted some time together, free from all the violence and torment that had defined our existences. She was right. It was the moments that mattered, and those moments were beautiful.

The afterglow of success faded, and the logistics of running a pseudomilitaristic organization during a time of reconciliation kicked in. The whole bureaucratic mess scrambled my brain as did the attempted diplomacy with Kaville. As promised, I withdrew the Falcons from any political influence or dealings and allowed Kaville to reenact the old nobility system that had been established prior to Namion's rise.

Outraged by the citizens' apathetic indifference to it all, I put Horuce in charge of diplomacy and logistics. I put Hawk in charge of our fighting men and set him to enact a proper enlistment and recruitment pattern. Raven and I remained figureheads within the guild but relinquished functional control to those with minds more appropriately geared to such ends.

What should have been the best months of our lives were torturous and painful. The peace of it all drove me to madness, and on several occasions, Raven had to step in to prevent me from saying or doing something to cause irreparable permanent damage within the guild structure and diplomatic processes.

All of this is why when I heard news of Talon presence again being seen in the poorer districts, I systematically denied it and ignored it. I knew the reports were true. I knew Namion yet lived, and I knew I should've crushed them while they were still wounded, but deep down inside, I wanted Namion to rise again. I wanted the familiar contest and comfortable chaos he provided. I wanted to return to war, to killing. I hate that about myself, but I didn't know how to live otherwise. I didn't know who to be anymore aside from being the Falcon.

A villain is only a villain when contested. I don't count myself a hero, granted I'm the more desirable of villains when put to comparison to Namion, but I didn't use that to justify calling myself a hero. A hero without contest can stand on his principles and codes. Thus, a hero without a villain is still a hero. A villain without contest is not but another shit bag, isn't he? So that is what I felt of myself. I felt like a villain absent his contest, and it unsettled me.

A decent figurative illustration of my state of consciousness would be the one in which one angel sits on a shoulder while a little devil sits on the opposing shoulder. I'm of the solid belief that my little devil skewered my poor little angel, grew to six feet tall, and now rides a chariot, carries a bullwhip and pitchfork, and progresses me along the course of my existence via constantly sodomizing me with aforementioned pitchfork.

[Narrator] Callahan needed some air after a particularly difficult bout of maintaining calm in the face of a guild meeting. That meeting had mind-numbingly consisted of nothing more than attendance costs to the newly opened fighting pit in the underground valley established for gambling purposes. Callahan walked as though he had a purpose through the streets of the city he called home.

While he barely had a glimpse, movement from a nearby alley caused Callahan to withdraw two throwing daggers. Callahan held the daggers flat against the underside of his wrists in an attempt to not startle other passersby as he shifted in toward the alley in question.

"Peace for the time being, Falcon. These people have witnessed more than enough death for a lifetime. Namion is again on the move and will meet opposition with brutal force. He is not plotting against you at this point." Owl revealed himself from the shadows, hands held out in peace. Maintaining a two- to three-body distance from the Falcon, Owl continued, "I would forewarn you that quite the grudge is being held against Raven, though, and plans are already well into the process in regard to her permanent removal."

Rage boiled within Callahan. "Clarify yerself with quickness lest I show ye the appearance of yer nuts removed from scrotal obstruction."

Owl smiled. "I do not come to you offering peace. I do not come to you pleading. I come because Namion is willing to barter division lines within the city districts to establish guild territories. If those lines can be negotiated and upheld, plots against Raven will be put to rest. He said that you are to meet him tonight in the place where it all began just after dusk." Tossing a pouch to the ground, Owl darted off as Callahan leapt back from the small explosion of smoke.

[Callahan] Seriously! That little turd. Apparently, Owl had been undergoing ninja lessons from Reader 1 or, should I say, Sean. Either way, like I've told ye before, love is the greatest of all brain-damaging emotions. Knowing it was a trap, knowing that it encompassed untold amounts of danger, I was en route. He had found me in what I knew was a well-prepared time window, for even at a full sprint, it would take me until the appointed time to arrive at the desired location. I believe that my love for Raven, boredom with the recent length of peace, and the culmination of all of my mental oddities were the contributing factors that led me, unthinking, to the place I had once called home as a child.

[Narrator] Concerned for the well-being of her beloved's mind, Raven traveled into the city to search out Callahan. It wasn't long before she noticed her shadow. Someone was following her motions through the streets. Taking a few quick turns and doubling back through a crowd, she cornered her tail on a nearby street with little citizen traffic.

Drawing her cutlass, Raven prepared herself for the worst as she approached the heavily cloaked individual. "Speak your purpose quickly and clearly."

"It is I, dear Raven." Veracliff lowered her hood. "I come to you because of the love and devotion I have for your husband. You know I speak honestly of such. Namion plots his end, but there is another way. I have arranged a meeting with Namion on your behalf to discuss possible territory divisions that will assuage his murderous desires. I do not want harm to come to the Falcon, and I know that he will not listen to such a plea. So I appeal to his better half."

"I hope you understand my reluctance in regard to trusting you." Raven kept her cutlass prepared for combat.

"Namion predicted such a reaction and has already begun the process of his plan's fruition. I implore you to join me in plea in Falcon's behalf. Time is of the essence, or I would do whatever necessary to ensure your trust. He will succeed if not for your intervention. He delays but only a few hours at Falcon's childhood residence. Please come with me. I know you love him, and I know that you are well aware of Namion's capabilities when set to purpose." Veracliff's eyes lent evidence to her sincere concern for Falcon.

Against her better judgment, Raven sheathed her blade and sped to keep up with Veracliff's rushed pace as they traveled to Callahan's childhood residence.

[Callahan] I wish there were more to say. I wish I had placed more thought into the whole thing. I wish that what is about to be read had never occurred, but wishes are as futile as prayers when they fall upon deaf ears. My heart sinks at the recollection that because I had been so unsettled in peace, I had lost my preparatory edge.

[Narrator] Entering the front door to his childhood home, Callahan found surprise at Raven's presence. Fearing the worst, he silently took the seat Owl bade him to.

Callahan sat next to Raven at the square table, waiting for Namion. Veracliff, in her sheer negligee-like dress, stood with her back to the corner of the room. Owl stared across the table from Raven. Nearly shouting, Callahan opened the negotiations. "Come out, Namion. This ends today. Enough blood has been spilled on account of our feud."

"I will say when it is enough, Falcon. You, who were once a lowly boy. You, who found yourself purpose as one of my elite. You, who rose to such fame and esteem as to achieve a guild of your own on the back of my guidance. You, who now spits in the face of all my favors, are now seeking peace. Was it not your order to take my city that led us to this? Your guild, your wife, you yourself started this war, not I. Now you seek to shy back from it. No, boy! Reap the whirlwind you have sown. Savor the sounds, drink in the sights—it will be glorious bloodshed yet again." Namion's eyes gleamed with fanatical light as he dropped into the common room from the loft. "Does my entrance inspire memory, dear friend?"

Catching Veracliff's subtle hand movements out the corner of his eye, Callahan tried to reach for his throwing daggers. The distraction provided by Namion's entrance had been just enough to allow Veracliff to conjure paralysis in both Callahan and Raven. Fighting against his muscles' stasis, Callahan's mind reeled in anger. The charm Veracliff had given Callahan to ward off magic had apparently been crafted in such a manner to still leave opening for her powers. Thinking quickly, he recalled that she had slyly asked for him to remove that charm the last time she had preformed magic upon him. She must have done so to further secure his trust in the device.

Tossing the book of Entearra Gharu on the table, Namion continued, "No, my beloved Falcon, or, should I say, Callahan? I will not let you die. Our pact, fashioned in regard to that indecipherable book, prevents me from such, does it not? Even under penalty of death, the mages, scribes, and assortment of intellectuals I gathered could not find hold of its ever-shifting script. The words alter and change every time it is opened. For reasons unknown, you are the only one the gods cursed with the ability to decipher its words. We were chosen, you and I. Chosen to battle each other at the cost of countless innocents until luck would finally catch up to us. Today, my friend, is not that day." Namion threw open the book before Callahan as he spoke. Walking casually behind Callahan, Namion spoke again. "Watch. Watch her eyes." Turning Callahan's chair to face Raven then turning Raven's chair to face Callahan, Namion smiled from ear to ear.

"I told you, you would be mine. I told you I would have you. You left me no choice, young Falcon." Veracliff's dark seductive voice could be heard outside Callahan's vision.

A dagger slid through Raven's throat, and Namion visibly shook as her life was siphoned into him. Callahan's world collapsed. His old voids and demons lit to life in monumental proportions. "Hmm, she had held your son inside her."

[Callahan] I would have willingly given my life in that moment. I would sacrifice every moment prior and after to regain what was taken from me in that moment. Paralysis or not, a tear ran down my cheek. I knew that never again would I love. I knew that with her died any hope for my soul. The darkness that plagues the recesses of all men's minds reached up to grasp me. I embraced it wholeheartedly. No longer would I quiet my demons, no longer would I seek the betterment of my fellow man. No, death was all I saw and all I knew in that moment. I embraced that pain, locked it deep inside, where my humanity had once been. It was and forever would be mine and mine alone. Some burdens are not to be let go. Some burdens carry on with us and echo through eternity.

[Narrator] A small voice in the back of Callahan's mind whispered, "You are Callahan, leader of the Falcons. You are a god among men. No magic outside that of the gods themselves should be able to contain you. Fight back. Seek your just due."

Drawing the plague bringer, Callahan thrust it forward, ripping through the outside of Namion's right thigh, just above his dagger's sheath. Drawing his short sword in a sweeping strike, Namion's body was dropping to its knees, his blade headed on for Namion's exposed neck. Crashing into the wall, Callahan twisted under Owl's grasp. Dropping both his swords, Callahan shifted his hands in, grasping Owl's wrists just as the tip of Owl's dagger entered his skin, meant to pierce up under his rib cage. With inhuman strength fueled by his unbridled rage, Callahan threw Owl back on to the table. Leaping upon Owl, Callahan smashed his fist into the wrist of the hand holding the dagger. Listening to bone snap, he watched the blade skitter free just before Owl's lurching roll caused them to reverse positions. Reaching for Callahan's throat, Owl's eyes shot wide as he felt himself launch airborne. During the predicted roll, Callahan had shifted his feet between them and, when steadied, used them to launch Owl into the window in front of them.

Following the push through to his feet, Callahan drew and released two of his throwing daggers. One found a home in Owl's left eye, the other in his throat. Lurching forward, Callahan grasped Owl's twitching body that lay in the broken windowsill; wrenching it upward with his madness-born strength, he watched the broken shards of glass still attached to the window frame pierce down into Owl's chest.

Two more daggers in hand, Callahan released them at Veracliff. Swirling dark tendrils shot out of her hands, grasping the blades in midair. Charging forward, Callahan hardly shrugged as the first blade lodged itself inside his left collarbone. The second blade buried itself in his right leg. Callahan roared in the face of Veracliff's terrified expression as he grasped her windpipe with his right hand. Roaring

283

again, he wrenched his hand back, exposing her throat's inner workings to the world while simultaneously head-butting her.

Callahan turned to find Namion's rapier hilt deep in his gut. Lifting the skewered Callahan bodily, Namion turned and, with a solid jerking motion, launched him onto the tabletop. "How can you break pact? You have breached the Entearra Gharu, and now I will finally have your death!" Namion pinned Callahan to the table and thrust his dagger toward Callahan's heart.

Frozen, the two stared death upon each other. An echo emanating from the book spoke Namion's past words: "Yes, Falcon, that is what I say. I order you to seek fatal reprisal upon any who would bring harm to my daughter." A dark vortex swirled to life atop the book's open pages.

A skeletal hand emerged from amidst the vortex, followed by the skull and torso. An unholy crackling voice split the air. "Greetings, my priests. Sit. Be comfortable while we chat." In ethereal form, Namion and Callahan watched as they were pulled to opposing seats on either side of their frozen bodies locked in what should have been Namion's killing blow. "Heathens that you are, I feel a proper introduction is in order." Seeming to seep from the bone itself, flesh fashioned and formed itself around the skeleton until standing atop the head of the table was a man in a tuxedo. His hair shifted color several times as he paced down the table to stand before the two men's ethereal forms.

"I am Zen." Removing a top hat that had not been previously present, he bowed slightly. "I usually have such pathetic followers. You two, though—well, you're different, aren't you?" The book of Entearra Gharu leapt to the man's grasp. Flipping to the back of it as though looking for something, Zen continued. "Successful and honorable conclusion to an unsanctioned pact."

The two watched Namion's dagger rip into Callahan's heart, drawing his life and siphoning it to Namion. An image then arose before them of Namion writhing in a bed until, suddenly, he fell stiff. "That is a week from now, Namion. You are resilient and the dagger is powerful, but so is the disease which you were infected with by Callahan's rapier. So neither of you wins. You both die due to the events of this day. Callahan, how sad it must be to know that at the end, you really were inferior. Namion, what a shame it must be to die such a slow and dishonorable end." Again, their bodies locked in battle appeared before them as they had been when frozen. "But wait. There is another way. Immortality is boring. You two have brought my purpose to Calarr better than every priest and follower of mine combined throughout the generations."

A tall elf wearing shimmering elven ceremonial armor stood where the tux-wearing man had. "In that regard, I find you both to be the most interesting specimens I have ever laid eyes upon. The council, in respect to the masterful manner by which you've complied with your made-up pact of Entearra Gharu, has granted me the right to offer you a bargain."

A bearded man with bright red hair wearing a kilt with an attached sash dropped the book to the table as it turned to a page containing only two x's with lines next to them. "What, might you ask, do I mean by made-up and unsanctioned?"

A sturdy dark-haired dwarf in a leather jerkin fashioned for forging was the image now displayed. "Well, seeing that the council had not sanctioned your entry into the pact of Entearra Gharu, you were never actually engaged in it. Nope, my dear friends, everything you two did, you did of free choice."

Hardly contained between the roof and the table crouched the form of a blue-skinned giant in a loincloth. "Granted, I laid several promptings and guiding thoughts, but never did I force either of you to keep pact."

Beautiful and dark-skinned, a woman adorned in a sheer black dress similar to the one Veracliff had worn continued, "As I said, your choices that upheld Entearra Gharu impressed the gods to such extent that they allowed me, my plea."

Twirling in a multicolored cape, a young girl in a yellow dress now sat before them with crossed legs. "Sanctioned and binding, I offer the two of you a real pact of Entearra Gharu. Each of you will possess a rapier imbued with the power to unravel pact when driven through its opponent's heart."

A dark-skinned man in animal skin clothing was now the vision. "Other than those rapiers, there will be nothing that can cause permanent death, and you will remain through the ages as you are now. Short of your wounds, of course."

A middle-aged man in shining silver armor stood before them with shoulder-length blond hair flowing atop his head. "That said, death can still take you. If it does, three days are your penalty. Three days in which you will join me in my realm."

Dirty blond hair atop a youthful man wearing gold-toned full plate armor, the next vision spoke. "Three days in which you will suffer the penance for each and every sin you've committed from your birth until that said death."

A middle-aged man with short black hair wearing a full suit of dark crimson armor continued, "I can slow time so that a second can seem an eternity, so please, do not think this light cost."

An aged and wizened man with gray hair, balding not having taken its toll, stood in a full-length brown robe atop the table. "The council allowed me to make such an offer only on the grounds that I would make a counteroffer as well."

A man with dark gray skin peeking out from beneath a black hood and a full black robe stood ominously in the place atop the table. "If you are to turn down the gods' sanctioned pact of Entearra Gharu, then you will be granted amnesty. You will be allowed an eternity of peaceful rest, absolved of any and all sin but harbored by no god. You will be cast forever to slumber."

Zen was once again the image of the tux-wearing gentleman. He set Namion's and Callahan's ethereal forms free to move of their own accord. "Choose, my friends. Craft mark toward a new pact, or set yourselves to an undeserved, peaceful, and eternal slumber."

[Callahan] For an inkling of a second, I almost, kind of, sort of, somewhat thought about, thinking about, maybe . . . nah! Fuck it! Where do I sign?

[Narrator] Following Callahan's rushed signing, Namion did likewise. Both watched the tuxedo-wearing god smile ear to ear. "See you soon, my dear friends. See you very soon." The god vanished back into the book, which in turn, twisted into itself, disappearing. Upon the book's disappearance, Callahan's and Namion's ethereal forms were drawn back into their bodies, and time unfroze.

The dagger drove home into Callahan's heart. Weakly, giving his wry half grin, Callahan whispered in his dying breath, "Let the game begin."

Epilogue

[CALLAHAN] WELL, HOW 'BOUT you?

[Narrator] What do you mean how 'bout you?

[Callahan] I rightly mean how 'bout you? This was a tale of my beginning. This was a tale of my origin. It's painful and difficult in the retelling for me. So how 'bout you?

[Narrator] I'm still not quite grasping your meaning.

[Callahan] The leading character of this tale, which is but one of many tales we could tell, is you. Yer the storyteller, the narrator, the creator, and yet of all the characters, we know the least about you. So one more time, how about you? What of yer origin, and why now?

[Narrator] What do you mean why now?

[Callahan] It's like talking to a brick wall all of a sudden. I mean, why did ye choose now to disclose our story? Why didn't ye tell it earlier?

[Narrator] You know why.

[Callahan] Like extracting teeth, this is. Of course I know why. The readers don't, though, do they?

[Narrator] The readers don't want to hear me prattle on about myself.

[Callahan] If they don't, they can count this as their warning 'cause that's exactly what we're about to do. Further telling of my tale overlaps with our next story, so if they want that, they should await our next book. I mean, why not try to capitalize on this shit. For now, the retelling of my story is only complete if told in partial conjunction with yers. Of all the situations we've walked, we've come a long way from when I found ye alone in that empty room, staring at empty walls.

[Narrator] Aye, I imagined you and your stories between the ages of twelve and fourteen, but you are only a side character in the general scope of Calarr.

[Callahan] A badass side character. So why did ye feel the need to craft an artificial world?

[Narrator] Because those empty walls you spoke of screamed despair and hopelessness to that young man. In that room, I found what it was to stare into the hungry maw of oblivion and found myself longing for its embrace.

[Callahan] Faded scar on the back of yer left hand. I remember that day. I sat with ye that day. Ye'd hidden a small modeling knife within a watchcase just so ye could end it when it became too much. I mean, really, what the fuck did ye intend to do with that piddly thing?

[Narrator] I was a little fucking kid now, wasn't I? I didn't know what the fuck I was going to do. I just knew that I didn't want to do it.

[Callahan] Thinking yerself a coward, ye carved that blade through the back of yer hand in frustration toward yer inability to draw it up and across yer wrist. Ye chose to turn yer back toward that maw of oblivion and face the unknown of life.

[Narrator] And I embodied all my pain, anger, and frustrations into an imaginary world called Calarr. I subjected the residents of said fantasy to untold amounts of suffering and triumph.

[Callahan] Being that ye created me as image of yer personality and desires, ye chose to write my story first despite the fact that though first in the chronological order of things to occur in Calarr, my story is one of the least developed within yer mind. Why did ye choose me?

[Narrator] Your story reflects how I feel in light of my current life. I scrape and fight for survival. I dream of living. Then I look at the little girl condemned to live her life with me as her sole guardian in the wake of her mother's passing due to cancer. I cannot tell that little girl that she is free, that she can be whatever she wants to be, if I have not first lent a sincere effort toward my own dreams and freedom.

[Callahan] Whoa, yer in the running to be a daytime talk show tearjerker for lonely fat bonbon–eating housewives everywhere, aren't ye?

[Narrator] Actually, far too much of you is expressed through me. So that's not a practical situation. I've only allowed our conclusion to encompass this topic because the truth is you saved my life. Not just once, but tons of times. I'm prone to depression and have sought to drown myself with chemical sedative in the form of alcohol. Throughout my existence, life has often scripted me the villain, be it of my own actions or of existential opposition forced upon me. I am not a good man. I am not an evil man. I am just one among many lost in the rapid course of life. Throughout all of my lowest and darkest moments, you've stood beside me, carrying me forward. The strength I imagined in you, though often depicted through villainous means, lent to me the ability to rise above my present.

[Callahan] Yer absolutely bat-shit crazy. Ye know that, right?

[Narrator] Yes, but no more or less than any other. I look around me today and see a world not so unlike how I depict yours. Humanity has formed a societal structure in which people who entertain live like kings, while people who provide functional purpose for life barely scrape out an existence few would call life. We are told we are free. We are told to be proud. We are told to close our eyes, plug our ears, and pretend that some great celestial janitor is going to make it all OK.

[Callahan] Fuck all. Really, ye wrote my story in some lame attempt at rallying revolution?

[Narrator] Not at all, quite the contrary. I wrote yer story to depict the desperate, painful, and pointless costs of such an endeavor. I'm arrogant, but I'm not so arrogant as to say I've anyone's answer. No, I wrote this because out there, it is very likely that there is at least one other suffering person who might find a bit of solace in you. I crawled from the brink of that abovementioned oblivion a couple of different times now. This time, I hold a little girl and know that returning to that edge, that failure, is no longer an option in my reality. I struggle to keep afloat, I struggle to maintain sanity in an insane world, but despite all of that, I find myself in a life of so much worth that I no longer need to selfishly cling to your protection. I share my words that maybe one other can find comfort in them. I share fatal truth hidden beneath snarky, cynical, pessimistic humor written amidst a fantasy in hopes of inspiring just a little thought.

I write this because there is a tiny sliver of hope at the slight possibility that maybe I am the sane one, and it is the rest of the world that is crazy. The more likely truth is that I am completely out of my mind, but it's my sincere belief that my madness is no more or less than that of the founding fathers of this system in which I find myself imprisoned by. Founding fathers who believed, against all odds, that taxation and law without proper representation is a crime and that such a thing is intolerable. Tyranny is not to be quietly adhered to but loudly protested against.

I find myself forced to be a member of a system in which I do not feel properly represents me or those like me. It doesn't properly represent the voice of its people. It subjects them to forced law and taxation without giving them any real say. Our representatives are doing so as career men, blinding themselves to anything but the continuation of their paychecks. A career in which individuals must undergo systematic brainwashing through institutions of excessively priced ignorance in the guise of education.

So, my friend, I find myself, in my own eyes, a patriot. I understand that I am most likely mad. Even with that in mind, I refuse to meander with the other sheep. I am a wolf in wolves' clothing. I'll not go quietly into the night. I'll lend my voice to at least one proclamation that we are still human. We do not have to adhere to oppression and tyranny just because it is what it is. I'll be deemed treasonous, I'll be deemed blasphemous. I'll be called a lot of things, but fuck those people. Just like you, I live against the grain.

I state what needs to be stated because I find myself sickened by profit made upon others' misery. I find myself sickened when attempted aid is called socialism and dismissed as such. I find myself sickened by the rampant lack of compassion and empathy for our fellow humans in light of profit and convenience. This is why I script this—not to inspire revolution, but to inspire a bit of thought. To allow others to do what they will with it.

Unlike your world, Callahan, my world still has opportunity. Much like you, I don't really want to see the world burn. I don't want to see people damaged and hurt. We have an opportunity in my world to avert the revolution that is on the brink. Change is on the wind. People are unsettled. We have opportunity before us to shift and change before unnecessary bloodshed. This, Callahan, is my dream. My dream is that people awaken to reality that change is needed. Awaken to the reality that it's needed now.

Unfortunately, I just don't see that conclusion. I just don't see the world in which I exist coming to that understanding. No, I see the world being set aflame. I see the world going to war. I see horrible acts of nightmares forced upon us, and if and when it occurs, I will not necessarily delight, but I will not shed tear. I'll watch this world burn, and I may not find pleasure in it, but it'll inspire no sadness within me. It's the inevitable logical conclusion to the courses people currently allow to exist because they just don't think they have the voice to say no. They don't think they have the right to call bullshit, bullshit.

I'd ask that any who read this take the time to be who they are, but be compassionate to your fellow man. Understand that we are humans before we are our nationalities, sexual preferences, or religions. We are just humans. We are just humans who should respect our fellow humans. We're all confused, we all just seek a course, we all want to exist and love. In the recognition of this, let us call bullshit what it is, and let us come together to fashion a world worth existing in and calling our own.

So many times have I said truth as I see it to people in my reality to see the reactions. The looks that say, "Really? We can say that? That's allowed?" They give this pondered look as though they are actually under some kind of restriction as to what can come out their mouth. Though I am a bit exaggerated and a bit extreme, it is very difficult to fully disagree with me. So most who listen come to the recognition that though I may not be right, I'm not entirely wrong either; they may even find that, like myself, they are not fond of accepting sodomy with a smile and a thank-you.

Still somewhat youthful, I refuse to accept the death of my humanity and my ideologies as yet. You may have accepted your circumstances in your world, dear Callahan, but I've yet to come to that understanding in mine. I still hold hope. I hold faith that maybe, just maybe, I can be proven incorrect. Maybe the world will not construct its own rapid destruction in chaos. I hope because perhaps we can aid in inspiring one voice that will whisper forward, "It isn't right. This isn't OK." That one whisper might turn into the low murmur of a few hundred. Then that low murmur might turn to dull roar as thousands take up the call. "We need change." Those thousands might turn into the deafening cry of millions, then no longer would they be able to ignore us. No longer would this world turn a blind eye to its tyrants just because they wear nice clothes and speak politely.

People are unsettled and in pain. Change is needed. Perhaps that change can come about without the world having to drive itself to an absolute destructive end. It is a ridiculous thought and a ridiculous hope, but still the same, it's a dream, and any with a dream cannot hope to see that dream come to life unless they first undertake the steps necessary to put that dream to action. That is what this document is to me.

[Callahan] Wow! I mean, good thing I gave that little disclaimer earlier in the epilogue about this being about yerself 'cause wow. Ye really haven't paid one little fucking iota of attention to anything we have written in my story, have ye? I've kind of illustrated the complete idiocy of being that one voice amidst the crowd now, haven't I? And more importantly, readers don't really give a shit what you believe or what you want, do they? They just want mindless entertainment. They want to feel that their substandard, sad, sappy existences aren't so fucking bad. They want to delight in fantasy and excite themselves with an existence not their own.

Why do they want to listen to ye whine on about yer pitiful existence? That completely defeats the purpose of fantasy now, doesn't it? They don't give two shits about ye? It's me they want to hear about. It's me they delight in, and it's me our literary endeavors should keep on being about.

[Narrator] You had your story. Now fuck off. Now it's my story, and I'll say what I want to say. By the way, don't forget you brought this all on with your persistent questions.

[Callahan in a really sarcastic and horrible singing voice] It's my story, and I'll cry if I want to, cry if I want to.

[Narrator, unable to suppress laughter] Oh, bugger off, ye bastard. You make light of the most serious moments. I was in a real grade-A rant up there. Really in the swing of it, ye know. I mean, that was a good "let's rise up and get better / why can't we all just get along?" spiel there meant to show people that I'm not actually entirely heartless. You are the most wretched pieces of my personality in culmination. Argh, I absolutely adore you.

[Callahan] In the afterglow of that wondrous and heartfelt garbage that sounded like a rant of lunacy, I really want, I really . . . oh, what's the word? I really . . . I really just want to vomit. Yep, that's the word, or ye can use *puke*, if ye prefer. I want to projectile-vomit and expel all of that rubbish that ye just raped the reader's eyeballs with. It all really just hurt my brain.

[Narrator] Yep, fuck you too, Callahan.

[Callahan] That's the general gist of what I was getting at. So readers are aware, this man holds no degree in anything. He is not a shrink, not a therapist. So please, for fuck's sake, don't fashion yer life by his word. Just take it as entertainment, and if ye do get something out of it, then all's the better.

[Narrator and Callahan] Thank ye to all who read these words. Thank ye to all who participated throughout our life in keeping Calarr alive; yer far too many to mention individually, so instead, in mass number, thank ye. If people actually choke this shit down, there is far more where this came from.

About the Author

I AM A THIRTY-YEAR-OLD nihilistic narcissist from Kitsap County, Washington, in the United States of America. I am not a good man, but I am not an evil man. I am just one among many lost upon this course we call life. I find myself a single father of a little girl in the wake of her mother's passing due to cancer. I cannot justify telling my little girl that she can be anything she wants or that she can do anything she wants unless I first attempt to chase my own dreams. I spent the better part of the last decade lost in the grip of the sedative known as alcohol. As stated, I am not a good man—just one fighting for redemption and renewal. Know that with your purchase of my book, you not only pay for your own entertainment but also make a purchase of yet one more step toward said redemption and ascension, which, all jokes aside, is met with the utmost respect and gratitude.